Perfectly Reckless

Perfectly Reckless

by Brigit Rosé and Nikki Haras

Copyright © 2021, 2023 by Krystyna Fenner and Nikki Haras

Prisma Isle™ is a claimed trademark of Two Realms Publishing LLC.

Published by

Two Realms Publishing LLC

Irmo, SC 29063

https://tworealmspublishingllc.com

Cover Designer: Sweet 15 Designs

Interior Designer: Two Realms Publishing LLC

Editor: Cassandra Fear

Illustrator: Nicodemus Holroyd

Cartographer: Jog Brogzin

Ebook ISBN: 978-1-955106-02-3

Paperback ISBN (Amazon): 978-1-955106-03-0

Paperback ISBN (Worldwide): 978-1-955106-18-4

Printed in the United States of America

Content Warning

Welcome to Prisma Isle, a realm not for the faint of heart.

Humans may not exist, but that doesn't mean villages don't have any fucked up shit happening inside their walls. We would warn you of everything, except the list is extensive. And we could be here far longer than necessary. All you need to know is that shit gets bad and escape isn't always possible.

On the brighter side, because let's face it, there has to be one. There's a lot of sex to counteract all that dark.

Yes, we agree.

Balance is the necessity of life.

Perfectly Reckless

PRISMA ISLE™ SERIES
BOOK ONE

BRIGIT ROSÉ & NIKKI HARAS

TWO REALMS PUBLISHING LLC

TERMINOLOGY

Adolescent: term in shape shifter culture for children ten years of age to twenty years of age

Antekilio [ant-E-keel-oh]: library of the Sirens

Chicane Village: village of the guilers

Demeter [dee-MEE-ter]: the goddess of fertility, earth, and harvests; protector of marriage and social order; daughter of Cronos and Rhea; mother to Persephone; and creator of the sirens

Full-fledged: term in shape shifter culture for adults; those twenty years of age and older

Galenus [gah-LEE-nus]: male, canine shape shifter, deceased

Informant: soldier to the shape shifter king, Markham

Hades: the Greek god of the underworld; sometimes used as a sort-of curse word by the shape shifters

Kriah [KREE-uh]: a female nymph who lives in Migas Village

Marana: the second cycle (month) of the year

Métamorphe [met-a-mor-fey]: the shape shifter village

Migas Village [MEE-gahs]: the hidden hybrid village and a place of sanctuary

Nestling: term in the shape shifter culture for children one year of age to five years of age

Newling: term in the shape shifter culture for newborns to one year of age

Pteryina [ter-EEN-uh]: home of the sirens; adjacent to The Clouds

Solaris: year, which comprises sixteen cycles (months) for the inhabitants of Prisma Isle

Vasilia [vuh-SILL-ee-uh]: female siren that is the Elder of the sirens and lives in Pteryrina

Verdant Grove: home of the fae

Youngling: term in shape shifter culture for children five years of age to ten years of age

Zancle's Rock [Zan-kuls rock]: bar and restaurant in the marketplace run by Ambrosia; known for their venison stew

Chapter One

Beginning of the month of Marana, Year 1027

Ambrosia reached up and grabbed onto the first craggy rock with a route planned out in her head. Something she forgot about from her last climb. She hauled herself up and ascended the cliff, placing her foot onto a pointed stone several inches from the bottom. The holds lessened the further up she got, but she would be damned if she stopped.

Sweat blossomed on her forehead, and slowly, her anger over her sister's face ebbed. Mostly because she no longer thought about it. Instead, her entire focus shifted to the climb ahead of her. She was precise in each movement, ensuring she captured the right spot. Her breaths came out in ragged puffs as she paused midway to the top and calculated her next maneuver. If she wasn't careful where she placed her hand—she went for the next stone and lost her grip, her arm getting scratched ever so slightly. "Dammit."

That was *precisely* what she was trying *not* to do. Okay, that hold wouldn't work. Which way did she take before? Her gaze fell to another option. It was a little higher than the hold she had previously went for, but it should work. Configuring her next couple of steps, Ambrosia pushed off one foothold to reach the handhold and missed it. Her other foot slipped, slamming her body into the cliff and scraping her knee.

Ambrosia screamed. She quickly tried to reclaim her prior selections with her feet and failed. Her fingers loosened around the rock as she tried again to find a place for her feet. Instead of repositioning herself, she lost her hold and fell backward.

This is going to hurt. There was no one to blame except herself.

But she didn't hit the ground. A pair of furry arms came around her body.

"I got you," the male said.

"Thank you." Ambrosia shielded the sun from her eyes. She winced as her gaze drifted to her savior. *Oh shit.* She was *not* in the arms of a shape shifter. Yep. And not just any shape shifter, a damn wolf.

"You are hurt," he stated. "I have a cabin close to here. I can treat your wounds." The male's dark ears twitched.

He wasn't handsome. Yes, he was. Ambrosia swallowed the lump in the back of her throat. The last thing she needed was to be attracted to a shape shifter, let alone a wolf. Besides, she could get treated back in Migas. She might even have some herbs in her knapsack; if she had her knapsack. She'd been so pissed that she had left without it. Crap. "I appreciate it, but if you set me down, then I can certainly take care of it myself."

"That gash on your arm is pretty bad. It looks like it will require stitches. Can you do that yourself?"

Ambrosia ground her jaw. Who the fuck was this guy? She dropped her gaze to her forearm. Okay. So, he was right, but she could still get it treated back home. Of course, it would take her an hour to get back to the village, and it could get infected the longer it went untended. "How far away is your cabin?"

"Fifteen miles, give or take."

Damn. She hoped it was far away. It would give her an excuse to head back home instead of taking the male up on his offer. She needed to decide. Her arm throbbed. His place was closer. And he had saved her from a cracked skull or broken spine. "Fine. I'll go with you."

"Good choice." He turned and strode toward the main path.

"What are you doing?"

"Carrying you to my cabin."

What the fuck kind of answer was that? She walked here so she could walk to his cabin. It wasn't like she twisted her ankle or anything. "I gathered that much, but you can put me down now. I have two feet."

"Yes, but you might hurt yourself again."

It wasn't like she was clumsy. Ambrosia scowled. "Excuse me? I fell off a cliff. I didn't trip over my own two feet. Now, put me down."

His aquamarine eyes fell to hers. "If you insist." He dropped her in a pile of leaves. Smirking, he cocked an eyebrow at her. "Better?"

"No!" Ambrosia snapped as she pushed herself from the greenery and got to her feet. Brushing out her burgundy-colored hair, she narrowed her gaze at him. "What kind of messed up shit was that? I said to put me down, not drop me."

"I put you down. You did not specify to set you down on your feet."

As much as she hated to admit it, he had a point. Frowning, Ambrosia eyed the male and drank in the full sight of him for the first time since he caught her. Gods, he was tall. He stood almost four feet taller than her. She didn't even know shape shifters got that tall. Ambrosia watched as he crossed his arms. His biceps bulged from the maneuver, although the black fur covering his body hid his muscles well. She bit the inside of her cheek. She shouldn't be checking him out. Although, it was good to know something about the male who rescued her from potential death. "What's your name?"

"Logan. Yours? Or should I simply call you, 'Your Highness?'"

"Oh, 'Your Highness' will do nicely." Ambrosia grinned. "Now, lead on." Arrogant prick. If he hadn't been snarky about it, she would've given him her name. No, he had to be a butt. It didn't matter how hot he was. With an attitude like that, he could patch her up, and she'd go right home without giving him another thought. *Bullshit. Oh, shut up.*

"Why did you not take the path to the top?" He started back up the trail. They passed a bit of topiary before he cut off to the right and trekked through a menagerie of trees.

"I thought it would be fun." Yeah, that wasn't the truth, but like she would tell him, it was so she could blow off steam. Her anger had probably been more of a hindrance than an advantage. Distractions weren't suitable for climbing, especially without safety equipment.

"That is a lie," Logan claimed.

How would he know that? Did he have some kind of ability that told him it was? No, that wasn't—then again, Santos always knew when people were lying. Maybe it was conceivable, more so than she thought. Ambrosia sighed. "Fine. I was trying to cool down."

"That I believe."

"Why do you believe that and not that it was for fun?" She attempted to cross her arms and grimaced. Damn it. Her forearm throbbed. The gash on her arm hurt worse than when it first happened. How was that possible? Ambrosia eyed the red stripe along the front of her forearm. Dirt. Probably from the leaves or when she got to her feet. Great.

"No one would climb a cliff for fun when they could hike it."

She rolled her eyes. "Is that your general assessment or your 'I-have-all-the-answers' assessment?" The last time she climbed had been for fun. This male knew little about people.

Logan raised an eyebrow at her. "I have never claimed to have all the answers."

"Really? Could've fooled me. You *are* the one acting like an insufferable know-it-all." The smug ass spoke like he knew everything—the isle, people, what they did for fun, and a lot of other shit she was sure she heard in his words.

"You are right, *Your Highness*. One as wise as yourself only surrounds themselves with those of equal or greater knowledge."

Ambrosia's eyebrows knitted together as she replayed his words in her mind. Was that sarcasm? "Are you trying to say you're smarter than me?"

"Well, you are the one who fell from the cliff, not me."

"You're an arrogant ass! Anyone ever tell you that?" And she was the idiot who walked beside him to his cabin. Not that he had any clue she was part shape shifter. Nothing about her gave it away.

Logan let out a soft chuckle. "Yes, I have heard that before. Still, I am the *arrogant ass* who is helping you."

"Oh, and that's supposed to make it all better, right?" Good grief. Today turned out to be screwed up. First, her twin and those damn bruises, and now this. What did she do to deserve it all?

"It makes me feel better."

"La-te-da. Good. For. You." It didn't change the fact that he was a cocky dipshit. One who didn't have to catch her. One who didn't have to treat her injuries. Regardless of how minor they were, he could've left her back there.

"Would it not be good for you as well?"

A sneer crawled across her features as she glared at him. What was with this guy? Either he was just a natural-born smart-ass, or he knew exactly which buttons of hers to push. "If I didn't know any better, Logan, I'd swear you were trying to piss me off."

"It is just my natural charm." He grinned.

"Then you must have the ladies swooning." Gods, she was ready to get her arm patched up so she could go home. She didn't care that this added more time to her travel. It gave her ample time to cool off.

"Only you."

"Ha! I don't swoon. Even if I did, I definitely wouldn't *swoon* for you." Lies, lies, lies. All lies. Except for the swooning part. Not once had she ever melted for a male. And she saw plenty—one idiot after another in the village and the bar. Yeah, falling for a male was low on her priority list. Not to mention, they were all morons.

Stopping in front of her, Logan leaned in close. "Your knees may not have buckled yet, Your Highness, but I promise they will."

"In. Your. Dreams." Ambrosia punctuated each word to ensure he understood that nothing he did would make her fall at his feet.

His lips twitched. "I am counting on it."

She'd slap him just to wipe that smirk off his face if she didn't enjoy looking into his eyes so damn much. They were the prettiest aquamarine she'd ever seen. Not that she'd ever tell him that. Pompous ass. Ambrosia dropped a hand to her hip and tapped a claw against the ground. "Are you going to keep gawking or are you ready to lead on?"

"I enjoy staring at you, but I would like to get that gash tended to. It is looking a little angry." Logan winked and continued forward.

Blinking, Ambrosia eyeballed him as he walked away, his tail happily flicking back and forth, not too far from his—her eyes snapped back to his neck as she stomped after him. The arrogance of that male! If she hadn't hurt her arm, she'd slap the cockiness right out of his mouth.

"Keep up, Your Highness. We are not too far now."

"Good! The sooner you patch me up, the sooner I can get away from you," she retorted. The nerve he had to think he could make her *want* him. Oh, but she did. No, she didn't! Okay, okay, okay. Maybe, just *maybe*, he was nice to look at, but that didn't mean she could contemplate anything with him. She didn't have the time to entertain someone as arrogant as Logan.

Logan glanced over his shoulder. "Here, I thought we were becoming friends."

"Like *that* would ever happen." Nope. As soon as he found out she was part shape shifter, he'd be like every other purist in that village. She knew what her father had sacrificed. No way would she disrespect him by associating with a shape shifter. Not that she associated with Logan. They weren't even companions.

Yes, he had likely saved her life, but that didn't mean they had to be friends, associates, or any of the above. Not that she would mind associating with him. Her eyes drifted to his ass again as she bit her bottom lip. Good gods, she had to *stop* ogling him. With her good arm, she dragged a hand down her face. Honestly, this was getting just a tad ridiculous.

Traipsing across a few broken branches, she followed Logan into a clearing. Her eyes shifted to a large cabin with a small front porch wrapped around one side. It only had one modest window. Not big enough that anyone could see in, but certainly large enough that an occupant could see out. Not what she expected.

How did she not know about this? She and her twin sister went to the basin often. Indeed, with it buried a way back, she would've crossed this place by now. Ambrosia ascended the staircase after Logan, pausing long enough to appreciate the craftsmanship of the woodwork. Somebody had put innate detail into the handrails. It was quite exquisite.

"Are you coming, or do you plan to stand outside all day?" Logan asked as he held open the door.

If nothing else stopped her from drinking in his assets, his attitude should do the damn trick. Holding back a snarky comeback, Ambrosia strode inside the cabin and took in her surroundings. The living room to her left comprised a simple brick fireplace, a couch, two chairs, and two small tables on either side of the sofa. The dining room was to her right. A table that easily sat six immediately drew her in—another piece of furniture with ornate detail. She ran her fingers gingerly across lilies painstakingly carved in the table's trim.

"Admiring my handiwork? I am good at other things, too," Logan said, his voice right behind her.

Ignoring the words that sent a blast of heat to her core, Ambrosia turned and faced him. "You did all of this?"

He stared at her through hooded eyes, a low growl rumbling in his throat as he gripped the back of his neck. "Yes. I did." Rolling his shoulders,

Logan headed into the kitchen. "Sit while I gather the items to treat your wounds."

That shouldn't have turned her on, yet it did. Not that she would vocalize her attraction—something she didn't have time for, anyway. Get patched up and leave. That was her aim. Inhaling and exhaling another deep breath, she sat in one chair at the table.

Logan returned with a few washcloths, a bowl of soapy water, and a few other items. He set everything on the table and sat in the chair across from her. Gently lifting her arm, he inspected the gash and cleaned it first. "Will you tell me your name?"

"I don't know. I kind of like you calling me *Your Highness.* It's quite fitting." No, it wasn't, and she hated it, but again, she wouldn't admit that. It was bad enough she found him attractive. She didn't need to hear how her name sounded rolling off his tongue.

His eyes met hers. "You do not have to tell me, but please do not insult my intelligence, either. We both know you dislike it." Logan returned to tenderly cleaning the injury on her arm.

Ambrosia ground her jaw. He was getting on her nerves. How could he tell she lied? There was something about him. Something she couldn't quite see. It wasn't like she knew nothing about his species—their shared species. "Why does it matter to you so much?"

"I would simply like to know who I am stitching up. Nothing more than a simple courtesy."

Courtesy? Oh, what a crock of shit. She didn't believe that for one second. Narrowing her gaze at him, she frowned. "I might believe the first half, but I don't believe the second."

He chuckled. "You do not believe it would be courteous for you to tell me your name? I told you mine. I would think you would reciprocate."

Damn. Logan wasn't wrong about any of that. It was the courteous thing to do when someone introduced themselves. Her mother raised her with proper manners. It would be rude to continue this path and refuse to give him her name despite her annoyance with him. He gave her no reason to suspect he would run to his *whatever* and offer her up to the slaughter. "Ambrosia."

"Ambrosia. That is a beautiful name." Logan smiled. "I believe you may need a few stitches on this. I can prepare something for the pain, if you would like, beforehand."

Good Demeter. He just needed to say her name again. Gods, it sounded like he served the stars on a platter the way it came out of his mouth. So silky smooth. She swallowed. What did he ask? Something about stitches? "Umm... what?"

"Would you like something for the pain before I start on stitches?"

"Oh, no. I don't think it'll be necessary." A few stitches never hurt before. She'd had them once or twice. Her twin received them more, and she was usually the one doing them.

"Alright." He offered a slight nod, stood, and disappeared back into the kitchen with the needle in hand. Lighting a match, he quickly sterilized the needle and returned to the dining room table. With everything set up, his gaze fell from hers to her arm. "Have you climbed the cliff before?"

"A few times. I typically have the equipment, but the last couple of climbs I've gone without." Today was no different, except her thoughts distracted her. If she hadn't been, the fall would've never happened. *That would be a shame.* Ambrosia bit her bottom lip as she watched Logan's nimble fingers move in one continuous motion.

"Any reason?"

"Just to see if I could do it." At least for the first time around. Though it had been risky, if she'd been smart, she wouldn't have risked her life by climbing without equipment. Maybe she was just as cocky as Logan. Maybe. Maybe not.

"So, you did something dangerous to see if you could? Sounds a little irresponsible."

"Oh, and what are you, the guard of responsibility? You don't know a damn thing about me, so please don't judge me." And what if it was true? He didn't have any right to pass judgment on her actions. They were hers and hers alone to take.

"Well, that is not true." Logan snickered. He tied off the end of the stitch, cut it, and set the materials aside. "I know your name. I know you agree with me on a couple of things, not that you will admit them, and I know you are attracted to me."

Her eyes widened. How did Logan know all that? She told him her name and nothing more. No way he saw her checking out his ass. Even if he, by some miracle, caught that, how would he know about her agreement? Ambrosia rose to her feet, the chair scraping against the wood floor. "Excuse me? I don't know where you got half of your *allegations* from, but it's a bunch of crap." She stalked away from the table and stormed out the door, slamming it shut behind her.

Chapter Two

Logan swung the ax and split another piece of wood. He should've chased after Ambrosia yesterday afternoon. Why didn't he chase after her? Because he'd been a jackass and would've only made the situation worse. He picked up the two logs and tossed them onto the pile before moving on to the next piece of wood. It didn't stop him from hoping, beyond hope, Ambrosia would make her way back out here. Not that she'd been at the cliff earlier, or even the basin. Hades, who was he kidding? She wouldn't come back out here. Maybe she found him attractive, but that didn't mean she wanted to spend time around him voluntarily. If she hadn't needed her arm stitched the day before, guaranteed she wouldn't have given him a second look.

He couldn't explain what it was about her that so quickly brought out his sarcasm. He couldn't remember the last time he bantered like that, well, with anyone; not since he left Métamorphe, for sure. Maybe before his brother became an Informant. Gods, talk about a long time ago. Eighteen years since he saw Pierce and their two sisters—Dahlia and Zinnia. Eighteen years since he saw his mother.

His gaze fell to the two new logs, and he stared at them for a moment. It had been difficult to stay away all this time, but there was only one thing that awaited him if Informants found him or he returned to the village—death. Still, he needed to get his family out of there. He didn't know if things had worsened in his absence. Although it was all he—

His ears twitched at the sound of leaves shuffling. Had someone found him? Had an Informant stumbled onto his grounds? Logan lifted his nose to the air and inhaled deeply; the sweetest scent filled his nostrils—smelled like vanilla. He smiled and set the ax aside. Although he didn't want his hands full, the cabin wasn't all that warm. The cold slowly left the isle. The spring equinox just passed, but they still had a few days before welcoming warmer weather.

Collecting enough wood to get a good fire going, Logan walked toward the front porch with the bundle in his arms. His smile brightened as his eyes fell upon Ambrosia standing at the door, mumbling to herself. Now that was a sight to behold. Her burgundy hair swept into a ponytail with a few loose strands framing her face. Jeans and a t-shirt mainly hid her body, but he could see the figure beneath. "I knew you could not stay away."

Her amber eyes swung in his direction. Ambrosia smirked. "I didn't come here to pay tribute. I just thought I owed you a thank you for yesterday. So, thank you."

"You are welcome." With the logs tucked under one arm, he strode to the porch and ascended the short staircase. "Are you certain that is all?"

"Yes, and now that I have done what I came to do, I can leave."

"I do not believe you came all of this way for a simple thank you." He reached around her and opened the front door. "Would you like to come in?"

Ambrosia raised an eyebrow at him. "Why are you being so nice?"

"I would think that was obvious." He winked at her. It was probably a bad idea on many levels, but he hadn't had company in a long time. Not that being lonely was a good excuse for inviting a stranger into his home, even if that stranger was the most beautiful female he'd ever seen.

"Anyone ever tell you that you're infuriating?"

Logan paused for a moment and tilted his head. The corners of his mouth tugged into a wide grin. "Yes. My youngest sister used to all the time." He couldn't count the number of times Zinni screamed those exact words at him, only to apologize and hug him moments later.

Blinking, Ambrosia gawked at him and nodded. "Well, as long as you know."

Her reaction amused him. He couldn't recall the last time a female outside his sisters entertained him. "Are you planning to come inside? Or are we going to continue standing out here?"

"Normally, I'd say stand out here, but since you so graciously offered…" Her words trailed off as she crossed the threshold.

Good to know Ambrosia was as much of a smart ass as he was; he liked the fact that she could dish it back to him. Logan followed her, shutting the door behind himself. He walked over to the fireplace, carefully arranged the logs and some kindling on the grate, and got a good fire going. "Would you care for something to drink? Or eat?"

"What do you have to drink?"

"Tea and water." It wasn't much, but he had to limit his trips to the marketplace. Unfortunately, he spotted Informants around the area once or twice, and he couldn't take the chance they'd catch his scent.

"Water is fine, thank you." Ambrosia strolled into the living room. She stopped at the back of the couch and ran her fingers along the woodwork. "You really built all of this?"

"Yes." Logan crossed the living room and headed into the kitchen with the fire burning. He wouldn't have had furniture otherwise, not to mention the cabin itself. Nothing, except the forest, existed here before his arrival. It was one of the many reasons he figured it would be a safe place to hide.

"It must've taken you months of labor to complete."

He never really thought about how much time had passed. It kept him busy—his hands and his mind. Logan shrugged. "I am not sure. I did not track the time."

Ambrosia raised an eyebrow. "How's that possible? Unless you did nothing else?"

"I did not." He collected a cup from the cabinet and poured some water from the pitcher he always kept full. It was easier to keep cool water in the house during the fall and winter months. Not so much during the spring and summer. He poured a second cup for himself and carried both across the room to where she stood waiting.

"Thank you." With a slight nod, she accepted the cup and took a sip. She stepped around the couch, her gaze flicking from one piece of furniture to the next before she turned back toward—Ambrosia bumped right into him, water spilling all over his fur and the floor as the cup fell from her hand. "Oh, gods! I'm sorry."

"That is okay. Just a little cold," Logan said.

He crouched on his haunches at the same time she bent over to pick up the cup. She slipped on some of the water, knocked him backward, and fell on top of him. Not only could he see the flush in her cheeks, but he felt her embarrassment. It amused him. He liked her tiny frame on top of his larger one.

"Oh, gods!" Ambrosia pressed her hands against his chest to get to her feet in a scrambled attempt.

"Mmm, we should have fallen to the ground sooner." A deep growl rumbled in his chest; he relished her touch. It was a turn-on.

Her eyebrows knitted together as she stared at him in utter confusion. "Why would you say that?"

Although she wasn't pushing against his pecs any longer, she stopped trying to get up. How honest should he be at the moment? Lifting his head close to hers, Logan wrapped an arm around her waist. "I enjoy having you against me like this."

Ambrosia's eyes widened, her body a little hotter. She shook her head. "Nothing about this is a good idea."

"Says who?" Every part of him thought it was a great idea. He wanted her, and she wanted him. Where it went from there... well, that, he wasn't sure was a good idea. He'd been on Markham's list since he left Métamorphe. She deserved more than a hunted shape shifter.

"Your leader, for one," she snapped.

Logan barely kept his snarl in check. He didn't want to scare her off. "Please do not associate me with *that* male. I am no longer a part of that village." Even if he were, he would never serve under Markham. He made that quite clear eighteen years ago. It was the reason he lived alone, away from his family, hidden away like a well-kept secret.

"I thought all of you backed him and his... purist lifestyle."

"No. We do not all agree. Most simply are too afraid to go against him." Informants hunted those that did. But he didn't want to talk about that. Logan tucked a loose strand of her hair behind her ear. "I do not think there is *any* reason we should not explore this... attraction."

She bit her bottom lip. Those bright amber eyes of hers stared at him.

It took every ounce of resistance not to pull Ambrosia down or lean up and kiss her lips. As much as he wanted her, he'd never take a female against her will. That happened way too often in Métamorphe. It wasn't something he supported.

"That I'm a hybrid… it doesn't bother you?" Ambrosia asked.

"I think you are beautiful. That is all that matters." He didn't care that she was a mixture of species because, in his eyes, she was stunning. With her burgundy hair swept back in a messy ponytail, the soft sea green scales along her back and shoulders, her tight, round ass, and smooth, long legs that led to a set of talons he'd love to feel digging into his back. He was desperately trying to keep a particular part of his anatomy from reacting, but damn, his imagination made that problematic.

"What if I still don't think this is a good idea, but I'm partial to a little fun?"

Logan slowly sat up with Ambrosia now in his lap, but that affected him less than he imagined it would. There was something else in her emotions that he felt besides attraction. Was it a concern? Was there someone she worried about? Maybe. He hadn't bothered even to ask if she had—"Do you have a mate?"

"What?" Her eyes widened. "Gods, no! If I had a mate, coming to thank you again in person would've been the *furthest* thing from my mind."

Thank Hades. He let out a sigh of relief. That wasn't something he wanted for her either, not when he tried to claim the spot for himself. Wow, two days, and he was already thinking that far ahead. Logan shook the thoughts from his head. "That is good to know."

Ambrosia inhaled and exhaled a deep breath. "It's not that. We have a unique experience with shape shifters, my sister, and me. I worry about how getting involved with one would affect her. That's all."

A unique experience? He didn't ask if she had experience with shape shifters at all. It never came up. Not that she shied away from him before. Or even now. But he didn't want to ruin the mood and ask either. There would be a time for it. After all, he was pretty patient. He could accept what she offered for now. Logan cupped her cheek. "I can handle a little fun."

"Gods, I was hoping you'd say that." Ambrosia sat up a touch and pressed her lips to his. Her tongue swept along the seam of his lips as she coaxed them open and deepened the kiss.

Fuck, she was hot. Logan wrapped an arm around her waist and quickly got to his feet. Damn. They were just kissing, and he was already hard as a rock. If all he had was *fun*, then he planned to take his time and enjoy every inch of her body. Logan lowered his hands to her tight, round ass and squeezed as he stepped forward, stopping when something crunched under his foot.

Breaking off the kiss, Ambrosia looked down before lifting her eyes back to his. "I think you just broke the cup."

"Better the cup than the table." He grinned. His lips crashed against hers as he walked around the couch and carried her to his bedroom. Although it wasn't necessary, he kicked the door shut with his foot before heading to the bed in the middle of the room. Her legs remained hooked around his back as he climbed onto the bed and lowered her body against the mattress.

The pads of his fingers skimmed across the scales on her shoulders as he broke the kiss. Both of their chests heaved with ragged breaths. Logan stared into those bright, beautiful amber eyes and caressed the top of her head. "Are you sure about this?"

"Absolutely," Ambrosia said. As if to emphasize her decision, she fused their mouths once again. Her arms unlinked from around his neck and stretched above her head. She released the kiss and nipped at his bottom lip. "Do I need to take it off myself? Or do you think you can handle that?"

"Oh, I can handle it, *Your Highness*." Grinning wide, Logan skated a trail of kisses down her neck, over her collarbone, and ended at the dip between her breasts. He undid her ponytail as he continued the path down her body. He fisted a handful of hair, his fingers playing in her silky, burgundy locks as he pressed a kiss to her belly button. His cock hardened more at the prospect of just seeing her even half-naked. Hades, he bet she was exquisite.

Her body arched beneath his lips as her talons gently scraped over his ass. A low growl left his mouth at the tingling sensation that crept along the length of his spine. Hades, he loved the way her talons felt against his skin, especially as they slipped through his fur. His hands slid beneath her t-shirt and grazed her abdomen. The feel of her creamy flesh beneath his hands was like satin. It was soft and completely hairless. Hades, would her whole body be like that?

Logan groaned as he pushed her t-shirt up. He brushed a trail of kisses and licked her soft, hairless skin. As her back arched, he wrapped his arm underneath her and tugged the top up and over her head. His gaze fell to the most beautiful pair of breasts he'd ever seen, each with a pert pink nipple.

"Like what you see?" Ambrosia asked.

Without hesitation, he nodded.

"Maybe you should show me how much," she whispered and brought her hands to his arms. Her fingers sifted through his fur, inching their way toward his biceps, collarbones, and chest.

A deep rumble escaped his throat. He didn't think his cock could get more erect, but, sure enough, it felt fucking stiff. He was more than ready to have her sex sheath his length, but he also wanted to take his sweet time. Logan lowered his head to the dip between her breasts as his fingers curled around her shoulders. He caressed the smooth green merfolk scales there, at her shoulder blades, and down her back as he wrapped his mouth around one of her breasts.

Ambrosia's body bowed with a gasped moan, pushing her breast further into his mouth. Her hands found their way to his shoulder blades, and she dug in with her nails, her grip on him tightening. As she slid a leg along his side, her talons raked across his ass.

Hades, she tasted like utter perfection. It took every ounce of willpower not to rip her jeans off her body and drive his tongue deep into her sex. Logan switched to her other breast and sucked on her nipple as he kneaded the breast he'd just had in his mouth.

"Oh, gods!" Ambrosia cried out, wrapping both of her legs around his waist. She tugged him closer, her jeans creating friction and heat between them.

Gently brushing his thumb across her pebbled nipple, he licked a path from her breast over her collarbone and up her neck before he fused their lips. Fisting a handful of her hair, he caressed her thigh. He encouraged her to unhook her legs from around his backside with his touch. He unbuttoned and unzipped her pants, then stretched his body out as he released the kiss. Her glassy gaze stared back at him. "If I do not take them off now, then I am going to rip them."

Her only response—she lifted her hips off the bed. "Then take them off."

She didn't have to tell him twice. Logan's lips crashed against hers again in another deep kiss as he gripped the sides of her pants and underwear and tugged them down over her hips. He skimmed her neck with his tongue and brushed kisses down her body as he peeled her bottoms down the length of her legs.

Tossing her pants and underwear to the side, he slid down until his knees hit the edge of the bed. It was a good thing the bed was as big as it was.

Not that he cared. His eyes raked over Ambrosia from her long, luscious, burgundy-colored hair to her bright, amber eyes and plump lips before taking in her slender neck and exquisitely smooth sea-green scales. Finally, he took in her beautiful round breasts, her flat belly, and her hips before his gaze widened at the sight of her hairless sex. "You are stunning."

He heard her heartbeat quicken, and heat radiated off her body. Her vanilla scent permeated his nostrils until he could no longer contain himself. Logan licked her slit from end to end, keeping his hands across her abdomen to hold her in place as he sucked on her nub and drove his tongue deep into her sex.

Ambrosia cried out in ecstasy as she gripped the back of his head. Her talons scraped his shoulders, and she gyrated her hips against his tongue. "Oh, gods! Don't stop!"

With the way she tasted, he didn't intend to. He nipped at her nub, switching his hold from her belly to her hips, swirled his tongue, and drove at her harder and deeper. His eyes lifted so he could watch. He wanted to see what she looked like when she came.

Her hands moved to the bed, and her fingers curled, balling up the sheets as her body bowed and her hips bucked beneath his continuous assault of her sex. She moaned as his hands skated up her sides until he reached her breasts, pinching her nipples before he kneaded both of them.

"Oh, gods! I'm coming!" Her talons dug into his shoulders until little bites of pain shot straight to his cock as she exploded into his mouth.

With her juices coating his tongue, he lapped at everything she had to give him, sucking on her sex until he swallowed every drop. He'd tasted nothing so sweet before. Her taste was as intoxicating as her scent. Something he could get drunk off time and time again. Something he'd never get enough of having.

As he crawled up her body, he pressed soft kisses across her abdomen. Logan sucked on each nipple and licked up her neck. When he hovered over her, their gazes met. Her lips crashed against his. He deepened the kiss as he lowered his body to hers until her breasts pressed against his pecs. Angling his cock at her slick entrance, he thrust inside her in one swift move. Fuck, she was tight.

She moaned into his mouth as her nails scored his back, and her talons gripped his ass. Feeling her sex sheathed around his cock stilled him. Her hips rocked against him. Ambrosia certainly seemed to know exactly how to get him moving.

Their tongues entangled as he fisted a handful of her hair, and he pistoned in and out of her. His cock never entirely left her slick folds. Hades, she felt terrific. The way she enveloped him was utter perfection. They fit together in ways he hadn't imagined possible.

Breaking off the kiss, her back arched, pushing her breasts more against his chest as she met him thrust for thrust. Her nails raked down his back, and the grip she had on him with her legs tightened. Through ragged breaths, loud moans filled the surrounding air.

Logan buried his face in her neck. With one hand, he grabbed hold of her hip, and the other curled around her shoulder as he drilled into her faster and faster. He couldn't tell where she ended, and he began. Her scent thickened in his nose. "Come for me, Ambrosia. Come for me."

He gently dragged his canines down her neck and sucked on her shoulder for emphasis. He wasn't marking her, though some part of him, deep down, felt the desire. That was something he wouldn't do without her permission. Hades knew he wanted to. Now that he had a taste of her, he knew for sure she was his, and he wanted others to know who she belonged to, even if she didn't realize it yet.

Her talons dug a little more into his ass as she cried out. The walls of her core seized around him, and an orgasm pulsated through her body. His set-off, exploding out of him in endless waves. Though their breathing remained ragged, it took several long moments for both of their bodies to still. Once their breaths settled, Logan nuzzled her neck and brushed a soft kiss across her pulse point. "Amazing."

"Yes, it was," she whispered as she stroked the back of his head and along his ears. Neither of them made any effort to move. Ambrosia pressed a tender kiss to his cheek. "It's something I'd like to do again."

Logan grinned widely. "Me too."

Chapter Three

Ambrosia leaned her head back under the spray of the waterfall. Going to the basin this time of night was probably reckless, but she'd done it for years. Many of the merfolk hybrids in her village opted to go out into the ocean, but she preferred the basin for several reasons, like her sister. It was private, so she didn't have to worry about peepers while she swam naked. Plus, it was peaceful and held plenty of splendid memories for her.

Although, at that moment, those heart-warming memories weighed on her heavily. She'd been seeing Logan for a couple of weeks now. They had gotten together practically every day since the first time they had sex. No talking, just sex. That was their agreement. Why did she want to tell him about her father? His death? About her twin sister? That they were shape shifter hybrids? That it was the reason she hadn't thought their involvement would be a good idea? Gods, all these things she purposely avoided.

Ambrosia ducked beneath the water. Gills opened on the sides of her neck, allowing her to breathe without issue, and she swam forward. Unlike other merfolk hybrids, she didn't have a merfolk form. Just the gills when she swam underneath the surface and light green scales along her back. Nothing more. As she popped above the surface about halfway back to the basin's edge, her gills closed and blended back into her neck. Her ears twitched when she heard leaves crunching above the din of the waterfall.

Logan stepped out from the treeline. He shifted from his animal form to his humanoid form. Although she heard the cracking and popping of his bones over the rushing sound of the waterfall, it didn't bother her. She saw her father go through the same transition multiple times before his death. Ambrosia chewed on the inside of her cheek. Damn. She hoped she'd have more time to figure out her feelings for Logan before she saw him again. "What're you doing here?"

"I was on my way home from the marketplace, and I caught your scent." He strode a little closer and sat on a nearby boulder. "What about you? Kind of late for a swim."

"Yeah, well, after a long night, I find this is the best place to be. Not only do I get my scales wet, but I get to relax a bit." Not that it was the stress of running a karaoke bar that brought her here tonight. Nope. That belonged to him.

"Long night?"

Right. It was her decision not to discuss anything. "You said you came from the marketplace, right?" She paused and didn't continue until he nodded. "Then I'm sure you passed by Zancle's Rock. It's a karaoke bar that my mom owns. Both my sister and I work there. I run the bar and handle most of the day-to-day activities, and my sister is in charge of the music." Ambrosia half-shrugged. "I'm good at listening, and she's good at socializing."

"You? Not good at socializing?" He chuckled. "I do not believe that for a second."

Smirking, she rolled her eyes. "Regardless, listening to nymphs, satyrs, and the occasional merfolk can get tedious. Anyone really." This was why she had her office built behind the kitchen, as far away from the customers as possible.

"I imagine if you must listen to nymphs talk about their sexapades all night, it very well could get tedious. Mind if I join you?" Logan gestured to the water.

Ambrosia busted out in laughter. Sexapades. That was a good one. The water hid most of her body, but if he got too much closer, he'd probably see more. She opened her mouth and snapped it shut. It was a simple request. Why couldn't she give him a simple answer?

"If that is not okay, then maybe I can just stick my toes in the water?"

She couldn't deny him sticking his toes in the water or joining her either, could she? She wanted him to, but she also needed to tell him what weighed on her mind. It wasn't a big deal. Her physical desire for him could remain in check. Ambrosia swallowed the lump in the back of her throat. "Um, it's okay. You're welcome to join me in the water."

"Thank you," he said as he stood. Closing the distance between them, he got into the water until it rose to his chest. His gaze stayed on her the entire time. "There seems to be something else on your mind. Care to talk about it?"

Ambrosia sighed. How did Logan know that? Either he was good at reading her facial tics, or he possessed an ability they hadn't discussed. Seeing as he'd done it since they met, the latter seemed more likely. Not that she intended to ask. "Am I that easy to read?"

"Sometimes."

She didn't know what to make of his answer. It didn't seem like much of one. Sighing again, she tilted her head and studied him. His aquamarine eyes lit up, sparkling against the night sky. A shiver shot down her spine. Good gods, when he looked at her like that, she could almost swear he saw every secret. She bit the inside of her cheek. There didn't seem to be any good reason not to tell him the truth. No matter how much she questioned the decision.

Except he wasn't an Informant. They carried marks on their right shoulders. And Logan didn't have one. He just had scars. Not that she ever asked about those. Part of her wanted to know how he had gotten them. She even wanted to know about the one sibling he had mentioned. "Things are... changing between us. I just don't know how to handle that."

"Why does it have to be handled at all? Why do you not just follow the path and see where it leads us?"

Moment of truth. Ambrosia bit the inside of her cheek again. "You know how I told you that my sister and I... we have a complicated relationship with shape shifters?"

"Yes. I remember that."

How did she tell him this? Gods, she didn't know. Just blurt it out. No. That didn't feel right. Her gaze dropped to the rippling water in front of her. Ambrosia opened her mouth and snapped it shut. Her eyes lifted back to his. "We're what makes it complicated. Our father... was a shape shifter. My sister and I are hybrids."

Logan stood there in silence, his eyes widening as he stared at her. "No part of you even looks shape shifter."

"I know. That's where it gets complicated. My sister and I are twins, mostly. I take more after our mother with the siren and merfolk ancestry, and my sister got more of our father. She has canine ears, just on the side, like mine." She tapped her ears. "There are a few other things that differentiate us, not that any of that is the point. I guess it's just... someone killed our father when we were young. That, combined with the fact that we hide that part of our genes, complicates our relationship."

Inhaling and exhaling a deep breath, he scrubbed his face with his hand. Slowly, he nodded and stepped a little closer to her. "You are worried what she would think if she found out about our relationship," he said, more than questioned.

"A little, yeah. Just by being who we are, we're already targets. I know what happens to shape shifters who mate outside their species." At least if anyone ever discovered them. Not that she wanted to admit it, but her attraction to Logan went beyond sex. She wanted a genuine relationship with him where they held hands in public and went out to dinner in the marketplace. But they couldn't have that. Not with Informants constantly searching for hybrids like her. "My sister was closer to our father than me. She took it harder than I did when he died. You and me, I think if she found out, she'd see it as a disgrace to his memory, to everything he sacrificed to protect us."

"Even if she saw you happy? Something I am certain your father would have wanted for both of you."

No. Maybe. Her sister swore she'd never mate. That didn't mean she had to follow the same path. Not that she was even thinking about mating Logan. It was way too soon for that. But she couldn't deny that she cared for him. "I don't know."

He closed the distance between them. Reaching up, he caressed Ambrosia's cheek with the back of his knuckles. "Do you think it would be worth it to find out? See where this goes?"

Part of her screamed, *yes*. The other part, the more logical part, understood everything he risked just by having sex with her. The last two weeks had been nothing short of amazing. If she were smart, she'd cut off all ties with him and end things before they couldn't turn back. "I don't get you. With what I just told you and how things work with your species, you're still willing to risk being with me?"

"I have learned that some things in life are worth the risk." Leaning in, he brushed a soft kiss across her lips. His mouth tugged into a smile as he stroked her cheek with his thumb.

She hoped that was true. No matter how much she told herself otherwise, it was already too late to turn away from Logan. Grinning, Ambrosia wrapped her arms around his neck and pressed her body against his. "I guess there are."

A soft growl came out of him. "You are very naked."

"That, I am." Hooking her legs around his waist, she fused their lips together. Something about this kiss was different. It was unhurried. Even the desire she felt coming from him was different. It wasn't the urgent, uncontrollable need she was accustomed to feeling.

Shivers ran down her spine as his hands gingerly traversed her back and cupped her ass. He turned them both around, deepening the kiss and starting toward the edge of the basin.

Ambrosia caressed the nape of his neck as their tongues entangled and the kiss deepened further. Good gods, this wasn't like anything they shared with one another before. It was like they both wanted to take their time and genuinely enjoy each other. Not that she thought for one second they'd make it back to his cabin. Besides, they were utterly alone.

Logan climbed out of the water, and it sluiced off both their bodies. His fingers skimmed along the small of her back, inching up the length of her spine. He followed the pattern created by her scales.

It was nothing more than a tender touch, yet she arched into it. His caresses sent blasts of heat to her core. She moaned into the kiss and gently raked her fingers along his shoulders as he eased her back onto the grassy area of the ground. Not that it felt cold in the slightest against her bare skin. Every part of her body was warm, and he'd barely touched her.

With a low rumble in his chest, he broke the kiss, trailed a path down her jaw, and nipped at her shoulder. Lowering his body to hers, he continued the trail he'd started and swirled his tongue around her pert nipple, then latched onto her breast. As one hand fisted a handful of her hair, the other kneaded her other breast.

Letting out a soft gasp, her back bowed, pushing her breasts into him. Heat radiated through her body. It just made her want to touch him more, to learn every nuance. She gently dragged her talons across his ass, skimmed her nails over his bunched-up shoulders, tracing each muscle. It didn't matter how much of him she felt beneath her hands; she still yearned for more. He seemed all too happy to comply.

His mouth switched from one breast to the other, not that it stopped him from paying both breasts attention. He used the tips of his claws to caress her collarbone and brushed a thumb over her nipple.

Between the way he touched her and the desire that rolled off him, her body was on fire. She had an inferno building in her core. Ambrosia's nails skated up his spine, along the nape of his neck, and across the backs of his ears. Her talons raked over his ass again until they reached the small of his back, splitting her thighs wide.

Logan growled. He gently traced a path along the valley of her breasts, down her abdomen, and then across her belly with his claws. Retracting his claws, he rubbed her nub with his thumb as he slipped one finger inside of her.

Moaning, she rocked her hips against his finger as his lips crashed against hers. She swept her tongue along the inside of his mouth. For the first time since they'd met and agreed to a sexual relationship, she felt every emotion coming off him in small waves. It wasn't like he just poured his feelings into the kiss as he deepened it once more. No. This was something more. Something she'd never felt before. Something she couldn't quite explain. Not that she was sure she was ready to, either.

Her talons dug into his back as he slipped another finger deep inside of her. As his fingers slowly penetrated her sex repeatedly, she rocked her hips against him. Ambrosia broke the kiss, both of their breaths ragged as she tightened her grip on his shoulders. "Oh, gods. Don't stop."

Burying his face in her neck, he nipped at her shoulder and rubbed a small circle around her nub. He licked along her neck and then nibbled on her ear. "Come for me."

Somehow, her body heard his instruction. She didn't know if it was the way he whispered the words, or if it was the jolts his tongue shot straight to her core, or a combination of both. Whatever caused it, the inner walls of her sex clenched around his fingers. An orgasm pulsated through her body as she cried out his name.

Logan kept his fingers inside her and helped her ride out the release. His gaze fell to hers as he pulled his fingers out and licked them clean. "I love how you taste."

Her eyes widened ever so slightly, and she bit her bottom lip as she watched his tongue work over his fingers. For a moment, she almost swore she could feel the gentle roughness of his tongue at her slit, but his head was nowhere near the apex of her thighs. Logan nuzzled her neck before his lips fused to hers once again. He stroked down her side, gripped onto her hip, and slowly eased his cock deep inside her sex.

Skimming her fingertips down his back, she rocked her hips as he slowly drove his cock into her repeatedly. As their tongues entangled more, she couldn't tell where her breath began and his ended. Gods, she loved the way he felt with his body pressed against her like this. Despite their height difference, they fit together like perfect puzzle pieces.

The gentle strokes of his shaft against her inner walls were torturous, but she wouldn't change any part of this. It wasn't just how good he felt on a physical level. It was more profound than that. Somehow, he had wiggled his way into her heart. This time between them expressed everything they both felt. Even if neither of them could speak their truth, it didn't change how sensuous this was between them—something she never wanted to end.

Her hips lifted to meet his thrust for thrust as a low growl rose in his chest. She loved that sound and desperately wanted him to make it again. Ambrosia dragged her hands across his back, his fur sifting through her fingers as she explored every contour and inch of his muscles. Her talons raked down his ass, splitting her thighs wider, which allowed him to penetrate her deeper.

Another growl left his mouth as he buried his face in the crook of her neck. He tightened his grip on her hip as he braced himself with his other arm. He pistoned in and out of her sex, faster and harder.

Each stroke of his cock sent a jolt of lightning through every synapse of her sex. It was like she felt him deep in her core. Arching her back, she dug her nails into his shoulder blades. Her thighs tensed, and a powerful orgasm slammed through her body. Ambrosia cried out in ecstasy.

Logan bit down on her shoulder with a roar as an orgasm exploded out of him. His fingers dug into her hip as the two of them rode out their releases together. A moment passed, and he licked the mark he'd left on her shoulder.

Both of their chests heaved with ragged breaths as they lay there in silent bliss. She lazily stroked up and down his spine. There wasn't any hurry for either of them to move. That he marked her kind of surprised her. It was something she'd seen on her mother's shoulder. According to her father, it was the way a canine shape shifter marked their mate. That didn't seem likely. She and Logan hadn't mated. Despite that minor fact, his action didn't bother her. Not in the least. As her breathing steadied, she pressed a kiss to his forehead. "Just...wow."

"I could not have said it better." Logan's gaze met hers. He brushed a loving kiss across her lips.

Staring into those bright aquamarine eyes of his, Ambrosia smiled. She saw the change between them, even felt it. Maybe this was the beginning.

Chapter Four

Once afternoon meal passed, Derrick met Gabby at the river right outside the borders of the territory of Métamorphe, just like they did anytime they could. But she'd been distant lately, avoiding him, refusing to tell him what was wrong. The situation what it was, these moments they could steal away were so precious.

She stood at the water's edge, her arms crossed over her chest, the sunlight glinting off her pure-white fur. The tip of her tail flicked back and forth ever so slightly as she stared into the aquamarine water of Ryn River. Derrick's ears twitched as he listened intently, searching for any sign that another was nearby. Nobody followed him, but he had to be sure. Confident they would remain alone; Derrick shifted to his humanoid form and crossed the grass where she stood. As he came up behind her, he placed his hands gently on her shoulders. She flinched away from him, and he frowned.

"Gabby..." Placing his hands on her shoulders again, he gently turned her around. She refused to look at him. Fear spiraled in his gut. "Tell me what is going on. What is wrong?" She didn't speak, not even as he placed a finger under her chin and tilted her head up, trying to catch her emerald-green gaze. He towered two feet taller than her in either form. But she had never appeared afraid of him. Never jerked away from him. Not once. They'd been together three years now, despite their different forms, his Informant status, or how it affected their relationship. The punishments were more extreme for those in his position than for the regular inhabitants of the village. Should Markham discover he had mated without permission, the punishment would be more severe. Yes, many openly frowned upon the different forms together, but no one in the pack was ignorant of what that truly meant. Neither of them ever cared about any of that, though. They only cared about being together in whatever way they could.

"Please, talk to me."

"I do not know how." Gabby's voice trembled. "This was not supposed to happen, Derrick. This, this was not..." She visibly swallowed. "I was taking the herbs. I do not know what happened." Tears spilled onto her cheeks, disappearing into her fur.

A slow chill spread through him as a sinking feeling filled him up. Derrick closed his eyes and drew her body against his. "Oh, Gabby... Oh, gods. You are with child." It wasn't a question. It didn't need to be.

"I believe so. I cannot confirm it for a week or so longer. But I think so. I..."

As she dissolved into sobs, he held her even tighter against him. So many emotions rolled through him all at once he almost couldn't sort through them. Having a young, especially with your true mate, should be joyous news. A life they created together; their love made manifest. But they could never have children and raise a family. Not here. Not under Markham's rule, with his laws such as they were.

Especially for a couple like them.

Lowering their bodies to the ground, Derrick held her on his lap, stroking her ears and the back of her head, letting his touch drift down her side. He kept his senses on high alert, ensuring he would hear anyone who drew near. He was quiet as he allowed her to calm. After several moments, he spoke, "Everything is going to be alright. I am going to make this alright."

"How in Hades' name do you expect to do that, Derrick? If I am truly with child..." She shook her head. "As soon as Markham discovers it, you and I both know I will be no longer. And you—"

"Stop it, Gabby. Do not speak of that. It will not happen." But he was fooling himself. Markham didn't allow the different forms to mix. Period. The male's obsession with purity of blood would never allow that. If she was with child and refused to leave the village because he couldn't, there would not be another outcome. And that outcome was not something he would, or could, allow. "I was going to tell you. I got a lead on Logan."

"Another one?"

"This time is different. I am sure of it." At least he hoped. It was all he had to hold on to these days. "He has stayed hidden for this long. Perhaps he can help us. He may even know how to leave the isle." Or kill Markham. Not that it was likely even possible. Leaving the isle, though, maybe he would know how to do that. If they could manage that, his Informant status wouldn't matter. Sure, if a shape shifter deserted the pack, Informants hunted them across the isle and dragged them home to make an example of, but he doubted Markham would send anyone after him and Gabby if they left completely. Too much work. If they could figure out how to escape and he could get their families to come too, he knew Gabby's twin would come; those two would follow each other anywhere. Her mother would be the issue.

"If Logan knew how to leave the isle, he would not still be on it. I never knew him well, but even I know that."

"His bloodline is still here. His family lives in torment like the rest of us because of the ways of our king. I do not think he would leave without them. I am going to seek him out and attempt to speak with him."

"And what if nothing comes of it?" The weariness in her voice made his heart break.

"Then I will continue to search for a solution until I find one." Derrick lifted her chin until their eyes met. "I will not give up on life with you, Gabriella. Never. You *are* my life. I will do whatever it takes to spend eternity in this world with you. And *if* there is a child within your womb, I will do whatever it takes to keep them safe as well." She opened her mouth to speak again, but he cut her off with a kiss. "Do not worry," he said against her lips. "I am going to take care of everything. I promise."

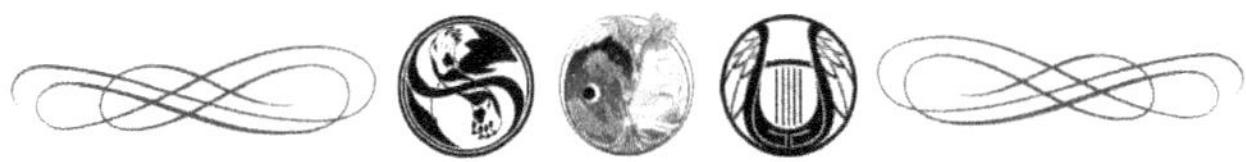

Derrick broke away from the group of Informants he scouted with. It wasn't uncommon for Informants to do so, but it was something he rarely did. Hopefully, he didn't arouse any suspicions regarding his true intentions. He weaved in and out of the trees until he got far enough away from the pack to make his way in the direction he truly wanted to go.

When he neared the marketplace, he shifted to his humanoid form and threw on his camouflage, staying in the shadows as much as possible. People were wary of shape shifters, especially Informants. They were even warier of those searching for information. It took too long, too many months of solo scouting missions to get even a fraction of the information he sought.

Though he had a vague idea of where the fighting ring was, he didn't even know if Logan would be there. All he knew was that someone had spotted a male shape shifter with aquamarine eyes in the fight ring at least once. The fur color didn't match, but the eyes did. This was probably another wild goose chase, and he was more than likely going to end up going back to the village no further along in his quest than when he started. But he had to try. All would be lost if he didn't try. He couldn't go down this path any longer. The danger of his position was constant. He twiddled his thumbs just waiting for the ax—claws, and teeth, instead—to come down upon him, and his mate. It was only a matter of time.

Too much death, pain, and misery. A love he couldn't reveal without bringing oblivion to himself and Gabriella. Orders he refused to follow. Punishment after punishment. His sister's quest for freedom that would never come while Markham still had a beating heart.

Not to mention his mother's most recent miscarriage. She still wouldn't rise from her bed.

He could take no more and could numb himself no longer.

Derrick finally located Belly of the Beast and ducked inside the ominous building. The entrance, shaped like the head of a beast, made it fairly easy to find within the marketplace. Removing his camouflage, he situated himself in a corner, leaned against the wall, and waited.

Either Logan would show, or he wouldn't. If he didn't, Derrick would go home. If he did, hopefully, he would talk. Logan was one of the few shape shifters to have a death sentence on his head and escape detection. And Markham hunted him so relentlessly. Yet Logan remained hidden for a long time; he had to be alive. If Markham found him, his death would have been a public affair.

The sound of a door opening out of sight reached his ears. Searching beyond the crowd, Derrick eyed the front entrance. No one came in that way.

Looking around, he caught sight of the one who entered the establishment from a back entrance. It was a canine shape shifter, standing just over nine feet tall, with dark brown fur. It was Logan. His fur might have changed somewhat, but it was him. The male kept to the shadows, crossing his arms as he scanned the throng of people.

Derrick pushed slowly off the wall and tried to catch Logan's eye across the room, but he was busy surveying the crowd. Sticking to the wall and in the shadows himself, Derrick moved to the other side of the room. His eyes didn't stray from Logan, so he didn't risk losing him in the mass. Not when he had searched for him for so long.

He hadn't laid eyes on the male in over eighteen years. Not since he warned him of Markham's declaration and told him he had no choice but to go into hiding. Perhaps the gods were finally smiling at him.

When he fully crossed the room and stood in front of Logan, he couldn't quite decide what to do first. A hug? A handshake? Neither seemed appropriate, so he just folded his arms across his chest. They'd once spent time together regularly and had been as close as brothers. Derrick opened his mouth, then closed it again. His eyes dropped to the floor, then lifted to Logan's face. Derrick finally found some words, but they seemed weak and failing. "I need your help."

Logan flicked his gaze to him. "Help is a broad statement. Care to be more specific?"

Oh, how to word this? How to put it all into words, without saying something that would have the male writing him off entirely and walking away. It had to be good, too, because he would not get another chance. It had taken him this long to find Logan, and there was no doubt in his mind the male would likely be even more careful after this. If Derrick located him—albeit with difficulty—any of the others could, too.

"You did something few have ever accomplished. You have stayed hidden without detection. No matter what you say to me, I will not out you. I need to do you one better. I need to get off the isle, or I need *him* to die. One or the other, I care not which. Preferably the latter. With circumstances what they are at present, I cannot continue going on as I am. And I have no one else to ask for help with this."

Logan scrubbed a hand down his face and shook his head. "There is no way off the isle. If that were possible, I would have grabbed Pierce, my sisters, and my mother a long time ago and gotten them off this abyss. And killing Markham, Derrick, please do not tell me you believe it is possible. Because, if it is, I do not know how."

Derrick's body sagged against the wall as he pinched the bridge of his nose. He sighed with exasperation. "I do not. I just... I do not know what I expected. I just had to try. Devin has exhausted herself, but she has found no answers either. Things are... I envy you, your banishment, honestly." Gods, he didn't know. Logan didn't know about his mother. More than likely, he didn't know of his youngest sister's existence either.

"My life is not something to envy. A life alone is practically nonexistent. I have searched for many *solaris*, and there only seems to be one place Informants will not go."

"Where?" That he was desperate was on the tip of Derrick's tongue, but he was reluctant to utter the words. He didn't act out of desperation or fear. But if Gabby indeed was pregnant, she couldn't stay in the village. She and their child would not be safe.

"I will tell you, but you must first tell me of my family. My brother, my sisters, my mother—are they well?"

Oh, gods, Derrick didn't want to be the one to tell him. It should come from Pierce. Too many times, they got into arguments on the very subject. Not that he didn't understand why the male stayed away, never attempting to find Logan and make contact. But it still didn't make it right. He wouldn't lie to Logan, though. About any of it.

Derrick inhaled and exhaled a deep breath. "Dahlia and Zinnia are well enough. However, neither would make you overly proud as their older brother. Pierce suffers in silence, though he would never admit to it. You have another sister. Her name is Lillianna, and she is nearing her sixteenth *solaris* of birth. She is beautiful, bright, and very gifted. She came into life after a series of miscarriages that left your mother very ill. I suspect Lillianna's birth was too much for her to take. I am so very sorry." The words were meaningless, though apologies like that always were. But not even he could hide the sorrow he felt at telling another their mother passed away. Over fifteen years ago. And no one told him until now.

Logan stood there and stared wide-eyed at him. The veins in his neck throbbed. Derrick heard the male's pulse quicken. Logan balled up his fists, his claws digging into his palms. The need for vengeance practically bled from his gaze. Anger rolled off him in waves. Logan growled. "Migas Village," he spat out and shoved off the wall.

"Logan! Wait!" The male stopped but didn't turn around. "Can I find you again? Please? There is much you do not know, and there is too much at stake."

"Here." Without another word, Logan headed straight for the ring.

Derrick stood there as he could do and say nothing more, not tonight. Shaking his head, he kept to the shadows and made for the exit. Curse Pierce to Hades and back. Fuck Markham and fuck the male's father. Pierce should've found the courage and told Logan the truth of it all long ago. One visit wouldn't have jeopardized the safety of his sisters any more than what he already did behind their *king's* back. Pierce was very skilled, but Derrick knew him well enough to know the male didn't follow Markham's orders any more than he did.

He reached the back exit, slammed the door open, and stormed into the alley. Derrick leaned against the wall for a bit, gulping down air to ease the ache in his chest. He took a few moments to steady himself, then threw on his camouflage. Pushing off the wall, he headed back the same way he'd come.

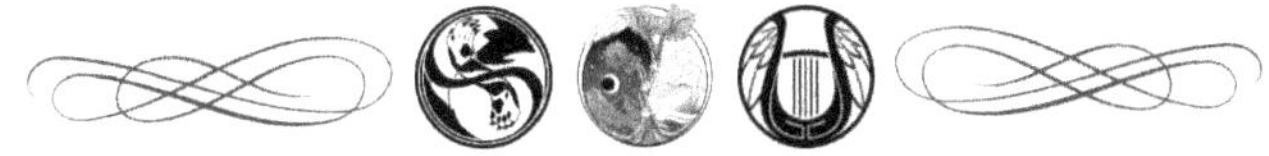

Logan gripped the back of his neck as he strode down the path to his cabin. Getting in that wire cage hadn't been the best idea. It took him too long to knock the troll down. Not that the creature didn't get in a few good hits. That was the point.

His mother was dead. A sister he knew nothing about. *Damn it!* All these years without that knowledge, all of that time gone. Why hadn't Pierce sought him out? Tried to find him and at least tell him what happened? His brother could've had the fucking courtesy to do that much. Logan swiped at the tears that rolled down his cheeks again and winced. His right eye had swollen shut. Not that it stopped the damn leaking.

His fury got the best of him in the cage. If it hadn't been for the rules, he likely would've killed the troll. It wasn't the troll's fault his mother had died. Or that he lost all this time with Lillianna. No. His father and Markham were the ones to blame. His father for forcing so many pregnancies on his mother. With all the miscarriages his mother had suffered,

Ailwin still got her pregnant again. And Markham for forcing him out of Métamorphe.

Logan wiped at his face again. Why wouldn't the damn tears stop? He didn't want to feel this anymore. He barely noticed the smoke billowing from the chimney, stepping into the clearing. Stopping halfway to the staircase, he sniffed the air. Something sweet mixed with something savory? His gaze flicked to the door. Shit. He forgot Ambrosia took the night off and planned to spend it with him. Although maybe this was a good thing. He wouldn't mind holding her.

He hadn't told her about his family yet, and he only learned of hers a week earlier. Even after she told him, he couldn't believe her father was a shape shifter. Not that he asked for details either, and that nagged at him. Maybe it would be an excellent night to clear the air. Swallowing the lump in the back of his throat, he headed to the front door and entered his cabin.

"I was thinking…" Ambrosia's words trailed off as her gaze flicked from the stove to him. "By all the gods, what happened to your face?"

"I uh… I just…" The words didn't want to come. That wasn't true. The words were there; he couldn't get them out. Closing the distance between them, he enveloped Ambrosia in his arms and buried his face in the crook of her neck.

Ambrosia's arms came around him. She gingerly stroked the back of his head. "Okay. Hey, whatever happened, we'll work through it."

If only it were that simple. How did he explain? How did he tell her he lost his temper? After receiving the worst news, he had jumped into a cage and beat the shit out of whomever volunteered. Curse his brother to Hades and back. Damn Pierce! He shouldn't have found out like this.

Logan's body shook ever so slightly as he tightened his hold on Ambrosia. He had to calm down. It was the only way he'd be able to tell her anything, but he didn't know how. Not when his blood was boiling like this. All he could think about was his mother. The last time he saw her, the last words he ever spoke to her.

Markham's announcement had been crap. The male forgave no one for their so-called transgressions. Least of all, Galenus. No way could Logan stand by and do nothing. He had to find the male and warn him. Stopping in the front room of their small hut, Logan pressed a kiss to his mother's cheek. "I need to go, Mom."

"I thought we agreed you would stay. You cannot go against Markham, not again."

They agreed on nothing, even if they had discussed it twice since Markham made his declaration. Yeah, the consequences of his previous actions had been dire, but he couldn't watch a wonderful male get killed. Not when he could stop it. "I have to go. If Galenus returns, he will not leave alive."

"Please..." No matter how many times she tried, she couldn't get another word out.

"No. That male has been nothing but good to us. He does not deserve what is coming. If you had not insisted on trying to help Dahlia so much, we would not be in this situation!" Logan snarled and stormed out of their hut. In all his twenty-three years, he never once yelled at his mother. Nor had he ever refused to comfort her when waves of anguish rolled off her. He stood by her side and cared for her through multiple miscarriages, but he couldn't stop to console her.

Not this time.

A soft melody resounded around him. Was Ambrosia singing? Yes. The voice belonged to her. She wasn't just stroking the back of his neck and along his ears, but she sang too. It wasn't a lullaby he recognized, but that was precisely what it sounded like—a lullaby about sailing across the sea.

Inhaling and exhaling a deep breath, her sweet scent filled his nostrils. Slowly, his anger ebbed. With his rage gone, Logan shifted his hands, cupped her thighs, and lifted Ambrosia off the ground. He walked out of the kitchen and headed into the living room by memory alone. He didn't dare move his head. Not yet.

The tension in his shoulders eased. He sat down on the couch just as tears rolled down his cheeks. Burying his face further in the crook of Ambrosia's neck, he wrapped his arms around her waist and replayed the last time he ever saw his mother in his mind again. He'd never be able to apologize. Never tell her how sorry he'd been. Never hug her one last time. She'd been concerned for him, and he'd been so focused on trying to help someone else, someone he had failed. He hadn't found Galenus. Instead, Markham had the male killed and claimed he was responsible.

He'd only hurt someone he loved, which forced him to run and hide for eighteen years. And for what? He always thought he could go back for his family one day. Now his mother was gone. Zinnia... Pierce... He sobbed harder. He had lost them all forever.

"Shh, it's okay." Ambrosia caressed the back of his neck. "I've got you. I've always got you."

She had him, didn't she? Just as he had her. But Ambrosia wasn't all he had. *You have another sister.* Derrick's words replayed in his head. Another sister. A sister who probably didn't even know he existed. Not once had Derrick mentioned anything negative about his brother. Did that mean he hadn't lost Pierce yet? That he could still get some of his family back? Not that it would change the facts. "She is gone," he whispered.

"Who's gone, love?"

He couldn't say it. The moment he said it aloud, it would become real. All too real. Except it *was* real. Derrick wouldn't lie to him. Not about something like this. The male had been the one to warn him of the threat upon his life. It didn't matter that he planned to apologize to his mother. If he hadn't run, he would have forfeited his life. And Markham would have killed more of his family. Logan swallowed. Ambrosia's gentle touch and sweet scent soothed him. "My mother... I just found out she died. I can never apologize. She will never know how sorry I am."

"I'm so sorry, love. It's never easy to lose a parent." Ambrosia pressed a soft kiss to his forehead. "No matter how ugly our words get, mothers have a way of knowing that we don't mean them."

"What if I meant them?" Truthfully, he meant them. He had meant every single word. As shocked as he acted with what Derrick told him about Dahlia, it didn't surprise him at all. Zinnia did, though. Yeah, she followed him around before he left, but he always thought she had a strong will and a mind of her own. How could she have fallen in with Dahlia? He didn't understand. It didn't sound like his *Zinni*, the one he remembered.

"Then they forgive us." Ambrosia's fingers lazily stroked up and down his spine. "I'm sure that, no matter what you said, your mother forgave you before she passed."

Hades, he prayed she was right, that his mother forgave him. Maybe not for what he said, but for how he said it and for not consoling her one last time. He left Métamorphe for the last time only a few days after Markham punished him and his mother for his decisions. Then they suffered all over again for his choices. If Markham had never discovered his ability, then it would've all been fine. Another moment he'd never forget.

Standing there in Markham's hut, Logan glowered. He didn't know how the male found out about his empathic abilities, but he'd be damned before he used them to benefit their so-called king. "There is nothing you can do that would ever make me become one of your minions."

Markham said nothing as he sat on his throne and stared at Logan. Silence stretched between them for several moments. "Nothing but the truth. That is unfortunate. But you will regret your refusal."

"That depends on the perspective." Sure, his father would be upset that he turned down the Informant position, but he didn't care. He wasn't his brother. He'd gladly accept whatever punishment came his way. It still wouldn't be enough to make him become an Informant.

"I suppose it does. We shall see."

Two pairs of jaws grabbed his hind legs and yanked him from Markham's hut. He stayed in his animal form the entire time he'd been in there. It had seemed like the best decision. Not that the two Informants now with him—a familiar female voice drew his attention. His gaze flicked toward his family's hut as someone dragged his mother out the door. Logan lunged forward. "No! She has nothing to do with this!"

His words had fallen on deaf ears. Markham hadn't cared. The male probably still didn't care. Derrick told him things had gotten worse. Worse than someone raping his mother because he declined the Informant position? All this time had passed, and he still couldn't get those horrid images out of his head. It had been one of the few times Markham punished his brother, too. They chained Pierce down next to him. They both had scars because of it.

Slowly, Logan lifted his head and scrubbed his hand down his face. If things were worse, then he needed to get his remaining family out of that place. His brother and the sister he knew little about. They deserved a better life. If he could do that, then at least it wouldn't feel as if his mother had died for nothing.

With just the tips of her fingers, Ambrosia gently touched around the swollen part of his face. "How did this happen?"

Staring at her through his one good eye, he caressed her cheek. He had to be honest with her, even if she got upset with him. "I went to Belly of the Beast."

Her amber gaze narrowed at him. "Why in all the gods would you go to *that* place? It's nothing but a place to brawl."

"I went to find some old friends. I was hoping..." His words trailed off. That wasn't right. His reason for going was so much more important than that. "I needed to reconnect with my family. To know they are okay. I have not seen them in a little over eighteen *solaris*, and the way I left things, well, we did not part on the best of terms." A few days after the punishment Markham delivered, he got into an argument with Pierce.

"You should have just said yes. You think I do everything he tells me to do? I pretend more than most in this godsforsaken place," Pierce said.

If Markham didn't know the truth about his empathic abilities, it would've been one thing. But that knowledge altered everything. His brother didn't understand what it would mean. "No. I could not."

Pierce scoffed at him. "That is bullshit! You need to go back there and tell him you changed your mind. Before this gets worse."

"There is nothing that could ever make me wear that brand. I am not our father, and I am not you."

Maybe his brother hadn't thought everything through back then, but Pierce was right about one thing. It had gotten worse. As a result, a wonderful male died.

"I don't understand," Ambrosia replied.

He explained none of this very well. With a heavy sigh, Logan scrubbed his face and winced. That damn eye. Not that he wouldn't live, but it was still irritating. He frowned. How did he make all this clear for her? His gaze met hers, and he tucked a loose strand of hair behind her ear. "The day we met, I mentioned your attraction to me, which you promptly advised me was 'crap.'" His lips tugged into a small smile at the memory. It even made her light up.

"Yes, I remember that."

Of course she did. He didn't think she would've forgotten something that occurred only a few weeks ago. "I saw that because I am empathic. I do not just sense a person's emotions; but I also get impressions of things that happened to them." He paused, stroking her cheek so she didn't interrupt. He needed a minute before he went on. "Eighteen *solaris* ago, the shape shifter's so-called king offered me a position as an Informant. I say 'offer,' but one does not get to choose. Both my father and my brother were Informants. It seemed natural I would follow, but neither of them has my ability. Markham made it clear he knew I was an empath. I could not allow him to twist what the gods intended for good into something dark. So, I declined. He dealt punishments out accordingly."

"The scars on your back?"

Although his fur covered most of them, it didn't mean they went unnoticed. Logan nodded. He wouldn't go into details of all that transpired. It wasn't something she needed in her head. "A few days later, I got into an argument with my brother, and then my mother, the day afterward. When I left our hut, I expected I would return. Instead, Markham accused me of something I did not do. I had no choice but to run. If I had gone back, he would have killed me. I have not seen my brother, my sisters, or my mother since."

Her eyebrows knitted together. "You've gone all this time without one word?"

"I thought if I stayed away, they would be safe." Ironically, that hadn't happened. His family wasn't safe. No. He just lost them differently. "Finding out my mother died almost sixteen *solaris* ago, and I have a sister I knew nothing about. I did not expect that. Nor did I react to the news very well." Not that he expected anyone in his position would've reacted any other way. Maybe they wouldn't have jumped into a ring to fight someone. Then again, he supposed that depended on the person.

Ambrosia cupped his jaw with her hand and stroked his cheek with her thumb. "I don't fault you for trying to check on them. I just wish you hadn't gone to *that* place; it has a reputation."

He leaned into her touch. Hades, her concern for him, no one worried over him like this in a long time. He wasn't sure what to do with it. Though he liked it. "It was the best option I had to find any of my former friends." Not to mention, it was the last place Informants would think to look for him. Since they actively hunted him. "With what I know now, somehow, I need to get my family out of Métamorphe." At least the family members he could.

She stared at him. After a moment, Ambrosia nodded. "I get that. I do. And I'll do whatever I can to help. Just promise me, you won't go back to Belly of the Beast. I don't want to see your face messed up again."

Logan rubbed the back of his neck. Shit. That was going to be tough. He'd told Derrick to meet him there. It wasn't like he knew of another place they could meet in secret. However, he could stay out of the ring from now on. How could he promise he wouldn't go back? Maybe all he had to do was word it carefully. "I promise you will not see my face like this again."

"Logan, I'm serious. Promise me you won't go back."

There had been a good reason he found her attractive. Smart and beautiful. He caressed her cheek with the back of his hand. "I promise."

"Thank you."

Chapter Five

After another fruitless scouting mission, Derrick arrived at the village with several others. He didn't know what Markham hoped to accomplish with the assignments. The Informants found none of the ones the king sought. Not anymore. A decade had passed since they found any Informant deserter. But the male was adamant. He swore some half-breeds contained shape shifter blood, and he claimed there were still deserters out there. Maybe there were, but that didn't mean they'd ever find them. Markham wanted their blood, though; all of it. Probably so he could play in it, the sick fucker.

Derrick could attest to the existence of one of them, but he'd never admit to it. He'd never out Logan to anyone, not even if it brought about his death. Which it probably would. It pained him he'd been the one to deliver the news of Sabina's death. About a week had gone by, but the look in the male's eyes when he uttered those words still haunted him and likely would for a very long time.

Once they finished their report to Markham, Derrick barely sustained a shudder as he walked away from the hut. That male reeked of evil. He didn't allow his eyes to linger on the Informant still chained in the middle of the clearing. Four days ago, Maddox pissed off the king. A couple of hybrids accidentally stumbled upon their territory, and in Markham's eyes, that warranted torture and death. It wasn't the first time it happened, but it got no easier to witness, no matter how many times it occurred. When it was over and Markham allowed the second male to leave, he ordered the body of the dead male and those of the fallen Informants prepared for evening meal. Maddox refused. The feline wouldn't help take the bodies to the kitchen house, and he refused to eat a single bite either.

After they placed an iron collar around his neck attached to a chain buried deep beneath the ground, Markham had Maddox whipped dozens of times. Blood still caked Maddox's dark blue, white, and black-striped fur. Markham ordered that he remain there without food or water for five days. That, perhaps then, he *would not be so quick to refuse a meal so graciously given to him*. Then Maddox yelled at Markham, screamed at the top of his lungs the entire time when a female entered the clearing to avenge the two. Either she knew nothing about Markham, or she'd been rather unintelligent. Maddox had been an idiot, too. Not that Derrick disagreed with them wholeheartedly, but going outwardly against Markham in such a way was just foolish, especially for someone you loved deeply, as the female had obviously loved the two males.

Outside of his whipping, Maddox had paid dearly. After their king sent Maddox's half-brother and stepfather away with the creatures' wings, Markham called the male's mother, Cecily, out of their hut. He chained her down and incinerated her right in front of her son. Maddox strained against the collar, causing it to cut into his skin. Blood leaked down his chest, and his fur singed from the flames. When Arman and Ramsey returned, Markham forced Maddox to tell them what had occurred. As a result, Ramsey threw him out of their hut. Maddox hadn't moved from his spot since. He just sat there in his animal form, head down, staring into the dirt.

Shaking all his thoughts away from that horrible day, Derrick continued to his family's hut. As he neared it, his younger sister peeked around from behind and gestured to him with her eyes to come to her. Frowning, he went behind the hut. Devina used her teeth to pull his ear down lower, then leaned up and whispered into it.

"River. Now. I will cover for you if need be, say you are cleaning up before evening meal or something."

As he pulled back slowly from her, their eyes met. It wasn't necessary, though; he knew what the exact trouble was. For a while now, he felt Gabriella was in distress. Derrick gave her a nod, then left the village and entered the woods before taking off at a dead run.

When he came upon Gabby, she was kneeling in her humanoid form at the water's edge, bent over at the waist. Her fingers gripped her arms so tightly she was likely to leave bruises. Her body shook with sobs. Derrick rushed to her and shifted to his humanoid form before taking her into his arms. "Oh, my love," he whispered against the top of her head. "Shh... Do not weep. My love, do not weep. It is going to be alright."

"No, it is not," she sobbed out. "It will not be alright, Derrick." Taking his hand, she placed it over her lower belly and fully opened up to him.

He heard—no, felt—a steady, fluttering beat from inside her, the pulse of a heart that was not her own. What they previously suspected was now confirmed—the heartbeat of their young. Tears stung his eyes, and his breath left him in a gasp. "Oh... Oh, gods..." He had no other words but those, and they were insufficient. There was life growing inside of her, a life they created together. They should have celebrated.

"He will take him from us. Markham will take him," she wailed. "He will find out and take him from us, then he will take you from me, too."

Derrick roughly shook his head. He wouldn't accept that. Never. "My love, you cannot think like that." Taking her face in his hands, he raised her head so their gazes met. "You *must* not think like that. I told you I would take care of everything, and I will. I am going to make all of this okay."

"By all the gods, how? How can any of this be made okay?"

"Logan told me of a place called Migas Village. He has not told me where it is or how to get there yet. I assume he is waiting until I say yes. But he told me our kind does not go there, which means Markham does not go there. I want to go there and ask for refuge for you. For you and our young."

"*And you.* I am not leaving the village without you, Derrick. I told you that, and I am standing by it. Nor will I leave my mother or my brother behind."

He let out a harsh sigh. "There is no other way, Gabby. If I leave, they will hunt me down; just like Logan, only worse. Markham cares not for females, so he will not hunt you down so hard. But for me? He will refuse to lose an Informant. It *does not* happen. Never. Except by his hand. I will put you in no further danger than our relationship already has."

"And I will not leave you to be slaughtered when he finds out the truth."

"And how do you expect that to happen?"

"Because it will. He always does, eventually. Secrets always come out here, no matter how long anyone keeps them. We have been fortunate so far, but he *will* find out the truth, and he will kill you for it."

"He will not find out if you are not here, and I am. But, even then, better me than you and our child. I would take a thousand deaths to ensure your life and the life of our young."

"And I refuse to allow that."

"So, you would have the *three* of us killed?" He despised putting reality into words, but there was little choice. Gabby *had to* understand. They had to do it this way. "Because that is going to happen if you stay, Gabby. How long do you think you can hide your condition? And when the child is born? A mixed child would be impossible to hide. I will not allow him to take our child from us."

Derrick kissed her as he moved her out of his lap and helped her to her feet. "I am going to speak to Logan again tomorrow. Then we can make a plan, and everything will be okay for us. For you." He kissed her again, and she moved out of his arms. The fear he felt from her made his heart shoot straight up into his throat. She was angry, irritated, and hurt, as well.

He could tell her not to worry, not to be afraid repeatedly. But it would make no difference. Neither of them could put their fears to rest, and for a good reason. They couldn't agree on what to do either, and they likely wouldn't. Which would only bring one outcome—one he couldn't even fathom.

Silence stretched between them. Without another word, Derrick turned back toward the village. Gabby would follow soon. He felt her calm herself, saw the rippling of the water through her eyes. She tried holding onto the hope he gave her, but he could barely hold it in his voice, let alone his heart.

The more steps he took, the more she closed off from him until he felt nothing from her. Neither of them knew how this happened. And the herbs were supposed to have worked. They had worked for so long. Not that any of it mattered. He had to focus on what they could do now.

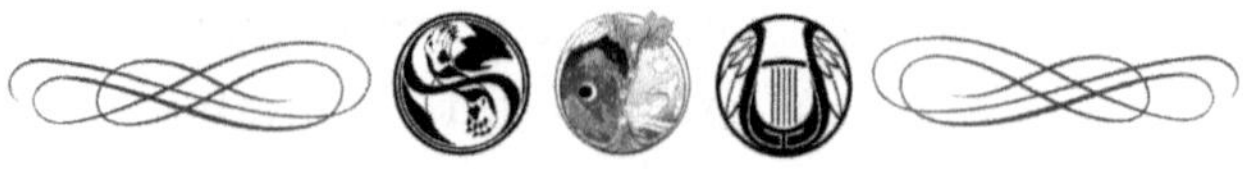

Gavin watched the strange creature with wings. He was in his animal form and always camouflaged when he did so. The female used the same tree and did nothing but survey the marketplace. She would sit on a low branch, watching as the various species paraded through and gained a multitude of items. Some got clothing, others picked up fruits and vegetables, and just now, another who had disappeared into the metal shop came out with a tiny precious item in their hand. The place bustled in a constant exchange of goods or young playing games. Young didn't play games in his village. He'd never been to the marketplace, though his twin sister Gabby had, and he barely paid it any attention now. Gavin couldn't take his eyes off the female he watched. It was like that from the moment he first caught sight of her. She was like a song calling out to his soul. Just being in her vicinity felt like he found a missing piece of himself.

Sometimes he caught her arrival, other times, she sat in the tree. If she ever noticed him, she never made it known. He saw no one like her. From the beginning, he wanted to get closer and investigate, or—dare he even think it—meet her. However, it was against the shape shifter laws to associate with other species.

Gavin watched the female kick her legs out, then glance over her wings. Her feathers were different shades of brown, a perfect mixture of varying hues. She wore clothing, which he only knew about from Gabby's descriptions. The female wore a light green top that went around her neck, leaving her arms bare. The skirt she wore was a dark blue material. He knew she couldn't see him with his camouflage on but, if he hazarded a guess, she couldn't sense him either. She bit her bottom lip, then swept her mahogany hair back before leaping from the branch she roosted upon and drifted down. As her taloned feet hit the ground, she poked her head around the tree she hid behind. With just the trees in her line of sight now, she tiptoed over to another tree, then another, until she moved much closer to the marketplace.

As he watched her move along, it was as if her aura called to him. He wanted to see her eyes, longed to hear her voice. He climbed quietly down through the tree branches. As apprehensive as he still was about getting too close, he couldn't stop himself from following her. He migrated silently from tree to tree, unable to hold himself back any longer.

"What secrets do you hold?"

The sound of her voice sent a shudder through his body. He slunk closer, mentally easing the camouflage off his body, no longer invisible as he materialized out of nowhere. Jet black fur covered his body. When the sun hit him just right, his barely discernible spots would be visible. His emerald-green eyes glowed as he moved quietly to a branch above the female's head and laid down. His front paws dangled over and his tail wrapped around the branch. "If you wonder what secrets it holds, why do you not go find out?"

Jumping back, she gasped. As their gazes met, her dark brown eyes glowed. She blinked. "I'm, um, I'm not allowed."

Gavin could only stare into her bright eyes. They were such a gorgeous shade. The glow of his eyes intensified. Her feathers ruffled. Her eyes, everything about her, captivated him. "I should not even be talking to you, but I cannot help myself. As they say, rules are made to be broken, yes?"

She canted her head and stepped nearer to the tree. "To a degree. But if you want to be successful, you do everything in your power not to get caught."

Gavin smiled at the enchanting creature before him. "That is very true, and we cannot have that. My name is Gavin. What might your name be?"

"I'm Parthenia." She returned his smile, bending her knees as she bowed her head. He didn't know what one called the gesture.

Her name resonated through his senses. He could envision her quickly becoming a sort of addiction. The more time he spent watching her, and now the closer he got to her, the more he wanted—needed. "I have observed you for some time. That does not frighten you, I hope. I have longed to meet you, but even this would anger my King."

"Not at all, Gavin. Though I feel we're in somewhat of the same predicament. My Elder, she wouldn't look too kindly at our interaction."

"In my village, interaction is to be strictly out of necessity, but even then, my king frowns upon it." Unable to stay away, Gavin went down to where she was. He stood up on the branch and leaped to the ground. On all fours before her, she was about a foot taller than him. He stared up at her for a moment, and then he transformed.

His joints loosened and his bones shifted until he stood upright on two legs. He now stood three-and-a-half feet taller than her at his full height of eight feet. His paws changed to hands with fingers and feet with toes. His face shifted to appear humanoid, though his feline ears and tail remained.

Fur still covered his body and, as his shift completed, his tail wrapped naturally around and between his legs.

"I rarely change into this form." The only time he did so was when he and Gabby spent time together in the treehouse. Gavin leaned against the tree, minimizing their height difference, so it was easier for them to look into each other's eyes.

Parthenia hooked her thumbs into the front pockets of her short skirt. "I… uh… can't imagine why." Her brows furrowed together, almost as if the words she spoke surprised her. She dropped her gaze to the forest floor. "Sorry. I feel like I've put a talon in my mouth. I'm probably the first siren to even step foot on the isle in centuries."

He bent his head, hoping to catch her gaze again. "Please do not apologize, it is alright. I have seen no one like you. A *siren*." Trying the word out on his tongue, he decided he liked it very much. "I have never heard of your kind, but you intrigue me."

Her gaze lifted to his, and her brown eyes widened. "You're a shape shifter, correct? I mean, I only know what I learned from books, but other than that, I've met no one outside of my species. This visit has proven to be the best for many reasons."

"I am glad for it. Also, glad I finally found the courage to approach you. As to your question, yes, I am a shape shifter. There are different forms in my village, not just feline like me."

"I'm glad too. Your village sounds colorful. We're not like that. Our wings, eyes, and hair are pretty much all the same, or some version thereof. We even dress the same. I mean, not this." She gestured to the clothing she had on.

"I love what you are wearing." Especially her top, the color made her eyes stand out.

"Thank you. I've seen some females in the market wear clothes like this. I thought it would help me blend in," Parthenia admitted.

Gavin didn't think she would blend in anywhere, and that wasn't an insult. To him, she was breathtaking. He wanted to spend every moment just drinking her in. "We do not have fabric coverings like that. Well, I think some may, but I do not know. They hide them and never wear them in the village if they do. They are unnecessary because of our fur. What kinds of things do you normally wear?"

"White gowns. We wear them for most things. The color changes for matings or celebrations."

"That sounds lovely. What made you travel down here?"

She paused for several moments. Her expression shifted many times, then she ran her fingers through her hair. "A lot of reasons, I guess. My people, nothing's the same. I know we'll eventually have to react, but no one seems to be in a hurry to do so. I suppose I wanted to be ready when they finally decide that we can't sit still and idly watch as our species dies off."

Gavin tried to hide his frown. It seemed silly; he'd only just met her. Before today, he didn't even know what one called her species. Before he first caught sight of her, he didn't even know someone like her existed. Her words worried him. "That sounds ominous. What is killing off your species?"

"Old laws, lack of mates." Her cheeks tinged pink. After a slight pause, she shuddered.

What had she been thinking? "We may have that same problem before too long. Our species is forbidden to mate outside of our own. Mating outside our form is frowned upon, but not wholly unheard of. Our king is the only bear. When he passes, bear shape shifters will be no more." He wouldn't say it aloud, but he couldn't wait for the day when Markham would only be a memory. Nor could he say he believed it would happen, but it was nice to think about as a possibility.

"Yeah. Sounds all too familiar," Parthenia replied. "We've become a society full of females, and most of us are approaching or have hit mating age."

"That must be difficult. I cannot imagine, well, maybe a little, the prospect of not finding a mate. All the female felines are already mated or are younglings. The oldest youngling is just nine, I believe." This was nice. They just met and already spoke as if they'd known each other their whole lives. He didn't know how it was possible, but he enjoyed himself.

Covering her mouth, Parthenia stifled a giggle. The sound warmed him as nothing else ever had. "The last male siren was my father. I completely understand. And being surrounded by females, it gets rather lonely."

"I know what loneliness is like all too well."

"Perhaps that's why we met."

"Maybe. Do you believe in fate, Parthenia?"

"More than you know." She flashed him a pearly white smile and glanced around. "You know, people watching has proven fruitful, but perhaps there's something else we can do around here."

"I think I would do anything with you." Okay, that came out wrong, but there was no taking it back now.

Another blush rose to Parthenia's cheeks. She lifted her gaze to the sky. Flicking her eyes back to him, she extended her wings and flapped until she was just off the ground. "I can't stay much longer, but I'd like to see you again. If that's okay."

As she hovered before him, her scent intensified, wholly consuming him. His eyelids lowered almost imperceptibly. He wanted nothing more than to drown in it. "I would love nothing more." The words left his mouth before he could stop them, but they were the truth. He realized he spoke more truth here with Parthenia than anything he said before meeting her. Except perhaps during private discussions with his sister. Gavin stretched a hand toward her until his fingertips almost touched her face. Energy sizzled between them, and he dropped his hand quickly. What was this? "When? When can I see you?" he asked, not caring that desperation laced his voice.

As she bit her bottom lip, a strange thought went through his brain, but he knew the certainty of it almost so much as he knew his name. She wanted him to touch her. She wanted to touch him.

Parthenia stared at him through hooded eyes. "Tomorrow. Noon. I can sneak down then."

Could her lips possibly be as soft as they looked? "I will be here."

She tilted her head. "Do you eat fruit?"

"I can, yes."

"I'll bring some snacks then. Until tomorrow."

As his gaze lifted and he watched her rise into the air, he knew one thing he'd enjoy snacking on, and it didn't involve food of any kind. He shook his head swiftly. This was insanity. Never had he experienced anything close to what he had in her presence. But their eyes glowed, which was a once-in-a-lifetime phenomenon. How could it be possible? It was so rare, at least in his village. True mates just so seldom occurred. Hardly anyone was lucky enough, and they were not even of the same species. Could it be?

Shifting back to all fours, Gavin turned and leaped into the tree again, going back the way he'd come. He would have to shield his thoughts of this encounter once he reached home, but he shielded a lot while he was in the village. He couldn't wait to see Parthenia again, and hopefully, the time didn't take too long to pass until noon tomorrow.

Chapter Six

Logan scrubbed his face as he stood in the alleyway around the corner from the fight ring. He shouldn't go back. He promised Ambrosia he wouldn't. But, by Hades, until he had crossed paths with Derrick, he had heard nothing else about his family. His mother, gone. A sister he didn't even know.

He had to go back, hoping that he saw Derrick there again. The male told him he didn't know how bad things had gotten. He was right. Promise or not, he had to know. Maybe he could find some way to help his family from this side. They deserved a better life.

Steeling himself, he slipped out of the alleyway and made his way once again to the fight ring. Even if he didn't keep his promise, he'd at least stay out of the ring this time. As he opened the door, he spotted Derrick sitting at a corner table nearby, his head in his hands. The male looked up at him, then lowered his gaze again.

Logan rubbed the back of his neck. Over the years, he learned to deal with the emotions that came off people, but there was a ton of conflict coursing through Derrick. It hit him like a boulder in the face. He inhaled and exhaled a deep breath and strode across the room. Stopping at the table the male occupied, Logan dropped into a chair that allowed him to watch what was going on. "You seem troubled. More so than usual."

"That may be the understatement of the century, my friend." Derrick gave him a sideways look. "If I can still call you that?"

Logan opened his mouth and snapped it shut. A lot of time had passed, but the two of them had once been quite close. "We used to be like brothers. The time apart has not changed that."

Derrick closed his eyes for a moment and nodded his head. "Thank you. I am glad to hear it. You have never stopped being a brother to me, either." Silence stretched between them for a moment. "I have a mate."

Taken aback, Logan raised an eyebrow. It should be something to celebrate. Then he considered his own situation and Markham's laws. "Let me guess. Not canine."

"No. Feline. And..." His eyes squeezed shut. "She is with child."

Something that should be joyous, but Markham would never allow. What the male would do if he ever discovered this news. Logan sighed. "Have you looked into the place I told you of?" He knew little about the half-hybrid village. Growing up, they called them half-breeds. With Ambrosia on his mind and all he had learned, he couldn't bring himself to use the term any longer. Although he scouted the area many times long before he met Ambrosia, he had never found the village. Even now, he hadn't been there. What little he knew came from her.

"Not yet. I will not do so until I can safely, and I have not had the chance. Markham..." He rubbed his eyes. "He is always watching. And I would daresay some of his Informants are as brutal as he. I am going to, though. And I thank you for telling me about it." Derrick sighed heavily. "She is too afraid to leave the village and, so far, refuses to do so without me, her mother, and her brother. But I cannot. Not without being hunted down. I have to convince her it is the right course of action. She knows what will happen when Markham finds out about the young she carries. It would be impossible to pass off a canine-feline child as pure."

Logan smirked. "They may be fairer, but they are far stronger than we give them credit for." Shape shifters often had complicated pregnancies, but praying Markham didn't find out just muddled matters even worse. "Informants do not go near the village. Someone or something protects it; I am unsure how, but as many times as I have scouted the area, I have not once seen an Informant close to those lands. The—" He paused. "The hybrid village would be the only safe place for both of you. Playing both sides, Derrick, you cannot expect it to end well. It has not done so in the past for others."

"I know. I know that. Leaving, despite the inherent risks of staying, would leave too many unprotected. Alone. Markham's ways grow increasingly brutal. Rarely does anyone step out of line, and for a good reason. Pierce will not walk away from your sisters, most especially after he almost died to make sure Lillianna could live. And Dahlia and Zinnia would never leave."

"I do not expect..." His words trailed off as he fully processed Derrick's statement. Logan shifted in the chair and narrowed his eyes at the male. "Dahlia has never wanted to leave, but why would Zinnia not leave? How did Pierce nearly die for Lillianna?" He'd been too angry to hear anything else last time they met, and then he jumped into the ring straight away. He fought with a troll for several moments—the exact time it took for the male to go down. Although the creature tagged him a few times, he welcomed the pain

"Neither would make you overly proud as their older brother. Dahlia is much worse than you might remember. And Zinnia is a follower, nothing more. Though she would never admit it, she is too frightened to do anything else. She would do nothing that Markham or Ailwin would consider unsuitable. You are not the only one that has changed over the *years*."

Derrick ran his hands over his head before he continued, "After Lillianna was born and your mother passed... I believe Lillianna came earlier than expected. She was sickly. You remember what happens when newlings are born sickly," he said, his voice laced with disgust. "Right after her birth, before Markham could come to do his inspection, Pierce stole away with her somewhere onto the isle. To this day, he has never told me where he went to hide her away or how he cared for her. Not that those details are important. On Markham's orders, Informants hunted him, but no one could find him. Your father did your mother's death ceremony almost immediately, as if all he cared about was getting it out of the way. When Pierce returned, Lillianna was almost a month old and as healthy as could be. Markham had him brutally punished for fleeing. He received so many injuries that he almost succumbed to death. But he returned willingly to the fold, so Markham *allowed* Pierce to live. And given our numbers and the fact that Lillianna was thriving then, Markham *allowed* her to keep her life. Pierce has raised her. Your father has taken no part in her upbringing. Zinnia is, well, Zinnia. After that, I think Dahlia feels as though Pierce betrayed the family, the pack, and Markham, all for a child not destined to live."

Logan balled his fists up, his claws digging into his palms and drawing blood. The acidic scent did nothing to calm his nerves as he listened to everything Derrick told him. He sat there in silence when the male finished. He could use the rage surrounding them to fuel his own, but it would put him back in that ring. It would accomplish nothing. Before Ambrosia, he would've jumped in the ring without a second thought. Much as he did a week ago. But she didn't even know he was here. He couldn't go into the ring a second time, especially as it seemed the atmosphere had changed.

His brother endured much in his absence. He failed the male. Even if he'd stayed, nothing good would've come of it. That wouldn't be the case now. He despised the idea of leaving any of his family there, but Derrick hadn't lied. Dahlia wasn't the female his mother always prayed she would become.

A long time passed before he spoke again because he planned in his mind, though it would take time and cooperation. As much as it pained him, he had to ask. Afraid to hear the answer, he shut his eyes. "Do you think Zinnia would leave if given a chance?"

Derrick didn't answer at first. The longer the silence stretched between them, the more his answer became apparent. "Truly?" He shook his head. "No. I do not. She is too attached to Dahlia, and…" He paused. "I will say that only Dahlia is in her element in the village. I think, given the chance and the choice, Pierce would try to convince Zinnia. But, no, I do not think she would leave."

Logan leaned his elbows on his knees. He scanned the growing crowd. "Based on what you have told me, I would not even suggest it. It would jeopardize too many lives." And he wouldn't risk his mate's life to save his family. Instead, all he could do was attempt to rescue the ones he could. "I need to speak with Pierce." Maybe if he got Pierce and his youngest sister out, Derrick would follow with his mate. It wasn't much of a plan, but it was the best he had.

"I will try. He does everything he can to protect your sisters. But if he will come, then I will bring him. Pierce has not let his soul go dark. I think he would want you to know that. He takes the orders, but he does not follow them. I am with him enough on scouting missions to know that much."

"I should not have left them there," he said before he stopped himself. Ambrosia was right. He understood now, all too well, the weight he left his brother to carry. It wasn't something he should've done alone. Eighteen years. He would never forgive himself for that. Logan shook his head. No one could alter the past, but he could change the future.

"Do not blame yourself. Pierce does not, and he never would. You had no choice. Life just sometimes has a way of bringing terrible misfortune. I will talk to him. It is long past time the two of you had a conversation."

Logan sat up and squeezed the male's shoulder. "We all have choices, brother." He could've gone back after he built his cabin. It was big enough to accommodate their family. It didn't cross his mind at the time he worked on it, but he didn't want to think about things much back then. He could have sought his brother out sooner. Perhaps if he had, they wouldn't have lost Zinnia. So many things he couldn't change. "If there is anything I can do to help you, I will."

Derrick reached across and squeezed his shoulder in return. "Thank you. Truly. That means much. And I extend the same to you. If there is anything I can do to help you, I will."

To get his brother and youngest sister out was the only thing he needed. He prayed to the gods Zinnia would come. He hated to think she would follow Dahlia just to appease those who could never be pleased. "Just do what you can to convince Pierce. I will take care of the rest."

"Thank you. Again. You were always the worthiest of males. Your father never deserved you." Derrick sighed and stood up. "I should go. We are not allowed out after hours, as you well know. Not unless Markham sends us on longer scouting missions. When will you come back here?"

"A few days." He hated lying to Ambrosia about his presence here, but she didn't need to know. He had to protect her.

"I will be here."

"Until then, be safe."

"You as well," Derrick said, then left the fighting ring behind.

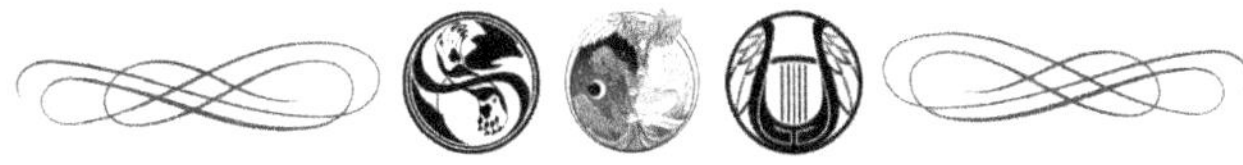

Derrick camouflaged in the alleyway before shifting to all fours. He would move faster through the marketplace this way. Wait. Someone was watching him. He couldn't catch a specific scent because there were too many creatures here and too many smells. But he sensed eyes upon him—if he got it right—a fellow Informant. He shook it off. It didn't matter. He had his camouflage on, and he would wait to remove it until he reached the trees. No one would know what he'd done or who he met in Belly of the Beast.

He weaved in and out of the marketplace, past vendors and creatures, through alleyways and around shops. Some felt him brush past, but they couldn't tell who he was. He reached one pathway that led out of the marketplace but veered away from it. There was no direct pathway into the shape shifter boundaries, but it wasn't necessary for anyone that lived there, especially Informants like him. They knew almost every nook and cranny of the woods and much beyond it.

With so much on his mind, way beyond just his conversation with Logan, he focused less on his surroundings as he headed toward the forest. As he breached the trees and made his way through them, he removed his camouflage and picked up his pace. It wasn't long before footsteps pounded behind him. He paid no attention to who it was. Informants roamed the forest almost constantly. It wouldn't be unusual for others to see him here.

A black blur caught the corner of his vision, and he barely had time to face it before someone slammed him in the side. His breath left him in a rush. Derrick rolled across the ground, his body and another twisting around each other. He snapped his jaws and got a snarl in return.

"Stop it, Derrick!" Pierce shoved off his body, moving away from him.

Derrick whipped around to face the male. "You are the one that slammed into me. What is your problem?"

"What in Hades' name were you doing back there?"

"Back where?"

Pierce rolled his eyes, a harsh chuckle leaving him. "*Back where?* Do you think I am that stupid? *The marketplace.* Specifically, the fight ring."

Derrick said nothing for a moment. "You were the one watching me."

"Yes. I was the one watching you. I watched you last time as well, but you did not appear to notice me." His lip curled. "I watched you go in. You left with no injuries. I watched you go in today. You have no injuries now." Pierce lowered his voice. "I know who went inside the establishment after you." Another stretch of silence passed between them. "You did not go there to fight. What in Hades' name are you thinking, Derrick?"

The two of them stared each other down. They used to be as close as brothers. Look at them now. Gods, much had changed over the last twenty years. It started with their Informant status.

Not that he should say it, but he wanted to bark out that it wasn't Pierce's business what he did. But that was false. It *was* Pierce's business. And he promised Logan. "He wishes to speak with you, Pierce. He *needs* to speak with you. You must meet with him."

Pierce growled. "You are insane. Utterly insane. Do you have any idea what kind of position that would put me in? *Any idea?* I cannot even think about doing that, let alone doing so."

"Do you think I care what *position* it puts you in? I have problems of my own. Problems I seek to find a solution for, which is why I sought Logan."

"And what can Logan do for you?" he sneered.

"*That* is truly none of your concern. I will not share what I spoke of with him. Only that I told him how you and your siblings are doing." Derrick paused. "*All* of your siblings."

Pierce's eyes widened, and a low snarl rose in his chest. "You told him of Lilli? How. Dare. You." He advanced on Derrick, snapping his jaws at him. Derrick moved out of the way just in time. "You had *no right*! You had no right to speak to him about *anything* concerning my family! They are *mine*, not *yours*!"

"And they are his as well! He deserved to know! He deserved to know what kind of female Dahlia has turned into."

"I will listen to no more about Dahlia."

Derrick growled and snapped his jaws in Pierce's face. The male didn't even flinch. "When she stops sending my sister home bloody, I will stop speaking of her to you."

"What Dahlia does is no fault of mine. I do not control her!"

"Someone had better, and soon. Or I am going to take care of it myself."

Pierce bared his fangs. "You will not touch any member of my family, Derrick. No matter our relationship, now or in the past. I will not abide by it. They are my blood."

"Oh, yes. That is right. Blood is *so* thick to you. So thick you will not go see your own *brother*."

Several long moments passed before Pierce spoke. "You know why I cannot." A low growl permeated his words. "Dahlia aside, I cannot risk my other sisters. They go through more than enough."

"I told him about Zinnia, too. About how her spirit has dwindled since he left—"

"Was thrown out."

"Whatever. I told him about Lillianna, but I did not tell him what she suffered. That would have been cruel. And I told him about your mother's passing."

Pierce's eyes darkened, and he let out a growl. "With that, you truly crossed a line, Derrick. A line you had *no right* to cross."

"Were *you* going to tell him? No? Then shut your mouth and back away from me. You had eighteen *solaris* to find him; sixteen *solaris* to tell him he has another sister, and no longer has a mother. *You* chose not to do so. I do not care what your reasons were. The truth of it, the only part that matters, is that you did not. He requested the information for the information I needed. I could not say no, and I would not have, anyway. He was innocent of the accused crime. He did not deserve any of what happened to him."

"There was nothing I could have done! Nothing I could do to save him! I do what I can with my sisters, but even there I fail miserably, and—"

"I am not blaming you," Derrick said, cutting him off. He waited until their eyes met before he continued, "But I will not endure blame from you or your fangs in my face because you are angry at me. What I have done is done. I have relayed the message that he wishes to speak to you. He will be back there again in a few days. I plan to meet with him there again." Silence stretched between them. "You should join me. It would bring him joy to see you, and I know it would bring you joy as well."

"I cannot. No matter how much"—Pierce visibly swallowed— "How much I want to or how much joy it would bring me, I cannot see him. What if they saw me there, as I saw you? One other Informant is all it would take. For all the other things I do behind Markham's back, chasing after my brother, who was banished from the pack and disowned by my father, even named a traitor would be the greatest dishonor to our king, and he would kill me for it right where I stood. Where would that leave Lillianna?"

"Logan spoke of a village, a village where Informants do not go near. He said it is protected—"

"There can be no such place so protected that Markham could not gain entrance. He is too powerful."

"So, you think your brother is lying?"

"I do not know what I think. Whether he is lying, it has been almost two decades since we have laid eyes on each other." Pierce shook his head. "I do not know him anymore."

"The three of us used to be as close as brothers, though I do not share blood with the two of you. That still means something to me. Even though it appears to mean little to you." Derrick took a step back from him. "You are a fool, Pierce. A fool."

"You must stop going to see him, Derrick. You will be caught. And when Markham finds out, he will slaughter you in front of everyone. He will use your death as a warning to the entire village."

"I do not care. I have reasons for doing what I am, and nothing can deter me. If I die in my quest, so be it. At least if that happens, I will know I did not lie on my back and let the atrocities in our pack continue." He sent a pointed glance at Pierce. "Like some." With that, he turned and took off deeper into the forest, leaving the male behind.

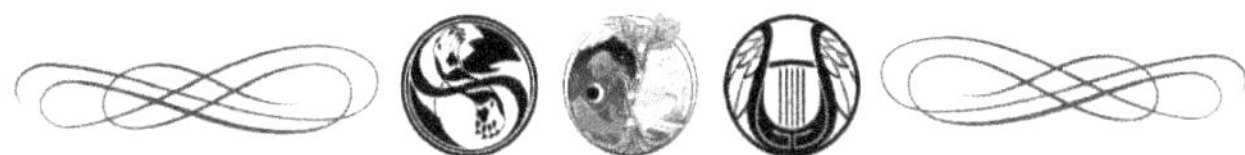

Shit. Shit. Shit. Ambrosia grunted as she hiked the path to Logan's cabin. She was late. She planned to arrive an hour ago, but her sister had to have an issue. And it wasn't as if Jo could stitch her own arm. Nope, of course not. Or go to Kaylina. Nope, that would've been too easy, probably because the female would've chastised her sister again for her irresponsible nature. Not that it was entirely Jo's fault. Leo and his attitude issues were partially to blame. Honestly, she would've knocked the male on his ass a long time ago if she thought it would've accomplished anything other than a sprained wrist.

Hitting the end of the path, she practically raced across the small clearing and up the staircase to Logan's cabin. They had spent the last month together and officially labeled it a relationship a couple of weeks ago. The more time she spent with him, the more she saw a future that included him. Who was she kidding? She couldn't go a day without seeing him now. No way they wouldn't be together for the long haul. Not that either of them uttered the big L-word. Of course, that didn't mean she wasn't feeling it.

She threw open the front door and closed it behind her. Logan wrapped an arm around her waist, scooped her into his arms, and brushed a soft kiss across her lips. "Hi."

"Hi." The simplest of words, yet there was so much said in it. "I'm sorry I'm late."

"I am just glad you are here."

If anyone told her a romantic sap hid beneath the sarcastic exterior he portrayed when they had first met, she would've called them a liar. She noted other changes in him as well. His fur had lightened—going from black to dark brown. She asked him about it a day or two ago. According to him, he hadn't noticed. She reached up and caressed his cheek. "Me too. It's been a day already, and the day is just starting."

"Care to talk about it?" He set her back on her feet, draped an arm across her shoulders, and kissed her forehead as they headed into the kitchen together.

"It's just my sister." Ambrosia groaned. "She's never handled our father's death very well, even though it was a long time ago. It used to be that she got into trouble any chance she got, and I'd rescue her before she wound up dead. Then, when we hit our teens, she took up sparring. Unfortunately, it usually means she ends up injured, and I'm the one who has to patch her up."

"How old were you when he died?" Leaving her side for a moment, he picked up a folded dishtowel from the counter and pulled a pan of meat and sliced potatoes out of the oven.

"Five." He'd been a magnificent male, as far as she remembered. He cherished both her and her sister. Taught them both how to swim and encouraged them to take chances. She watched Logan as he moved around the kitchen with the final preparations for breakfast. Her father would've liked him.

"Can I ask... with his death, what, eighteen *solaris* ago?" A slight frown crossed his face. "Why do you still look after your sister instead of letting her take responsibility for her decisions?"

Ambrosia collected the pitcher of tea, along with two cups, and followed Logan into the dining room. Gods, had it really been eighteen years? Yeah. Three months prior, it had been eighteen years since her father's death.

Her gaze flicked to Logan as she set the tea and cups on the table, and she half-shrugged. "I'm the oldest. It's my responsibility to make sure she's taken care of."

He raised an eyebrow and placed the pan on the table between the two settings. Both plates were at the head of the table. He sat down first and then pulled her into his lap. "I thought you were twins."

"We are, but I was born first by a few minutes, so it still makes me the oldest. And as the oldest, sometimes we have to sacrifice to make sure our younger siblings are taken care of." And she certainly did that over the years. She sacrificed relationships and job positions all to make sure she was there whenever Jo needed her. "I do whatever is necessary to help her, even when she doesn't realize everything I've done."

"I never thought about it like that. The decisions of an older sibling being a sacrifice." He laid his head on her shoulder and buried his face in the crook of her neck.

Younger siblings usually didn't. And she'd never tell her sister of what she'd let go of to be there for her. Ambrosia stroked along Logan's ears. He was probably the first decision she made for herself. Not that she told her sister or her mother about him. Although, they probably knew something was going on, since his scent was all over her. "Older siblings rarely announce it. They just decide and suffer the consequences in silence. Especially when there's a missing or inactive parent."

"May I ask... what was your father's name?"

It wasn't a strange question. Or even an out-of-the-blue question. Her father was a shape shifter and was born and raised in Métamorphe. Not that he ever spoke of that place. Her knowledge of it came from rumors she heard around the marketplace. Still, a sense of unease, or maybe concern, radiated off Logan. Getting a glimpse of his emotions was unusual. Though she supposed, as more time passed, she'd get accustomed to it. It hadn't started all that long ago. Ambrosia shook the sensations off. "Galenus. His name was Galenus." She sensed a change in Logan's emotions. "Did you know him?"

"Yes," Logan whispered as he sat up. Tucking a loose strand of hair behind her ear, he caressed her cheek. "I knew him. He and my mother... they were friends."

Okay. That made sense. Logan was seventeen years her senior. But there was something else. Something he wasn't—her mind returned to the conversation they had a week earlier. *Eighteen years ago.* Logan said someone forced him out of Métamorphe eighteen years ago after being accused of a crime he didn't commit. Ambrosia rubbed at the tightness in her chest. It couldn't be true. No. She had to be wrong. *Very* wrong.

He inhaled and exhaled a deep breath before lowering his gaze. "Yes, they blamed me for your father's death. It was a lie. I was not even in the village when Galenus arrived to speak with Markham. I was out trying to find Galenus, to warn him."

Tears pricked the corners of her eyes. It couldn't be true. The male she—no, she didn't want to believe him. It made little sense. None of this could be possible. She shook her head. "No, it can't be."

"I am so sorry, Ambrosia." He pulled her close and ran his fingers through her ponytail, letting them fall to brush up and down her spine as he held her in his arms.

Her sister begged their father not to go, but he told them both he had to—for them. Several hours passed without a word from him. Not that they hadn't known what happened. Or at least suspected it when their mother passed out in the kitchen. He had been gone over a day by the time they received word of his death. Both her mother and sister had been inconsolable after that. As she sat up straighter, tears rolled down her cheeks. "His body... do you know what happened to his body?"

"No. I am sorry, my love, I do not. He had—" He halted, staring at her for a moment. "Are you certain you wish to hear this?"

"Yes. I need to, for my sister and my mother." She loved her father with all her heart, but for her family's sake, if she could get some answers, even after all this time, then maybe it would give them closure. "Please," she pleaded softly. "Please, tell me." Her lips trembled as more tears streaked her face. She needed to know.

Logan pulled her close again, stroking her back with the tips of his fingers. "Someone had already killed him, and the accusation made. I had not even gotten near the boundaries when a friend found me. He told me what happened and to run."

Oh, gods. This wasn't something she could ever tell her family. No body to lie to rest. What had they done? Just left him to—gods, no. She couldn't even—Ambrosia jumped from his lap, ran down the hall to the bathroom, and threw up in the toilet. Her arms hung over the sides of the basin as she sobbed. So close to factual information, and she failed again. For years, she did everything she could to hold her family together. All she hoped for was something to give them, something to help them move past the pain. They lost him eighteen years ago, but it was a wound that never healed. And it seemed like it never would.

A pair of warm arms scooped her off the floor and carried her into the living room. Logan sat in the chair and held her as she wept. How was it possible to cry so many tears? Even when they found out about her father's death, she didn't weep. She stayed strong. At least as strong as any five-year-old could be. It was what her mother and sister needed. They needed someone to help take care of them, and that's what she'd done. She still did, but more so for her sister than her mother.

There were so many things she wanted to know, but she didn't have the strength to ask him. Not yet. Instead, she just sat there curled up like a small child with his arms wrapped around her. She never leaned on anyone like this. It was comforting, like she'd never imagined.

It was impossible to tell how much time passed. The food Logan prepared and kept warm for her was likely cold. Ambrosia sniffled and wiped at her face. "I'm sorry. I didn't mean to break down like that."

"You do not need to apologize." He caressed her merfolk scales. "Morning meal will keep. For however long we need to sit here."

"Thank you." Whatever she did to deserve a loving male like Logan, she was grateful for it. Despite how things went down the day they met; she wouldn't have traded any of it. And when she was ready, maybe he'd tell her stories of her father. Things she could share with her sister and mother. One day. Wiping more of her tears away, she slowly lifted her head. "Can you do me a favor?"

"Anything, my love."

She swallowed the lump at the back of her throat. "Should you meet my mom and my sister, whenever that day comes, don't tell them anything regarding my father. Not that anyone blamed you for his death or that you knew him—none of it."

Inhaling and exhaling a deep breath, Logan nodded. "If that is what you think is best, then I will say nothing."

"Thank you." Maybe it was cruel, but she was confident it would do more harm than good if they had only pieces of information. At least this way, nothing changed, and she could keep her sister from trying to find a place they had no business being near.

Chapter Seven

Parthenia's eyes snapped open to Gavin in his humanoid form right in front of her face. He jumped, lost his balance, and fell from the tree. *Oh, poppies!* She'd fallen asleep, hadn't she? On the bright side, she the snacks remained untouched. As Parthenia poked her head out from between the branches, she caught the end of his graceful landing on all fours. He must've changed forms midair.

Gavin stared up at her for a moment, and before she could speak, he started laughing. "Oh, I am sorry," he called up. "I am so sorry. I did not mean to startle you."

His amusement sent her into a fit of giggles. Once she gained control, her mouth spread into a wide grin. "I didn't mean to fall asleep."

"You are lovely while sleeping. Well, you are beautiful regardless. I mean, well, what I meant was…" He chuckled nervously. "You are beautiful."

Parthenia blushed as she tucked her legs beneath her bottom. No one had ever told her she was beautiful, not even her father.

Gavin scaled the tree trunk until he was on the branch once more and sitting. The grin faded from his face as he sobered. "I did not mean to be late. I feel terrible for making you wait, but I am so delighted you did."

She would've waited longer if that was what it took, as long as she got to see him again. "Thank you. And, uh, I suspect you couldn't help it. Any more than my dozing off, but you're here now."

"I am, and so are you." He shifted, straddling the branch and leaning against the trunk. Her feathers ruffled as his eyes raked the length of her body. "I could not help it, no, and I came as quickly as I could. I-I dreamed of you," he whispered.

His tender voice sent shivers down the back of her spine. She sat there for a moment as she drank in the sight of his form. It didn't matter which one she saw him in because they were each stunning—the way the sun caught the sheen of his dark fur and the subtle beauty in his green eyes. Either way, she quietly appreciated each in its uniqueness. "I dreamed of you, too."

Gavin gently caressed her cheek. That electric sizzle seemed to radiate through the air between them still. His hand remained there as she leaned into his touch. "I feel as if I have known you for so long, though we have just met. Being away from you was painful. I do not mean to sound so intense, but..." His words trailed off.

Parthenia pressed a tender kiss to the inside of his palm. She didn't know where the desire came from, but it was one among many things she yearned to do with him. The night had been strenuous, but if she had many more days and perhaps nights with him, she'd suffer through the difficulties they were bound to face. "I know what you mean. It's almost like half of me was missing."

"*Yes*." He drew the word out. "I wish I knew what to do. Just the thought of being away from you is unfathomable. But this... us—is this an *us*? Whatever we are, it is risky."

Rising on her knees, Parthenia scooted a little closer without losing contact with his hand. His limbs were much longer than hers, but she desperately longed to be closer. "It's perilous, yet it feels so right." Nothing they shared sent him running away. Perhaps it was time she told him what she sensed upon their meeting yesterday. "I've heard stories among my people of those who knew the second they met, they found their true mate. Their eyes glowed as ours did. It seems impossible for *us* not to make this work. I can't imagine not being near you."

"I cannot imagine that either." Heat radiated from his body, and his chest heaved with each inhale as though it were difficult for him to breathe. "So, you think it was fate that we met? That we are each other's true mate?" His thumb brushed gently across her lower lip.

Oh, sweet, succulent poppies! She felt nothing as potent as this before. Her breath hitched in the back of her throat as she nodded. The scents between them intensified in her nostrils, almost as if their aromas cocooned her. The combination of her cherry blossom and vanilla scent and his rich oak set her skin on fire. "Yes," she said in a heady breath.

"May I... please... may I kiss you?"

Her lids lowered as she stared at him through hooded eyes. What would his lips feel like against hers? This connection was how it was between mates. It was why all sirens remained pure until that day, so they could share every first with one person. Even if that wasn't how things had been for centuries, the goddess created them that way. Parthenia swallowed to wet her parched throat. "You should know, I've never, I mean... I'm untouched."

"Oh," he whispered. A visible shudder passed through him. "I am as well. There has been none that has ever caught my attention. I have felt nothing even close to what I feel with you."

Parthenia blinked. She didn't expect that, but it thrilled her to no end that it was an experience they could share. To answer his question and make her intentions clear, she scooted closer until she sat on her knees between his legs. Forgetting the fruit, she stroked the top of his head and rested her fingers at the nape of his neck. His body trembled, his eyelids fluttered closed, and a soft noise rumbled out of him—a sort of purr. It was the most exquisite sound she'd ever heard. She wanted to make him do it again. "I'd very much like to kiss you."

"I—oh." Gavin opened his eyes, and their gazes met. His tail wrapped around her waist and sent shivers down her spine. Closing the distance between them, he brushed his lips across hers. For a moment, she enjoyed the pleasure of his tender kiss, and then the world got flipped upside down.

Some unseen force knocked Gavin out of the tree and threw her backward. Her talons snagged on a branch and kept her from falling, though she still heard him hit the earth with a thud. As soon as she collected herself, she flew to his side, kneeled on the ground beside him, and checked him over. Not that she could do much to help. It took her less time to gather herself than it did him. Of course, he fell out of a tree.

"Good Demeter, I'm so sorry. I don't know..." Her words trailed off.

"Maybe... in the future... we may need to steer clear of trees."

She couldn't explain what had just happened. And yet, a small smile touched Gavin's lips. Cupping his jaw, she gently pressed her forehead to his. "For you, I can deal with the ground."

"Mmm, well, that is good to know," he said, caressing her cheek. "Despite the misfortune of falling from the tree, that kiss was truly wonderful."

She leaned into his touch and bit her bottom lip. Something invisible may have thrown them apart, but it didn't stop her from thinking about that moment of bliss and how much she wanted to do it again. No. She wouldn't put him through that. It wasn't right.

"Yes, it was." Parthenia brushed a soft kiss across his cheek. "I wish I knew what caused it."

"As do I. I would love to kiss you again." His fingertips grazed the spot her lips just touched. "It appears we can kiss each other in other places, though." He propped up on an elbow, pressing a soft kiss right below her ear, and slowly inhaled her scent.

Her eyes closed as goosebumps crawled across her skin. His hot breath against her neck tickled, and it was the most beautiful sensation—a moment she could cherish forever—one of many first as they discovered their limitations. "Yes, it does. As much as I would love that, I couldn't bear to see you hurt."

"I could not bear to see you hurt, either. If I could spare you that, I would gladly take the pain to feel your lips against mine again."

"Then maybe, for now, we explore other options. Until we can find some answers." Unfortunately, it meant time apart. But if it meant she could one day indeed kiss him, then she'd gladly accept that temporary emptiness.

"I am up for anything. What would you suggest?" His hand trailed down the tips of her wings.

Her whole body shook. Parthenia stretched out her legs and gingerly stroked his shoulder, the pads of her fingers running through his soft fur. That deep, low purring sound came out of him again. Sweet, succulent poppies. She loved that sound. It was better than the taste of her favorite fruit hitting her tongue on the first bite. "I suppose this is a good start." She cleared her throat. Their touches were challenging to override, with so many new sensations coursing through her veins. The synapses in her brain misfired as she attempted to collect her thoughts. "I, uh, potions. I can make them. See if that alters anything. Or research. Antekilio, it might have some answers." The words poured out. Not that she was positive they held any semblance of meaning.

Gavin laid a hand against her hip as the tip of his tail danced across her bare leg. Her thigh muscles tightened. "This is an *excellent* start." His voice sounded a bit strangled. "Is there anything I can do to further your research?"

They were playing with fire. No way he didn't realize it, too. Not that it would stop—he had watched her. That's what he told her yesterday. Parthenia settled her palm against his pecs and stilled her fingers. "You watched me, but I didn't see you. How?"

"I can camouflage. Shape shifters come into that ability at different ages. I was quite young, around my eighth *solaris* of age, but there have been those who come into it younger than that."

"Hmm, does that mean you blend into your surroundings? Any surroundings?" She snuck no one in, only ever sneaked out. But it was one option. Of course, the other could be that it was something in his species' history, but she didn't quite believe that. She spent half her life in their library and, of all the books she read, no one ever presented a complete account of her species' history.

"So far, yes. But it is a little more than that. I did it every time I watched you. I did it today in case anyone tried to follow me when I left the village." His thumb traced a slow circle along her hip, bringing a soft hum out of her. "Would you like to see?"

"Yes. Very much." She smiled at the idea running around her brain, but she wasn't sure it would work yet.

Gavin held her against him as he rolled a bit, then lifted himself from the ground. His hands went to the small of her back as she fluttered in the air before him. He leaned down and kissed her cheek before letting her go. Going to stand next to a tree, he—

Parthenia's eyes widened, and she gasped as she watched him disappear before her eyes. She never witnessed other phenomena except what her sisters could do. It was amazing. "Wow." She surveyed their surroundings, still not seeing him, and sought a woodland creature. He'd shown her something of his, so she wanted to do the same. It was just a tiny deer, so that it wouldn't take much.

"What is it you are looking for?" Gavin asked in her ear, inhaling her scent again.

She jumped. She knew he was nearby, but not that close. Parthenia glanced over her shoulder at him, and he reappeared. His ability made her giddy with joy. She gestured toward the woodland animal a way off from them. "Do you see that deer?"

"Yes, I see it."

"This won't be as neat as yours, but it's just a small fraction of mine." Turning to face the creature's direction, she whistled a gentle tune that carried over the breeze to the deer. The small animal galloped toward them and slowed upon approaching. It walked right up to her and allowed her to stroke its head.

"It is lovely." He kneeled slowly not to startle the creature. Reaching his hand out, he stroked its back. "I want to know everything about you and the world you live in."

"Wait right here." She flew up to the spot they shared earlier in the tree and collected the knapsack of fruit. The breeze danced around her as her talons hit the ground with ease.

"You are just..." He shook his head. "You are perfection." Gavin took her hand. "Are those the snacks you said you would bring?"

"Yes." Keeping their hands together, she held onto one part of the knapsack, and opened it. Parthenia dug inside and produced a green-yellow apple with a sweet, tangy smell. "It's my favorite. Always crisp, quite juicy, and just the right mixture of sweet and acidic."

He accepted it and then took a small bite. "Mmm, I can see why it is your favorite. It is delicious." Gavin held it out to her. "Would you like to share it with me?"

She bit what he offered, moaning as the juice hit her palate, still her favorite. She sensed a shudder pass through him, and his eyes glowed brightly for a moment like they did the day before. "Mmm, I think I found something sweeter than my favorite fruit."

Gavin let out a low growl full of need as his body moved flush against hers. He brushed the fingers of his free hand through her hair. Their gazes locked on one another. "That sound you just made could get me into heaps of trouble."

Heat speared through her body with him so close. He dipped his head and took another bite of the apple, his tongue catching the tip of her finger where the juice still lingered. The slight roughness of his tongue brought another soft moan from her mouth. Of their own accord, her wings wrapped around him, cocooning them together. "Sweet, succulent poppies. I'm thinking we're going to have to find some answers quick."

"Yes, we are." He took another bite of the apple, and when juices escaped the fruit and slid down her finger, he captured it in his mouth. Gavin let out another deep growl as his tongue stroked it, catching every drop before releasing her finger. "You taste incredible."

"We... uh..." Her words trailed off. She didn't know what they needed to do. That wasn't true. She knew what they should do, but suspected it would be near impossible. Good Demeter, the things she imagined. This was why mates never strayed too far from one another.

"We what?" Gavin lowered his head to her neck. "I wonder if I can kiss you here," he murmured against her, nuzzling her flesh a bit. "I am sorry. Things are getting more difficult."

"Library. Answers." It was all she could manage. Her grip on the knapsack loosened, and it fell to the ground. Parthenia tilted her head, giving him more access as a moan escaped her. "I can't... I can't imagine this is easy on you, either."

"It is not." He purred as he nuzzled her neck some more. Both of her hands ran up his chest, pulling a growl out of him. "I like it very much when you touch me." His tongue extended, and he ran it lazily up the side of her throat, a deep rumble emerging from his chest.

"I enjoy touching you. Soft and hard at the same time." She ran her fingers up the sides of his chest. Her head dropped back as her wings tightened their grip and tugged him closer. Her body was as warm as his. It was as if she stood directly beside a massive fire, one that she didn't know how to quench. "More."

"I never want to stop touching you." His hands slid lower until they settled on her rear, and he drew her tighter against him. Gavin licked over her ear, and the tip of one of his fangs grazed her earlobe. He dipped his head lower, his lips and tongue snaked a trail down her neck, collarbone, and to the valley between her breasts. He was very gentle.

Her fingers dug into his shoulder blades. The silky caress made her moan deeper. Good Demeter, she wanted him so badly. Being so close to him felt amazing. The way his fur brushed against her skin. She shuddered at the mere thought of his tongue trailing further along her body.

"I want to taste more of you than your skin. I want to taste every inch of you," Gavin murmured. His tongue moved slowly up to her neck and ear. Both of them panted with want and need. "We need to find those answers, Parthenia. Quickly."

Yes, they did, like right now. She wanted nothing between them. No clothes for a week, maybe longer. Sneaking him into the library no longer seemed like the worst idea ever. "Quickly." Parthenia swallowed. "Gavin, how would you feel about joining me in our library?"

"If it means I get to spend more time with you, I am ready for anything."

"Yes. It's quite vast." She hadn't even read a small portion of the books the library contained. And she spent a lot of time there over the years. Come to think of it; maybe they only needed to go through the ancient texts. It was a smaller selection, though still significant in its entirety.

"We should go then."

"Yes, we should." He didn't appear to be in a hurry to move, and, if she were honest, neither was she. She wanted to hold him this close just a little longer. At least until the fire in her belly settled, especially as she would—her eyes closed. She almost forgot. "I have to change."

"Change? Oh, your clothing. Would you like me to turn away while you do so?" His hands went back around her waist, stroking her skin just barely underneath the hem of her shirt.

Oh, Demeter. That was a tough question. A considerable part of her wanted him to see all of her, but the other part felt it would be torturous for both of them. Although they were in the middle of the forest, her naked form was meant for his eyes only. They'd been careful, but she needed to ensure they didn't get caught. "Normally, I would say no, but given our current situation, it might not be fair to either of us. And when you see me, it should be somewhere that only *you* can see me."

Gavin straightened and caressed her cheek with the back of his knuckles. "One day, hopefully soon, I will take you somewhere where it can just be the two of us. You can show me all of you, and I will touch every inch. Until then..." He bent his head and placed a kiss on her cheek, lingering for a moment. "I should let you change your clothing, but I find it difficult to move away from you." He breathed in her scent and took a step back, albeit a small one.

"I know what you mean." Time alone together, where no one could find them. The idea pleased her greatly. She couldn't wait to discover how to make it happen. It would undoubtedly be one instance where he would put out the fire surging through her body. Perhaps reviewing dull, old books would ease the ache between her legs. Even the tiny distance between them felt wrong.

Gavin stepped back a little farther, frowning as he put a hand against his chest. He inhaled deeply as he shifted to all fours and laid at the base of a tree, facing away from her.

Parthenia bit her bottom lip and stared at him. She couldn't help it. It took every ounce of willpower she could muster not to go up to him, stroke his head, and curl up beside him. Forcing her feet to move, she located the knapsack she dropped. She dug around the other pieces of fruit she brought along and removed her white covering. As quickly as possible, Parthenia stepped out of the skirt and tank-top she wore, slipped into the gown, and pulled it over her shoulders, tying the gold belt around her waist. The dress itself tied at her shoulders with a deep plunge between her breasts. It was a soft, shimmering material that split down each leg.

She shoved her other clothing into the knapsack and strode over to where Gavin lay. She sensed his breathing picking up a little the closer she got to him. So as not to get the bottom dirty, she gathered the hem of the dress in her hand and kneeled beside him. He rolled over onto his side and turned his head to smile at her. As his gaze passed over her, his tail slid up her bare leg through the split in the side.

"Are you ready?" he asked.

Setting the knapsack aside, she ran her fingers delicately over his tail with one hand while the other rested against his exposed side. "Yes. Not my preferred choice of attire, but it's what we all wear in Pteryrina."

"You would look wonderful in nothing. Um, anything. Oh..." Gavin bit down on his lower lip; his fangs exposed—quite longer now than they'd been before. "I've put my tail in my mouth again. Although, I doubt there is any question as to my feelings."

Parthenia brushed a soft kiss upon his muzzle. "No, there isn't. And in case it wasn't clear, the feeling is mutual."

"I have no doubts," he pressed his forehead against hers.

She closed her eyes, allowing the sensations and his exotic scent to wash over her. Her heart swelled with the memories they created and the new ones within their grasp. "Then let's go find some answers."

Chapter Eight

Parthenia slipped behind the willow leaves hanging down over the secret passage to Pteryrina. Gavin stayed right behind her, camouflaged. Although they ascended the long staircase in silence, they spoke about the differences between their species and their families the entire way here.

No part of the stone had broken, despite its age. Each step was still perfectly even. Nothing about the rock eroded over the years. Parthenia stopped two steps away from the top. It wasn't quite a door, but more like a large boulder between them and the library. She crooned a few notes of the right octave. Otherwise, the passage wouldn't open. The doorway shifted, and tiny rays of light filtered in.

As Gavin followed her inside, his footsteps came to a halt. The boulder closed behind them. "There are so many."

With its towering shelves, dim lighting, and musty scent of aged books, their library obviously awed him. The number of books they'd collected lost its allure to her years ago. The good news was that they didn't have to scour through every single book here. It would take them months to go through the small section they wanted. "I've practically lived here since I could read. Not that I've even touched a quarter of what's here."

"I can understand why you would want to spend time here. It is magnificent. Books are scarce where I am from. Where should we start?"

"My father was the one who got me started." It was a shame they were so rare with his species. Maybe he could take one or two back with him. There couldn't be any harm in—the sound of talons against the marble floor at the library's entrance echoed. "Stay here," she whispered. Quickly, she grabbed an apple out of the knapsack and quietly tossed the bag to the floor. Shoving aside a couple of books in the row closest to where they stood revealed a single vial. Parthenia poured a tiny amount of liquid in one hand, rubbed it along one arm, and then did the same with the other. She grabbed one book from the shelf and flew closer to the front stacks.

"Parthenia? Are you—oh, there you are," a deep feminine voice said.

"Fagonia, what can I do for you?" As she spoke, she took a slow, deep breath. She sensed it as Gavin bared his fangs, just barely suppressing a hiss. Strange. To him, Fagonia radiated danger. Thankfully, he made no noise.

Fagonia laced her fingers together in front of her body. "Elder Vasilia sent me to get an updated report on The Poppy Field."

Parthenia's eyebrows knitted together. The request made little sense. She did that before she left. Hadn't she? Whatever she did, she had to keep the woman from stepping farther into the library than necessary. "I spoke with Elder Vasilia this morning."

"Oh? She didn't show you'd spoken with one another."

Right. The female pulled that trick again. How many times over the last few months had they done this dance? Too many to count. "I'm sure she didn't, Fagonia. Since you asked so kindly, we've lost another block. I removed the dead plants this morning and added nutrients to the soil. I'll keep track of it to see if there are improvements."

"Very well." Fagonia turned to leave, then stopped.

Good Demeter, why couldn't she just go? What did she want now? "Was there something else?" Parthenia bit into the apple so the fragrance would combine with the cleansing potion on her arms. It had worked perfectly for years, but she was optimistic the exchange with Gavin earlier might have left an imprint.

"I was just wondering what that smell is. It's… different."

"A new perfume I'm trying. You don't like it?" Parthenia tilted her head and tried to keep the smile off her face.

"No, not really."

"Then I guess it's a good thing you don't have to wear it. Now, if you require nothing else, I have a long night of studying ahead. You know, The Poppy Field." She took another bite of the apple, effectively dismissing the female.

Fagonia smirked. Her talons clicked against the marble floor as she left the library.

Parthenia's shoulders slumped as she set the book and apple down on a nearby table. That was close.

Gavin laid his head on her shoulder and buried his face in her neck, breathing in her scent. "I did not like that female," he mumbled. "Just being in her vicinity..." He shuddered. "Who was that?"

Having him close eased the tension from her body. It had taken every fiber of her being to keep from shoving Fagonia out the door. She didn't have to see him as she spun toward him and wrapped her arms around his waist, which was easier now with him in his humanoid form. "No one cares for her. That's Fagonia, and she's the one who keeps convincing our elder that we shouldn't stray from our laws."

He drew her close to him, stroking her spine as her wings enveloped him. "If no one cares for her, how can she influence the elder so?"

"Because I'm the only one willing to stand against her." Although she suspected there was something else going on with the female, she'd never been able to pinpoint what exactly. "Some feel sorry for her. To this day, Fagonia is unmated, and she has one reproductive cycle left. Even my father, as the last male, wouldn't touch her."

"Well, she did not seem friendly. If that is the case, it is strange that she would wish for the laws to go unchanged. If there are no male sirens left and she is so close to being unable to bear children, hm."

"Yes, it does." She snuggled into him a bit. It was dangerous to get this comfortable. They'd get nothing accomplished, but she couldn't help herself. He was soft and smelled wonderful. Parthenia pulled back a touch, her eyebrows knitting together as a thought crossed her mind. Fagonia was rather masculine. "It seems strange. We've had sirens in the past born asexual. If she were, I'd suspect she would've produced children by now. Unless..."—Parthenia glanced toward the front entrance—"There's another male siren out there somewhere. So many families left here hundreds of *solaris* ago that it could be possible."

"Yes, maybe. Although, based on what you said earlier, it may not be possible unless their mate has passed. Or there are unmated children out there." Gavin laid his cheek on top of her head, his fingers still stroking her.

"I suppose it's possible. They tracked none of the families after they left."

"Should we look through the books?" he asked, his voice husky.

Mmm, she loved when his voice got low like that. It was as hot as when he growled. Her feathers ruffled as tingles crawled up the back of her spine. Parthenia unwrapped her wings from around him. "Yes, we should. Um, the ones we want will be the back rows on the left side. There are about ten rows of ancient texts."

"Then let us begin." He captured her hand in his and brought it to his lips as his tongue ran over her knuckles. "Lead the way."

A shudder passed through her. Shaking away the dirty thoughts swimming around her brain, Parthenia strode toward the back, the opposite side of where they came in. Each aisle was nearly thirty feet high, even where the older books lived. It was dimly lit, and the air was more controlled to a perfect temperature. She stopped in the first row and eyed the other nine. "This could take months to go through."

"We will search until we find the answers we seek." His tail wrapped around her leg, caressing it. "I am not as familiar with the written word as I wish I were. What words should I look for?"

Stroking his tail, she tapped her chin. Her eyes danced across the various bindings as she considered what they would need to seek. She scanned the titles, searching for something that would stand out. "Interspecies, mating, shockwave, shock, barriers, forcefield. Those are probably a good start." Parthenia handed him a book, and he took it carefully. As she retrieved another, he sat in a chair and drew her into his lap.

"I promise to focus, but I need you close to me," Gavin said in her ear, resting his hand on her thigh.

She nuzzled his neck with her nose and pressed a soft kiss on his cheek. "I'm pleased to be close to you."

He let out a low growl, his chest rumbling again. Oh, sweet torturous bliss. That sound again. It took everything she had not to respond in kind. The library echoed, and if they made too much noise, somebody would surely catch them. That thought alone temporarily stilled her desire, although not by much.

His whole body quivered. "That pleases me greatly." He gave her thigh a soft squeeze. Neither of them missed how close his fingers were to a particular part of her body. Opening the book, Parthenia ran her fingers lazily up and down his arm as she skimmed through the volume's contents.

Her brows knitted together as she flipped to another page. It took her a few tries to comprehend the words she just read. She could feel every hard plane of Gavin's muscles beneath her body. His thick thighs underneath her bottom. The breadth of his chest at her back. The strength in his arms around her body. And the gentle grip of his hand on her thigh. The slits in her dress were high, to begin with. They made the dresses to remove quickly. She swallowed and attempted to focus on the words in front of her. At some point, they would make sense.

She shifted against him, and he immediately hardened more against the outside of her leg. His hand slid further along her leg, closer to her inner thigh. Parthenia jerked as an intense shock of electricity shot straight up her arm and traveled down her wing.

"*Ow,*" Gavin hissed. He shook his arm out and used his other hand to rub up and down her arm. "I am so sorry. I cannot seem to help myself."

Her nose wrinkled as her gaze dropped to the bottom tip of her wing. Had one of her feathers singed? The barest hint of smoke stained the air. How was that possible? Parthenia closed the book and leaned back against him. "That makes two of us." A lot of images ran through her mind. All of them started with her straddling him and ended with unsnapping the straps of her dress. "I don't think I understood anything."

He groaned and dropped his head into her neck, nuzzling her throat. "I did not either. Are you alright?"

Good Demeter, she was warm. Heat radiated through both of their bodies. The blatant desire between them was as clear as the sky. Both of their bodies craved what they couldn't give one another. She caressed his cheek. "It'll heal."

"Do you think... would it be possible... could I take a few of these with me? Not that I wish to leave you, not in the least." He brushed his hand down her arm. "But I fear this will get us nowhere."

"I don't see the harm in you taking a few books. No one will notice them missing because I am the only one here. I don't want to part either, but I don't know we'll get anything done otherwise."

"It is impossible, when I am near you, to focus on anything else. I promise I tried, though."

"I know you did, as much as I did." Neither of them could help it. It was that simple. She readjusted in his lap. She could feel every part of him, even if she couldn't see him. Still, she wanted to look into his eyes. "We're truly alone if you want to... your camouflage."

Gavin removed his camouflage, revealing the smile on his face. At least now she could see him. Although, she felt other parts she may not have noticed as much before. Not that it stopped her from wanting to face him. She enjoyed gazing into his eyes too much.

As if he read her mind, he took the book from her hand, set it aside on the nearby table, along with the one he read, and turned her around in his lap, so she straddled him. He swept a strand of hair from her face and tucked it over her ear. "Is this love? What we feel. I feel as if it is, but we just met. It seems impossible, but even more impossible, that it could be anything else."

"I don't know. Maybe. All I know, I'd do anything for you, kill anyone who tried to hurt you, and that I never want to be apart."

"I feel the same way. I know I would die for you. Nor do I want to part from you. When may I see you again?"

Parthenia gently pressed her forehead to his as she warred against her body. But she didn't want to draw attention to them. It would cause way too much harm. If this was how they had to live for the time being, then it's what they would do. "What if you come back later tonight? After everyone is asleep. I could show you the most beautiful part of Pteryrina."

"The most beautiful part of Pteryrina is you." He kissed her cheek. "But yes, I will return. Nothing could keep me from you."

Parthenia blushed. She didn't think she'd ever become accustomed to the compliments. "I might have to disagree with you, as you're here. It certainly makes me look forward to showing you more."

Gavin growled. "I look forward to seeing every single inch of you." He buried his face in her neck and breathed in her scent. "Oh, gods, we should go. I am going to get us caught."

Tightening her grip on his shoulders, she bit her bottom lip to quiet the moan as she arched ever so slightly against him. "Demeter, I wish this library didn't echo so bad."

"Mmm, as do I," he murmured against her. Gripping her hips, his tail slipped around one of her bare legs. "We could always go back to the forest. I can take some books with me when we have to part ways. But then we would not have to worry about being so quiet. I do not want to stop touching you."

"I think that's a good idea. The last thing I want is for anyone to find you here." While Cipriana might understand, Fagonia wouldn't stand for it. She wasn't sure about any of the other sirens. Mating desires wasn't something she discussed with, well, any of them.

Focus. Books. What books? Parthenia eyed the two books they discarded on the table. Both would be good options. One addressed mating rituals, and the other was a general history of the isle. At least what the sirens knew. Though, perhaps, they should bring one other. She got out of his lap and walked over to the first aisle of ancient texts. Her eyes flicked to the books on the shelf behind his shoulders. Flapping her wings, she reached behind him, collected a book on barriers, and eased her feet to the floor.

"I will take good care of them. Should I camouflage as we leave, or do you think we can slip out unseen?"

She trusted he would. Later, when she returned, she'd scour for a couple of books to give him permanently. They had so many it seemed pointless not to gift a few. "I think we'll be okay. Everyone knows how easy it is for me to get lost in here. There has been many a time I've spent all day in these aisles. They've learned not to bother me when I'm in here. And the forest on the other side is uncontrolled."

"Then I will stay this way so you can see me." Taking her hand, he laced their fingers together. Gavin pulled her to him. He dipped his head down and nuzzled her neck. "Feel free to ride on my back this time as we leave."

A shiver ran from her neck down her arms. She loved when Gavin did that. It was a good thing she left the knapsack over there. They could tuck the books inside of it before they departed. "Are you sure? I mean, I'll be careful with my talons."

"Am I sure I want you sitting on top of me? Absolutely."

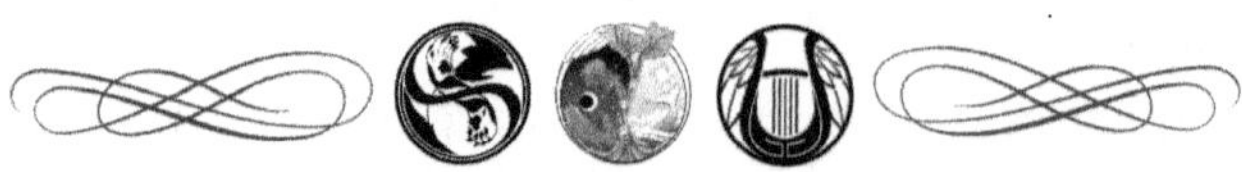

"It is just straight up. You will know it when you see it. Though it is not much to look at, we managed one decent-sized room," Gavin said as they stopped in front of a tall tree. "Would you like to race up?"

"I'm quite certain you might beat me, but I love a challenge." Parthenia pushed off his back and shot straight into the air as her wings extended to their entire ten-foot span. His laughter below her caught her attention. It was pure freedom to race him to the top while watching him propel up the tree with such speed. It didn't matter who got there first. In the end, they would be there together.

Gavin reached the top first.

"Wow. You are magnificent in flight," he said as Parthenia joined him on the platform. He laid on the floor of the little room in his humanoid form.

She removed the knapsack from her shoulders, tucked her wings in tight as she set it on the floor, and then walked over to him. Dropping to her knees and laying on her side, Gavin purred as she curled up to him. "I don't think I've enjoyed flying like that in so long. Although, I can't decide if I enjoyed that more than watching you move through the branches with such grace."

"You were the graceful one. That was an incredible thing to watch." Gathering her into his arms, he drew her close, gazed down at her, and slowly stroked her hip. "I wish we could stay just like this... for always."

"Me too." Making herself quite comfortable, she snuggled against him and draped a leg over his, her knee against his inner thigh. Goddess, she couldn't imagine never being with him like this for the rest of their lives.

"I love you draped around me like this." He wrapped his other arm around her and kissed her forehead, temple, cheek, and the spot beneath her ear. "I love you," he whispered.

Her heart swelled at the words. It was so much more than that. For the first time in her life, she felt complete, whole. Like she found her other half. Parthenia nuzzled his cheek. "I love you too."

"I have felt so very empty for so very long. For forever. But no longer. Not with you. You make me feel truly alive."

"I feel the same way. It's like I found the joy in life again."

"I have never felt such happiness as I feel with you."

Parthenia caressed the back of his head, bringing a deep purr out of him. "I shall do everything to ensure the feeling never changes."

"I believe you. And I shall do whatever it takes to ensure you never lose this feeling as well." He growled as he stroked her neck with his tongue.

Her body arched of its own volition. "I believe you, with all my heart and soul."

Rolling over, Gavin hovered over her as their gazes met. The smoldering look in his eyes brought forth the heat that had settled in her body. She angled her neck to give him more room, moaning at the sensation of his lips and tongue against her skin. It would be easy to undo the straps of her dress from this position. Although she hadn't done it before, she couldn't stop herself this time. Maybe they didn't know how little or how much they'd be able to share concerning a physical connection, but she desperately wanted to find out. Reaching to her shoulder, Parthenia undid the clasp that held the straps on each side in place.

A deep rumble vibrated in his chest. The barest hint of the side of her bosom exposed. His mouth moved further down her arm, his eyes on the creamy swell of her breast the entire time. As he extended his fingers towards it—so wildly close—some force threw him hard against the wall of the room. A pang shot up her spine.

Gavin quickly scrambled back over her. "So. None of that, it would seem."

"Good Demeter. I'm so sorry. So, so sorry."

"Do not be." He moved a strand of hair over her shoulder, his fingers caressing it. "You did nothing wrong. And it is good to learn boundaries, yes?"

His words didn't stop the guilt she felt. Every boundary they discovered caused him harm. His fingers and purring warred with the concern in her head and heart as he continued to light her body up with his touch. If only she hadn't read that stupid journal, except then they—the journal! Her eyes lit up. Parthenia arched into him and gave her wings room to extend ever so slightly. She pressed a gentle kiss to his jaw. "I have an idea."

He slid his arm around her lower back, holding her to him, and burrowed his face against her neck. "Oh? What might that be?"

Another moan escaped her lips as she plucked a feather from one of her wings. Being so close to Gavin distracted her from the minor burn associated with the removal. It was a small price to pay. She held the feather up to him. "For the places you can't touch me with your hands, lips, or tongue, until the day you can. And all the places I can't touch you."

His eyes glowed slightly for a moment. "I very much like the sound of that." His fingertip brushed along the length of the feather. "That did not hurt you, though, did it? Removing your feather?"

She trailed kisses from his chin up the length of his jaw. "I hardly noticed it."

"G-good," he breathed out. Gripping her waist, Gavin rolled them over and settled her just above his hips. "You may touch me anywhere you would like." His fingers gently curled around her knees, his thumbs stroking them. "And I will touch you anywhere that you will allow me to."

With the tip of her talons, Parthenia teased his outer thigh. With the straps of her dress undone, the top half fell to her waist. She almost forgot all about it. His eyes immediately strayed to her breasts, both fully exposed now. Leaning forward, she raked her fingers along the length of his arm. She snaked her tongue across his collarbone. "Everywhere. You may touch me everywhere."

Taking the feather from her, Gavin brushed the tip down the valley between her breasts and across he sweetly curved mounds. He trailed the fingers down her bare arm, side, then lower, across her hips, and over her belly button.

Parthenia moaned in ecstasy. It felt so good. Tracing her fingers across the lines of his pectoral muscles, she continued along his abs. Her thighs tightened around him as she caressed the length of his legs with the tips of her wings.

He rolled them over again, carefully, so he hovered over her. His lips and tongue moved across her belly button and stomach. "We should probably stop, though I do not want to," he breathed against her hairless skin, his voice husky and strained.

She stroked the back of his head, running her fingers along his ears and at the nape of his neck. The pain within him was the last thing she wanted to cause. She wanted to see him release—the same way it spoke of in the siren's journal. They may not yet be able to do some of the other things she read about, but this they could. "I do not wish to stop either. You are in pain. Let me ease it."

"You may do anything to me you would like." He licked a trail up her stomach, stopping before he got too close to her breasts.

Her body felt like an inferno as he spoke and moved. Maybe she couldn't do everything she wanted, but she would explore as much of him as she could and use the feather for the places she couldn't until she could freely trace every crevice and muscle he owned. She planned to know his body better than she knew her own. Parthenia pushed on his shoulders to urge him onto his back. As he did so, he propped himself up on his elbows, not taking his eyes off her.

For a moment, she considered removing the dress the rest of the way, but she feared it would be too much of a distraction. Straddling him just below the waist, she trailed her fingers from his forehead and down his nose. She pressed a soft, moist kiss on either side of his lips and continued to make a path down his chest and abs with her mouth as she raked her fingers down his arms.

His entire body shook. Hisses, moans, growls, and other sounds of pleasure came out of him. Gavin clenched his hands into fists. "Do not—oh, do not stop. Parthenia!"

She had no intention of doing that. Driving him crazy pleased her to no end. She stopped just above the tip of his sex. Her gaze focused on his size and girth. A moan escaped her lips at the mere thought of where it would one day be. He proved earlier that they couldn't touch each other's sex, but she could indeed stroke the sensitive skin around it, lick and nip his thighs. While she inched her body lower, she raked her fingers down his chest. To ensure she kept the total momentum going, she caressed the length of his calf muscles with her talons and grazed her fingernails along his hipbones.

He growled loud, and his hips bucked as she got ever so close to where his body was begging her to be. Just enough for his claws to extend, he shifted slightly. He dug them into the wood floor, leaving gouges as he panted. His sex twitched, and she knew he was on the edge of an orgasm.

As Parthenia sucked on his inner thigh, she dragged her hand along the curve of his rear until she found his tail. She licked across his thigh and sucked the tip of his tail into her mouth; not that she could say where the urge came from. All she knew was that he looked magnificent, and he was almost exactly where she wanted him.

What started as a moan quickly turned into the loudest growl he had uttered. His claws dug more into the wood, not only leaving mere divots this time but cracking the floor. Gavin's head jerked back, banging into the wooden surface as his sex kicked. Over and over, he came, covering his chest and the ground on either side of him. When the orgasm ended, he laid there panting, his chest heaving.

Parthenia rolled her shoulders as she shuddered and slowly crawled back up his body. She licked at his chest and lapped at the sweet, sweet taste of him. "Mmm, I've tasted nothing better."

A low rumble left him. "You may have more to taste if you keep doing that," he murmured. He caressed her face. "I want to make you feel what you just made me feel. I want to make you release, and I want to taste every bit."

She pressed a kiss to the inside of his palm. "I believe we can arrange that." Sliding back down his body, she got to her feet and untied the belt around her waist. Letting her dress fall to the floor, she bared herself to him completely. Her entire body was hairless, except for the mahogany waves that spilled over her shoulders and cascaded to the middle of her back. Her porcelain skin was flawless, from the top of her head to the bottom of her calves, where her bird-like feet began.

Gavin stared. His tongue snaked out across his lips. He kneeled before her, caressing her talons and feet, calves, and thighs. His lips and tongue followed each of the touches his fingers gave. The contrast between his soft hands and rough tongue sent endless jolts of lightning to her sex. He moved outward to her hips, letting his fangs graze across them. Her eyes stayed on him until he moved around behind her. Shivers shot down her spine.

He continued his touches, kisses, licks, and grazes along the curve of her rear, as she'd done to him with her hand. He slowly inched up her body until he towered over her. Standing between her wings, he moved her hair over her shoulder and slid his arms around her, caressing her belly as low as he dared. Parthenia moaned.

"You are exquisite. I plan to worship you now, as much as I can." He kissed and licked her shoulder, then her neck. "Would you lie down for me?"

Slowly, she faced him. Biting on her bottom lip, she pressed a kiss to his chest, took a couple of steps back, and lowered her body to the ground.

Gavin's gaze didn't leave her. He joined her, crawling up and over her body. After picking up the feather again, he slowly caressed her breasts with it. He moved it down her stomach, then between her legs. He watched for a moment as he moved it over the slit of her sex, then licked at her neck as he did it again.

One of her legs cocked naturally, and she angled her neck as she opened herself further to the sensations. Her nipples pebbled, and her back arched as she gripped the floor above her head. When her talons curled, she scratched against the wooden boards beneath her feet. The mix of every-thing set her body ablaze. "Oh please, don't stop," she groaned.

The sound of his growl sent a wave of heat straight to her sex. He moved down until he laid between her legs. Spreading them wider, he grazed his fangs down her inner thighs as he kept going with the feather at her sex.

"Gavin!" His teeth against her tender skin sent her over the edge. Her thighs tensed as the inner walls of her sex clenched. She cried out some exotic chirping sound as an orgasm slammed through her body. Cream gushed from her sex onto the floor and down the inside of her thighs. Parthenia panted as the last of the explosion pulsated through her veins.

Growling against her, Gavin licked up both of her inner thighs, as high as he dared to go, getting every single drop he could. "You are the sweetest thing I have ever tasted." He kissed and licked her stomach, around her breasts, then up her neck. Placing a kiss on either side of her mouth, he laid down beside her and pulled her into his arms.

She had no words as heavy breaths left her mouth. At no point had she thought once about what they couldn't do. Her mind had gone silent as they explored each other's bodies and soared together to new sensations. Being with someone she felt so deeply for was the best feeling in the world. She never wanted to leave. Her eyes drifted shut as she curled up to him. "That was amazing."

"It truly was," he whispered, stroking her hair. "You truly are. You honor me by giving me such a gift as yourself."

Parthenia pressed a soft kiss to the underside of his chin. She couldn't imagine doing anything differently. The world outside waited for them, but she didn't want to think about that. She was content just being here with him. "Can we just stay here?" Although, if they did, some repairs would be necessary. She giggled at the broken boards. Those may not go unnoticed.

"I am going to have to explain those to my sister." He kissed her temple. "I would stay here with you until the end of my days if we could."

His absence would go as noticed as her own would. If she didn't return at some point, her mother or Cipriana would come looking for her and conclude the worse when they didn't find her. She chewed on the inside of her cheek, wishing she knew of a way that she and Gavin could reach out whenever they were apart. A way to ease the pang they'd each suffer without the other nearby. "I believe there will come a day where we can spend our time together freely. Until then, we'll steal time whenever we can."

"Yes, we shall. And I shall enjoy every moment."

"As will I."

"I will come tomorrow; when I am able and look through the books, we brought here. Hopefully, I will find something that will help us."

Resting her hands on his pecs, Parthenia laid her chin on her hands. He had agreed to return to Pteryrina later that night. Initially, she planned to show him The Poppy Field and The Reflection Pools. She could check a few of the books when she returned, but she also had to work on strengthening the potion. It got her thinking. "Will you still come back later?"

"I will come back whenever you wish me to. Though I will need you to let me in. I am no singer."

"There's something more... me. It's the closest place I have to call my own. I'd like to share it with you. And I will always let you in." Parthenia beamed brightly. She hadn't ever shown it to anyone before. Cipriana used to share her love for potions but hadn't in several years. Much had changed since then. He'd be the first to see it.

"I would love to see it and anything else you want to show me. I wish I could show you my village, too, but it would be much too dangerous."

"Understandable. Perhaps one day I can see it when things are safe for both of us." Her gaze drifted across the room where she left her dress. She should go soon, but she wasn't ready yet.

"I long for that day. When we will both be safe." He buried his nose into the crook of her neck. "You are my beloved, my fate, and my destiny."

His words struck a chord with her. In her species, they were the promise one made to another during a mating ceremony. Did he realize that? Parthenia propped up on his chest, looked him in the eyes, and caressed his cheek. She could see he meant every word. "You are my beloved mate, my most trusted companion, and the father of our future children."

Gavin placed his hand over hers, entwining their fingers. Something passed between them just now and, though she'd known it already, the knowledge washed over her in waves. No matter who went first—though it wasn't a thought either of them wanted in their heads—they would both have no other, ever. They loved each other wholeheartedly, and with everything in them, until death parted them.

She had only ever heard of how females shined when the exchange of the mating words occurred. She hadn't believed it until then. Even if she couldn't see her face, she saw the love reflected in his green eyes. The promises made between them were perfect.

"Do you think there will come a time when we will have young? I want that with no other but you."

She squeezed his fingers within her own. "I do. I want to have them with no other but you."

"Our children will be beautifully perfect because they will come from you."

"They will be a perfect mixture of us." She couldn't wait until her first reproductive cycle. They would have beautiful children. And she hoped they got his eyes. But they would be perfect no matter how they appeared.

He kissed her forehead, cheeks, nose, and chin softly before leaning his head against hers. "When should I come tonight? Once they account my presence, I should be able to sneak out."

"Midnight. Everyone should be asleep by then." Parthenia brushed a small kiss across his nose. She didn't know how long they'd been gone, but she needed to return before dinner preparations began. "I should get dressed."

"I wish you did not have to." Gavin kissed the side of her mouth before reluctantly releasing her.

"I wish I didn't have to go, either." As much as she didn't want to leave him, she had no choice. She stood, strode across the room, collected her dress, and stepped into it. It felt wrong to be pulling the straps over her shoulders and snapping them back into place.

"We will see each other soon. I pray the time passes quickly." He caressed her leg.

"Yes, we will." Shivers shot down her spine. It would take a lot of willpower to leave him, but it was something she had to do. She suspected the time might feel as if it would drag on forever, regardless of how quickly it passed. Completely dressed, she crouched down and removed the books from her knapsack. She set them on the floor, placed a pair of oranges on top of them, and closed the distance between the two of them. "Small snack. Just make sure you peel them first."

He pulled her to him, so she sat on his lap and circled his arms around her lower back. He swept his tongue up her neck to her ear. "Until later."

A shudder passed through her. If Gavin kept that up, she'd never leave. Not that she was ready to say goodbye, either. She snuggled against him. "Yes, later."

"As soon as I can let you go." They stayed like that for a while. It was utterly perfect. She could've quickly fallen asleep in his arms, listening to the steady thrum of his heart. She remained awake and, after some time, though she was unsure how much time had passed, he unwrapped himself from her. "We should both get home before suspicions arise. Besides, the sooner we part, the sooner we will be together again."

"I look forward to it." She hooked a thumb over her shoulder. "Save the orange peels, please. Bring them with you, if possible. If not, leave them here, and I'll collect them the next time we're here."

"I will leave them here, but will collect them before I come to you tonight."

"Thank you." Before she couldn't make herself leave, she climbed out of his lap and tugged her knapsack over her shoulders. "I'll see you soon."

"Yes. Soon." He picked her feather up off the floor, holding it to his chest for a moment. Crossing to one of the four walls, he placed it on a shelf. "I will keep this here. I would keep it with me always if I could." Gavin faced her. "Be safe, beloved."

She understood. It was safest if it remained here where no one could find it on him. "You as well." Parthenia turned to the exit and, with one last look at him over her shoulder, she took off.

Chapter Nine

Parthenia sang the right notes with no enthusiasm, and the door slid open. She stepped into the library. As the door closed behind her, she accessed her cleansing potion nearby and used it on her arms, chest, neck, and legs. It seemed wrong to wipe over the places Gavin had touched her, but it was necessary for both their survival.

"Ugh. Where are you?"

She poked her head around the corner. What in the world? "Cipriana?"

Her sister stomped between the aisles and came into her view. "Good Demeter, there you—" Cipriana's eyes narrowed, and she crossed her arms. "You've been out again, haven't you?"

How did she possibly know that? Parthenia blinked and sighed. Right. The cleansing potion didn't entirely cover Gavin's scent. Not that she'd openly admit that. "Out where? What are you talking about?"

"Oh, come off it. I know you've been sneaking down to the isle." Cipriana frowned.

"Shh, keep your voice down." Someone could hear her. Slipping out from behind the bookshelves, Parthenia peered down the long aisle. She listened for any sign that someone else wandered around the library. Confident they were alone, her gaze flicked back to Cipriana. "How'd you figure it out?"

"Because I know you better than anyone else. Besides, it's not like there are a lot of places you can visibly hide around here."

Her sister had a valid point. There were only so many places to search for her, which wasn't something her sister usually did. It wasn't like she was late for dinner or preparations. "Why were you looking for me?"

"Fagonia was asking questions. I think she's vying to be the next elder."

"What?" It made no sense. No way would Elder Vasilia appoint Fagonia to take her place. No one cared for the female, and she constantly undermined the elder. Even earlier, when the woman showed up in the library unexpectedly to check the progress that she had already discussed with the Elder.

"You and I both know the idea is farfetched. Regardless, Fagonia was seeking you out, and I covered for you."

Parthenia exhaled a breath of relief. One she didn't realize she even held. A tiny smile fell across her mouth as she rested a hand against her throat. Of all the females in her life, she could always count on Cipriana. "What did you tell her?"

"That you were holed up in your apothecary and asked not to be disturbed. Now, let's go back to my place and get you cleaned up before you go home."

"What about your mother and sisters?" Cipriana might understand, but she suspected anyone else in the female's immediate family wouldn't be so accommodating. It was a chance she couldn't take.

"They're all in the gardens, but we need to move fast if we plan to slip by unnoticed."

"Thank you." The two of them left Antekilio out the side exit and headed toward the group of white stone homes they all shared. Each house had minimal decoration. They had enough to sleep, bathe, and gather for meals.

It didn't take long for them to make their way to Cipriana's house. The two of them slipped inside unseen and went straight to the household bathing hole. Steam poured from the water in the tub. She flipped her gaze to her sister.

Cipriana shrugged. "I prepared when I couldn't find you."

Parthenia threw her arms around the female and hugged her tightly. Her sister went out of the way to protect her without once asking for details.

"Alright. Come on, you need to bathe before you go home. I'll get you a new dress while you wash." Cipriana tapped Parthenia on the back. Once she let go, she walked out of the room.

Left by herself, Parthenia glanced at the warm water, took off her knapsack, and quickly stripped. For the future, she'd have to find some freshwater to bathe in before returning home. Unfortunately, the map she sketched out in her apothecary covered very little. Maybe Gavin would know of some place close to the treehouse he and his sister had built. She'd have to remember to ask him later.

Easing into the water, Parthenia reached for the soap and washed her body and hair. She'd have to put it up once she got out, but it would be a risk not to clean her mahogany locks. Her heart broke with every soapy run across her skin. It felt like she was attempting to rid her body of his memory. Of course, it was the furthest from the truth, but the knowledge didn't make it hurt any less.

Satisfied with the minor effort she put forth, Parthenia climbed out of the bathing hole and dried herself using nearby linen. She shook the water from her feathers and preened them as much as she could manage.

Cipriana returned with fresh drapery. "I brought you something to pin your hair up, too."

"Thank you." Without hesitation, she dressed and pinned her hair up into a chignon. As much as she preferred to wear it down, with it still wet, it wasn't an option.

"You're welcome." Cipriana dragged her fingers through her hair. "Can you just do me a favor from now on?"

"Anything." The response came out of her mouth before she gave it much thought. But, in all honesty, her following answer would depend on the request.

"Tell me when you're leaving. I don't need the specifics, just that you're going down to the isle. It'll make it easier for me to cover for you."

Her eyebrows knitted together. She didn't know how to reply. The female didn't want to know what she did, who she saw, or how long she planned to be gone. All her sister asked was to be notified when she left. Parthenia swallowed. Cipriana never gave her any sign that she'd betray her; somehow, her sister even figured out that she'd been leaving. "Yeah, I can, uh, I can do that."

"Thank you. Now, get going. I'm sure your mother's looking for you by now."

Parthenia departed, and not a minute too soon. Voices approached as she tiptoed around the corner, just in time to see Cipriana's mother and siblings return. She cut it close this time. Not that she would've traded the hours she spent with Gavin for anything. She was ready for it to be midnight.

As darkness settled over Pteryrina, she took advantage and moved between the shadows to her own home. Parthenia hurried through the door and stopped just inside the doorway. Her gaze fell to her mother, who busily sliced vegetables at the dining table.

"Look who graced me with her presence finally."

"My apologies, Mother. I'll put my knapsack away and come help."

Her mother scowled. "Really? Now that I've done most of everything?"

This kind of exchange occurred before. It likely wouldn't be the last. She could only do one thing to restore the peace. Grimacing, she lowered her gaze to the white floor beneath her feet. "My apologies, Mother. I'll be certain it doesn't happen again."

"Oh, I'm sure you won't. Move quickly. You can dice the herbs, finish the stew, and wash the dishes."

"Of course, Mother." Parthenia bowed her head and darted to the small box that served as her room. She kept little here. Several dresses and gold belts hung on the wall. A simple cotton strip on the other side of the room served as her bed. As she glanced around her quarters, her thoughts drifted once again to Gavin. Had he made it home safely? Did anyone notice him before he made it back, and did he feel as empty as she did?

"Parthenia!"

She jumped at the orotund sound of her mother's voice. "Coming, Mother." Dropping her knapsack to the floor, she spun on her heel and rushed to the dining table. Out of the corner of her eye, she saw the fire burned well. It was ready for the pot. Parthenia picked up a knife, diced herbs, and tossed them into the stew.

As she worked on dinner, Gavin continuously crept into her thoughts. She wished they could communicate even with the distance between them. Wouldn't that be something? To hear him in her head and to speak with him. Pausing with the knife in her hand, she rubbed at her chest again. She felt the same pang earlier. No. That wasn't right. This one was different. The pain from before had been because of the distance between them. She couldn't explain this sensation.

"Parthenia! Stop dawdling."

She snapped back into action and went on with getting dinner together. "My apologies, Mother."

The pangs continued as she got the pot on the fire and stirred the stew. While she attempted to focus on their meal, her mother set out a couple of bowls, spoons, and cups with water. The two of them worked in silence. Once dinner was ready, they ate in silence, too. She grew accustomed to this over the years. They didn't converse. She used to draw her mother in with questions, but they always went unanswered. Instead of a mother and daughter relationship, they became roommates who moved around each other.

Her mother left her to her own devices after dinner. Parthenia collected the few dishes they used and went about clearing away the remnants of their meal. It was for the best. They had nothing to say to one another as it was. As soon as she finished with the dishes, she planned to leave. The few books she and Gavin picked out earlier were back at the treehouse, but there were so many more to go through.

Plus, it would be wise to seek the journal she'd forgotten about. She might find a piece of information in there that explained the forcefield that yanked them apart multiple times. Although, now that she thought about it, she curled up to Gavin naked, and nothing happened. Not to mention the other stuff they'd done. She shuddered at the memory.

Parthenia laid out the last of the dishes to dry, carried the dirty water outside, and dumped it out. Her gaze drifted to the stars shining above in the dark blue sky—still a few more hours before he arrived.

Her mother strode out from the back and scanned over the table. "Don't forget to wipe this down."

"Of course, Mother." She shut the front door and put the washing bucket up. She grabbed the damp cloth and took it over to the table. Confident the wood was spotless; she stepped to the side and awaited her mother's inspection.

Bending over, the female ran a finger across various spots on the table. Then, rising to her full height, she smirked. "It'll do. I expect you back for breakfast in the morning. Bring some fruit with you."

"Yes, Mother." It had been years since she spent a night in this house. She only returned to endure quiet meals with the female who gave her life and to bathe. Other than that, she spent her time on the isle, in the library, or her apothecary. At night, she slept there, surrounded by her potions, books, and more. Until Gavin, it was where she called home.

Gavin practically flew through the secret entrance, breathing in deeply as soon as Parthenia's scent flooded his nose. She was close. He leaped up the stairs and, when he reached her, curled his head up under her arm.

Parthenia smiled and stroked his head. "I missed you."

"I missed you as well." He inhaled her aroma, allowing it to wash over him and ease him the rest of the way. Once his nerves and fear settled, he gazed up at her. "I hated being away from you."

"Me too." Her fingers sifted through his fur. "I've got tea ready to heat if you're ready to go in, but I get the sense you need another moment."

"I just need to be here with you. It does not matter where, just as long as I am with you. If you would like to go in, we can."

"We can wait a minute. No one will come across us." Leaning into him, she pressed a tender kiss to his shoulder. "Was it bad when you returned to your village?"

"Only normal. At least, I do not—" Gavin stopped, shaking his head a little. "I do not know. But Markham, he watches me. Not just me, but everyone. When his eyes are on me, I feel like I need to bathe. He just radiates evil. I have felt nothing like it. And when I got back to the village ..." He hesitated for a moment. While he didn't want to worry her, he didn't want to keep anything from her either. "I still had my camouflage on, but it was as if he could see right through it. Like he could see me even though he should not have been able to."

"Maybe there's something I can do to help." Parthenia stood.

"I would welcome that. Thank you. You are wonderful."

"I would do anything for you."

He tilted his head back and gave her neck a small lick. "I am okay. We can go upstairs now."

With a smile, she ascended the staircase. Parthenia sang the right notes two steps from the top, and the door opened to the library as it did earlier.

"Your voice soothes me." He followed her inside.

"I've never been told that before. Siren songs manipulate, allow us to convince an enemy or an unfriendly to do our bidding." The door closed behind them. She strode through the library and led him past all the aisles of books to the actual entrance. She pushed on the heavy wooden door, opening to a stone staircase. To the left was an enormous structure built with tall columns. Opposite the library appeared to be gardens. He noted a splash of red just beyond that.

"Well, whatever it does, it soothes me like nothing else." He could tell that his words pleased her, and that knowledge warmed him. He nuzzled her side before staring around at what was before him. Everything was white, except for the gardens and beyond. "Your home is truly wondrous. What is that red?"

She rested her hand on his shoulder. "The Poppy Field. I spend my mornings there cultivating the flowers and checking the levels of The Reflection Pools."

"I would love to see it." The tip of his tail caressed the edge of one of her wings. "White is clean to me. Pure. Calming. The opposite of everything I feel at home. And it is the color of my twin. While I am fully black, she is pure white."

Parthenia stared out across the land. "It's amazing how we can view things so differently. You see peacefulness and purity. I see vastness and emptiness." She descended the stairs and started toward a tall tree with the same orange fruit on it she gave him earlier.

Gavin followed beside her, taking in their surroundings. "In my village, the vastness and emptiness have nothing to do with the scenery."

"Your parents? They do nothing to aid with that?" She led him to a white stone pathway just on the other side of the orange tree. A small garden with various vegetables was to the left of the path. To the right was a garden with fresh fruits, including two large apple trees.

He could identify some fruits and vegetables, but not all of them. They were far from his mind, though, at present. "They are not very warm. I wonder, sometimes, if that is because of the way Markham affects people, or if it is just my father's way. My father is one of his Informants, but they do not give him many orders any longer. He had to get permission from Markham to mate my mother, and he has never been friendly toward us. Growing up, others often looked after us in the village. As for my mother, I do not remember her ever having much warmth towards us, though I know she yearns for it." He shrugged. "I have only ever known warmth from my sister."

"The more I learn about you, the more I realize how much we share." Parthenia continued down the stone path, leading him past an herbal garden. It seemed large, with rows of wheat on one side and barley and mint on the other. The flourish of red stood out like a beacon from where they stood.

The aromas here were so far beyond anything that had ever assaulted his senses. There were scents he knew, but plenty that he didn't. And they all paled compared to Parthenia. She smelled of cherry blossom flowers, mint, vanilla, something he only knew about since Gabriella got some in the market, and something else he couldn't quite place, but it was heavenly. "I agree. You are the only one who has ever truly understood me."

They strolled toward The Poppy Field. Three nine-foot-squares were bare, aside from dry soil, but the fields of red on either side of them brought a smile to Parthenia's face.

Gavin inhaled deeply; he couldn't have held the grin back if he tried. "This place smells just like you."

A small chuckle left her mouth as she stroked his head. "I'm not surprised. This is where I spend most of my time."

"What happened in the empty spaces?" They were nearly at the center of the field, and the clean smell of freshwater was present.

"Those are the lots where the poppies completely wilted. I had to remove the dead flowers, and I've begun a nutrient-rich regiment to rejuvenate the soil."

"That is so sad. I wish I knew something that would help. My sister has the green thumb, though. I wonder what is causing it. Oh, I brought the orange peels with me too, as you asked." After leaving the village earlier, he stopped at the treehouse to eat the fruit she left for him, hoping it would settle his nerves some. It hadn't helped, though. He put the peels in a little bag and hung it around his neck before heading here

"Wonderful. Thank you." She slowed her pace as they approached nine circular pools made of stone. Each interconnected as they stacked on top of one another and led to the top of a waterfall. There was no water running over, though. Only the two bottom pools held any; a beautiful teal color. "Unfortunately, I have this grave feeling that the issues with the poppies links to the drying of The Reflection Pools."

"Did they all used to be full of water?" He'd seen no water quite that color before. He wanted to reach out and touch it.

Parthenia closed the distance between them and the bottom pool. Staring at the empty ones for a moment, she dipped her fingers into the calm waters. "Yes. They hold magical properties, even when they aren't all flowing, but they're at their most powerful when the waterfall flows freely." She gestured to the bottom level. "You may touch it if you wish."

"Thank you." Gavin brushed his tail against her leg, then moved closer to the pools. Laying down on the ground at the edge, he dipped his paw down and ran it through the water. It was the perfect temperature. "Oh, it is not cold, like the river."

She crouched down next to him. "The temperature of the pools never changes. That's part of what makes me believe they're connected to the magic of Prisma Isle."

"It seems very mysterious. But I bet it would be a lovely place to bathe. Bathing in the river is so unpleasant."

"Is it cold? Not fresh?"

"On a hot day, it is not too bad. Nice. But it can get chilly, especially in the winter. It freezes in the winter sometimes too. Unfortunately, it is the only place we have to bathe, so many choose not to during the frigid months."

"We have our bathing holes inside the house. We get the water from the springs. If we need to heat it, we use fire, but it isn't essential. We have to use fresh water because salt is harsh on our feathers."

"I do not know if the river has salt in it. It might, though. I think it may connect to the ocean, or so I have heard. I have not seen it, though I think it surrounds the isle."

Parthenia got to her feet. "I believe so. I haven't mapped out enough of the isle to confirm that. And I haven't come across anything in our books here either. Though it would certainly make sense."

"You have mapped out some of the isle?"

"Yes. I keep it in my apothecary, away from wandering eyes."

"I would very much like to see it. If you would not mind my wandering eyes."

"I'd be more than happy to share it with you." She strode toward the path they had taken to get to The Reflection Pools.

The corners of his muzzle lifted at what he felt from her. He had things he kept to himself that he shared with no one else, not even Gabby. But he wanted to share all of them with Parthenia, and he planned to do just that. Excited to see everything she would show him, he followed her.

Parthenia led him back out through the gardens, past the trees, and into the open area between everything. They strolled along to the left toward a group of several white buildings. About fifty feet away from the buildings, they veered off to the right and continued until they approached a lone white structure with a wooden door. A garden of herbs and spices sat next to the building. On the door hung a sign that read, "In Session." She tugged on the handle and opened the door to let him in, only closing it once they both entered.

Gavin removed his camouflage, then shifted to his humanoid form to make it easier to look around. He couldn't explain why, but just being in here made him feel giddy, like a child who had discovered a hidden gem to explore.

Although the outside of the house was white, the inside was an explosion of color. All the walls were bright red. The shelves and cabinets were a dark blue, close to the color of the night sky. The ceiling went fifteen feet high, with two windows built into the back wall. Each window had wood shutters, both currently closed. Directly in front of them, beneath one window, hung metallic moon phases. A wreath of lavender and chamomile hung on the back of the door. It filled the room with a sense of calm.

A multitude of jars with various herbs, spices, fruit peelings, seeds, kernels, and roots filled racks, along with a few scrolls among the cubbies. Several flowers hung from hooks attached to the bottom counter. Aligning the shelves were also small vials of liquids in various colors. They held jars of twigs, leaves, and small bones as well. More shelves lined the wall closest to them, which contained books, tins, empty jars, gemstones, seashells, and a metal implement with holes. Bowls of varying sizes, a couple more books, a few small knives, and a mortar and pestle sat on the counter. A book sat open on a round wooden table, a furled scroll, and another journal lay next to a few sticks of charcoal. Four chairs surrounded the table. The other window was next to the fireplace, which crackled with small flames. Oversized bedding lay on the floor just beyond the hearth.

Gavin ambled around the room, gently brushing his fingers against a few different objects as he looked at everything. "I think I could spend days in here. Did you put all of this in here by yourself?"

"With some help from my sister. I had a minor accident about six *solaris* ago. That's why it's so far away from the other houses." Parthenia collected an iron pot with a handle from one cabinet. She poured water from a large glass into the kettle first. Scanning the various jars, she pulled down one with lavender seeds and another with honey.

"What kind of accident?"

"I had just started learning potions. To see what they would do, I mixed a few different ingredients. I only left for a minute. The next thing I know, *boom*! Took out half the roof, blew out the side of the house, and charred the outer walls of the house next to it."

"Oh, goodness." He let out a small laugh, though he was sure it hadn't been amusing. "Well, it seems like the relocation was probably a good idea," he teased. Stepping behind her, his hands found her hips, and he laid his head on her shoulder. "What are you making?"

She reached up and caressed his cheek as she leaned in a little. Then, with a contented sigh, she gestured to the bag of orange peels around his neck. "May I?" Once he gave his permission, she carefully removed the bag. "Tea. The lavender has a calming effect, the honey sweetens it, and the orange peels..." She added them to the water last. "Will give it a slight citrus flavor."

He nuzzled her neck a little. "That sounds lovely. I have not had tea before."

"It's one of my favorite things to drink. You can use dried orange peels, but fresh peels are better." She flashed him a warm smile, placed a cover on the pot, and carried it over to the fireplace. Mindful of the flames, she hung the pot on the hook. "I'll take it off once the water comes to a boil and let it steep."

"I ate the oranges right before I came here, so I hope they are fresh enough."

She strode back over to him and wrapped her arms around his waist. "Yes. Even if you'd eaten them earlier, they'd still be fresh enough."

Beaming, Gavin embraced her. "Good. I am glad. I rather enjoyed them." Though not nearly as much as he enjoyed her. Nothing could compare to her.

"I'm happy to hear that." Taking his hand in her own, Parthenia tugged him toward the table where a piece of parchment lay with a map drawn on it. She'd sketched trees, a path, and the treehouse on it. "I enjoy sharing new things with you."

He ran his fingers gently over her drawing of the treehouse. His body warmed as the memories of what they'd shared there came fresh to his mind. "I like it too. I love every new thing I get to experience with you."

"We have so many more to look forward to." Her gaze flicked to the map on the table. It contained little besides some parts of the marketplace: a clothing shop, a fish vendor, apothecary, inn, and a few other miscellaneous shops. She had included the uncontrolled part of the forest around the market, but nothing further. A couple of unique pieces of parchment lay beneath a complete sketch of the treehouse.

His fingertips grazed over the blank spaces of the parchment. "I would like to explore these places with you. Help you fill in your map. I want to see much more of this place than I have."

Her face lit up. "I'd like that. The books here only teach so much. I can't imagine exploring these places without you."

Turning, he drew her against him. "It is funny. Before I met you, I had little urge to explore. Now, I want to discover the world with you beside me. I want to see everything with you that this place offers."

She cupped his jaw. "Before you, I thought my books, my potions, and my dreams would be the culmination of my life, of my existence. I didn't think I could ever explore much of anything. But, for the first time, I can see all the possibilities." The boiling water caught her attention. "I need to get the pot."

"I am glad I can make you see those possibilities." He bent down and kissed her cheek. "Get the pot, then I can hold you again. Is there anything you would like me to do?"

She bit her bottom lip. Turning toward the pot, she grabbed the hand-sized linen by the fireplace. "There's a stack of cloths in that first drawer. Can you pull a couple out and set them on the counter?"

"Of course." His tail caressed her wing before he moved to the drawer. Opening it, he took a few out.

Parthenia wrapped the linen around the handle of the pot and then transferred it to the cloth he set out. "That just needs to steep for thirty minutes to an hour, then I'll strain it, and we can have our tea."

"What should we do until then?"

"I can work on that ward I told you about. Or…" Her eyelids hooded.

A low rumble left him as he gently tugged her body against his. "Or?"

"We could make use of the bedding I have over there." She brushed a soft kiss to the bottom of his chin and jawline. "It's stuffed with feathers."

He tightened his hold on her. "That sounds like an excellent plan." Scooping her into his arms, he carried her to the far side of the room and laid her down.

The bedding was quite comfortable. Gavin hovered over her, just taking her in. It didn't matter how many times, or how long, he looked at her. He could never get enough. Arching up, Parthenia kissed him on either side of his mouth. One day, they'd be able to kiss on the lips. It would be more wonderful than anything they could imagine.

Gavin swept her hair over her shoulder, then licked up her neck. "I cannot wait for the day that I can truly taste every part of you," he whispered in her ear.

"Me either. When we can both taste each other." Parthenia moaned as he grazed his fangs down her neck and over her shoulder. She slid one leg out from beneath him and rubbed his hips with it. Slowly, she raked her nails along the backside of his arms.

He growled and stroked the side of her neck with his tongue as his tail caressed her thigh. "I love the feel of your nails on me."

"Oh, goddess. I love your growl. It's like a song. I can't get enough of it." Her back arched, pressing her breasts against his chest.

"I cannot get enough of your voice, either. I love it when you sing. And your skin…"

Her skin heated beneath the ministrations of his tongue. She groaned and dragged her nails across his shoulders. Gripping his rear with her leg, one of her talons grazed the back of his thigh. He ran his tail along her inner thigh as he gently licked around one breast, then the other.

Parthenia smoothed her hand down the back of his ears. She traced his taut back muscles as far as her fingers would go. Her dress bunched up between them as she lifted her other leg from beneath him and gently dragged a talon along the back of his thigh.

He hissed. Kneeling between her legs, he retraced the same pattern down her neck to her collarbone. Spreading her legs apart, his sex throbbed as he crawled down her body and grazed his fangs along her inner thighs. Every one of her moans, sighs, and touches had him panting for more. He longed to close his mouth around her sex and taste her sweet honey straight from the source.

She dug her nails into his shoulder blades and arched her back as her thigh muscles tensed. "Oh, Gavin."

"I love your nails in me. And I love when you moan my name." He licked up her inner thigh as he skimmed her legs and hips with his fingertips and scraped his fangs back down again.

"I love how you feel. Oh, goddess, don't stop." She cried out in pleasure and scored his back with her nails. Her talons curled as an orgasm pulsated through her body, gushing down her thighs.

His growl amplified. Something he just couldn't help. His eyes glowed as he ran his tongue up Parthenia's inner thighs, catching every drop that he could. He wanted to roar at the taste of her. He yearned to bury his face in her sex, drive his tongue in deep, and taste her until she released again and again. It was a struggle not to do just what he wished, but he had no desire to be parted from her now.

As his tongue stroked her skin, her orgasm intensified, and her thighs trembled as another release slammed through her body. Gavin let out a roar so loud the windows rattled behind their panes as more of her honey gushed down her thighs.

"Oh, yes," he grunted. Parting her legs further, he licked up her thighs once, and stopped just before he reached her sex. Her back bowed more. He moaned with want as he held himself back. Her talons scraped his shoulder blades as her nails dug harder into his shoulders. "Gavin!"

"Parthenia," he whispered against her skin. His entire body was trembling. Moving from one leg to the next, he didn't bother to pull his tongue back into his mouth; he wanted it back against her skin as soon as possible. The tip of his tongue brushed against her sex. He froze, expecting the electricity or, at the very least, to be thrown back again. But nothing happened. Whatever this was, whatever was preventing the previous reaction, well, he intended to take full advantage of it.

He gazed up at her. The shape of her breasts coupled with her glistening sex, her moans, his name leaving her lips. All of it had his sex aching. Extending his tongue, he ran it over her sex, and he exhaled a moan of pleasure.

She groaned, and he let out a rumble of pleasure. Sliding his hands to rest against her stomach and using his shoulders to part her thighs, he didn't hold back. Who knew if this would last? If it was a fluke? He would not waste it, that was for sure. His tongue slid deep inside her sex. A loud growl vibrated through her as her taste exploded on his tongue. Oh, she was heavenly. If he couldn't have her any other way just yet, he'd undoubtedly have her like this for as long as he could.

Parthenia balled the bedding into her hands. She ground herself against his tongue. Another cry of pleasure left her as another orgasm pulsated through her body.

He moved his tongue all over inside her, in and out, his growl continuous as she rode it. When her orgasm passed, he looked up at her. He licked his lips as her eyes caught his. "I would wear your scratches like a badge of honor," he said, then drove his tongue back inside her. Oh, gods, he couldn't get enough of her taste. It consumed him, making his brain fuzzy with the need to do nothing but drink down the honey she gave only to him.

"Oh, goddess…" Her hands grabbed hold of him, her nails digging deep into his biceps. He couldn't hold back the moan he let loose against her. Her body vibrated with each orgasm he milked from her.

Gavin didn't know how long he stayed there between her legs. When his head finally lifted, she lay there, limp on the bedding. Their chests heaved as they panted in unison. The remnants of her orgasms covered his lips and his chin, and he licked them away. "I do not think I want to leave from down here."

"I don't think I can move."

"You do not need to." He laid on the bedding beside her. "I wish we had known before that we could do that. The whole thing is bizarre. Some things seem to be allowed, while others are not." He propped himself up on one elbow, his free hand caressing her hip and belly.

She grinned as her breathing settled to some normalcy. "It is unusual. I wish I understood it more, but I believe we'll find answers. Perhaps the siren's journal will have some."

"There is a journal? Now, that is intriguing."

"Yes. I came across it a couple of *solaris* ago. It's been interesting." Her gaze flicked to his as she rolled onto her side.

He growled at the look in her eyes and rolled over onto his back. "Please, experiment," he said, still smirking at her. Just the thought of the possibility that her mouth and tongue could be against his sex made it twitch.

Her feathers ruffled ever so slightly. "Demeter, you do not know how much I love that sound." She slowly climbed on top of him and nipped at his ear. "Or what it does to me." She trailed kisses along his jawline and sucked on his neck.

His head fell back, and he groaned. "You do not know what everything you do does to me." He ran his hands down her side until they fell on her hips, gripping them lightly.

"Oh?" Brushing her lips across his pecs, she licked at his nipples and followed a path down his abs. Her talons grazed along the length of his legs as she shimmied down his body.

"Yes," he replied in a slow, steady hiss. "Everything you do drives me to distraction. But in such a good way."

"Mmm, I like the sound of that." She pressed a kiss to the soft skin at the apex of his thighs. Extending her tongue, she stroked the base of his sex and raked her nails over his thighs. No shock. Dragging her nails over his rear, she sucked one of his balls into her mouth and licked up the length of his sex with a moan.

His hips bucked, and his sex jerked, her name leaving his lips on a groan. His hands fisted around the bedding.

She gripped his behind and licked around the tip of his sex before she took him in her mouth. She gently scraped her teeth over his length, popping him out between her lips, and wrapped her mouth around him again. One hand holding tight to the roundness of his butt, she continued the repetition and caressed his tail with her free hand.

"Oh, gods," he cried out. He repeatedly growled as her lips and tongue caressed his sex, her mouth sucking on him as her hand moved up and down his tail. "You are going to make me—" A moan cut his words off.

Her nails dug into the base of his rear, where it connected with his tail. She popped his sex out of her mouth, her teeth grazing his length as she sucked both balls. After giving them plenty of attention, she licked up his sex again and wrapped her mouth back around him, taking his sex to the back of her throat. She moaned, the vibration traveling through his sex.

"Parthenia..." He could no longer tell where his groans ended and his growls began. His hips rose and fell, pushing his sex in and out of her mouth as she sucked on him. He dug his claws into his palms, not wanting to rip her bedding, as his sex hit the back of her throat. His balls tensed up, his hips punched up again, and he let out a roar as his orgasm exploded from him.

Beautiful noises left her as she swallowed everything he gave, refusing to even let one drop slip from her mouth. She kept at it until she milked him dry. Once he was completely limp, Parthenia released his sex from her mouth and licked her lips. Slowly, she crawled back up his body, pressed a tender kiss on the side of his mouth, and curled up against him.

He lay there, unmoving, not speaking, until his breathing eased. He drew Parthenia into his arms and laid his head on hers. "That was incredible." He kissed the top of her head, then her temple, then her forehead. Lifting her chin so her eyes met his, he stared deep into them, knowing that if they ever parted, or if anything ever happened to her, he would genuinely perish. All that they meant to one another was in their eyes. What they'd shared in the last hours meant more than words could express. "You are incredible. Parthenia, I love you. I truly do."

"I love you too, Gavin. More than anything."

His heart swelled at her words. He could see the truth of them shining brightly out of her eyes. Eyes that could see straight through to his soul, see the true him as no others could. "I wish we could leave this place. Go somewhere, just you and me. I want to have a long life, and I want to spend it with you by my side."

She blinked. "Leave Prisma Isle?"

"I would go anywhere with you, Parthenia, if it meant we would never be parted. Here I fear we will be. It is only a matter of time. Markham is smart, conniving, and evil. He will discover us, and he will rip us apart. Our souls are joined for life; he cannot touch those. But he is a destroyer."

"I would go to the edges of the world to keep that from happening, but I fear leaving Prisma Isle won't be an easy feat." She kissed him on the cheek. "I need to show you something." Parthenia climbed from atop him and waltzed across the room. She flew up, plucked a book from the topmost shelf, and returned to the floor. Walking back to the table, she pushed aside the map and other pieces of parchment and opened the book.

Gavin joined her at the table, but the other pieces of parchment she pushed away caught his attention. He picked them up, a smile crossing his face. They were drawings of him. "You did these? I-I have drawn you too. I planned to show you the next time we went to the treehouse. That is where I have them hidden." He beamed at her. "These are wonderful."

Her gaze flicked from him to her charcoal sketches and back to his face. A small smile tugged at the corners of her lips. "Thank you. I had a compelling subject." She stepped in close to him. "I can't believe you've drawn me, too. I just, I've met no one who sketches or even enjoys it."

"Nor I. My sister is artistic, but not in the same way. Have you ever seen a feline dance?"

"No, but I bet it's exquisite to watch."

His gaze drifted from the drawings to her. "This is how you see me?"

She rested a hand on his arm. "It is."

He carefully laid the pieces of parchment back down and drew her into his arms. For a few moments, he held her, needing to have her against him. When he pulled back, he kissed her forehead, then either side of her mouth. "What is it you were going to show me?"

She pointed to the book she opened and set upon the table. "There's a barrier that surrounds Prisma Isle. I'm sure it can be broken, but I don't know how. I've seen it from our springs. It's like a thick fog separating us from whatever is on the other side."

He scanned the part about the barrier and shook his head. "I have never been that far from the village. I have not even been to the marketplace. Gabby has; she and her closest friend go all the time. They are constantly exploring, though Gabby does not go out as often as she does. I am not sure how much of the isle they have seen. I have always stuck closer to home, though I cannot say why."

"Possibly the same reason I never strayed too close to the marketplace."

"It looks like we have two mysteries to solve, then."

With a heavy sigh, she closed her eyes and leaned into him. "I don't even know if our books will have more information on the barrier. This is all I've ever found in nearly seven *solaris*."

He lifted her chin, so her gaze focused on him. "We will keep looking until we find the answers we need. I will never stop fighting to be with you, my beloved." He kissed her forehead, then laid his head atop of hers.

"You're an amazing male, Gavin, my love. I'm quite grateful you approached me." A small chuckle escaped her.

"I am so glad about that as well." He smiled. "I feel like I had been searching for you for many *solaris*. And when I saw you... it was like I finally found myself, everything that had been missing." Whatever happened, they were in each other's souls. That was something no one could ever take from them.

She stood there a moment with her ear pressed against his chest. "I'm thinking you're reading my mind. I swear I was just thinking the same thing." She paused. "How would you feel about some tea, now? It'll be cold but flavorful. And then afterward, I can show you the springs before you have to go."

He glanced at the pot of tea and laughed. "I completely forgot about the tea. That sounds wonderful, though. And I would love to see the springs." He turned his gaze back to her. "Sometimes, it is as though I can read your mind. Not your thoughts, but it is like I can feel what you do."

Parthenia kissed his chest, right over his heart, then turned toward the counter where the pot sat. She dug around one cabinet and brought out a sieve. She peered at him for a moment, then returned to straining the lavender seeds and orange peels from the tea. "I wonder if it goes both ways. I mean, feeling what the other is feeling." Once she had everything separated, she poured the tea into two cups and handed one to him, taking the other for herself.

He took the cup from her, careful not to spill it. "It is possible. Have you felt things that did not align with what you were feeling at the time?"

She sipped the tea and let it sit on her tongue before she answered him. "Yes. I don't genuinely feel much when I'm preparing a meal. I simply focus on the task."

Gavin said nothing in return for a moment. "What did you feel?" he asked quietly.

"An ache in my chest as if I was alone. Even the thought of you felt like a dream. One I was eager for."

He slowly took a sip of his tea. "This is very good," he whispered, smiling a little at Parthenia. He took another sip. "Thinking of you, of coming back to you, was the only thing that got me through until I left to come back here. I felt very alone. Alone and afraid. Markham frightens me much more than I care to admit. When I left the village, I ran. I ran to the treehouse. I ate the oranges you gave me, and that helped calm me."

"That's good. I'm glad they helped, but I hate he makes you feel that way. I wish you could just stay here or in your treehouse." She glanced around at all the herbs, spices, and other items scattered across the shelves. "I don't think I have time before you must go, but during the day, before we see one another again,"—Parthenia returned her attention to Gavin—"I can make a protection ward."

He smiled and drew her against his side, kissing both of her cheeks. "You are wonderful. I would love that. I would keep it on me as much as possible. Thank you." He sighed a little. "I wish it were only Markham that I had to fear. Some of his Informants can be quite brutal when they are *carrying out their duties*, as they call it."

She leaned into him. A touch of fear went through her. "What duties would be brutal?"

"When he punishes the males in my village for an offense, they are forced to fight Informants that outweigh them in strength and skill. Often over, one at a time. As for the females, they have different punishments, and they usually are not so public. Most of the females are very submissive. Honestly, the males are as well. It is rarely anyone in my village steps out of line. I suppose my sister and I are exceptions to the rule." He smiled some, but it didn't reach his eyes.

She sipped at her tea. Silence stretched between them. "I wish I could give you some of my power."

"What powers do you have, my beloved?"

Her eyes lit up. "You know how I whistled to call that deer to me? Well, with my voice, I can convince anyone that they never saw me, that I was a mere figment of their imagination. Some of us can even use our voices to control the wind. I can call a small breeze, but nothing more, yet."

His eyes widened. "That sounds amazing, and like it could come in handy. Your voice sounds like a melody to me and is very calming."

"It can. It certainly makes it easier to get information or get someone to do one's bidding."

"Oh, I can imagine." He drank the rest of his tea and set his cup down on the table. "You would never have to use your powers on me, though. Just by gazing at me, you put a spell on me." He bent down and nuzzled her neck. "And I love every moment."

Setting her cup aside, Parthenia wrapped her arms around him. "I would never use them on you, but I would sing for you any time you wished."

"Any time you wish to, my love. I would never say no to hearing you sing." Oh, gods, he didn't want to leave her. He never wanted to leave her side, never wanted to be parted from her. But he would have to go soon, and it was already breaking him.

"Come. Let's go to the springs."

Gavin took her hand in his. "Lead the way." She could lead him anywhere, and he would follow without hesitation.

She picked up her cup, finished the tea, and set it aside on their way out the door. Pausing in the doorway, she ensured no one was around before they left and rounded the corner past the small garden by her apothecary. She led him toward the group of white houses but veered before they got too close, continuing beyond them and leaving them in the background. Up ahead, there was a collection of large trees with long white willow leaves hanging.

Gavin ran his hand over the leaves as they walked beneath the trees. He didn't have to duck under them, but they were close to his head. He'd never seen a tree so beautiful before. Parthenia's features brightened, and she brushed a kiss across his knuckles before bowing low. Then, rising to her full height, she opened her mouth and softly bellowed the first lines of a love song.

He turned toward her and froze. Immediately, all the nerves and fear about going back to the village and parted from her left him. Instead, her voice filled him with a calming peace that he had never truly felt anywhere else.

She continued the aria, executing each note flawlessly. Her focus was on the words as she expressed their emotions. How her heart beat only for him. That they had a love made for the stars, destined to collide. With each word she sang, her whole body moved. She gently sang, reached for him, and physically grasped his hand within her own.

Gavin clasped both of her hands tightly. Her song radiated through him, from the tips of his ears to the end of his tail. A tear pricked his eye as the love she felt for him swelled within him. Not knowing if she could handle it from him or not, he sent all of his love back to her.

A smile lit up her face. Parthenia moved into the next verse and vocalized how others might see their relationship as strange, but it wouldn't stop them from always wanting more. Continuing the melody, she reiterated, reaching out for him. She intertwined their fingers and led him farther through the trees. She lifted her voice to him, all the while describing that he called out her name, and their stars came together. As she bellowed more of the song, she extended their arms and spun into him.

He slid his palms down her body until they were around her waist. Lifting her, he spun them around, then lowered her back to the ground. His fingers intertwined with hers again, and he turned in a circle before pulling her against him. His eyes never left hers. Nothing in the world existed outside of the two of them in this place and at this moment.

She echoed the last of the chorus as she stared into his eyes. The moment between them was absolute perfection. Their love would light up the world. As the song's last word left her mouth, they arrived at the springs. Gentle bursts of steam rose at her back, the warmth of the light green waters surrounding them. Reaching up, Parthenia caressed his cheek.

He cupped her face, brushing her cheeks with his thumbs. "Parthenia, my beloved," he whispered. "My love for you reaches higher than the tallest mountain and goes further than the deepest part of the ocean. I will love you and be loyal to you, long past when the seas dry up and the rocks decay. Until the end of my days, my heart and soul will belong only to you. This vow I make to you." His eyes glowed as he spoke the words. There was no more tremendous oath he could utter, every word the truth to this female who'd stolen his heart and captivated his soul. She was indeed his other half, everything he'd ever been missing and everything he would ever need. She was his true mate, his forever destiny.

Parthenia's eyes glowed as she spoke, "My love for you knows no end. Its only equal is the endless sky. I will love you and always be loyal to you from this life until the next. All of my days, heart and soul, belong only to you. This promise I make to you."

He bent down and kissed her forehead, then on both sides of her mouth and neck. Nothing more needed to be said. Lacing his fingers with hers again, he led her toward the spring. It didn't matter what happened now. They mated each other in their hearts from this moment forward.

Nothing and no one could take that away from them.

Chapter Ten

Gavin took his time getting back to the village, though it was likely a mistake. He'd already been gone much longer than he should've. He didn't care, though. The time he spent with Parthenia was priceless and precious. He would do it again, over and over, no matter the consequences.

He wasn't naïve about the fact that his relationship with her would most likely result in his death. They only met days ago, though it seemed as if they'd known each other for a lifetime. It wouldn't be long before those who would disapprove did everything in their power to destroy them.

He neared the edge of the village, and the wind shifted. He stopped in his tracks, catching the scent of one...two... three shape shifters. And Markham. He wasn't wearing his camouflage. He hadn't thought to throw it on as he left Parthenia's home, nor had he thrown it on during his trek back. It made no difference now. They knew he left, and they knew he returned.

They were waiting for him.

He took a deep breath and moved again. Each step after another forced until he broke through the trees. They stood in a semicircle, Markham behind him—his massive black bear form stood taller than Gavin on all fours by a foot-and-a-half. His dark gray eyes glinted. The crescent moon shape on his chest stood out brightly, though the moonlight hid behind the clouds. The crown atop his head gave off glints and flashes of red.

Gavin bowed his head, looking up at Markham from his lowered gaze. As he stood there, staring at his *King*, something rustled behind him and he whipped his head around. Three more than he originally sensed joined them. There might have been more, but only three entered his line of sight.

"Your arrival is late, Gavin."

Markham's voice, as always, sent shivers through his body. Each word seemed to slink through him, slithering across each of his nerve endings. It brought fear to him swifter than anything else could, leaving his senses on edge. Slowly, he turned his head back and fixed his eyes on Markham. It would offend the bear if he didn't.

"I lost track of time, is all, Your Majesty," he practically whispered. Although he tried, he couldn't keep the trembling out of his voice.

"I do not tolerate excuses. I never have, and that will not change." Markham let his words hang in the air for a moment. "Where have you been."

It was a statement, not a question. This was just Markham's way of humoring him, giving him a chance to confess to whatever he'd done. Markham ultimately didn't care. When one broke the rules, he dealt out punishment. It would come, and it would be harsh. Either there would be severe pain and injury or death. There was no gray area. You could be completely innocent, and it wouldn't matter.

Gavin kept his head bowed and his tail lowered, a sign of submission; he inhaled a deep breath and exhaled slowly to calm himself. He couldn't appear any more nervous than he already did. And he must keep his mind shielded.

Markham tilted his head to the side, a slight smirk upon his lips. "Well?"

"I was merely exploring, Your Majesty. Despite my age, I have seen little of the isle. I have taken to wandering during the daylight hours when I do not have duties here at home."

"Ah. And yet, it is well past midnight, Gavin. You left after curfew." He chuckled low. "Whatever did you see on your *wanderings*? What did you see that called your attention to where you disregarded a command from your King? A command put into place for your protection, I might add." His tone was condescending, a hint of laughter in it. He stepped toward Gavin, the Informants moving to the side to give him room. "You are lying to me."

The nearer Markham got, the more Gavin cowered closer to the ground. He visibly shook by the time Markham stopped, the male's snout in his face. Gavin tried to hold it back, but the whine escaped his throat all the same.

Markham's voice lowered as he spoke again. "There are creatures that lurk around the isle in the dead of night. Creatures that would rip your throat out and drink the blood that runs through your veins without a second thought." It went without saying, but Gavin knew Markham was one of those creatures spoken of and possibly the most dangerous. "I care not why you defied me. Ultimately, it matters not. As long as your heart beats in your chest, your blood runs through your veins, and you call my village your home, you *will* obey me." Markham paused. "You fight tomorrow when the sun is highest in the sky. You will remain in The Pit until it is time. If you are lucky, a female may take pity on you and bring you morning meal."

He let out a low chuckle, then lunged. Gavin yelped as jaws closed around the nape of his neck. Not enough to puncture the skin, but a pain shot through him all the same. Markham lifted him from the ground, carrying him across the village like a disobedient nestling. The Informants flanked them, hissing and barking, growling and snapping. When they reached The Pit, two of the Informants removed the heavy iron grate off the top of it before Markham tossed him in. Gavin landed on his side with a yowl and the wind knocked out of him.

Almost thirty feet deep and less than five feet in diameter, it indeed was a pit. Even if they hadn't replaced the metal grate over the top of the hole or the Informants didn't stand guard, he couldn't escape without help.

"Until tomorrow, Gavin. We are all very much looking forward to it."

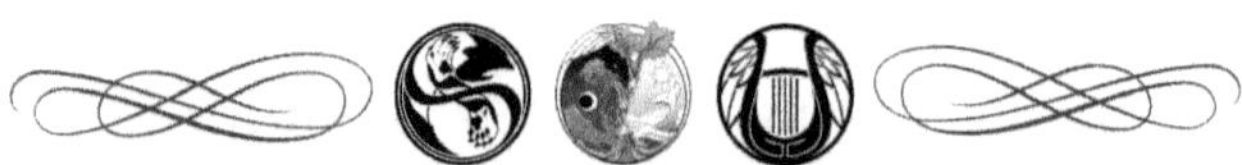

Gabby snuck him food for morning meal, but she couldn't stay. The Informants snapped and growled at her, refusing to let her get close. She tossed the food through the grate, narrowly getting it through their outstretched claws. Their behavior enraged Gavin. He jumped as high as he could, trying to get his claws to catch into the walls, roaring at them as they goaded her until she left. His actions did nothing, only caused them to laugh at his attempts.

The intense sun parched him, and his body cramped from lack of water. When a rope finally lowered into The Pit to help him up, it took him a couple of tries to grab it with his teeth. They moved it every time he almost had his jaws around it, which didn't help.

As soon as he got out and, on the ground, jaws snapped at his ankles. Calls and jeers of Informants followed him as someone forced him to the larger ring set up for fighting. It was a good fifty feet in diameter, plenty of room for conflict, and ringed with a fence many repaired more times than he could count throughout his lifetime. Mostly Informants, but other pack members enwrapped the cage as somebody pushed him into it. A paw reached out and tripped him, sending him sprawling into the middle just as Gabby shoved her way to the front of the crowd. She had a few choice words and a growl for those who tried to keep her back.

"Gavin! Gavin! It is going to be alright!"

He only nodded, not trusting his voice at the moment, as three Informants entered the fence before it was closed off—cousins Arman and Chaz, two of the bulkiest felines in the pack, and Pierce, one of the few full-grown wolves with all black fur. During these fights, they couldn't shift to their humanoid forms, so they all stood two- to two-and-a-half feet taller than he did and were all several hundred pounds heavier.

He wanted nothing more right now than to cower down and back away from them. He couldn't do that, though. Any appearance of weakness would be detrimental. They were going to take him down. There was no question about that, but he didn't have to make it easy on them.

They tried to circle him, to get him in the middle, to attack him as one, but he was quick. Dodging to avoid their assaults, he kept all three in front of him for quite a while. They snapped at his ankles and tail, slashed at him with their claws, and Arman almost slammed him in the head once or twice. He was tiring, though, especially after spending the night in The Pit and having no food or water in his system.

All at once, pain shot up his tail. He yelped as someone jerked him back, slamming his body into the fence. A crack rang out. Ripping his body away from whoever held him, he spun around and ended up taking a paw to the side. Scratch marks streaked down his flank. He rolled to his back and kicked out, catching one of them in the chest, only to be bitten on the ear. When they released him, though, it seemed his ear remained intact.

So, they didn't intend to take chunks from him, only to poke holes, cause pain, draw blood.

Pierce took a step back, allowing Arman and Chaz to lead. He circled the fence, watching as if he were waiting for an opening. With only Chaz and Arman to deal with now, Gavin fared better than he would've otherwise, but still not very well. His ability to duck and avoid shots lessened as his strength faltered. For every blow, scratch, or bite he doled out, he got three in return.

He didn't know how long the fight dragged on, but he saw Markham behind it all. He stood on his hind legs, watching it unfold, his expression darkening the longer Gavin held out. With his gaze on Markham, he saw the King's eyes flashed red for a moment. A force of nature crashed into Gavin's side. He howled in pain as teeth sank in. His first instinct was to spin away from what held him, but he couldn't afford to lose a sizeable chunk out of his side. He likely wouldn't survive if that happened. Rolling into the jaws that held him, his back rammed into the fence. The teeth released, and he got up, only to have the teeth sink in again—ferociously this time—before they let go.

"Stay down, you fool," Pierce hissed. "Stay down, and this ends."

Gavin didn't think he had the strength to move anymore anyway, so staying down seemed like an excellent option. His chest heaved with the effort it took to take each breath. Finally, he nodded almost imperceptibly and let his head fall to the dirt.

The noise of the surrounding crowd went on for a couple of minutes before a hush fell over them. Heavy footsteps sounded. The ground trembled. Gavin opened one eye, only to look up into Markham's dark gaze. Without meaning to, he whined. Which turned into a yelp as Markham put a heavy paw upon his side, right over the bite mark Pierce had left.

"I thought a decent lesson was in order. Just in case you had any notions about breaking any more rules or laws. Hopefully, this has been a lesson well learned."

He lifted his paw to Gavin's face, claws outstretched, and left scratch marks down his cheek. As blood ran into his eyes, the void that threatened to overtake him won, and he slipped into darkness.

"Father! You cannot do this! You cannot bar him entry! He is your son!"

"As usual, he lost the fight. He is a disgrace, Gabriella. This day, he will not stain my doorstep. Take him elsewhere if you insist on caring for him."

"He was up against three! And they are massive, much larger than he!"

"Markham was punishing him. I do not know what for, and I do not care. It is not my concern, and it should not be yours either. You make it yours, so you shall deal with it, without my help and without that of your mother's. Go, Gabriella. Now," he snarled.

The door of their hut slammed in her face. Not that it should surprise her. Her father never cared about either of them. Looking around the village, everyone within sight avoided her gaze. A curse roared through her head. How could they continue to live like this? Gavin could very well die without aid, and she wouldn't leave him to lie in the dirt. As someone nudged her, she spun around in defense, only to rear back before she struck out with her paw. "Devin... oh, I am so sorry."

"Do not apologize. We are going to take Gavin to our hut. Mother is preparing a meal, Father is elsewhere, and Derrick is scouting. It is empty. Come." Moving her body underneath one of Gavin's front limbs, Devin waited until she did the same on the other side. It took some time, but they finally got him inside. Devin shut the door behind them while Gabby moved him to the pallet in the front room's corner. Transforming to her humanoid form, she gathered a pot of water and some cloths around the room. "I do not have any medicament here at the moment. I have to get more for myself and Aradia at the marketplace, but you can at least clean him up some. There are extra linens to hold over that bite on his side. And I have a needle and thread to stitch him up, so he heals properly. I would stay and aid you further, but I have to go."

"No. You have done enough. Thank you. Where are you going?"

Devin shook her head. "You always ask that, and you know I will not tell you. I cannot. If you know, it makes you culpable. And I think you have enough secrets to hide." She gave Gabby a pointed look. "There will be no one else here for a couple of hours, three at most. So do what you can to wake him and get him out of here until he heals."

Gabby nodded. She knew the drill. This wasn't anything unfamiliar to her or Gavin. "Thank you. Again. Be safe wherever you are going."

"I shall." Devin came to Gabby and pressed her forehead against hers. Turning around, she slipped out the door, shutting it firmly behind her.

Gabby cleaned her twin as best she could, but he was still bloody and bruised with one swollen eye shut. It took over two hours to get him to come around, which was enough to worry her close to sickness. Finally, though, he stirred.

"Treehouse... Have to get to treehouse, treehouse now. Have to go. Have to get there now."

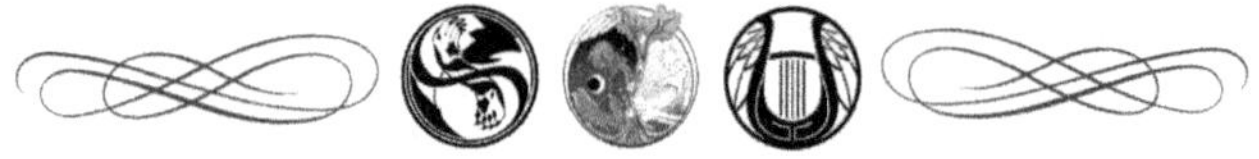

It took longer than Parthenia expected, putting the two protection pouches together. Once she blessed them both, she tucked them into her knapsack and raced to the hidden staircase. She didn't waste time changing out of her dress. All she could think about was getting to the treehouse and Gavin. She flew through the treetops as if her life depended on it. The vice grip around her heart eased the closer she got. She released a breath as her feet hit the landing of the treehouse. It was empty, so she wandered in farther. He wasn't here yet. Where was he?

Parthenia waited. Nothing would keep her from seeing Gavin. Even as the sun began its descent into the sky, she didn't care. It wasn't like her mother would miss her, anyway. She busied herself around the treehouse and hung one pouch she brought along. When she finished with that, she read through one book she always carried in her knapsack. Some items remained in there since her first trip down to the isle. She never knew when they'd be necessary.

The longer his arrival took, the more fear gnawed at her belly. She repeatedly told herself he was strong and she wouldn't lose him so soon. But it did little for the grip around her heart, one that told her something had happened.

The smell of blood had her on alert. She didn't have to see to know it came from her mate. Darting toward the entrance, she skidded to a stop before she ran over whomever approached.

A white form leaped over her, claws scraping wood as the shape shifter glided to a halt in the middle of the room. The female faced Parthenia and froze. "He said your name was… Parthenia? I am Gabby."

His sister! She didn't waste time with formalities, something to address later. Parthenia grabbed her knapsack and tugged it over her shoulders. If he hadn't come himself, she would need her potions and herbs for aid. "Where is he? How bad is it?"

"At the base of the tree. It is serious. I do not know how Gavin made it this far, but he insisted. Nothing I said would deter him."

Parthenia didn't wait for Gabby. Instead, she dove out of the room and flew to the bottom of the tree faster than she thought possible. She came to a dead halt an inch from the ground and immediately went to his side. "Oh, goddess." She shrugged off her knapsack. Her gaze flicked to Gabby as she leaped the last few feet down to the ground and shifted to her humanoid form. "I have healing potions."

"Those will be helpful, thank you. I have things to help with pain and to help him avoid infection. His arm is most likely broken, and he thinks his ribs as well."

Gavin looked up at Parthenia and raised his good hand to her face. "I did not want you to see me like this, but I could not stay away. I am sorry I was so late."

"Stop it, Gavin," Gabby said. "She does not seem the type to be angry about that. Especially considering your condition."

Parthenia took his hand in her own. Her heart ached for what he had endured. "I don't care about that. Save your strength, my love, while your sister and I work on your wounds." His condition worried her greatly; broken ribs could cause a punctured lung. They had to work quickly to set his arm. She dug into her knapsack for the vials she kept with her. He required both. Grasping the cork between her teeth, she yanked it free and brought it to Gavin's mouth. "Drink this. It will help."

Gabby helped him tilt his head back so he could drink. "Be of care," she said to Parthenia. "Besides his scratches, they bit him at least once. There were three of them." She barely contained the anger in her voice.

"Three of them?" Parthenia glowered. Fury flooded her. It took every ounce of power she had to keep the shaking out of her wings. One look at Gavin reminded her this wasn't the time or place.

When Gavin finished drinking the vials, Gabby pulled things out of the bag she brought down with her. "What was in those?"

Settling down, Parthenia exhaled a deep breath. "Herbs mixed with water from The Reflection Pool… magical pools with healing properties. If we need to set his arm, then we need to hurry."

"I do not think the bone is fully broken. Perhaps just fractured. He moved it, but it caused him great pain." Gabby finished getting the herbs ready and mixed them with a jar of water, helping him to drink them as well. "While he may get sleepy, he will remain conscious. He should tolerate all we need to do to dress his wounds now. How long will it take for what was in those vials to work?"

"Not long. The pools have regenerative properties when fully functioning. Even in their current state, they will begin healing within minutes." She feared an improperly healed bone would be harmful. Regardless, she had no intention of leaving him. "The full timeframe will depend on the gravity of his wounds. Including that which we cannot see."

"Will it close his open wounds, or will we need to do that? I stitched a couple of them, but our resources are limited." Gabby carefully checked the bite on his side.

"It'll close his open wounds." Goddess, she didn't know what brought this on, but the more wounds she saw, the deeper her hatred for those who caused them burned. Parthenia pressed a tender kiss to his forehead and stroked his cheek. Those who harmed her mate should pray they never crossed her path. She'd use her song to bring them to their knees and beg for mercy.

"How much has he told you? About our village, our way of life?"

"He has told me many things. I believe when he spoke of this yesterday, he indicated it was a form of punishment instituted by your so-called king." She spoke derisively. One of her feathers shot out into a nearby tree. Parthenia blinked and glanced over her shoulder to find the feather protruding from the trunk.

Gabby's head jerked in the feather's direction. "Does that happen often? I would hate to be on the receiving end of that." Her gaze shifted back to Parthenia. "As for Markham, he is not a king. He is an abomination."

Parthenia swallowed to wet her parched throat. She couldn't allow this to happen again. Demeter, she prayed the pouches she prepared would help. Because she knew neither of them would handle not seeing one another well. She peered back at the feather lodged in the tree. "It's never happened before. I suspect I didn't contain my anger as well as I had hoped." She returned her attention to Gabby. "Abomination is too kind. He is a monster, one that should die."

"Oh, yes. Surely. Gavin thinks he is untouchable. But death is inevitable; anyone can be killed. The way just has to be found first."

"Yes. That's quite true. Death can take anyone." She readjusted her position and made herself comfortable. "My apologies for my earlier reaction, Gabby. Gavin has told me about you. I'd hoped we would one day meet, though under very different circumstances."

"No apology needed, I assure you. I admit I did not know of your existence until we arrived here, and Gavin told me you were waiting. That he has found a mate, though, pleases me greatly. He has spent a lifetime in sadness and loneliness. If you will forgive my rudeness, what are you?"

A soft smile crossed her face. The question didn't surprise her. Her species kept much to themselves. "I'm a siren. And forgiveness isn't necessary. As your laws forbid you from interacting with other species, ours do as well."

"I was never big on following the rules. But when they are filled with cruelty and ridiculousness, that is something I want no part of."

"I understand. I consider ours antiquated and harmful to the species. Yours, though." She paused. "Will you tell me about those that he forced Gavin to fight?" The female likely understood exactly how she felt about them. What she wanted to know was about the males that fought her mate.

"I watched the whole thing, though it pained me more than I can say because one day I will make sure they receive all that they gave." She reached out a hand, hovering over each fading mark as she named the one who had given it.

"Chaz. He is called a leopon, a leopard, and a lion mix. He stands seven feet tall on all fours, eleven in his humanoid form. His fur is orangish-brown and pale reddish-yellow, and he has brown spots to match a mane and tuft to his tail like a lion. His eyes are usually black, though they occasionally take on a touch of orange-like fire. Arman. A mix of a lion and tiger, he is called a liger. He is about six-and-a-half feet tall on all fours, about ten-and-a-half in his humanoid form, and he has brown stripes and facial markings, both golden and darker, and white fur. He has a dark brown mane. His eyes are yellow, like the gemstone citrine. They are two of the largest felines in the pack. The third, Pierce, is a wolf. His fur is all black, and his eyes are the color of rubies. He is the same height as Arman on all fours, but transformed, he only reaches nine feet."

Parthenia's feathers stood on end as she committed each description to memory. Her blood boiled as her eyes flipped from each closing wound to the next. "They should each pray for you to get to them first. I *won't* be merciful. Their size will mean nothing if I get my talons in them," she seethed.

A smile spread across Gabby's face. "That is something I would relish seeing. I want their pain to last ten times longer than the pain they caused him." She looked down at her brother. "More than that. I want them to suffer truly. Markham too, for ordering his pain and all the other pain he has ordered."

"Yes. Markham must suffer the most." She hadn't ever wished death, slow or swift, upon anyone before. Not even Fagonia, and she truly disliked the female. But Markham, he was different. She hadn't met the male, and she despised him with every fiber of her being. Shaking the feeling away, she clasped Gavin's hand within her own and refocused on Gabby. For the first time, she paid attention to the similarities between her and Gavin. Same green eyes. Same bone structure. Although there was a noticeable difference in their coloring. "I was told you have a mate."

"I do. Though it is difficult, they forced him into his position as one of Markham's Informants. He takes many punishments when he refuses to give them. And Informants especially may not mate in the village without Markham's permission. My mate is a canine, while I am a feline. So, even if he were not an Informant, we would have to remain in the village but shunned for our mating."

"I'm sorry to hear that. Gavin told me your relationship was complicated." It may not have been the exact terminology. She couldn't recall, but she knew the female had difficulties with her relationship. They hid much of their time together as she and Gavin did. "It should shame no one for whom they choose as their mate."

"No. They should not. I have told only one other, my closest friend and his sister. It isn't easy to hide our relationship. I love him so very much. I know, though, that you are one that I can trust."

"Yes, you can. I believe I can trust you as well." Parthenia beamed. "I love your brother very much. It is difficult any time we must part." Her gaze shifted to the knapsack on the ground. She dug inside it, removed a pouch of herbs, and held it out to Gabby. "I made a protection ward against evil. There is a second in the treehouse. I believe you should take this one. Gavin can take the other, and I'll make two more tomorrow. One for your mate and one for the treehouse."

Gabby accepted the pouch. "You are very kind. Thank you for this. How do they work exactly? I have never heard of such a thing."

"You should carry it on your person. According to my book, it creates a bubble that evil spirits or persons cannot cross. I've never made one until now." After her frustrations with the pouch, the second attempt improved. Then again, she got a different recipe than what she initially used.

"Is it detectable by evil, or does it just deter it?"

"It just deters it. I believe Demeter was guiding my hands earlier. I—" She paused. How did she explain? Gavin told her his sister had a green thumb. Maybe she would understand. "I used water from our spring to coat the pouch. Once it dried, I pulled fresh herbs and spices from my garden to create the ward itself. The water conceals the smell and intensifies the ward. I apologize. We do not use the bodies of water here on Prisma Isle. In Pteryrina, our sources are separate."

"Why do you apologize? The entire thing sounds fascinating. That it is undetectable reassures me, however. It would not be safe to wear if evil could detect it in the village. Markham radiates evil. Thank you for them, again." She smiled. "I would love to see this Pteryrina, but something tells me that would not be a possibility." She sighed. "What I would do just to leave this place altogether."

"I don't understand why it wouldn't be possible. Gavin has seen much of it already. We do not view it the same. Though, with what you've told me and what I've learned about him, I understand why." She turned to her mate and stroked his head. His wounds were healing nicely. If he didn't have the chance to tell Gabby about her, she suspected the female didn't know about their plan to leave either. "Your brother and I, we are seeking a way for that to be possible."

Gabby's eyes widened. "That would be wonderful. He is not built for the ways of the pack." She checked the wound on his side. It looked good. "Nor am I, if I am honest. If possible, I would love to go with the two of you when you find a way. I am sure Derrick would as well."

"I see no reason you shouldn't join us. It's something Gavin would like. I'm sure much of this he planned to tell you himself." Her eyes dropped to her mate again. It comforted her to see the physical changes in his injuries. "I don't know how long it will take to find a way past the barrier, but I won't stop until we find the answers."

"If there is anything I might do to help, please let me know. Derrick's sister, Devin, travels more around the isle than I do. She may have some ideas as well. I could ask her if you would like. Although, I am sure she would be open to meeting you. She often keeps to herself, though." Her attention drifted back to Gavin. "It is amazing how quickly he is healing. I was worried he would need to be nursed for days. We heal quickly, but the damage was still extensive."

"Yes. I would. Thank you. Our library is vast, but some days—" The sensation of Gavin's tail playing softly with her feathers brought a smile to her face. Praise Demeter. She gave his hand a slight squeeze. "I'm grateful I continued to carry them. Some say the pools are the only way to regenerate a wing. We can't survive without them."

"I would love to hear more about your kind sometime." Gabby grinned as Gavin's eyes opened. "Thank the gods. We were anxious about you."

"I did not mean to fall asleep. I feel much better, though."

Leaning over, Parthenia pressed her forehead to Gavin's. She didn't care that his sister was here. Not that it was anything inappropriate. Parthenia opened her mouth and closed it because she couldn't find the words to say. Not even to answer Gabby. Tears welled in the corners of her eyes. He was alive; he was well, and he had healed. The repeated thoughts did nothing to stave off the immense relief she felt. Or the gravity that the situation could've been much worse.

Gavin raised his hand and rested it against her cheek. "It is alright. I am okay." He brushed away her tears with his thumb.

She covered his hand with her own and shut her eyes. She allowed his voice, words, and touch to wash over her as she focused on the steady beat of his heart. It didn't completely stop the flow of tears, but they eased. And, somehow, she found her voice. "Goddess, I wouldn't survive without you. Can we please not do that again?" The question left her mouth of its own accord. After this, she planned to stock vials from her apothecary in the treehouse, just in case.

"It is most definitely not in my plans to do that again." He caressed both of her cheeks. "I could not survive without you either, my beloved. You are everything to me."

"I will leave you two. Markham will not expect you healed enough to be moved for a day or so. I think I should be able to make your excuses until tomorrow evening, at least. I will have Derrick vouch for you," Gabby commented.

"Thank the goddess," Parthenia replied. It warmed her heart to hear the words. To know he would do everything in his power not to put them in that position again. She eyed Gabby and reached a hand out to her. "Thank you. For everything."

Gabby clasped her hand tightly. "Thank *you*. I owe you a great debt. You saved my brother's life."

"It was not as dire as all that, Gabby," he interjected.

"We worked together, sister." Her potions hadn't been the only thing that helped. The female thought quickly on her feet. It made her proud to call the female sister. And, yes, when they found a way off this isle, they would take her with them.

Parthenia turned to her mate. It was unnecessary to contradict his statement. That was something better discussed in private. She didn't want to think about the what ifs. They were unnecessary. There was still much to be figured out, but they could save it for tomorrow. Right now, she just wanted to be with her mate, to feel his heartbeat with hers. Hear his heavy breaths. Feel his skin on hers. To be reminded, they were both alive and together.

"Thank you. I am proud to call you sister as well." Gabby hugged Gavin tightly and then Parthenia, and stood. "Until we meet again. Which I hope will be soon." Giving them both one more smile, she shifted, so she was on all fours and took off into the forest.

Gavin pushed himself to a sitting position and drew Parthenia into his lap. She immediately wrapped her arms around him and surrounded them together with her wings. "We should go up," he whispered.

"Yes, we should. I just need a minute." She encountered an array of emotions over the last hour. At the top of them were fear and anger on levels she had never experienced before. Her heart rate normalized, but the feelings in her soul hadn't yet fully settled.

"Take as long as you need, my love. Right here is just fine with me." He laid his head on top of hers and breathed in deep. "I am sorry I frightened you."

"It's not your fault. I know you're not to blame. Gabby told me what happened. I can't seem to get the rationale of Markham's actions to coincide with everything I'm feeling in my bones." Her body tensed as the description of the three culprits popped into her mind. Her wings shook, and three more feathers shot out, burying themselves in a tree behind them. Good Demeter, she had to stop that! She committed their descriptions and actions to memory for later. Now she just needed to hold her mate. Focusing on the sound of his heart, she attempted to sync their beats.

"Parthenia, darling, it is alright. Calm yourself, love," he said, rubbing her back to soothe her. "I am well, thanks to you and my sister. I am okay." He kissed her neck. "Why did that happen?"

Pulling back a touch, she lifted her gaze to his. "I want to kill them, Gavin. I want to hurt them. Cause them pain. I do not wish to be merciful. This..." She gestured to the feathers in the tree. "It seems to result from my fury."

Gavin ran a hand through her hair, then down her wing. His touch comforted and relaxed her. "I would feel the same if anyone ever even thought to harm you. I feel Markham brainwashed them, though. Some seem to enjoy it more than others, but I blame him. Not them."

Slowly, her wings unfurled and released their cocoon. "I wish for Markham to suffer the most."

He brushed his thumb from the corner of her eye down her cheek. "He will. One day. I have to have faith in that." He brought her face to his, pressing a kiss to her forehead and both sides of her mouth. "I love your spirit and how fierce you are. In anger, I can tell you are truly a force to be reckoned with." He kissed her neck, and then left his head there, breathing in deep. "I also love your scent. I cannot get enough of it. The memory of it soothes me when I cannot be with you."

The last of her rage ebbed from her body. Gavin's face in the crook of her neck reminded her he was alive. With a deep breath, she stroked the back of his head. "I love your scent, too. It helps me recall many things about you when we are apart. But I don't want to think about being separated right now. I can't think about it. So, I'm staying here for the night. With you."

Gavin beamed. "Yes. You are. And it is going to be wonderful." He nuzzled her neck and gave it a lick. She moaned as the sensation shot a blast of heat into her sex. "I am so very much looking forward to it, my beloved. Being separated is something I do not want to think about. I want to think about every moment we will spend together this night."

"As do I, my love." Parthenia smiled. "I believe I'm ready to retreat to the treehouse now."

"Then let us ascend." He licked down her collarbone, and then rose to his feet, still holding her in his arms. "Feel free to go first. Your rear is a beautiful sight to behold."

Chapter Eleven

Logan exhaled ragged breaths as Ambrosia rolled off him. How many times did they make love? He lost count. Having her on top was his favorite because it offered the best view. He wrapped an arm around her as she curled up close, pressed a soft kiss to her forehead, and then brushed one across her lips. Staring into those beautiful amber pools of hers, he caressed her cheek. Hades, he loved her so much, but he didn't know how even to utter the words.

Only a few days passed since she discovered what forced him out of Métamorphe. For all the help Galenus had given his family and his mother's death, the least he could do to honor them was get Pierce and Lillianna out of that village. Not that he was any closer to accomplishing that. Although he was pretty confident that he caught a whiff of Pierce's scent the last time he met with Derrick. There hadn't been time for him to follow the smell and find out.

"What are you thinking about?"

He didn't need to ask how she could tell something weighed on his mind. Over the past few weeks, she picked up more and more of his emotions, almost seeming to know when he needed just to hold her. Or what to say. It usually centered on thoughts regarding his family, as it did now. He pressed another tender kiss to her forehead. "I am thinking about my siblings. The sacrifices made to get them away from Métamorphe so they, well, so we all could have better lives."

Ambrosia cupped his chin and gently turned his face back toward hers. "Hey. You're not failing them. I know it's taking longer than you'd like, but that doesn't mean you're failing them."

"I know you are right up here." He tapped his head. "But I do not feel it here." Moving her hand from his jaw, he laid her palm on his chest over his heart. "I cannot help but wonder if there is something more I could be doing."

Her eyebrows knitted together as she stroked her thumb back and forth across his chest. "Honestly, I'm glad you're not. Not because I don't want you to get them out. I do, but I heard from one of my patrons last night that Informants have become more visible around the marketplace and even in the outer forest. Getting them out shouldn't end with you caught."

More Informants? Had others picked up on his scent? He tried to be as careful as possible and took different paths each time he went, which wasn't that often. Well, every few days anyway, even though he last saw Derrick about a week earlier. Besides, things changed a bit at Belly of the Beast, so he spent less time there. Logan sighed. "I know, love. I do not wish to be caught either. The last thing I would ever want is to be taken from you."

"That's good. I don't want that either."

If the information given to her was accurate, then he'd have to take extra precautions in the future. Camouflage in the marketplace itself would prove highly difficult, given the crowd. But, even if he took the back way to Belly of the Beast, it wouldn't make that much of a difference. And he needed to return in a few days to meet Derrick again. Although maybe he could push it for a week to be on the safe side. He meant what he said. "I will not do anything to put myself in harm's way."

"Good... that's good." She readjusted her fingers and played with his fur. "I've already lost one person I cared about. I couldn't bear to lose you, too."

Logan kissed the top of her head. "You will never lose me. I will always be right here. No matter what."

Still sifting her fingers through his fur, she nodded silently.

Although she said nothing, he suspected she started thinking about her father. Not that it surprised him in the least bit. He had, too, just in a different capacity. All he could think about was all the times Galenus helped them. One, in particular, came to mind.

The crack blared in Logan's ears. Their father shoved Pierce to the floor and repeatedly hit their mother; there was only one way to stop this. Turning around, Logan ran out the door and almost slammed right into Galenus. "You have to help!"

"Stay here with your sisters." Galenus handed Zinnia off to Logan and stormed into the hut.

As good as his hearing was, he didn't have to watch to see what happened. Not that it kept him from looking. As instructed, he remained outside with his two sisters.

Galenus yanked their father off their mother, slammed him into the wall three times, and twisted their father's arm behind his back until another loud crack filled the air. Finally, he knocked their father's face into the wall again and threw him to the floor.

"Lay your hands on your mate or those kids again, and I will get you outside of these boundaries, and you will not return," Galenus snarled at their father. "I suggest you stay down there."

Turning, Galenus scooped their mother up into his arms. By that point, Pierce got to his feet. They all left.

Pierce had been sixteen. He'd been eleven, maybe twelve; both Dahlia and Zinnia had been tiny. They all went to Aradia's hut together, and Galenus stayed with them the entire time. It was one of the few times he remembered his brother getting proper medical treatment. Same with his mother.

"What are you thinking about?" Ambrosia asked.

"Your father and mine." His gaze flicked to hers, and he drew her more against his side. His fingers gingerly stroked her lower belly.

"Oh?"

"Yeah. Just how different they were." It was the truth. Galenus was a wonderful male who constantly tried to take care of them and who got into regular fights with his father, which often resulted in Markham punishing Galenus. But he certainly didn't want to tell her that.

Her eyebrows furrowed. "You've never really spoken about your father."

"He is not a fit male. Everything my brother and I learned—how to treat females and how to be strong but good—we learned from your father." Galenus didn't just teach them how to fish, fight when necessary, or how to fend for themselves; he also taught them how to be respectful of females.

Ailwin hadn't taught them anything. He didn't care one bit about his children.

"How bad are we talking here?"

He was not as evil as Markham but fit for how their so-called king ran the village.

Galenus barged into their hut. He grabbed Ailwin by the shoulders, his dick way too close to Zinnia's mouth, and tossed him across the room.

Logan had been right behind Galenus. He didn't need to hear any instruction from the male. He dashed across the room, pulled Zinnia to her feet, and rushed her outside before she puked.

"She is seven, Ailwin! Just a child!" Galenus growled.

"She does not feel like a seven-year-old," Ailwin slurred.

Snarling, Galenus dragged Ailwin outside and beat the shit out of him.

Pressing another kiss to Ambrosia's forehead, Logan inhaled her sweet scent. Not that he needed to be this close to smell it. Her scent thickened over the last few weeks. Probably one reason here lately he couldn't keep his hands off of her. Her delicious aroma settled his nerves and quieted his mind.

He didn't like the memories that bombarded his brain. Not that he could change any of them. It was all in the past. Well, some of it was. Who knew what his father got away with when Pierce wasn't in the village? Getting Pierce and Lillianna out was the only answer. Logan blew out a deep breath. "Atrocious. Ailwin, that is my father, and he cares only for himself and what others can do for him."

"I imagine our fathers didn't get along then."

That was an understatement. It hadn't ever been hard to see how much Ailwin hated Galenus. A small smile tugged at the corners of his mouth. "No, they did not. Your father physically fought mine several times. Galenus typically won too. Do not be sad about it. Any time I remember Galenus coming after Ailwin, he deserved it." Well deserved. The only time he went after his father had been after Galenus made one last attempt to get his family out of Métamorphe before he left for good.

Logan sat in the front room of their hut. He and his brother agreed it was best to speak with their mother and try to convince her to leave Dahlia behind. Their father beat their mother again, so severely she almost died. All because Dahlia didn't want to leave their father, so she ran off and told him what they planned.

Now, he sat there and listened as Galenus spoke to his mother. She was still healing from her wounds. If Galenus couldn't convince her of what needed to happen, no one could.

"You must leave," Galenus proclaimed.

"I cannot. Not again. Not after this. I can never try to leave him again. She will not come. And I could never bear to leave one of my young behind. You know I cannot. No. My place is here. Go. Be safe. Please do not spend your life thinking you have failed me. None of this is your fault."

"She is not like your other children. I need you to think of them. Think of what is best for them."

"I have lost so many. I cannot leave one behind here. No matter how dark her heart is. Take Pierce, Logan, and Zinnia with you. They deserve a good life."

Galenus sighed. "You know they will not leave without you."

"I cannot go with them. I have to keep trying with her. Before she is truly lost."

"You know I cannot come back after this. My mate, she needs me. I will always help you in any way I can. If you change your mind, you know how to find me."

"You are truly the most wonderful male. And your mate is blessed to have you. But not everyone can be saved, Galenus. Leave this place behind. Have a good life. One day, I pray they will leave it behind too. But, while I have a living child in this village, I cannot walk away. No matter how much it hurts."

"It would never stop me from trying. We may not be related by blood, but you are my family."

"You have always been my brother, and you always will be. No matter what happens. I will never forget you or what you have done for my children and me."

Galenus was the one who told him about Migas Village. That day, now that he thought about it. Not that he used the information until the day he tried to find and warn Galenus of Markham's true intentions. Now, he needed to pick up where Galenus left off.

"I don't ever remember my father in a physical altercation. Well, unless a male went after a female. He'd always been protective of females, and he always made sure both Jo and I knew what was okay and what wasn't.

And that we could always come to him if we were ever uncomfortable with something that happened. He made us feel safe," Ambrosia said.

"That is how I remember him."

"You know… it's strange, but I kind of find it comforting that you learned from my father."

"Why do you say that?"

"Because it means he would approve of you."

Warmth flooded every part of him, down to his soul. His gaze met hers. His beautiful, fantastic female. "As happy as that makes me, I only need your approval."

"Then I guess it's a good thing you have it."

"Yes, it is." An excellent thing. Logan brushed a soft kiss across her lips. Hades, he truly loved this female; now, if he could tell her that.

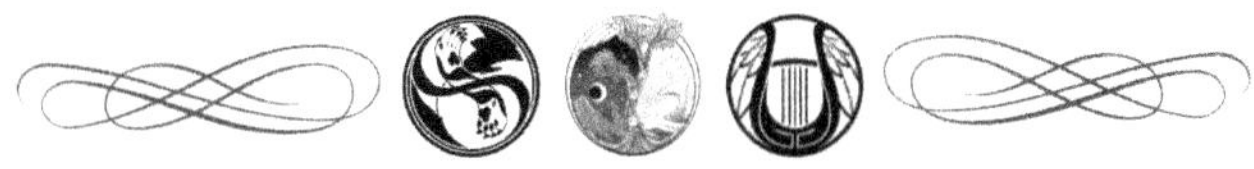

It was mid-morning when Derrick changed course and sped back to the territory. He didn't even register the shuddering sensation of evil as he passed over the boundary line. He felt his mate's pain for miles as he rushed home. The physical and emotional anguish from her. Oh, gods, he didn't need to hear the words to know; he wouldn't need to reach her to see.

He caught Devina's scent before he came upon the clearing. His speed didn't slow and, as he passed her, she turned and followed him. "You do not have to say it," he said, his voice strained as they ran.

"She is at the river. Derrick, I… I am so very so—"

"Stop. It was not your fault. It just is."

His sister fell silent for a few minutes. "I left food with her. Try to get her to eat. No one should expect you at the village yet, so you should have some time, but…" Her words trailed off. She didn't need to finish the statement. They wouldn't be able to stay away from the village all day. Anyone could come upon them, and someone would eventually miss them.

"I will see you later. I love you, brother mine."

"I love you too, sister mine."

Without another word, she veered off.

Derrick quickened his pace and neared the river in next to no time. Gabby kneeled on the ground by the water, sobbing, her arms wrapped around her belly. The copper scent of blood reached his nose, but he didn't see any. Either Devina had already cleaned her up, or she hadn't. He knew from others—too many others—in the village. Sometimes the bleeding passed quickly, and sometimes it took hours.

Too many others. Now it was them.

Hades, he could *smell* the loss.

As soon as he cleared the trees, he shifted to his humanoid form and rushed to her. Sitting on the ground next to her, he drew her into his lap and wound his arms around her. She leaned against him, her arms still clutching her belly. Burying her face in his chest, her tears soaked his fur. His own didn't take long to arrive as her sobs shattered his heart.

"I am so sorry, Derrick. Oh, gods, I am so sorry," she cried out.

He squeezed his eyes shut tight, but it did nothing to lessen the flow of anguish that poured down his cheeks. The feelings of guilt, despair, utter emptiness and loss that poured from Gabby and into him made his chest ache, made his throat so tight he could barely speak. "Oh, no. No, my love, please do not blame yourself. It is not your fault. You did nothing wrong. Do you hear me? *Nothing*. It just happens sometimes." Her sobs ripped through her harder, and all he could do was hold her, rocking her gently in his lap.

It was not supposed to be this way. Not with them. They didn't expect a pregnancy at all. But it happened anyway. Since she told him, they met here at the river and took walks through the forest. They spent time together as often as they could without arousing suspicion. But they didn't discuss the life that grew inside. Because if they couldn't agree on her finding safety, what was the point? If she wouldn't decide to go to Migas, if she wouldn't leave him, then the inevitable would come. They couldn't afford to become attached.

But that didn't mean they didn't want the young. It just wasn't something that Markham would allow to exist.

He hadn't even found the village Logan spoke about. He planned to find it and prayed they would grant Gabby entry so she would have a place to raise their child safely. Without him. Regardless of if she refused to part from him, he refused to bring Markham's wrath upon her and their young by deserting. But now...

If this was what the gods planned—for them to lose their young so soon—he could at least be grateful it occurred naturally, as opposed to... He barely held back the shudder. At least no one exposed Gabby to *that*. She didn't have the child forced from her. She didn't have to watch him die. Not yet anyway.

He still wanted to find the village as soon as he could. He still wanted to ask for Gabby to be allowed entry, so she could be safe. But he knew she wouldn't go without him. And he knew she also wouldn't go without her mother and her twin. Getting Gavin out with them would prove easy. Getting Gemma away, too. Well, that would be much more difficult.

Derrick rubbed Gabby's back as the shakes in her body eased somewhat. Although her tears continued, they slowed. They wouldn't entirely stop for a while. He'd already forced himself to stop crying and buried his pain. Gabby was in enough of it and felt too much unnecessary guilt. She didn't need to feel his. When he could get away and find some solitude, he would allow himself to break completely. But not now. Right now, his mate needed him and his strength.

Ambrosia stared at her reflection in the full-length, silver-glass mirror hanging on her bedroom wall. Her skin appeared a little paler than usual. There were dark circles under her eyes. She supposed that was partially because of the nights she spent apart from Logan. She always wanted to be around him. And it wasn't entirely because of her increased sexual drive as of late. She swore the last week they went at it three or four times before coming up for air and food. Plus, she was always hungry, even when she was just a little queasy. Not full-on nausea, just nauseous.

Since she had thrown nothing up, she told her sister she was feeling under the weather, not that it impacted her ability to work. Thankfully, Jo bought it. Standing here, staring at her reflection, it made little sense of how. Ambrosia inhaled and exhaled a deep breath. Whatever it was, she and Logan could deal with it, but she had to find out first. That required a trip to the medical building.

Taking in one more deep breath, Ambrosia left her bedroom and paused outside her sister's room. She didn't bother knocking; just opened the door. Her eyebrows knitted together at the chaos. A mountain of clothes covered her sister's bed, along with several pairs of jeans scattered all over the floor and a few different blouses strewn across the dresser. "What exploded in here?"

In only a t-shirt and a pair of underwear, Jo poked her head out from behind the closet door. "Nothing. I just can't find anything to wear."

"How is that even remotely possible?" She gestured to the stack of clothes on the bed. Her point would be easier to make if she stepped farther into her sister's bedroom. Except then, she might get lost among the piles of clothing that littered the floor.

"Here we go again," Jo smirked and crossed her arms. "You know as well as I do, no matter how many times we have this conversation, the answer never changes. I have an image to maintain."

Yes, they had. She couldn't count the number of times they'd had this same conversation over the last seven years. *Let the gods give me strength.* Ambrosia inhaled and exhaled another deep breath. The third in less than five minutes. That couldn't be good. "You can't seriously be this shallow."

Narrowing her eyes, Jo frowned. "I'm not shallow. Our patrons simply have a certain expectation. I'm the sexy karaoke jockey who likes to have fun, and you're the nosey barkeep who wants to know everyone's secrets. See? Image."

"Tell me you don't believe that." Her twin came up with some doozies over the years, but this one took the sweet roll. She wasn't nosey. Nor did she want to know everyone's secrets. She simply collected information, nothing more.

"Of course, I do."

Taking a step back into the hall, Ambrosia shook her head. "I can't even ..." Her words trailed off—nosey barkeep. She'd heard nothing so ridiculous. Sexy karaoke jockey. Whatever. None of that mattered. Her eyes flicked to her twin. "Find some clothes and be ready by the time I get back."

"Back? Wait. Where are you going?"

"None of your business." Good gods, when did her twin get so nosey? Jo never really asked her questions like this before. Then again, many of their conversations occurred telepathically through their mindlink. That afforded them a lot of information on the other.

"If I didn't know any better, I'd say you have a guy." Unfolding her arms, Jo crossed her bedroom. She stopped in front of the bed and began sorting through clothes.

"I don't." Lie, lie, lie—sort of. Logan was more than just *some guy*. She was pretty positive he was the one. "Even if I did, it's still none of your business."

Jo paused with a blouse in her hand and glanced at Ambrosia. "I'm going to remember that the next time *you* intercede in someone else's business."

"Hey. You're the one who has clothes all over the place because you think wearing the wrong top might ruin your career." With that said, she turned and started for the front door. It was a good thing she was going to the medical building because she had to get away from her sister.

"I'm still not shallow," Jo called out after her.

Whatever got her sister through the night. Ambrosia dismissed her with a wave of her hand and left the house.

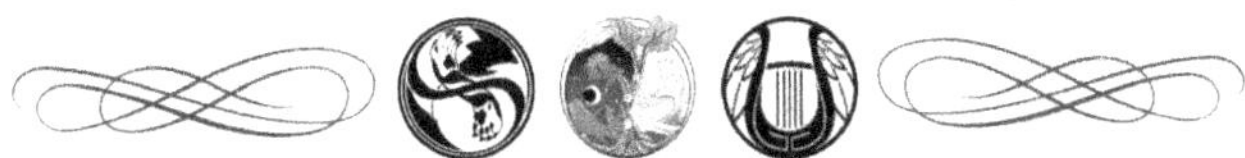

Parthenia ascended the hidden staircase. She spent last night and all day with Gavin. It was harder to part than usual, but, with almost a whole day together, she had to return to Pteryrina. She sang the notes at the top of the stairs, and the hidden doorway slid open.

"Where have you been?" Cipriana stood there with her arms folded across her chest, her brown eyes narrowed.

How did she answer that? She lied. She lied as if her life depended on it, and it did. Not that she suspected Cipriana would ever give her up, but she couldn't take the chance. "I fell asleep in a tree and then got lost on my way back."

"I don't believe you."

Of course not. Her sister couldn't just make this easy on her, could she? Then again, it would be nice not to have this conversation at all. But she had to be here for a reason. Parthenia stepped into the library, the secret door closing behind her. "I don't know what else to tell you."

"How about the truth? I've spent the last two days covering for you. The least you could do is to be honest with me."

With Cipriana here, she couldn't use the cleansing potion she hadn't improved yet. As late as it was, a bath in the spring was her only option. But she didn't want to be followed. "That is the truth." She paused. Hold on; she was certain no one saw her leave. "How did you even know I was gone?"

"You don't remember? I told you yesterday before you reported to the Elder that I'd bring you food later. I know how you get when you're in your apothecary. No one else exists."

Oh, poppies! The female said that, didn't she? Parthenia scrubbed a hand down her face. So much happened with her emotions yesterday that she barely noticed the female there. "I apologize, and I appreciate you covering for me, but I got lost."

"Do you truly think me a fool?"

"Of course not! How could you even ask me that?" She valued her sister. This was simply one lie she had to maintain, especially after what occurred. She couldn't chance that, somehow, word got out. It didn't matter that her sister didn't leave Pteryrina.

"Because you keep feeding me some crap line about getting lost." Cipriana stuck her finger in Parthenia's face. "No one up here, and I mean no one, has a better sense of direction than you. Stop lying to me and tell me the truth right now, or—"

"Or what?" Parthenia crossed her arms. The female would do nothing to cause her harm.

"I'll tell the Elder you've been sneaking off."

She gasped. "You wouldn't." If Cipriana did, what kind of trouble would she be in? No one dared to step outside their grounds in centuries. At least, as far as she knew. She noticed no one using the hidden staircase. It didn't even appear as if someone opened it in ages when she'd first found it.

"Wouldn't I?" Cipriana huffed and stormed off.

Good goddess! Couldn't they get through a few days without one crisis? She couldn't risk her sister saying something, but she couldn't tell her about Gavin, either. As much as she loved Cipriana, she didn't think she'd understand. But she had to give the female something other than the lie she had unceremoniously thrown into the mix. Parthenia chased after her sister and grabbed her arm. "Fine. I didn't get lost, but I can't tell you what happened either."

Cipriana spun around to face her. "Why not?"

Raking a hand through her mahogany locks, she groaned. "I'm trying to protect you. For me to do that, I can't tell you exactly where I've been."

"Protect me? From what?"

"Goddess, I can't tell you that either."

"Then what can you tell me?" Cipriana glowered at Parthenia.

If she was honest, nothing. She couldn't tell her anything. At least, nothing more than she already knew. The female knew she went down to the isle, but nothing more. That was precisely how it had to be kept. At least, for now. Maybe she could tell her about Gavin in the future, but it wouldn't be soon. "Only what you already know."

"Which is nothing."

"Cipriana, please. I beg of you to let this go. It's best for all involved if you don't know where I have been." What else could she say? Nothing, absolutely nothing, would make her divulge the details of her dalliance over the last two days. The female would make her choice and, if she reported her, she'd deal with the repercussions.

Crossing her arms, Cipriana inhaled and exhaled a deep breath. She stood there in silence and scrutinized Parthenia. "Fine. I will say nothing for now. Do not think this is the end of the matter. There will come a time when you must explain yourself."

"Thank you. Thank you, Cipriana. I owe you greatly." One day, she'd repay her for the reprieve granted. Not that she knew how or when, but eventually, she'd figure something out.

"Don't thank me yet. You still have to show everyone tomorrow what you've accomplished, as they all believe you've been locked in your apothecary since yesterday afternoon."

Right. What she accomplished. Perhaps it was a good thing she rested well the night before. She expected it would be difficult to sleep without Gavin by her side. This simply gave her something to focus on instead of a failed attempt at rest. "I will come up with something."

"Then I suggest you get to work."

"Of course." She nodded at her sister and left the library. She could see it now; tomorrow would be a long day. A bath in the spring first, then a nutrient for the dried soil. Goddess, she needed to find an answer in a night when she hadn't found something in months.

An endless day, indeed.

Chapter Twelve

Logan paced back and forth in the living room of his cabin. Since yesterday, he tried to stay busy, but failed gloriously. This strange feeling overcame him, one he couldn't explain. He didn't even know it was possible. After Ambrosia left him for the day, something in her changed. An unease, or maybe it was nerves. What could've brought on the discomfort? It took every ounce of willpower not to go into the marketplace where she worked to find out what was going on.

Was this something that happened between mates? Even with this kind of distance, he could feel everything she felt. It wasn't like he saw true love between his parents. True mates rarely existed in Métamorphe. The only people he could even remotely think of that were true mates were Derrick's parents. Those two were a good match. He thought he had the same thing with Ambrosia.

He gripped the back of his neck. A bit of warning of what to expect might've been nice, especially from any of the males he had ever learned from. Hades, he didn't enjoy feeling so helpless, trapped, caged. Even with all the years he hid, he never got accustomed to those kinds of feelings. His ears perked up at the sound of leaves rustling. His heart pounded loudly in his ears as he sniffed the air. Ambrosia. Oh, that sweet, sweet nectar of hers, and something else.

Turning toward the door, he paused mid-step. Her scent wasn't the only thing he caught a whiff of. But it couldn't be. Not those herbs. No. Oh, gods. How many times had he smelled them with his mother? How many times had she returned to their hut with the same pouches? He lost count over the years. There had been so many. Logan scrubbed a hand across his face, inhaling and exhaling a deep breath.

If it was the case, he could handle it. They could take it. They would figure it all out together. He still stood in the middle of the living room when the front door opened and Ambrosia entered the cabin. His gaze flicked to her.

Shutting the door behind her, Ambrosia stopped and stared at him. "Hi."

"Hi." Part of him wanted to rush over to her and sweep her into his arms. The other part slowed his movements as he closed the distance between them. Gentle. He needed to be gentle with her. One wrong misstep and she could—Hades, he didn't want to think about that.

"You know, don't you? Not that I know how you could know because I haven't said anything or told—"

Tilting her head up, he brushed a soft kiss across her lips. "I smelled the herbs." He could've let her prattle on, but she should be at ease. Not nervous. That's what he sensed since yesterday afternoon. It must've been when she found out. Logan swallowed the lump in the back of his throat. She needed him to remain calm. "Are you truly..." He couldn't finish the question.

"Yes. I'm pregnant." Her shoulders tensed, and her lips trembled. Tears pricked the corners of her eyes. "Logan... I'm scared." She half-shrugged. "We both know shape shifter pregnancies... they usually... they don't—"

"Hey, shh, none of that." He enveloped her in his arms and gently hugged her against his body. "You and I are going to think positive." So many things they'd have to change, but he could do that. They could do that. She couldn't walk from her village to his cabin anymore. He'd take her to and from going forward. They'd have to make time so she could introduce him to her family. Maybe they could figure out living arrangements from there. And an official mating ceremony. Hmm, he should probably talk to her about all of that first. No. First, he needed to calm her down. She had to relax. Stress wasn't good for her.

Good vibes. If they had good vibes, everything would all work out. Logan rubbed slow circles across her back and kissed the top of her head. "That is what we will do. Think positive. And in, well ..." He hadn't asked how far along she was. Crap, he really should've asked that. "However, many months, we will have a beautiful little one."

"Four weeks. I'm ..." Ambrosia paused. "I'm four weeks."

Four weeks, he thought. Oh, gods. Hades, please keep her and the baby safe. All of his mother's pregnancies that had failed had never gone past six weeks. And Ambrosia wasn't even there yet. No. He couldn't let that get to him. His thoughts had to remain positive. It wasn't just for her benefit, but for his as well. Positive thoughts. "Then, in twenty weeks, we will have a beautiful baby girl or baby boy. And we will love them."

That was positive. Optimistic that Ambrosia would deliver their child safely. All of his mother's pregnancies that failed never went past six weeks. Inhaling another deep breath, he focused on the steady thrum of her heartbeat, the sensation of her fingers linked at the small of his back. Logan pressed another kiss to the top of her head. It would all be okay. He just needed to keep repeating that until he believed it. "I cannot tell you how happy you have made me."

"Really?" She sniffled and lifted her gaze to his.

Staring into her pools of liquid amber, he smiled and caressed her cheek. Hades, he loved this woman with all of his heart and soul. An aquamarine-colored light covered her face. Where was it—oh, it came from him. His eyes were glowing. "You are beautiful and kind-hearted. Maybe a tad sarcastic, but I kind of like that. Of all the males you could have chosen, you chose me. You have filled holes in my heart I did not know existed and repaired pieces of my soul I did not know were broken. Not only have you comforted me through the worst time in my life, but you have also allowed me to lean on you. You are everything I could ever want and more. I love you, Ambrosia."

"I love you, too." The corners of her lips tugged into a broad grin as she stared up at him. She bit her bottom lip. The green scales lining her spine and shoulders became rather vibrant as their color emanated out in a luminous halo. "You've got a good heart, one that cares deeply for others. No matter how much I argued against it initially, you reminded me I could have a life for myself. Helping my sister didn't mean I focused less on myself or the things I wanted. You showed me I could be happy and still be there for my family, too."

His heart swelled. Ambrosia uttered the most beautiful words—ones he'd cherish until the day he died. Cupping the back of her head, Logan leaned down and brushed a soft kiss across her lips. Dropping to his knees, he pressed a loving kiss to her belly and locked his gaze on hers. Hades, he couldn't get over the halo her scales created around her. "When you are ready, I would like to meet your family and to be officially mated. If that is something, you would want as well."

Tears pricked the corners of her eyes again. "Damn it," she muttered and wiped at her face. "I'd like that very much."

Although she cried, nothing but pure joy radiated across her face. The way she beamed almost had him jumping to his feet and swinging her in the air. Then he reminded himself of the baby. Instead, Logan kissed her flat belly again and stood. His lips fused with hers in a deep and languid kiss. Not only would he get to say before the world that they belonged to one another, but she was making him a father, too. Something he never believed would happen in his lifetime. With one last stroke of his tongue, he broke the kiss. "I cannot wait to share my life with you."

"Me, too, Logan. Me, too." Ambrosia beamed.

Lillianna sat on the floor in the corner of her father's hut, her arms wrapped around her knees. She glared at the male who spoke with her father across the room. He terrified her, but more than that, he disgusted her. She did nothing to him, but he caused her great pain. And her father helped him do it.

"That is more than last time. I am not paying that much, Ailwin. Others have used her beside me, and you do not allow the fucking I prefer. She is not worth what you are asking."

Lilli didn't know what all the words meant. She didn't understand what payment had to do with any of it. When a male and female lay together, she knew what that meant. She heard talk of it around the village. Some used the word "fucking" to describe it, but no one ever did that to her. No one ever put their thing inside of her—in that place. No, the males her father allowed in here just touched her and did things to her, in places and ways that made her miserable and scared. And it was so excruciating. She hated it, and she hated him, but she didn't know why he hated her.

"Then go find some other little bitch. It is no matter to me. If you do not want her, someone else will."

Cyrus gazed over at her, his eyes traveling slowly over her body. He had that look in his eyes—the one that made her fur stand on end and her skin crawl. Lilli was on the small side even for her age, covered in white and light tan fur, with amethyst-colored eyes. Cyrus licked his lips, sending a shiver through her. He was a hulking canine and one of Markham's Informants. His fur was black, except where dotted with a light golden color. His eyes were orange like fire, and they twinkled with a gleam that petrified her. Markham only chose the largest and strongest male canines and felines in the village.

"She looks just like Sabina. Does she not?" Cyrus smirked.

Her father let out a growl. "Yes, she does. A fucking mirror image. Do not speak her name in my home again." He jerked his head in Lilli's direction. "Do you want her or not?"

Cyrus let out an annoyed growl. "You know I do. I will pay what you are asking. She is a great beauty, her attitude aside. If you could curb that, I would take her as a second mate and off your hands for good."

"Believe me, I have tried," her father snarled. "The day I am rid of her will be a great day, to be sure."

He crossed the room, and though she tried to scramble away from him, he grabbed her wrist. With a tight grip, he jerked her to her feet. "Father, please do not let him do this. Please. I will be good, I swear, I will be good," Lilli pleaded. She glanced at Cyrus, and he rolled his eyes as he counted out coins.

Father tightened his hold, dragging her into his bedroom, and then flung her onto his bedding. She tried to escape and get back to the door, but he hit her jaw, throwing her into the wall.

"Stop this, Lillianna," he barked. "You will stop this nonsense immediately, and you will allow him to inspect you without fuss."

"No! I dislike him; he is mean and cruel, and what he does is painful! Do not let him do this! Please!"

"I care not what he does to you. His coin is more valuable than you are. And if he will take you off my hands, he will do. But your attitude makes it impossible."

"I do not want him to touch me! I do not want his hands upon me!"

"And I care not!" he roared. "You will do AS YOU ARE TOLD. And you will do it now."

"I will not." Her father came at her, and she snapped her jaws at him, causing him to hit her again. She tasted blood in her mouth. Oh, gods, Pierce was going to go insane with rage. He did so every time he saw marks on her.

Her father's hand closed around her throat, and he squeezed, not enough to make her unable to breathe, but enough, so she couldn't speak. "I. Said. Enough." He looked over his shoulder and called into the other room, "Cyrus!"

As Cyrus came in from the front room, she tried to free her arm out of her father's hold, but it was no use. He was an enormous male too, and much stronger than her. His fur was the color of night, and his eyes were usually the moon's color. However, they darkened and held a grayish tinge because of his anger toward her. She should stop fighting and let Cyrus do what he wanted. It would make her father less angry if she did. But she just couldn't. "Please do not, do not do this. Leave me alone. Please—" Her father's hand tightened on her throat again, cutting off her words, before he moved behind her. He gripped her wrists so hard she thought her bones would break and pulled them tight above her head. Cyrus moved across the room and overtop of her, forcing her legs apart.

"NO!" Pulling her leg back, she kicked out as hard as she could and caught him in the gut.

A deep growl emanated out of his chest, and he gripped her chin, forcing her to look at him. "You will lay still, and you will shut up, bitch."

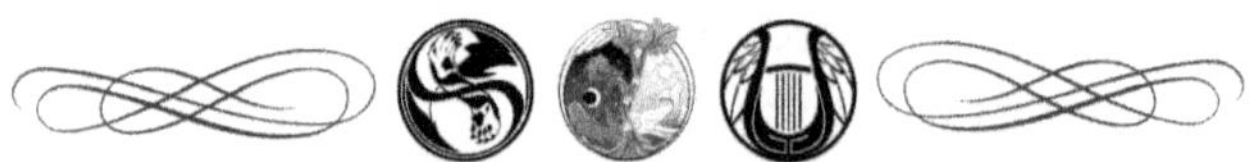

Pierce circled the outside of the larger fighting ring in his animal form, monitoring both of the adolescents inside. Reznor was a canine, and Storm was a feline. Both were on the older side of the age group, and both were still in their teens. Storm kept turning his dark purple eyes on Nova, a female feline watching from outside the ring. She was an older adolescent who had her front paws up on the fence boards again. Her sapphire eyes twinkled as she watched Storm. They both hoped to be permitted to mate once they left adolescence behind.

"Nova! Down!" he hollered. If she were still leaning on the fence, she would get injured when the young males crashed into it. It happened more times than he could count, and he wouldn't have a female wounded on his watch. Not if he could help it. Her ears fell back in submission, and she slunk off the fence, backing up enough that Pierce had adequate room to pass as he circled the ring. Out of the corner of his eye, he caught her slinking to the fence. He rolled his eyes. Love. From what he saw in his forty-five years on this earth, love between mates was pointless. There may be truth to it, but happiness never came from it. Not here in this village.

He looked back into the ring. Storm wasn't paying attention, and Reznor was going to, right now—Yup. Reznor launched himself into Storm's side, and a sickening crack rang out into the air. He yelped as he landed hard on the ground. Reznor rolled with the landing and leaped back to his feet.

"Get up, Storm," Pierce called out. "It was only a rib."

Gods, he fucking loathed this, every single bit of it. How he had to appear to lack empathy, and how he had to act like he didn't care. He hated he had to train young how to kill, because this wasn't just about fighting. Oh, no. Markham didn't want the young to know how to protect themselves. The male wanted them to become fighters that knew how to steal life. Pierce swallowed his feelings of disgust, burying them as deeply as he could.

With his aversion went his feelings of guilt. Although he had his survival to think about, it was an all-too-familiar feeling after he had to attack someone who genuinely did nothing wrong. He didn't know what the male feline did to warrant Markham's anger. He broke curfew, but Pierce could tell it was more than that. Gavin was no troublemaker. He wasn't even sure the male often left the boundaries. Yet Markham forced Gavin to fight him, Chaz, and Arman until the male could barely stand. He would've gone on fighting even longer and sustained even worse injuries if Pierce hadn't done the only thing he could think of to get him to stand down.

Knowing that he'd all but had no choice didn't appease his guilt any, though. Regardless, his emotions weren't something he could afford to have made known here. Not near Markham. The thoughts in the back of his mind—his conversation with Derrick, thoughts of his brother—were taboo as well. So, down deep they all went, buried further than his gut and far away from his mind.

As Storm struggled to get back to his feet, he saw Nova fighting with herself. She wanted to get in the ring and go to him. He glared at her, one that clearly said, *"Do not even think about it."* Then he glowered at Reznor, who looked like he wanted to attack the other male while he still lay on the ground. The male backed up, lowering his head in submission, until Pierce looked away.

He turned his attention to the smaller pen. The two younglings were nearing their transition into adolescence. Nine or ten years of age, he wasn't sure. Midnight and Thorn were both canines, but their teeth wouldn't cause too much damage until they matured a little more. As close as brothers, the two were best friends, so they weren't trying to harm each other, anyway. Just wrestling. They weren't the two he needed to monitor.

"Storm, enough. Get. Up." He sent a warning growl at Reznor, who still eyeballed Storm, looking for an opening as soon as the young male got to his feet again. "Reznor. Hold until he is on his feet. That is an order." Out of his periphery, he spotted a little ball of swirling black and gray fur. Whipping his head around, he barely had time to slam a paw down in front of Rainn before she crept under the bottom board of the fence. She stopped abruptly, running into his leg. He let out a low warning growl. Rainn was a tiny orphan canine, only in her fourth year of life. Nestlings weren't to wander around the village without a guardian close by, yet here she was. He shook his head. Rainn was always getting into some kind of trouble.

He lifted his head and let loose a loud bark. Heads from all over the clearing turned in his direction. "Where is her guardian?" Rainn made another attempt to sneak past his paw again, but he snapped his jaws in warning, causing her to yowl in fear. "Where is her guardian?!"

"Pierce."

He turned his head, his gaze meeting Devin's.

"I will take her." She walked over to him and used a paw to pull Rainn between her front legs. She looked way up at him as he stood two-and-a-half feet taller than her in this form. "You do not need to yell. If you had looked around some more, you would have seen me coming."

He stared down at her light brown and blonde form, his expression softening a bit. Usually, he would've kept his harsh tone, but they had a history together. Nothing romantic. He never felt those feelings for anyone, and neither did she. But they were a comfort to each other when words were impossible but also not needed. "Keep a better watch on her. She could have gotten seriously injured."

"Willow was watching her. She feels ill today. I will take her to—" A female's scream cut her off, making both of their ears prick up. It was faint and came from a hut across the clearing, and he knew exactly whose it was. He raced across the expanse, though he still heard Devin's parting words. "Go. I have Rainn, and I will get Zagan to watch the training."

Pierce sped toward their hut, ignoring all the eyes upon him. They didn't matter. All that mattered was saving Lilli and getting his jaws around his father's throat. Before he could burst through the front door, someone rammed him hard in the side. He and another canine tumbled across the ground; their legs tangled together. Through his rage, he didn't track who he fought. Loud growls filled the surrounding clearing. As they bit and clawed one another, another joined the fray, latching their jaws onto Pierce's hind leg and jerking him backward. He flipped onto his back and nailed the male in the face with his other back paw. Somebody released his leg, and he rolled, getting back to his feet. Three canine Informants circled him, keeping him from the door of his hut and his little sister.

Evan let out a low chuckle. "You are sooo stupid, Pierce. Did you think your father would not make it worth our while to ensure you did not get through that door? Some of us like it when they struggle, and taking you on gets us a freebie."

Yes, Evan taunted him. It was more likely that whatever male was inside the hut with Lilli paid these three to prevent an interruption, as Pierce had done to others before. But it didn't stop the overwhelming rage from roaring through him full force. He heard Lillianna screaming inside the hut, which only intensified his fury. He saw red. As his chest heaved, puffs of breath left his mouth. He lunged at Evan, latching his jaws onto the male's collarbone. As they rolled across the ground, the other two joined in as well. Teeth and claws tore at him, but he took no more damage than he dealt out.

Time stood still as they fought, ripping and tearing into each other as much as they could, blood splattering everywhere. He primed to launch himself—he couldn't move. Pierce watched as the bodies of the others lifted and flew through the air. Two of them smacked hard into the sides of a couple of huts. Several snaps echoed around them before their bodies fell. Evan landed somewhere beyond the huts, a thud announcing his contact with the ground.

Fuck. He always tried to avoid their King's anger, but that hadn't happened today. Markham forbade attacking an Informant unless the male ordered the attack. The reasons for the attack were irrelevant. The two Informants he saw didn't move, and he heard nothing from Evan either. But the instigator always received the worst punishment. He started the fight by intervening when he had no right to by their laws. According to Markham, females were the property of their mates, fathers if they had no mate, and only if neither of those existed did brothers have any say.

The ground beneath him trembled as Markham's scent drew nearer. From the position the male froze him in, he couldn't see Markham as he approached. But his shadow covered the surrounding ground, eclipsing his own, as the male stopped behind him.

His neck constricted, though no hands or paws touched him. Markham lifted him into the air, turning his body until their eyes met. The King stood on his hind legs, and his right front paw clenched into a fist. Pierce growled. Markham said nothing as the smirk on his face grew, the unholy look in his eyes sharpening. The red-black jewel in his crown shone behind the empty eyes of the skull. And then... *agony* wracked his body.

One by one, his bones snapped, starting at his back paws and moving upward throughout his entire body to his ribs. His growls, barking cries, and yelps resounded around the clearing. The constriction around his throat restricted the noise. Anguish speared through him as if the injuries actually happened. It didn't matter that he knew better. He saw Markham use his powers many times before; even had them used on him like this a time or two. That didn't stop the pain from roaring through him.

He heard Lilli inside the hut, but her cries grew quieter, more broken. He caught the growls of the male inside there with her as well. Those were much more audible. Tears of anger pricked the corners of his eyes. He squeezed his eyes shut tightly against them. It would be worse if he openly shed tears.

Next, it seemed like water filled his lungs. His eyes popped open, his breaths coming in quick gasps, bubbling noises, and wheezing escaped his lips. Sweat poured off of him. His gaze diverted from Markham's when he saw something red out of the corner of his eye. Glancing downward, he watched as blood dripped from his nose and mouth. His throat tightened as he choked on the non-existent liquid in his lungs until spots swam in front of his eyes. He tried to raise his front paws to claw at his throat, but he still couldn't move.

Markham gave a low, menacing chuckle, every one of his fangs showing as a grin spread across his face. The hold on Pierce released in a rush, and he crumpled to the ground, his face landing in the dirt. Intense throbbing and pulsating still filled his body, though he suffered no actual injuries outside of the ones he received during the fight. He had no broken bones except perhaps a couple of ribs. The blood that appeared to drip out of his nose and mouth no longer existed.

Pierce tried to get his legs underneath his body to lift himself off the dirt, but all four of limbs felt hollow, as if they would hold no weight. Markham's paw came down hard on his neck. He let out a hard breath, gasping as he tried to draw air into his windpipe. His claws scrambled and grabbed at the earth until the pressure on his neck increased, and he forced his body to still. Submit. They must always submit to their King.

He no longer heard Lilli inside, but he heard the muffled voices of his father and *Cyrus*.

"I grow tired of this, Pierce. The unnecessary altercations between you and your fellow Informants. You are a great asset to me and the pack. So you have not received death for your transgressions. Yet." Markham pressed down harder on Pierce's neck, and his vision blurred. "The ways of my village are the ways of my village. And you will respect them. It is *long* past time you accept that. Long past time."

The pressure on Pierce's neck lifted, but only slightly.

"In my village, fathers are to be obeyed by their children. No matter what that entails. You know this, Pierce. Personal feelings mean absolutely nothing here. If Ailwin earns coin by selling his daughters to my Informants, that is between them and is no concern of mine." Pierce struggled under the hold but stilled again when the pressure on his neck increased. "And it will no longer be any concern of yours. I hope I have made myself very clear." He paused in his speech. "You will obey my laws. Your sister, Lillianna, is Ailwin's property. When she is mated, she will become that male's property. I know you know this, but something tells me you need reminding of it. Maybe even from time to time."

The door of the hut opened, and his father and Cyrus emerged. They didn't even glance at Pierce, only bowed their heads to Markham as they strolled by, continuing to speak in low tones. Markham's paw stayed put until they were halfway across the clearing. Then he let Pierce go. Though the pressure left his neck, he couldn't move or get his legs to work. He just watched as Markham and the males, who had abused his sister once again, walked away.

A flash out the corner of his eye caught his attention, and he flicked his gaze in that direction. It was Devin. She glanced over at him but didn't speak a word as she went inside. When he finally rose from the ground, he dragged himself into the hut and closed the door. Lilli laid on her pallet in the front room, and Devin was in her humanoid form, shielding her with a blanket she tucked underneath her chin. He squeezed his eyes shut and bit back a growl at the copper scent filling the air—something he smelled far too often. When he opened his eyes, Devin pointed to the corner.

"Sit," she hissed.

He didn't have the strength to argue. Staying on all fours, he lurched across the room and curled up in the corner. Though he couldn't see what Devin did, he didn't avert his eyes.

"She woke briefly. I gave her something to help her sleep and something for the pain. When I go, I will leave more with you. I am just cleaning her up."

What could he say? Not that she expected anything from him. At some point, he shifted to his humanoid form, sat up, drew his knees up to his chest, and rested his arms upon them. He trailed blood in here, and it got on the wall. It would have to be cleaned up. He didn't want Lilli to see it whenever she awoke.

He couldn't ignore the stained cloths Devin tried to hide before she tucked a blanket around Lilli's sleeping form. Then, without a word, she strode over to a basin of water in the corner. Devin dragged the bay over to Pierce and kneeled in front of him with a few more clean cloths in her hand. She dipped the rag in the water, wrung it out, and cleaned the blood from his fur and the wall behind him.

It took her some time to finish, not that he could say how long. She gave him no chance to object—or, perhaps, his voice just refused to work—as she wiped up the blood on the floor as well. Devin dragged the basin outside, and he heard the distant sound of sloshing water. When she returned, she put the empty pot back in the corner. The filthy rags were nowhere in sight.

Devin kneeled in front of him. "I got most of it," she whispered. "You should go wash, though. I can sit with Lilli until you get back."

He shook his head. As her hand reached up toward his cheek, his chin dropped and rested against his chest. "I need you to go… please," he mumbled.

Reaching into a bag hung across her chest, she tucked two vials into his hand. "In case she needs them when she wakes."

Pierce just nodded. His throat had closed up, and words were no longer possible. Devin left, easing the door shut behind her. From the surrounding silence, no one was near the hut. He stared at Lilli's sleeping form. At least she rested, for now.

He folded his arms over his knees, laid his head on top of them, and let the dam break, allowing the tears to fall.

Chapter Thirteen

Ambrosia rolled onto her side and frowned. Without opening her eyes, she reached out to the other side of the bed. It was empty. She winced as another slight twinge shot up from her pelvis. This had been why she'd laid down. She'd cramped on and off for a few hours, but it was a normal part of pregnancy, right? Just part of the many changes in her body. Only nineteen more weeks left to go.

Maybe if she tried walking around, the sensations would stop. It wasn't like a nap had helped any. She flipped over to her back with a slight groan and slowly sat up. Another minor twinge blasted across her abdomen. "Okay, baby, I get it. You don't like this position."

Inhaling and exhaling a deep breath, Ambrosia got to her feet. A wave of nauseousness crept over her. Gods, she didn't know how she'd make it through nineteen more weeks of this. She hadn't been able to hold much down for days, even with the herbs Kaylina had given her. But they were remaining positive.

Optimistic that their worst fears wouldn't come to pass.

Optimistic that she'd carry to term.

Positive that she'd deliver with no issues.

She swallowed the lump in the back of her throat as she stood there staring at the floor. None of those positive thoughts comforted her at the moment. A tear trickled down her cheek, and she quickly wiped it away. She desperately wanted to believe these pangs were a regular part of pregnancy, but what if they weren't? What if their worst fear was already happening, and they couldn't—another wave of nauseousness came over her. Maybe she just needed to throw up. Not that there was much of anything in her stomach.

Ambrosia waited for the nausea to pass and then left the bedroom. As she stepped into the hallway, a new pain twisted in her lower belly. More intense than anything she'd ever felt before. She threw her hand out against the wall and wrapped an arm around her abdomen. This couldn't be happening. No. It couldn't be happening. Please, gods, please... Her eyes shut tight as her fingers clutched the wall. Something wet trickled down the inside of her thigh.

"Logan," she whispered. Although she wanted to cry out for him, she didn't have the strength. Tears streamed down her face as the pain intensified. It was like someone stabbed her repeatedly in her uterus. There was no doubt in her mind.

She was losing their young.

The front door creaked open and slammed shut. A set of feet pounded against the wood flooring of the cabin and headed in her direction. Logan's scent filled her nostrils as his arms came around her.

Her eyes flipped open, more tears streaking her face. "Logan," she said, her voice low as he reached for her. Moving one hand off the wall, she grasped onto him.

"Ambrosia?"

It seemed pointless for him to say more than that. He'd likely caught the smell of blood before he even walked into the cabin. Another bout of pain wracked her body. It was only in her abdomen, but it was like she felt it all over. Her grip on his arm tightened. More tears slid down her cheeks.

Logan scooped her into his arms. "We need to get you to your village now."

"It's too far. We'll—" Ambrosia cried out as another bout of agony pierced her pelvis. Her fingers dug into Logan's arms, not that she'd moved her one arm from around her belly. She couldn't. It would be like leaving their child alone, and she didn't want him to be. He should feel her comfort and the love she and Logan already had for him as he left them.

Ambrosia sobbed against her mate as the wetness between her thighs grew. There was no point in him taking her back to her village. They couldn't do anything to stop this loss. At least this way, they could mourn privately over her body's failure. It was her body that failed to hold on to their child. It was her body that was letting him go. Their son. The one they'd never get to carry. They'd never get to see thrive and grow up. It was her body…

Lowering to the floor, Logan sat and held her tight against his chest. His arms didn't move from around her. Not once did he leave her side. Instead, he stayed with her as the agony passed through her body and claimed their son.

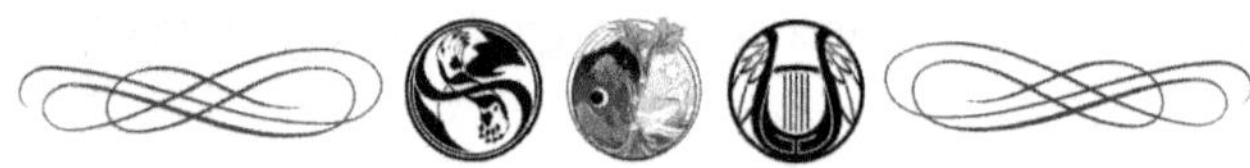

"You have got to stop doing this, Derrick," Pierce growled low as they moved through the marketplace. They were in their humanoid forms, making it easier to maneuver around the other creatures there, duck behind vendors, and through alleyways.

"Stop doing what? I am doing nothing, Pierce, and you know it."

Pierce snarled. "Do not patronize me. I hate him as much as you do, possibly more for what he has done to my family, but this is not the way."

Derrick turned and stared him in the face, forcing him to halt in his tracks. "And what is, Pierce? Your way? Ostracizing a member of your family, your blood, your brother, because of what our King accused him of? You know it was wrong. You know your brother killed no one, but you still will not speak to him."

"And you know exactly why. It has nothing to do with what they accused him of. I cannot put my sisters in harm's way. Not even for him. They are too vulnerable in the pack, as all females are."

Derrick scoffed. "Vulnerable? The only one of your sisters that might be what you consider vulnerable is Lillianna. You are being idiotic and cruel. Come and talk to Logan with me. Hear what he has to say."

"I will not. I could not save him from his disownment. Nor will I get myself killed, leaving my sisters defenseless by breaking more orders. I am already breaking them by not reporting you and him to our King." Not to mention everything else he did. "I will put my family and myself at no further risk."

"Then you are a coward." Derrick spat the words at him with a disapproving rumble. "You are a coward."

"Markham cannot be stopped!" He bit his tongue and lowered his voice. "He cannot be stopped. No one at present can defeat him. We must endure. That is all we can do."

"Endure? You are kidding yourself. Your way is going to be your demise. I will not sit back idly and watch him destroy our pack. Our innocents. Our future. If that is your way, then so be it. But I will have no part in it."

"Clearly," Pierce sneered at him. "Do what you must. I will be here. But do not take too long or I will have to leave you. We must be back by evening meal."

"I know when we must be back. Go. Do whatever it is you do. I shall find you."

Derrick ducked back out of the alley and disappeared. As Pierce watched him go, he just shook his head. He still didn't know where this alleged fighting ring was, and he had no desire to find out. He understood where Derrick came from, but it wasn't a direction he could rationalize going in. Not now. Not after the things he'd seen—and felt—Markham do. The power he had—no one came into that kind of power by natural means. Just the thought that the brute could have dark magic was sobering, but something he couldn't dismiss. There were no other explanations.

They couldn't fight magic. They had no power themselves. Shaking his head again, frustrated beyond all measure, he shoved off of the wall and exited the alleyway, only to slam right into a creature. Losing his footing, he spun around on one foot and almost bumped into another one as they passed.

"My apologies," he called out to whoever he had almost knocked over. He turned around to apologize to the original person he'd run into, only to freeze in place when he laid eyes upon a female. All he could see were amber eyes and flowing, crimson hair.

Logan had sat in the corner of Belly of the Beast for a good hour. His drink remained untouched. Although he'd asked, his brother had yet to meet with him. The last thing he wanted was to change course, but he would do what had to be done. Maybe today would be different. Maybe Pierce would show up with Derrick, especially if the rumors Ambrosia had shared with him a couple of weeks ago were true. Their conversation had gone further that day about her father, not that it currently weighed on his mind.

That was something else entirely.

And he couldn't go there—not tonight.

He watched Derrick practically shove his way into the establishment and make a beeline straight for the bar. The male pushed payment across the counter and downed first one glass, then a second, of whatever the barkeep gave him. His hands gripped the edge of the countertop while he waited for another, and then he grasped the glass, taking sips as he made his way to Logan's table.

Derrick eased himself into the chair, setting his glass down. "He will not come," he mumbled. "Pierce. He will not come. But it is not because he does not want to."

Sitting there silently, Logan swallowed the lump in the back of his throat. The male's emotions overwhelmed him—anger and sorrow. It was all he could feel, and it took everything in him to keep the tears at bay. A male only felt like that when he faced loss. It would've been worse if it had been his mate, which meant it could only be of the child Derrick had told him his mate had carried.

What happened with his mate a few days earlier only worsened the emotions he felt coming from Derrick. Logan gulped back his untouched drink. He had to focus; otherwise, the male's emotions mixed with his own would consume him. "I understand. It pains me, but I understand."

Derrick looked up at him, meeting his eyes, and it was like a wall inside him gave a tiny crack. He squeezed his eyes shut as he bent over, elbows on his knees, face in his hands. "I was not there. My sister was. She found me in a panic. By the time I got to Gabby, it was already too late." The words came out in a hushed tone.

Logan squeezed the male's shoulder tightly. "I am sorry, brother." Words did little with this kind of loss, but it was all he had. Nothing could make up for losing an unborn child. One loved them the moment one discovered their existence. And no matter how common they were in shape shifters; it didn't make it any easier to face. The heartache, guilt, and shame that they could've done something. That, somehow, they were to blame for the outcome. Regardless of how much it wasn't true, it didn't change the feelings.

Derrick opened his mouth to speak, but no words came out. Instead, a single sob escaped. The male's jaw clenched. Logan caught the coppery aroma of blood. Derrick rubbed his eyes hard for a moment. "Thank you, brother," he said. Derrick visibly swallowed, rubbed his eyes again, and then cleared his throat. "Pierce is adamant he can do nothing to jeopardize the safety of your sisters. Even the suspicion that he knows where you are and has not reported you would cause his death. He said he is already risking too much by not reporting our meetings, not that he ever would. And Lillianna avoids me, as she does all Informants but Pierce. Your sister is brilliant."

Swallowing, Logan sat for a moment to give the emotions swirling around his heart time to settle. Males didn't sob in public. Feeling what Derrick was going through only heightened his loss. If he didn't get his mind away from that—he inhaled deeply once, twice, three times, then sat up straight. His brother was being cautious, not that he blamed him. Logan leaned back in the chair and gulped the rest of his drink down. "Keep trying with Lillianna. If I can get her to leave, Pierce will follow. I will request sanctuary for them soon."

Derrick nodded. Picking up his glass, he downed every drop in it, and then set it down. "I agree. If Lillianna knew of your existence, I believe that would be all it would take for her to flee. I will keep trying to speak with her until I succeed."

Logan waved at the barkeep for two more drinks. He sighed heavily. "I hate that I have put you in the middle of this. You have more than enough on your plate."

"You have not put me in the middle of anything. I have put myself in the middle of it."

Someone set another round of drinks on the table, and Logan waited a moment before speaking again. "You should be aware; I have heard more of Markham's Informants are being seen around the isle."

Derrick took a drink. "Yes, I am aware. Part of why Pierce refuses to get involved. Thank you for telling me, though. Where were they seen?"

"According to what I was told, along the outskirts of the forest, around the marketplace. Some near Verdant Grove." Logan smirked. Of all the places they'd go, the fae forest, but his mate confirmed as much. Fae talked a lot. "As well as Viridescent Forest." Those were the ones that concerned him. It put them too close to Migas Village.

"I will keep that in mind." Derrick took a swig of his drink. "Pierce thinks I am being too careless. I am just doing the best that I can. Perhaps I should be a little more mindful of my actions."

"Pierce is right. You should be careful. They may be the stronger sex, but our mates need us as much as we need them." He lifted the glass to his mouth and realized his error. If he were lucky, Derrick would overlook his vernacular and accept it as a generalization. But the male was too smart for his own good sometimes.

Derrick lowered the glass he held. "Our?" He raised an eyebrow. A faint smile crossed his face, not that it reached his eyes. "You have mated as well. I am happy for you. Now the changes to your fur make sense."

Logan stroked the glass in his hand. He wouldn't change a thing about meeting her, but he'd discovered the true complexities of their relationship as time had gone on. "It had been truly unexpected. Well, her and the change to my fur."

"I know the feeling well. So I will pray to the gods for the two of you, for a life full of love and happiness. You deserve it."

"Thank you. I will do the same for you and Gabby as well." He didn't wish to add more detail about Ambrosia. Perhaps Derrick had kept their meetings to himself, but he needed to ensure her identity remained secret. Along with everything that had happened recently. "Do you know of other places than I have mentioned that the Informants search?"

"None that I know of have entered, or even been near, Chicane Village. And none go too close to the border. Those with wings have no affection for those of us stuck on the ground. Other than that, everywhere else is fair game except for the unknown places. Like Migas. Each year, he tells us to stretch our paths further." He sipped more of his drink. "Markham appears to be getting desperate. There is a prize on your head. You need to be mindful of your steps as well."

That didn't shock him. None of what Derrick told him did. "I watch every step. More so than I have in the past. It is one reason I need to get Pierce and Lillianna out as quickly as I can. If he finds out anything, he will use them to get to me." Just as he would use his mate, especially if he knew who she was.

"I know he will. And I share the same concerns for my sister and my mate. Devina is..." He let out a small chuckle. "As driven as always. She is the one who told me of your innocence. Not that I believed your guilt, but she confirmed my beliefs."

They each had a complicated relationship. "I did not know anyone knew, aside from you."

"She witnessed his death. Camouflaged way up in the trees. You remember how much of a climber she has always been? Barely walking, and she was scaling trunks." He snickered. "She was only three then."

Logan knocked back the last of his drink. "We should be more careful with our meetings here."

Derrick finished his drink as well. "I should go anyway. I need to get home and try to check on Gabby."

"Be safe and be well, Derrick." He had to space his time out more here. Watch the marketplace itself. If the Informants were hitting the outskirts, he had to be mindful of their presence for Ambrosia's sake.

"You as well, Logan. Until we meet again." Derrick stood and clapped a hand to his shoulder. Then, turned around and left.

Some time passed before Logan took care of his tab and exited the premises himself. The longer he waited, the less likely anyone would have seen him with Derrick. It was information that didn't need to get back to Markham at all.

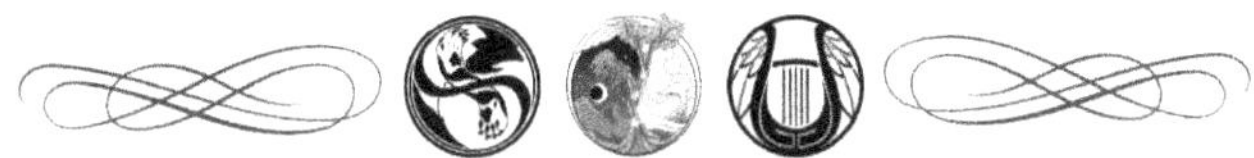

Gods, he couldn't move. Pierce watched a square wicker basket tumble from the female's hands as she fell. She let out a groan at the sight of the broken bottles now lying on the ground, surrounded by scattered herbs and potions.

Her gaze shifted to him, her amber gaze hardened, and she slowly got to her feet. "Good gods, don't you watch where you're going?"

Pierce narrowed his eyes as he forced the feeling in his gut down, *way* down. This female had a strange manner of speaking, but her voice, oh gods, her voice. He shook his head to clear it, trying to shake himself out of this stupor. She'd said something to him. She probably thought he was a complete idiot, the way he just stared at her, mute. He took a breath. "Normally, yes. Do you?" Why in Hades' name had he said that? That was so rude, and it hadn't been her fault. He hadn't watched where he was going. He kneeled and picked up the pieces of broken bottles. "Are you keeping these?"

"Oh, yes, because they're going to do me any good now."

Gods, her voice, sarcasm and all—maybe even primarily because of that. She crouched down on her haunches and searched through the mess. They reached for a piece. As their hands touched, something sparked between them, and she immediately yanked her hand away.

He let out a growl without meaning to and opened his mouth to say something when every single comeback he could've blurted seeped out of his head as if his mind were a bag of-of—Hades. Why wouldn't his brain work? "Why did you do that? It was a simple accident, and I am helping you clean it up. You did not need to shock me." He continued to pick up the mess he'd caused and realized she just kneeled there, gawking at him. "What?"

Her gaze didn't waver. All he wanted to do was continue to drown in her amber-colored eyes, which radiated warmth like the sun. She opened her mouth—

"Jo? Everything okay?" a male voice called out. Jo... Her name was Jo. Was that a nickname or her full name?

The female jumped to her feet and spun around to face a nine-foot troll who held two other baskets in his arms. Dropping her hands to her hips, she cracked a smile that made heat curl deep within him. "It's all good, Bruce. Just a minor accident. Go on ahead and take those to the bar. I'll be along after I go back to the apothecary."

Pierce kept his mouth shut. Even talking to someone of another species in anything more than a professional capacity brought punishment, usually a good whipping. And she was a half-breed, which would make the punishment even worse. How Markham didn't realize that half-breeds ran rampant here, he did not know. Or perhaps he only cared if they were part shape shifter. Who knew? Shape shifter half-breeds were the only ones Markham ordered them to bring back to the village if found. Either way, he wouldn't say anything about it, which would probably get him killed. Yup, this was going to get him killed.

He carefully picked up the rest of the mess and all the shards from the basket so the female wouldn't hurt herself. While he tried to ignore the scent coming off her—the one making his cock twitch. NO, oh NO, definitely NOT. He needed to get the hell away from here. Immediately.

"You sure?" the troll asked.

Pierce saw the male glance over at him out of his periphery, but he simply continued disposing of the glass in a large trash basin nearby. He could practically hear the female—Jo—grinding her teeth together as she crossed her arms. A smirk twitched at the corners of his mouth, but it didn't surface. Yeah, his mouth muscles hadn't worked that way in a very long time.

"Positive," she said.

"Alright." Without another word, the male left the alleyway.

The female turned around, bent over, and grabbed the edges of the wicker basket. "Thanks for the help, but I've got it from here."

Do not do it. Do not do it. Do not— "Are you sure? I do not mind helping you. And I will, of course, replace everything that I broke." And when Markham punished him for using pack funds for something that didn't pertain to the pack—like the king gave a shit about any of them—he was going to remember how stupid he was. Except right now, as her scent filled every synapse of his brain, the last thing he wanted was to move away from her. What in Hades' name was wrong with him? He did not act like this. Around anyone. Never.

With the basket in hand, she straightened to her full height of five-and-a-half feet. "What's your name?"

Standing upright in this form, he towered over three feet taller than her. *Do not give her your name. She does not need your name. This is going to get you into loads of trouble. You do not give your name out to anyone. Not one creature. Especially some random half-br*— "Pierce. What is yours?"

"Jocasta."

"Jocasta. That is a lovely name. Please, let me help you to where you are going. I will explain what happened and replace what broke." *NO, YOU WILL NOT! WHAT IN HADES' NAME ARE YOU DOING? THIS IS THE STUPIDEST THING YOU HAVE EVER DONE!* "Please. I feel terrible, and you should not have to pay for replacements because I was not watching where I was going." *WHY ARE YOU BEING SO NICE? YOU ARE NOT NICE.*

She blinked, then snickered and cleared her throat. As she cocked a hip out, that breathtaking smile tugged at the corners of her lips. "You've never been to the apothecary, have you? You don't have to answer that. I'm sure you haven't. Feel free to explain. I'd pay to see you talk to Kriah."

He rolled his eyes. "I am just trying to right my wrong. There is no need to goad me." Was she goading him? Did he care? No. Not really. And that was stupid. Idiotic. "And no, to answer your question, I have never been to the apothecary. It is not in my job description to visit apothecaries." Not that he ever followed his job description, at least to any degree, outside the village. Nor was he altogether sure what an apothecary was.

Her eyes raked over his body, and he almost couldn't hold back the growl that rose within him. She smirked. "I'm not the type to goad. I call it as I see it. And no offense, Pierce, in your job description or not, a big, tall male like you talking to a... well, it's priceless."

Oh, he did not want to *talk* at all. Not really. Far from it. He wanted to push Jocasta against the wall, pin her arms above her head, and put his face right between her—*OH, HELL NO.* What in Hades' name was *wrong* with him? Her grip tightened on the basket, and all he could think was that he wanted that grip somewhere else on him. *NO.*

"While I appreciate you trying to right your wrong, I can handle it myself."

Oh, he bet she could... Oh, for fuck's sake. He had to get out of here before he did something genuinely idiotic. "You know what?" He raised his hands for a moment and forced himself to take a step back. "It is just as well. I cannot afford to help you. I was merely trying to give into the nicer instincts I usually cannot exhibit. It will not happen again. I have helped you clean up, which is more than I should have done. You should carry on now, as should I."

But he didn't turn away, no matter how much he should. He couldn't seem to look away from those eyes of hers. He couldn't move away from her intoxicating scent that grew stronger, deepened, and invaded his senses the longer they stood here like this. Suddenly, she tossed the basket to the side and got into his face. Was she suicidal? Or did the brand on his shoulder just mean absolutely nothing to her? Oh, gods. A growl rested on the tip of his tongue, and he had to resist the urge to lick his lips.

"Good. Forget your nicer instincts because I don't need them. You can forget we ever met."

She stood there, stared up at him with her feet planted shoulder-width apart and her hands at her sides. Gods, she was breathtaking, her body just the type he would want to wrap his own around, run his hands all over, bury his face in—he gave himself a hard, mental shake.

"You do not want me to forget my nicer instincts." Hades, had he said that out loud? Yup. He had. He inhaled deep, the intensity of her scent caused his brain to misfire. A rumble of pure lust sounded deep in his chest. Her scent thickened. The aroma of arousal filled the air. No, he couldn't—oh, but he wanted to. "And I do not think that forgetting you would be possible, in all honesty. Though it would be an intelligent move on my part. But I am sure after you have had a good laugh with your clan, it will be easy for you to forget about me."

"My clan?" Jocasta scoffed as she folded her arms across her chest. She opened her mouth, then snapped it shut, inhaled and exhaled a deep breath, then unfolded her arms again. Her gaze softened. "I wouldn't laugh at you, Pierce. Ever. And forgetting you, it would be intelligent for both of us, but you are kind of unforgettable."

"Yes, clan, or whatever you call it. Forgive me for not knowing the proper vernacular. In my species, we call our group a pack." *SHUT. UP.* He clenched his hands into fists to prevent himself from reaching out to touch her. *YOU WILL NOT TOUCH HER.*

He looked her over from head to toe, committing every detail to memory. Her crimson hair flowed over her bare shoulders, a green sleeveless shirt that went around her neck hugged her torso, flashes of pink merfolk scales were visible between the bottom of the shirt and the top of her dark blue pants, and her feet were birdlike in appearance. His tongue slid just barely out of his mouth—damn thing had a mind of its own, just like something else on him—and licked over his lips. He would *much* prefer to run his tongue over parts of her body—many parts.

"Unforgettable, am I?" By all the gods, he smirked. He didn't smirk, not like this, not out of amusement.

"Hybrids. In our village, we just call ourselves hybrids." Her gaze dropped to his lips for a split second before she flicked her eyes back to his. She opened her mouth, but it was a minute before anything came out. "We prefer to go by our given names in my village."

"I see. In my village, I know your kind as half-breeds. But I felt that might be offensive." Not a term he'd ever enjoyed. His ears pricked up. Derrick was coming. "I have to go." But he didn't move. *GO. NOW.* But he didn't. He couldn't.

"I'm—" Her words cut off as the sound of Derrick's footsteps drew nearer. She stepped away from him and picked up the basket she'd tossed aside.

He forced himself not to move back toward her. All he wanted to do was bring their bodies closer together again, as close as possible.

"Zancle's Rock."

"What?"

"It's where I work. I don't think this is the last we'll see each other, Pierce," Jocasta said as she slowly backed down the alleyway, her gaze still on him.

He just nodded. It wouldn't be the least bit safe—for either of them—for him to seek her out. However, he knew he would. Whatever he was feeling, his body would push him to act. "Do not expect to see me." With great effort, he stepped back.

She stopped in her tracks, her eyes reflecting nothing but hurt. Gods, it felt like a dagger pierced his chest at that look. She heaved a deep breath and then tucked her hair behind one of her pointed wolf ears. He froze. *Holy Hades, what?* How on earth had he missed that?

"Goodbye." She let the word hang and then spun on her heel. "Pierce," she muttered as she started forward.

"Jocasta! Wait!" He lunged forward and grabbed her wrist. A tingling buzz shot up his arm at the contact. Not that he cared. He turned her around to face him, but kept a hold of her wrist. She yanked and pulled to release his grip. But he'd be damned if he was letting go right now. "Who are you?"

"It's better that you don't know."

"It is a little too late for that." She said nothing, just continued to pull her arm away from his. He hated he couldn't let her go. Not yet. Not until he knew. He knew that coloring, but it could not be. "I will not report you." Which would get him killed, but he knew with complete certainty that he would never reveal her.

She visibly swallowed. "I'm Galenus's daughter."

He dropped her wrist like it was on fire. Cursing himself to Hades and back, he ran a hand over his head as his tail flicked with agitation. Oh, this was bad. So terrible. Derrick was almost here. He would say nothing. This was far too dangerous. "Am I the only shape shifter you have met here?"

"Yes." She shook her hand out and tugged her hair back over her ear. "I avoid shape shifters here. And they don't exactly come to the bar."

Derrick would say nothing, but it was better not to risk it. "Go. I will find you. Go," Pierce said.

With a quick nod, she walked away. Pierce watched her every second until she disappeared from his sight. Every instinct he had screamed at him to follow her, not to let her move away from him. But he had to. At least, for now. Reluctantly turning around, he went to meet back up with Derrick. They had work to do.

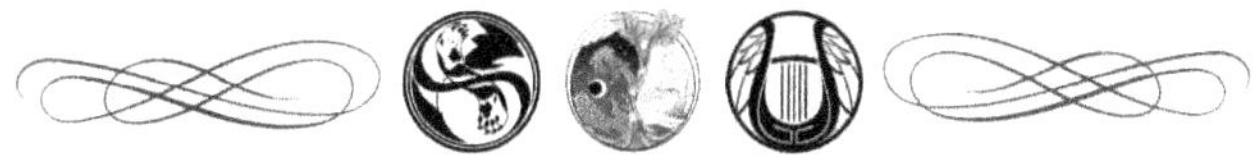

Jo practically ran back to Mystique Herbs. She pushed through the crowd milling about the market like her ass was on fire. With ragged breaths, she shoved the door open and closed it shut as she leaned against it. Her grip tightened on the handle of the empty basket. Her gaze barely focused on Kriah propped up against the counter as she attempted to collect herself.

Kriah's eyebrows knitted together. "Is everything alright?"

Good gods, what was wrong with her? Her sister had just returned after a few days of being gone, and she did something so idiotic. Her breaths finally settled. Jo pushed off the door and lifted the basket. Tiny flakes of herbs coated its bottom, along with a few wet spots. "I..." she squeaked out. Jo shook her head and attempted the words again. "I had an accident." Her gaze zeroed in on the basket. Had he picked out all the glass? No glass shards remained. Frowning, she shifted her gaze to the nymph. The female had always been kind, regardless of the few times she'd come in over the years.

"Accidents happen, but is that all that seems to have you so flustered? Or is there something more?" She swept her juniper-colored hair behind her pointed ear. Stepping away from the counter, Kriah picked up a stool, her dress shimmering with her movements, and set it to the side of the counter.

Standing there, Jo didn't budge at all until the female patted the stool, inviting her over. "I just feel awful about it." And it had nothing to do with dropping the basket. It had everything to do with revealing her secret. He was a shape shifter. By all means, if he followed his laws, he'd report her.

And she would be dead. Years. She had hidden her ears for years, and, in one stupid move, she'd screwed all of that up. There had to be something wrong with her.

"I will have Adrian get you another basket with the other half of your order, and we'll take that one to inspect for damage." She took the empty basket from Jo's hands and disappeared into the back. Returning a few moments later, Kriah came back with a glass kettle of water and two mugs. She placed the mugs on the counter, set the kettle on the single burner, and lit it. "I thought some lavender tea might be good."

"Why? Do you think it'll cure stupidity?" Jo groaned. So what if she found him attractive. She shouldn't. Shape shifter and half shape shifter didn't mix. There was a reason she avoided them. Her life depended on it.

"Well, maybe not stupidity, but it can certainly help you see a situation differently."

"I don't think there's another way to see this situation." She'd been out-right stupid. There was no way around that. Revealing her truth to a male she'd found—oh, good gods, he wasn't that hot! Yes, he was. *Shut up.* It didn't matter how attractive she thought Pierce was. Nothing, absolutely *nothing*, could happen between them. It would be entirely too dangerous. Gods, she could use a spirit. A good Ice Moon would be great, but that was back at the bar.

"Are you certain about that?" Kriah asked. It didn't take long for the water to get going. She pulled a small bottle out from beneath the counter, along with two tea bags. First, she placed a bag, then poured a little from the bottle, followed by hot water into each cup. Finally, Kriah slid a mug of tea over to her.

Her gaze fell to the spiked tea as she let it steep a bit. Gods, what was she thinking? She had to get this male out of her head. Nothing good would come from them getting to know one another. Still, this would be great. A fantastic deterrent from the crap running through her head. "Either you're a mind reader, Kriah, or Ambrosia talks too much." Not that she'd ever decline a spirit. Jo cracked a slight smile as she lifted the cup of tea to her lips. "Now, that's my kind of drink."

"Ambrosia talks as much as she needs to." A small chuckle left Kriah's mouth as she shut the burner down and picked up her mug. "Though that does not change how pale you look. If I did not know better, I would think you had seen a guiler."

Holding the cup in front of her face, Jo hardly concealed the smirk. That was the polite way of saying Am was a talker. There was a reason her twin worked the bar and the crowd while she remained comfortable in her booth and took care of the music. "That would've been easier," she muttered and sipped more of the tea. If only she *had* seen a guiler. They didn't travel into the market that often, but she could handle that at least. No. She had to run smack dab into a gorgeous—no, he wasn't, but tall, that was accurate—male shape shifter.

"Oh? So, you ran into something worse?"

"You could say that." Taking another sip of the tea, Jo nodded to Kriah. The female's husband, Adrian, a ten-foot troll, stepped out into the front room and set a fresh basket of the replacement items on the counter.

At least she wasn't thinking about all the dirty—nope, she wasn't going there. Not. At. All. Jo cleared her throat. She needed to get back to the bar. And she wouldn't talk about the situation any longer. They'd never see one another again. He'd never come looking for her at Zancle's, so it didn't matter. Jo sat there in silence as she finished the tea. "Thank you, Kriah. I appreciate the tea. What do I owe you for the replacements?"

"Well, you and your sister are one of my best customers. Seeing as you were ruffled, perhaps a third of our normal price."

She snickered at the pun. That amused her. "Thanks, Kriah."

"Of course." The female grinned. "I would not wish your booth to remain empty for too long."

Jo chuckled and took care of the payment. "You know I live to party." Her nerves settled. She picked up the basket and left. This time, it was easier to head through the maze of back alleys to the bar. Especially as she paid attention to exactly where she walked, ensuring a second accident didn't occur. Of all the years she'd made that short trek, not one had happened. At least now she wasn't thinking—oh, gods—yes, she was! Seriously, she needed to get that pair of ruby eyes out of her head. Now! Forcing the image of Pierce from her mind, Jo opened the front door to Zancle's Rock and strode inside.

Ambrosia jumped from behind the bar. "There you are!" She rushed over to Jo, took the basket from her, and set it aside on the closest table. Then, clasping Jo's hands in her own, she squeezed tight. "Are you okay? Bruce told me what happened."

Stupid troll. He couldn't just mind his own business. "I'm fine. It was no big deal. I handled it." Mostly. Sort of. Not really. Oh, yeah, she handled it all right. In the worst way possible, but she refused to admit any of that to her sister. Otherwise, the female would never leave her alone.

"Are you sure? I mean, really sure." Ambrosia narrowed her eyes and stared her down.

"I'm positive. Now, if you have no more questions, I'm going back to my booth. I've got prep work to do." Jo patted her sister's hand and walked away. Yeah, she lied through her teeth. Even if the female didn't believe her, she wouldn't utter another question. It wasn't as if they'd spoken of her three-day hiatus from work or disappearance from home; they wouldn't discuss that. At least not for tonight.

Chapter Fourteen

Not having anything else to do, Devin made her way to the marketplace and lazily perused through the shops and vendors. Gabby wasn't in a good place at all. Her miscarriage after the unexpected child had hit her extremely hard. Derrick had been quieter than usual, which didn't surprise her, but she hoped he could control his emotions better in the village. All it took was one slip.

While Devin had comforted Gabby again last night, the female had let it slip that she'd promised to go to the marketplace for Gavin. He'd wanted something to give to his mate, but didn't know what to get her, what she might like. He was still under seclusion in the village, unable to leave, and the little Gabby had spoken to him—out by Ryn River before their father had found her—she'd promised she would go for him, so he could take it to Parthenia the next time he saw her. She'd wanted to raise his spirits. Then she'd miscarried. Devin had told her she would take care of it.

She had no clue what to get either. She hadn't even known the male had a mate. But a trip to the marketplace had seemed like an excellent way to pass the time. Plus, she could pick up some things for Aradia while she was here.

Passing in front of a shop door, she paused in her steps, and then backtracked. She ignored the few curious stares she got as she weaved her way through the other creatures. It wasn't altogether common for females of her species to travel outside their boundaries—especially alone—but that had never deterred her. Or Gabby. Though Gabby's father didn't allow it, Devin's did. It made a difference.

The front door she stood in front of was a pretty plum color. How had she never noticed it before? Looking up, she read the shop's name—*The Four Muses*. Shrugging, she opened the door and went inside. There was a counter at the back of the store with a bright red curtain behind it. Shelves lined the remaining walls. Earrings were on the left wall, necklaces on the right, and two enormous cases sat toward the front full of rings.

She went to the right first. Jewelry hadn't ever interested her, not that their king permitted it in the village anyway, but Gabby learned from Gavin that Parthenia liked color. Particularly red and green. Pausing in front of one section, Devin stared at a piece set with an azure stone. It was rather beautiful. Everything here was exquisite.

The clicking sound of hooves against the wooden floor from behind the curtain reached her ears. A half-humanoid female stepped into the room. She grumbled slightly as a hoof got caught in the bright red material of the curtain. Coarse brown fur covered the lower half of her body. Her bright champagne eyes lit up. "Oh, hello. Welcome, welcome. All pieces here are unique. Please tell me if you do not see what you are looking for. I create to order."

Devin faced the female. "Hello. Honestly, I do not know what I am looking for." She gave a soft laugh. "I am looking for something for my close friend's brother to give to his mate. It is a bit of a long story. But neither could come into the market today, so I volunteered."

"Oh! Mates are my specialty. Tell me, tell me their names, my dear." The female beamed and tucked some wisps of brown hair behind her ears.

It was uncommon for her to meet someone so difficult *not* to smile around. And normally she wouldn't share names, but some instinct inside her told her to trust the woman. "His name is Gavin, and hers is Parthenia. They are true mates and very much in love."

"Oh, yes. They sound it. Hmm, let me think." She tapped her chin, and her heels clicked as she wandered around the store. "No, no. Special, yes, yes. Nothing I have, though, perhaps... green eyes? Yes?"

How could the woman know that? She hadn't described either of them. "Are you, by chance, psychic?"

The female giggled. "I will never tell."

As if that wasn't answer enough. "Yes, he has green eyes. Emerald. His mate is especially partial to red as well. Particularly the color of poppies. That is the extent of my knowledge, though."

She held up a finger. "I have just the thing. A piece I only completed today."

"Thank you. May I look around some more while you get it?"

"Oh, yes, yes, of course." With that, she turned, and her hooves clicked against the floor as she disappeared into the back again.

Devin browsed the shelves and cases, just taking in all the variety. There was a bit of everything. Almost every gemstone she knew of appeared in several pieces. She turned around when the clop of the female's hooves reached her ears. "You are an artist. Your work is beautiful."

"Oh, thank you." She held out a necklace with a green chain and a red rose pendant. "I believe this will be perfect."

Devin gently accepted it and eyed the piece. "I believe you are right. This is quite beautiful." She squinted, and then her eyes widened. The female had carefully engraved Parthenia's and Gavin's initials on one petal. She had to look closely to see them, but they were there. "Tell me you just put those on there. Because if they were there before I came in here, I may come back and have you tell me my future," she joked.

Pressing her finger to her lips, the female smiled. "Shh. It will be our little secret."

"I will never tell a soul." She made the mark of an X over her heart with her finger. "Cross my heart. Regardless of whether you read my future, I plan to return here. You have a beautiful place. Now, what do I owe you for the necklace?"

"Oh, no charge. You come back, and we will call it even."

"Are you sure I cannot pay you? Or I travel all over. Is there something I could bring you next time I come in?"

"Oh, yes. I am certain. I believe everything will make itself known in time. You come back, and I believe we can come to an arrangement."

She tilted her head in question. "Arrangements?"

"Oh, yes. I work on a barter system."

Despite not understanding what the female referred to, Devin nodded. "Well. I plan to return. I am already looking forward to it. Thank you very much for the necklace."

"You are quite welcome." The female turned toward the main counter and disappeared behind the curtain.

Devin stood there for another moment with the sudden realization that she hadn't asked the female her name. Somehow, though, she had a feeling the female knew hers. Tucking the necklace into her bag, she made her way out. She had already spent far too long in the marketplace and needed to head home. On her way, she stopped and left the necklace in the treehouse for Gavin to find, along with a note, then returned to the village.

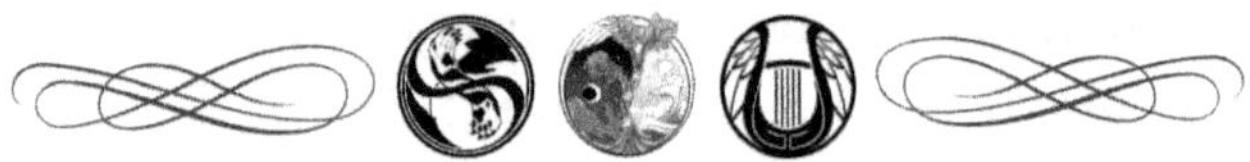

Jo rolled her eyes at the question her sister shot into her brain. Really? Fine, she'd check. She could use the distraction. A day had passed since she'd seen Pierce, and she still couldn't get him out of her head. Maybe if she numbed her mind a little, she could get rid of all these inappropriate thoughts. Leaving the comfort of her karaoke booth, she walked over to the bar, leaned over the counter with a slight hop, and scanned the bottles. She snagged the nearly empty Ice Moon and a shot glass before dropping to her feet. *Yep, the Ice Moon is out,* she replied to her sister through their shared mindlink.

The hair on the nape of her neck prickled, summoning her attention to the door. Her gaze fell on Pierce. The male leaned just part-way inside the door, staring right at her. He nodded his head in the alley's direction and then eased the door shut.

Caught off guard, Jo stood there. He'd disappeared as quickly as he'd appeared. However, he wasn't an apparition or something she'd conjured in her mind—outside; this was a bad idea on so many levels.

"Put it back," Am called out.

Setting the bottle and empty shot glass on the counter, she waved off her twin. "I'm stepping out for a few." Bad idea. But her body took full control. Jo strolled out of the bar and stopped just outside the door.

Pierce's low voice came from the alley next to the bar, but she had no problem hearing him. She'd inherited her advanced hearing from her father. "I can smell you. If you do not want to meet with me, stay where you are, and I will go."

"Not wanting to meet with you isn't the problem." She wanted to meet with him. The sound of his voice told her exactly where he was, and she turned in that direction. He paced the shadows in his animal form.

"I would beg to differ, but I am here all the same."

The material of the long-sleeved, low-cut, white blouse she wore tugged as she crossed her arms. It had a deep plunge and revealed more of her pink scales than the top she'd had on when they'd first met. "So, either we continue with our lives, or we figure this out. Whatever it is."

"I cannot stop thinking about you," he blurted. "You have invaded my mind."

That really shouldn't please her, yet it did. She glanced over her shoulder and moved closer to where Pierce hid. The last thing she needed was for her twin to pop her head out. "Nor can I stop thinking about you."

"I have never been in a relationship with anyone. While I have had relations with females, I have never committed to anyone. I cannot commit to you. This entire situation is dangerous, and we should both avoid it at all costs. If it is discovered that I have not reported you to my King, let alone that I have spoken at length with you, it will mean great punishment for me. Maybe even death. That being said,"—He took a deep breath—"I cannot get you out of my mind. You are all I can think about. And I cannot walk away and not see you again. Speak to you. Smell you." His last words rolled out in a low growl.

She didn't like the idea of him with another female. But at least he was honest. It was more than she could say for most males she interacted with daily. People in her village knew of her heritage if they'd known her father. One person knew of it directly. Then again, he'd seen her naked, so they had next to no secrets. She'd never tell him about this. "Canosa Ridge. It has a waterfall I visit a few times a week."

He raised his head and met her gaze. "You should not tell me this. We should not encourage this. You should tell me to walk away and never come near you again."

"I should ..." She dropped her hands to her hips. "And then I think about how you've taken over my dreams. How the idea of you with another female makes my blood boil. That the thought of forcing myself to be with another male makes me sick to my stomach and breaks me in half. Tell me you don't feel any of that, and I'll tell you to hit the road."

"I cannot tell you any of that. And I should not say what is on my mind right now." He briefly squeezed his eyes shut and then leveled his ruby eyes on her. "I know the place. When will you be there?"

She raised an eyebrow. Her curiosity almost got the best of her, but she stopped short of asking what thoughts danced across his brain. Her twin was still inside, and she could come looking for her any minute. Or pop into her head. That would be just as bad. "Tomorrow, after morning meal."

"I will try to be there."

"Until then." She turned to walk away and halted. Not that she knew why or what had prompted her.

He stared at her. Though he said nothing, he strode toward her. In his current form, he only stood a few inches taller than her. As he moved closer and she took a step back, he shifted to his humanoid form. He towered over her now, as he had the day before, and kept pressing forward until he backed her up against the wall. He bent down slowly and put his face in her neck, drawing in a deep breath. "I think it may just be the ultimate torture waiting until then," he whispered in her ear. He turned away and disappeared from the alley without another word.

Jo swallowed. It took every ounce of strength she had not to melt to the ground. Having him that close against her neck and body was torturous, all right. As she gawked at the surrounding emptiness, her sister piped up in her head. "Yeah, yeah." She glanced one last time to where Pierce had occupied and ambled back inside.

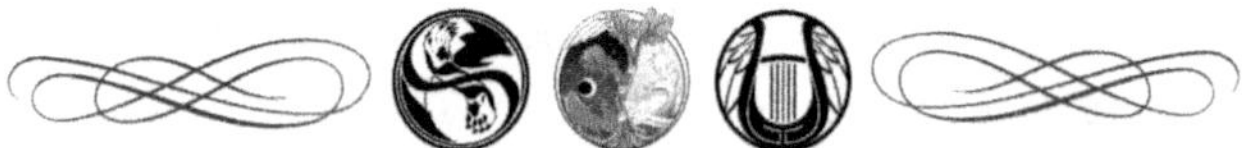

Gavin lay on the ground behind his family's hut, his head leaning against the side of it. The sun had set a while ago. At least it was springtime. The nights weren't cold, but comfortable. His stomach rumbled. His father allowed him no food unless he caught it himself, and he'd only caught two fish in the river this afternoon. But at least he had water.

Though he tried to shut out his parents' words, it didn't help. No walls, nor his paws over his ears kept the discussion from reaching him. Not even his mother's soft tone.

"Gembert, can you not at least let him inside? Please? He has been punished enough."

"Has he? Has your precious little male been punished enough, Gemma?"

"I think so, yes."

His father growled a laugh. "*You* think?"

"It was too much. Whatever he has done, it should not have warranted that."

"He should have received more."

"He was near death, Gembert. He faced *three*."

"He seemed perfectly fine to me when he returned—fully healed."

"Gabriella needs him right now. She is hurting. She could use his comfort," his mother whispered.

"I do not care! He disgraced me! He disgraced me, and he disgraced this family! As he always does! I care not for her pain, nor yours! I care not what he did!" His father crossed the room and smacked his mother. A thump followed. Gavin squeezed his eyes shut, barely acknowledging the tears that trickled down his cheeks. "He may have survived Markham's punishment, but mine is *not* over yet. And you will shut your mouth unless you want punishment as well."

"Is that what you want, Gembert? Truly? A submissive mate who cares nothing for her young?"

"You know exactly what I want."

His mother yelped. He couldn't take anymore. Moving around to the front of the hut, he banged hard on the door with his paw. It ripped open in seconds. His father stood there in his humanoid form. He saw his mother on the floor, in the doorway to her and his father's bedroom. She looked at him for only a moment. The apology in her eyes was loud enough she may as well have spoken the words. Then she turned her head away. Gabby laid on her pallet in the corner, facing the wall. The scent of her tears reached him where he stood, but she didn't say anything, glance his way, or even turn over.

"What in Hades' name do you want?" his father growled.

Using the mindlink that came with all twins, Gavin dropped the barrier he kept up only long enough to send his sister a telepathic message. Her walls were strong, but he sent it anyway, just in case. *Gabby, I love you. Everything will be alright. We will make everything okay. I promise you.* He shielded his mind again, then glared up at his father. "If you are angry at me, take it out on me. Leave them be."

"I will do as I please—"

"Take it out on me!"

"—and that does not include speaking to you. Get out of my doorway. Before I shove you out of it."

"Go ahead," he snarled.

Gembert bent down, putting his face close to Gavin's. "Unless you want me to take a bite out of you myself... Get. The. Fuck. Out. Of. My. Doorway."

Gavin let out a low growl. He wanted to do nothing more right now than bite down on his father's jugular. But he couldn't. His father was an Informant, though the male received few orders from Markham these days. Attacking an Informant, even his father—especially his father—would mean another punishment, harsher than the last. He couldn't return to Parthenia again, looking like he had. Or worse. He forced himself to step back.

"That is what I thought." Gembert slammed the door in Gavin's face, sliding the lock home.

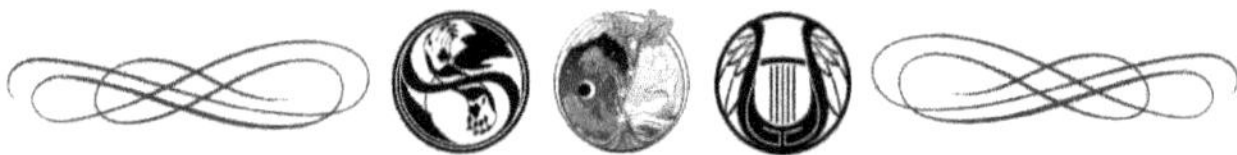

Pierce broke off from the group of Informant scouts like he usually did. He was grateful now that he'd long since made that a habit. No one questioned it when he diverted, all because he hadn't stopped thinking of Jocasta—the feel of her eyes upon him, her scent, the way her skin felt against his hand, and her voice. He had steered clear of Markham. That demon could read thoughts. Pierce could mindblock, but one could never be too careful. He'd gone about his duties, gone out scouting, supervised training when needed, and he'd thought of her. Her amber-colored eyes, crimson hair, pink scales around her hips, talons, and voice. Gods, her voice.

He should have told her yesterday he'd lied, and she hadn't been on his mind at all, that he hadn't thought about her day and night, reliving every single detail about her. Not that he would've told her he had given himself a hand job in the middle of the night while thinking about what it would be like to be with her, or that when he ejaculated, it was so intense he'd had to go to the river to wash.

He hadn't told her any of that. No. He'd agreed to meet her. He'd told her he would try to be here. All the while knowing there would be no way even the gods could keep him away.

It took some time for him to get to the falls. He stayed just behind the treeline when he made it there and spotted Jocasta. It was impossible not to watch her. She came up out of the water, brushing her hair out of her face, and he glimpsed her ears. His tail flicked back and forth. The water she was in wasn't deep, so she stood completely naked, and lust shot through him, hardening his entire body.

Water sluiced her bare skin and the scales covering her back, hips, and the top of her ass. Her breasts were full and plump, the tips erect. She had no hair anywhere on her body. His mouth opened as it became difficult to draw breath. Transforming to his humanoid form, he leaned against a tree, still unable to tear his eyes away from her as she dived back into the water. Oh, she was perfect. Just utterly perfect.

After he watched her for a while—longer than he should have, making him feel like a voyeur. He stepped out from the trees. "How does the water feel?" Though he tried to conceal his emotions, his erection was a bit more difficult to hide.

She stopped midway to the edge of the bank, narrowed her eyes ever so slightly, and licked her lips. "Perfect."

"Is it?" He stepped closer. His instincts pulled him in two *very* opposite directions. This was against the laws and could put them both in grave danger. But he couldn't have cared less. Whatever *this* was, whatever it would end up being, he wanted her.

He needed her in his arms, her body wrapped around his, their mouths and tongues all over each other. He needed to drive his cock deep inside her, hear her call out his name. Not that it would come to that. Nope, it would *not* happen. He would keep his self-control.

"Yes, it is." Her voice was husky as she responded. She swam forward until her feet hit the floor of the basin. Slowly, Jocasta stood. The water came to just above her hips. Droplets trickled down her skin. Her hooded gaze raked over his body from his ears, tail, the length of his cock, and his legs. Her ears twitched. "Are you going to stand there and stare? Or do you plan to join me?"

Joining her was a bad idea. *Do not join her,* he repeated to himself, over and over. But as the water slid down her body, teasing her breasts and dripping down her belly until it pooled in her naval, his self-control completely snapped. "I am not much of a swimmer. But swimming is very far from my mind right now." He strode closer. "If my intentions are not clear, tell me now, and I will be as descriptive as I need to be. If it is not something you want, then tell me to stop. Because if I come any closer to you, with the way you look and smell right now, I cannot stop what my body wants."

Her nipples pebbled. She gripped one of her shoulders and bit her bottom lip. "I don't recall saying anything about swimming."

Pierce growled and closed the distance between them. Joining her in the water, he practically yanked her up into his arms. His hands gripped her ass as her legs wrapped around his waist, and he crushed his lips to hers.

Jocasta moaned as she deepened the kiss, swiping her tongue along the inside of his mouth. Her arms came around his shoulders. She shuddered.

He slid a hand up into her hair, gripping it firmly, but not enough to hurt her. Their tongues twisted and clashed together. Her breasts pressed against his chest and her nails dug into his shoulders. His cock was so hard she probably could've perched on it, and it would have held her weight. Tilting her head to the side, he trailed kisses down her neck, and then leaned her back, taking her breast into his mouth.

"Harder."

As the scent of her arousal thickened, he growled against her skin. He sucked and licked at her breasts as he fisted a handful of hair, drawing a moan out of her. Stroking his tongue up her neck, he nibbled on her throat. "Do you like it rough, Jocasta?"

"Yes," she cried out. She dug her nails more into his shoulder blades and tightened her grip around his waist.

Pierce strode to the land. Picking her up off his waist, he put her down on the ground on all fours. He got behind her, lying on his stomach because of their height difference. Gently pushing her head down, he made her ass lift higher and spread her cheeks. Extending his tongue, he licked her slit from end to end. A deep rumble resounded in his chest as her taste exploded on his tongue. She moaned in ecstasy, bending closer to the earth.

He plunged his tongue inside her sex and held her in place. The noises she made as he devoured her had his cock pulsing. He slid a hand around her leg, found her nub, and rubbed it hard and fast.

"Oh, gods! Pierce!"

It didn't take long for her orgasm to fill his mouth. He let out a loud growl as he lapped up every drop. Keeping his hand right where it was, still rubbing her, he kneeled behind her. He slipped his cock between her thighs, brushing against her slick sex. Fisting a handful of her hair, he pulled her up so her back was against his chest. He licked up her neck and nipped her ear. "I enjoy it very much when you say my *name*." Emphasizing his point, he drew his hips back a little and drove his cock inside her. A loud growl left him when her sex fully sheathed him. "Hades, you are tight."

The walls of her sex quivered. Her entire body clenched as she grabbed his shoulders and curled her feet against the back of his thighs, splitting her legs wider. "I enjoy saying it."

"Then say it again." He bit down on her shoulder, though not enough to leave indents or break the skin. He wasn't marking her. That was something he couldn't—and wouldn't—do. This could never be that. Cupping his hands over her breasts, he pistoned in and out of her, hard and unrelenting.

Her talons scratched lightly at his thighs as she dug her nails into his biceps. Meeting him thrust for thrust, she cried out, "Oh, gods! Don't stop, Pierce! Don't stop!"

He did exactly as she asked. Demanded, more like, which he thoroughly enjoyed. Releasing his hold on her shoulder, he lifted her off his dick, turned her around and slammed his cock into her sex. He leaned her back, clenched her hips, and moved her up and down his shaft, hard and fast. His growls seemed to go on without end. Her body fit more perfectly around his than anyone he had ever been inside. More than that, though, this felt perfect and everything else he could not allow himself to feel.

She gripped his upper-arms as another orgasm rocked through her core and pulsated around his cock. "Oh, gods! Pierce!"

A burst of pleasure more powerful than any he'd ever had exploded from him. He held her against him as his head fell back, and he howled. Something he'd never done before during sex, but not something he could deny doing either. His orgasm seemed to go on forever. Her cum drizzled down his leg. When their mutual release ended, he collapsed to the ground with her on top of him. "I want you to clean me up." With his hand on the back of her neck, he fused their lips in a hard kiss.

Jocasta responded to the kiss with desperation. Her ears twitched, and she nipped at his bottom lip as she pulled back. She sucked on his neck and raked her nails down his chest, inching down his body until she reached the part of his leg coated with her cum. She licked up the insides of both of his thighs, sucked each of his balls into her mouth, and fully lathered them up with her saliva. Once she'd done a thorough job, she stroked the length of his shaft with her tongue, paying particular attention to the head of his cock.

Pierce's head fell back, and he let out a loud moan. Gods, she was an artist with that tongue of hers. His claws dug into the ground beneath him, and he put his free hand on the back of her head, guiding her up and down his cock as she licked and sucked his length. "Oh, yes, that is right. Do not stop." How he could have another orgasm inside of him so soon, he didn't know, but it wasn't going to take her long to draw it out of him.

She grazed his shaft ever so slightly with her teeth and then sucked him in again. Grabbing a hold of his thigh, she slid her fingers inside her folds. Jocasta moaned as he exploded in her mouth. Swallowing every bit of him she could, she rode her fingers to another release.

A sight he hadn't torn his eyes away from for one second. As soon as she'd swallowed the last drop of his orgasm, he dragged her over his face and drove his tongue inside her. He licked every inch of her sex, inside and out, thoroughly cleaning her off before running his tongue up her inner thighs. Once he'd finished, he laid her on his chest, so their eyes met. He swept his tongue across his lips; her taste still humming against his tastebuds. "Well. I have to say. That was a tad bit unexpected." No, it wasn't. He smirked, and a chuckle escaped him. When was the last time he'd laughed? At anything?

"I'll say."

"I would be lying if I said I did not want to do this again. You are too perfect not to get another taste." Pierce punctuated his words by stroking her neck with his tongue and nibbling on her ear, which made it twitch.

She nipped at his bottom lip. "You aren't so bad yourself. And I'd enjoy another taste."

He growled against her. Laying his head back down, he regarded her with a faint smile. How was that possible? Maybe because he'd just had the best sex and beyond that he'd ever had in his life. "So. How are we going to do this? And, just for the record, I did only come here originally to talk." *Liar. Such a liar.* "But I do not think I have to tell you I do not regret this one bit."

"I don't either. I'm here a few times a week to maintain the moisture of my scales. Or there's an inn in the marketplace."

"I cannot, and will not, risk us being seen together in the marketplace. We have done that enough, and it would be detrimental for both of us should anyone catch us. Others would question why I was visiting the inn, too." He shook his head. "I will come here, as long as it is isolated. Do others visit here as well?" As he spoke, he caressed her sides and hips.

Her head rested in the crook of his neck. "My sister and I are the only ones who come out here. The other half merfolk in our village prefer the salt waters surrounding the isle."

"Tell me when you will be here without your sister, and I will come." He snickered at the double entendre. "I will tell no one where I am going. It is not uncommon for me to go on scouting missions solo." Shit. He hadn't meant to say that. Not that she'd said one thing about the brand on his right shoulder, but if she hadn't known what it meant before, he'd just done an excellent job of revealing its meaning. His position within the pack could make things complicated between them. More so than things already were.

Her body stilled. She shot up off his chest and climbed out of his arms. "I need to clean up."

His entire body hardened, but not with lust this time. He made no move to get up off the ground. "Is there any point in me trying to explain myself? Or should I just go?"

Jocasta stopped and stood at the edge of the water. Her body tensed as she repressed the threatening tears he could already smell, and her shoulders steeled as she spun around to face him. "Go ahead. Explain."

Pierce sat up slowly and rested his arms against his knees. "I was not given my position by choice. Regardless, it is my position. Though I outwardly appear to follow orders, it is not my reality. I know what my pack leader is, and I know what he does. I have no power to take him down, and I have younger sisters to protect. Our father will not protect them. He is too far gone; evil has consumed him. I have already lost my brother. He is not dead, but he is lost to me. I may have to work in the shadows and risk myself, and I will not lie to you and say that I have never killed. But I have never taken a life where a true crime has not been committed. I do not shed blood based on genetics."

She stood there in silence for a moment. "I understand. Family is everything."

"They are. And I must protect what family I have left. Trust me, if I truly followed Markham's ways and his orders, fucking you is not what I would have done when I got here. Despite how I feel when I am in your presence." And out of it. The fact remained she was constantly on his mind while he was awake, as well as in his dreams. But he didn't say that out loud.

Jocasta smirked. "If I had heeded my father's warnings, I would've never revealed myself to you, regardless of my attraction to you." She paused a moment. "Every other day. Always after morning meal. That's how often I'm here."

He nodded as he rose to his feet. "I will come when I can." Crossing to where she stood, he placed his hand on the back of her neck and pulled her against him, crushing her lips in a hard kiss. His tongue plunged inside her mouth, entangling with hers as if they'd never get enough of one another. It was more than just a kiss. He staked a claim. A demand that she belonged to no one else.

When he broke the kiss, Pierce stepped back from her. He had to leave her now. The mere thought made it difficult for him to draw breath. "Your father was a wonderful male. I did not know him well, but I knew that. He did not deserve what happened to him." Pierce shifted to all fours and turned, sprinting back into the trees. He had to get away from her right now. The more he stood in her presence, the more positive he was he would make a deadly mistake.

Chapter Fifteen

"What should we work with today?" Leo asked.

Jo scanned over the weapons at hand. For the last week, Pierce's words about her father haunted her. She needed a sparring session to figure out how to approach the subject. Although they'd gotten together a few times, she hadn't found the courage to ask him what he'd meant. They hadn't spoken much at all. At least not in so many words. Their bodies had practically sung. Even with the way he towered over her, they fit together perfectly. Not that she wanted to examine that too closely.

"Hey!" Leo snapped his fingers in her face. "You've got that far-off look again."

"No, I don't." She hadn't spaced out. Not at all. Her gaze refocused on the weapons. She'd started these sessions for a reason. After her father's death, her control over her life faltered. Trouble always found her at school, around the village, and occasionally at home. The slightest irritation set her off. Sparring gave her a way to harness those emotions.

He chuckled and crossed his arms. "Oh, yes, you did. I know that look. You hook up with somebody?"

"Excuse me?" Her eyes shot from the mixture of swords, daggers, and bamboo sticks to her friend and sparring partner.

"You had that same look when we were together."

Scoffing, she returned her attention to the board. "We had sex. Sex doesn't constitute a relationship." *Are you listening to yourself?* Sex. It was all she had with Pierce. Mind-blowing sex. Nothing more. Oh, gods, the thought alone had a vice grip around her heart. Shaking the feeling from her body, she went for her weapon of choice. Jo tossed a bamboo stick to Leo and picked one up for herself. Yeah, she needed this session.

"But one can start that way." He caught the bamboo stick and took his place in the sparring circle. "So, come on. Who's the lucky male?"

"You know damn well I have no interest in any male around here. Now, shut up and put your hands where your mouth is." The male had said more than enough for her liking. He had her thinking about things she didn't want to think about, especially when she had something to talk to Pierce about. Eighteen years had passed since her father's death. It was time she got some answers. If anyone knew something, he did. Right?

She hadn't been ready to address the topic any time in the last week. But she was now. She didn't care who was at fault—no, that wasn't true. Deep down, she suspected Markham held that helm. Her father's murder fell on his shoulders. None of the sparring sessions had ever been about revenge. They had been about defense—liar.

Of course they had. Revenge entered her mind several times over the years. She dreamed about driving a blade into the heart of her father's killer. It wouldn't bring him back, but it would satisfy her desire for retribution. Or so she believed.

The lack of knowledge. All the secrets surrounding her father's death. The few years she had been with him. That her mother would no longer talk about him. Her anger over the situation bubbled to the surface. Swinging the bamboo stick in her hand, Jo took up her fighting position opposite Leo.

"Even me?"

Her smirk served as an answer to Leo's idiotic question. Nothing more needed to be said. Let them begin.

"Spar!" Jo called out. She didn't give him any other warning as she moved against him. First, she swung the bamboo stick high, which he successfully dodged, then below, which he parried again. Then she feigned a thrust to the gut with the bo stick.

He stepped back, and Jo spun around and struck him in the side. Leo groaned but quickly regained his footing and switched positions with him as the aggressor. Turning the bo stick in his hands, he launched at her. Their weapons came together again at the top and the bottom. He brought the bo stick around and swung it from above.

Their sticks didn't collide. Instead, Leo's bo stick slammed into her arm. It didn't break, but bamboo was tough. She winced at the pain that radiated up her shoulder and growled. Jo lunged forward. Their bo sticks clashed together at the top, the bottom, overhead, and then again in several swift maneuvers. At the last second, she changed the direction of the overhead and jabbed him in the nose.

As the bamboo stick connected, blood splattered everywhere. Stepping back, Leo rubbed the blood from his face and nodded.

The direction of their sparring session shifted. Either that or Leo finally understood precisely how it had started. In sparring, one rule applied—no abilities. He couldn't use his water manipulation, and she couldn't camouflage. Everything else was on the table. Jo smirked. Not waiting wait for him to make a move, she leaped right into a full-on rotating swing with the bo stick, forcing Leo to keep stepping backward.

His feet hit the edge of the circle, and he ducked just before she lobbed his head off with the bamboo stick. Despite his evasiveness, he overlooked the follow-up as Jo smashed the bo stick into the back of his calves and knocked him off his feet.

Dropping the bo stick, Leo landed on the ground on his back.

Jo tossed her stick aside and jumped on top of him. She pulled on his shoulder and wrapped her legs around his biceps. Squeezing with her thighs, Jo grasped his forearm in her hands and angled her body.

A sickening pop filled the surrounding air, but it didn't stop her. She couldn't hear anything aside from the blood pounding in her ears. Out of nowhere, her back throbbed. The crack of the bo stick snapped her out of her blind rage. As pain shot down her spine, she released her grip on Leo's arm and rolled away onto her knees.

With a loud moan, Leo held the side of his arm. "Good gods, Jo! Were you trying to break my arm?"

A slight grimace crossed her face, and she rose to her feet. "I'm sorry, Leo. I just..." She had lost control. Her anger had taken over, and all she'd seen was her enemy. Shaking her head in shame, Jo exited the sparring circle.

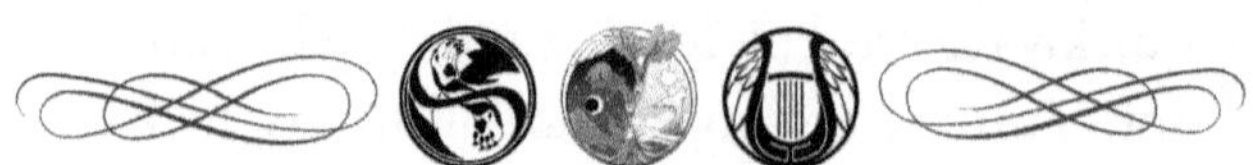

Jo wrung the water from her hair. She'd come to the waterfall earlier than usual, entirely skipping breakfast. The memories of her father's last day with them had crept up, altering the direction of the sparring session she had. Not that she blamed Leo for the bruises on her arm or the one on her back. The tank top covered that one.

It all started because of Pierce's comment about her father. It was time she asked him about what he'd said. Jo tossed her wet hair over her shoulder in her typical tank top and shorts. She heard the leaves rustle before he came through the trees in his humanoid form. Goddess, she'd wanted to see him, but she didn't want to have this conversation. She couldn't ignore it. Jo caught sight of his eyes first.

His eyes were never that dark. They had gone from the ruby red she enjoyed to a jet black. Was that anger she felt from him? That was strange. He stopped dead in his tracks, his gaze zeroing in on the bruises on her arm. "Who laid hands upon you?" he growled. "Tell me, and I will kill them where they stand."

"No one hurt me. I got them sparring."

"Sparring," he spat out. "Who were you sparring with, and how is it they do not understand how to be more careful? You can spar with a female and not leave marks such as those." His body shook as his claws dug into his palms.

The last thing either of them needed was him plowing into her village. Enraged would be ten times worse. And she wasn't going to give him her sparring partner's name. Inhaling a deep breath, she closed the distance between them and rested her hands on his forearms. His body stilled and his typical eye color slowly returned, but his fists hadn't unclenched.

"I don't blame my partner. The session got a little aggressive. That usually doesn't happen. My partner was just defending against me."

Pierce took slow, deep breaths, as though he had to force himself to calm down. "It angers me they marred your skin. Whatever the reason, whatever the situation." He took another deep breath. "It is probably an excellent thing that I was not present."

By the gods, she'd seen no one so furious. It wasn't the first time she'd gotten bruises from sparring, even if it was the first time she'd exposed Pierce to them. No one in her family ever reacted like this. Not her sister. Nor her mother. And she didn't spar with any of the females. None of them could keep up. At least they hadn't in years. She stroked the inside of his forearms. "Would it make you feel better if I told you my partner got it worse?"

"Maybe." His claws released from his palms. Tiny trickles of blood slid down the inside of his hands. Despite everything, one corner of his mouth lifted in a small smile. He stroked her cheek with the his knuckles. "I apologize for my anger."

Leo had gotten it worse, all right, because she'd broken his nose, possibly dislocated his shoulder, and nearly broke his arm. She leaned into Pierce's touch. "Just out of curiosity, is this a reaction I can expect if more bruises happen?"

"I do not know. Possibly. I have never reacted this way before. I have been angry, yes, but this is something new."

All unfamiliar territory. Apparently, for both of them. She supposed there was only one way to find out. Gods, this was a dangerous line to walk. Tightening her grip on his forearms, she continued stroking them with her thumbs. She opened her mouth and snapped it shut. Maybe she didn't have to tell him about the bruises on her back. There was no guarantee he'd see them. After all, she wanted to talk to him about his words a week ago. But what if they ended up naked, and he saw the bruises on her back? Goddess, she didn't know if one way was better than the other. She sighed. It was just best if she told him. "Okay. Well, I need you to stay calm. I have a couple of other bruises; other than the ones on my arm."

He let out a snarl, and his claws clamped down on his palms. "Show me."

Maybe she shouldn't have said anything, but it was too late now. Inhaling a deep breath, she released her hold on Pierce's arms and turned around. She swept her hair over her shoulder and lifted the back of her tank top. The black and blue marks angled across the middle of her back. If Ambrosia hadn't said anything, she wouldn't have even known they were there.

Her hands clenched at the snarl that came out of Pierce's mouth. She'd heard nothing so loud. It reaffirmed her decision not to utter one word about the identity of her sparring partner. And that she may want to ease up a little or learn to use weapons that didn't leave marks. Maybe both.

He took deep breaths, one after another. Several moments passed before he spoke. "Are. There. More."

Jo let her tank top fall back into place and faced him. His eyes were black again. "No. That's it."

He nodded, inhaled and exhaled a few more times before his eyes returned to their ruby red shade. "I need a moment." He moved around her and walked to the water's edge. Pierce just stood there, staring off into space, continuing those slow, deep breaths. After several long minutes, he kneeled and washed the blood from his hands.

Jo sat on a nearby boulder and waited. What else could she do? Go up to him and wrap her arms around his waist. Comfort him. Why would she do that? They were bruises, for crying out loud. They weren't the first she'd ever gotten and were unlikely to be the last. The urge to hold him made no sense to her. Yes, he'd gotten upset and threatened to kill Leo. What was this feeling about? All she'd done was learn to protect herself. "I broke his nose," she said, though she didn't understand why she offered the information.

"Good." His voice sounded off, rough and heavy with emotion that didn't make a single bit of sense. "It eases me to know you can defend yourself. And that it was a sparring session, not self-defense."

Something about what he said struck her—self-defense. She clasped her hands together in her lap. "Is that something you have to do? In the village? Defend yourself?"

"Not me. I have made sure I am feared, so it has never been much of an issue. Others, yes."

At least she didn't have to worry about that. Not that she should, but she did. Unwilling to explore the feeling too much, she thought back to her father. One of the many times she'd asked him about that place. "My father shared very little with me about the village. No matter how curious I was, he always shut the conversation down quickly."

"That does not surprise me. No good father would want to tell his daughter about that place."

Her father had only wanted to protect her and her sister. She canted her head. "Did you know him? Before he left."

"Not well. But, yes. He was a wonderful male. He and Markham—our so-called king—never got along."

Somehow, that didn't shock her. She recalled the use of the male's name mostly in derogatory statements. Despite her question, it wasn't really what she wanted to ask. It wasn't what she wanted to know. She shifted her gaze back to the basin. No. What she wanted to know about was his death. The truth. Not just what little information she had. "Last week, you said he didn't deserve what happened. What did you mean?"

Pierce didn't raise his eyes, or glance at her—just stared into the water. "As I said, he was a wonderful male. He did not deserve what happened to him." She opened her mouth to speak, but he cut her off. "Please. Do not ask me. It will benefit no one, least of all you, to know the truth of that night. The details are not something you should have in your head. And vengeance, revenge, is not something that you can find. Not now. Not as things stand." He turned his head and looked at her. "But I prayed to the gods for safe travels of his soul to the afterlife."

For days after they'd gotten the news, her mother had done nothing but lie in bed. She remembered the female crying all the time. Whether her mother knew everything, she'd never said. All she knew, someone had killed him. Even without giving her any details, Pierce confirmed her suspicions. Her father had died protecting her. A tear rolled down Jo's cheek. She turned away from Pierce as she tried to stop any further tears from escaping.

Without a word, Pierce joined her where she sat, wrapped his arms around her, and held her against his chest. She wasn't the type of female that showed vulnerability. She hated that he even saw an ounce. It made her feel weak, and as hard as she tried, she couldn't stop the flow of tears. As much as she didn't want to admit it, she only wanted to be in his arms as she cried.

His hold on her tightened when he sat on the ground, pulling her onto his lap. He rested his head on top of hers, allowing her to cry as long as she needed to. No words were necessary. Eventually, her tears subsided. No one had held her like this since her father had passed. "I miss him. It seems strange to say, but I do."

"That is not a strange thing to say. Not at all."

"You don't think so?" She felt like it was. She had all of five years with her father. "I don't have many memories of him, but my mother has always said I take after him. In more ways than one." Her ears twitched.

Pierre's hand rose, slowly stroking the back of her ears, her head, and down her spine. Up and down. Up and down. "Then you will make a worthy mate." He paused. "To someone. Someday."

His words hurt like a knife to the gut, which made no sense. It was almost ironic. She'd never intended to get mated. It wasn't something she'd ever wanted until now. But she couldn't ever truly have him, and he'd told her that himself. But it wasn't something she wanted to think about. Or the whole mate thing.

"In what ways?" he asked, his voice hoarse and choked.

His question came just as she'd intended to change the subject herself. She didn't want to think about what the strangeness of his voice meant, either. Just answer the question. "I-uh, I have his protective nature. I've knocked a male or two around occasionally." She cracked a small smile. "Very few will spar with me because of it."

"It brings me joy to hear that."

"Oh?" She was curious why. His earlier reaction to her bruises suggested otherwise. Then again, it meant she could take care of herself. That had always been her goal: to need no one. Funny. It didn't feel like that when she was around him.

"Yes. That you can protect yourself brings me joy. That, despite the bruises, I do not have to wor—" He stopped short and cleared his throat. "Was there anything else you wished to speak about?"

Part of her wanted to know what he cut off. Part of her didn't. Whatever this was between them, it wasn't supposed to include feelings. Despite her thoughts, she didn't ask him anything about it. "No."

"Then let us not talk anymore."

Pierce gently drew her face toward his, stopping when their eyes met and held. Something unspoken passed between them. He slid his hand to her neck, and their lips locked together. Something was different. It wasn't just the languid kiss that she felt deep in the pit of her stomach, but also something else. Something more. Something she couldn't put her finger on. She enjoyed him in a new way. Unlike any other time they'd come together, there was no desperation between them. As if, for the first time, it went beyond sex.

He trailed kisses down her jaw, neck, and shoulder, nipping her skin as he moved along. He took his time as though he were memorizing every inch of her flesh. "I love the way you taste." He growled against her as he laid her back on the grass and stripped her of her clothes.

"I love the way you feel." With the blades tickling her bare skin, she stroked behind his ears and lazily traced her fingers down his face. Yearning to remember every crevice, every hard plane of muscle, and every inch of his body, she took her time with each caress. She refused to acknowledge what she was feeling in the depth of her soul. She couldn't. It was the only way they would remain safe.

"Then do not stop touching me." Pierce kissed lower until he reached her breasts. Sucking and licking them, one after another, he left no part of them untouched as he moved his hand between them and found her sex. He slipped his def fingers inside her, expertly guiding them in and out of her, his thumb rubbing her nub.

With a soft gasp, Jo arched her back, pushing her breasts more into his mouth. Her hands never once left his body. She continued a path over his thick biceps, spine, and the rippling muscles of his back, as low as her fingers reached. Sliding her legs up over his ass and hips, she stroked him in the places she couldn't go with her hands. Her talons curled as lightning coursed through her body. Her inner walls clenched, and an orgasm pulsated around his digits.

His fingers worked her slowly through her release. Popping her nipple free, he thoroughly sucked her juices from his digits with a growl. He kissed and licked his way down her stomach, over her hips, between her thighs. Claiming her sex with his mouth, he drove his tongue inside, taking in every leftover drop of her orgasm. Her inner walls tightened again around his tongue. He turned her around right before she came and pulled her up, so her back was against his chest. He teased her with his cock before sliding it inside her until she sheathed him completely. Wrapping one arm around her waist, he brought the other around her chest and palmed her breast.

"I am going to fuck you now," he whispered. "But I am going to take my time with you. I want you to remember every second of my cock buried deep inside you. I want my cock to be the only one inside you."

Oh, gods, it was exactly what she wanted too. But she couldn't say it. She couldn't form the words, but she could show him that as he claimed her, she claimed him. That he would be the only male for her, just as she'd be the only female ever for him. Laying her arms over his, she leaned back and nipped at his lips. She licked up the side of his neck and gently bit him. Spreading her thighs wider, she ground herself against him and moaned. "The only one, Pierce."

He slid his hand between her thighs and rubbed her nub as he thrust in and out of her. "Your sex is mine, and only mine," he growled before his lips claimed hers.

Their tongues entangled, and Jo threaded her fingers through his. She reached up and stroked the nape of his neck with her fingernails, deepening the kiss until she could no longer tell where her breath began, and his ended. They were utterly insane. But she didn't think about tomorrow. All she could think about was this moment. Right now, right here. In his arms. His lips pressed against hers. His hands on her body as he unhurriedly pistoned in and out of her. Her fingers danced over his skin—nothing between them. No walls, no cares, just them.

Pierce slid easily in and out of her, her sex and thighs slick with wetness. He kissed her languidly, but urgently. Slipping his cock out of her, he turned her around. As she wrapped her legs around his waist, her arms around his neck, he slammed back inside her.

It was the strangest phenomenon as he laid back and relinquished control. Jo didn't dominate in many places, but it didn't feel like that with him. He gave himself to her. It wasn't something she had ever thought she'd want, yet she did. As much as she crave to leave her mark on him, she desired to take him like she'd taken no other. Bracing her hands on his chest, Jo spread her thighs wider, taking him deep into her core, and then rocked against him. Trailing her hands along his arms, she leaned down and sucked on one nipple, then the other, drawing out the orgasm that would come. What she wanted was a massive explosion, one that neither of them would forget.

His head fell back, and he let out a deep moan. He gazed at her, watching every movement she made on top of him. Loosely gripping her hips, he relinquished complete control. As she rocked harder against him, her pace remaining torturously slow, he groaned out her name. "Yes, ride me, my queen."

Sitting back up, she gently raked her nails down his chest and braced her hands against him. She lifted her hips and eased him back inside her, then ground into him. Spreading her thighs wider and wider each time, she did this until she could no longer stand the torment. The pressure was so thick in her core that that she nearly pitched right over the edge; she rocked harder against him and increased her speed. With a deep moan, she uttered a request she'd never issued before. "Come with me. Come with me now, Pierce."

Reaching up, he took her hands in his and intertwined their fingers. He thrust his hips up into hers until they orgasmed simultaneously. The noise he made shook birds from the trees. Jerking her face down, he kissed her hard, fused their mouths and tongues as they rode out their release together. When it finished, their bodies trembled against one other. His chest heaved, but he didn't move, nor did he remove his lips from hers.

As the kiss continued through ragged breaths, it seemed as if the exchange of air was giving her life, breathing energy into her spirit. How was this possible? How had they gotten this close? And how had they gotten here from that alleyway? Letting him in, giving herself entirely to him, wasn't what she'd intended, yet somehow, her heart opened up to him; her soul yielded to his. As if their hearts and souls had another plan altogether.

As their breathing eased, they said nothing, only stared into each other's eyes. Pierce brushed her hair back over her ear, then rested his hand against her cheek. "Jocasta... I..." His words trailed off as he clamped his mouth shut.

"You don't have to say anything." She could see it in his eyes. And she was sure it reflected in hers. Their feelings didn't require words. All the things they couldn't say, they said with their bodies. They already risked so much. Not that she regretted a single moment. The only regret she'd have was if she never saw him again. That was something she couldn't accept.

He lifted her up to lie beside him. Propping himself up on one elbow, he stared down at her, his hand caressing her hip and thighs. "For the first time in my life, I do not know what to do. But I know what I want, and I know what I cannot live without."

Without giving it much thought, she rested a hand on his chest over his heart. "I wish I could tell you I had the answers, but I don't. There are things I never thought I'd want, but I do, and I can't imagine ever being without them."

"This is something I never thought I would feel for anyone. Certainly not someone I have just met, nor someone of a different species. You know as well as I that we are in mortal danger if this continues." He shook his head. "No. Not *if*. I can no longer even entertain that thought."

His earlier comment about her as a mate—she didn't want to tell him her truth. Or how it related to everything in front of them. But she didn't want to hide either. He hadn't. "I never wanted to feel like this for anyone. After seeing what my mother went through, I was afraid to care for someone so deeply. And I know the danger this puts us in, but I can't imagine being without you, either."

"I never wanted a true mate. Not with all I have seen. I would have mated for other reasons, but not love. Now, though, things are very different."

"I always thought it would be through my twin if our line continued. But things have changed. And I don't know what we should do."

"Perhaps I should go until I come up with a solution, but I cannot. I do not think I wish to go home."

Jo closed her eyes. Pierce never leaving sounded heavenly. But he had a family in his village, sisters he protected. She wouldn't make him choose. Opening her eyes, she caressed his cheek. "You have to leave at some point. If you do not return, we both know Markham will go after your sisters. I won't have that."

"I know." Pierce pressed his forehead to hers. "I need to wash up. Then I should go. Before, I cannot force myself not to."

"I should clean up as well. I'll need to head back to my village soon."

He inhaled and exhaled a deep breath, kissed her quickly, and then removed himself from her arms and rose to his feet. Jo watched him as he headed to the basin to wash. He had raised the wall inside of himself again. The wall they'd both destroyed when their bodies joined. Letting out a soft breath, she took a moment before she got up to clean herself off in the water.

This was how things had to be for now. Maybe one day things would change, but she'd never forgive herself if anything happened to his family. It would be like losing her sister. She'd take this pain over the pain of losing him altogether. It wasn't the first time she'd faced heartache. As much as she hated it, she had to put some distance between them. Jo dove into the water and swam out to the bottom of the waterfall.

Though he didn't look right at her, she could feel him watching her as he washed all the remnants of their lovemaking from his body. When he was clean, he stepped out onto the bank. She mainly stayed under the water. When she surfaced, it was only briefly before she dove back under again. Her head surfaced above the water, and he called out to her. "I will return when I can." Shifting to all fours, he shook his body, getting rid of all the excess water. He looked back at her one more time, then took off into the woods.

She slide under the falls and stood there, letting the water wash away her tears. This was exactly as it had to be. Until they could meet again, she'd come here every day. It was a good thing her sister preferred to come at the end of the night—one less thing to worry over.

Chapter Sixteen

Parthenia snuck out a few hours past lunch. Somehow, she escaped the ever-watchful eyes of her mother and aunt and slipped out of the hidden staircase unseen. She only took a minute to change clothes before she flew straight for the treehouse. While she should've taken a less direct route, she was too eager to get there, hoping that her mate would be there today. A smile fell on her lips as her gaze landed on her mate. "Gavin."

He crossed the floor in moments. As he grabbed her up to him, a soft fluttering like that of parchment sounded. Gavin buried his face in her neck. "My beloved," he said against her. "I am sorry I was absent for so long, but I could not come. I have missed you."

Wrapping her arms around him tightly, she gingerly stroked the back of his head. "I've missed you too. I'm sorry I couldn't get here sooner."

"You do not need to apologize. I could only leave today, and I had duties in the village to attend to." He swallowed hard. "I have not been here for long."

Parthenia opened her mouth and snapped it shut. Something was wrong. Very wrong. She could feel the ache in his heart. Drawing back a touch, she cupped his cheek. "What's the matter?"

He rubbed his cheek against her hand, his eyes closing. "Gabby is not doing well. She ..." He sighed. "I did not even know. She did not tell me." Something flickered through his head, a pregnancy that hadn't come to fruition.

"Oh, goddess. I'm so sorry, my love." He didn't say all of it, but it wasn't necessary. She understood enough that his sister had to be suffering. The issues with pregnancies in her species had never gone unnoticed, no matter how well one hid it. Females born asexual. Pregnancies that didn't come to term. She hugged him and held him close.

Gavin laid his head on top of hers and deeply breathed in her scent. "Either way, it was doomed. Markham would have... he would not have let the young live. But the loss still hurts. It hurts too that she could not tell me, though I understand why. Markham has a way of getting thoughts from the mind. The more people that knew..." His words trailed off. "I am happy to see you."

Of course, it would hurt. Gavin was close to his sister. The female deserved to be happy. Perhaps they would find the answer to getting off the isle soon. And Gabby would come with her mate as planned. They would make a new home together.

He squeezed her to him. "Oh. I got you something. Well, not directly, but it is from me."

"You didn't have to get me anything. I'm quite happy just spending time with you." Indirectly or not, she only needed him.

"I know, but I suppose I just wanted to." Keeping her close, he brought his hand out from behind her back. "I do not even know if you will like it. I did not know what you would like. We cannot wear such things in the village. I told Gabby that I wanted to get something for you, and she must have told Devin. She left it here for me." He opened his palm, revealing a necklace nestled carefully inside it.

"I'd love anything—" Parthenia gasped. Her eyes widened as she drank in the necklace. It had a green chain with a rose-shaped pendant dangling from it. The pendant was a bright, poppy-colored red. It perfectly combined his eye color and her favorite color. Hesitantly, she lifted the charm in her fingers. Were those their initials? "Gavin, it's beautiful."

"I am glad you like it. I do not know where Devin might have gone to get it. But I wanted you to have something from me when it was not possible to be with me." He stroked the small of her back.

"Gavin, it's perfect. I love it. Will you?" She swept her hair to the side. Although she couldn't wear it while in Pteryrina, she would wear it whenever possible.

"Of course, love." Stepping behind her, he draped it around her neck. It took him a few moments to fasten the clasp, but he managed it. "I do not even have to see it to know it is perfect on you." He dropped a kiss to her neck as she turned in his arms. "How were things for you since we last saw one another?"

She leaned into him as she wrapped her arms around his waist. "They have kept me quite busy. Yesterday was the first chance I had even had to leave the grounds." Another lot of The Poppy Field had wilted in her absence. "It was only for a couple of hours."

"Are you being watched more, too?"

"Yes. My sister was waiting for me when I returned a few days ago. I lied to her about where I had been, but she didn't believe me." And she didn't know what that could mean for them. Though she didn't expect Cipriana to say anything, her conversation with her sister still lingered in her mind. As it weighed on his mind that Markham paid more attention to him.

He stroked her spine, then across her wing. "Do you and your sister have a good relationship?"

"Of all my sisters, I have the strongest relationship with her. I suppose it's why she didn't believe my lie. She knows me too well." Parthenia sighed.

"Perhaps she is just worried about you and does not want to see you get into trouble."

"Or she doesn't wish to get into trouble herself for covering for me."

"That could be true, too." He ran his fingertips along her soft brown feathers, silent for a minute. "Do you think, if she knew what you were doing... she would tell your Elder?"

"I don't know. Cipriana has always been one to follow the rules." The slight sensations of his touch soothed her.

He nestled his face in her neck. "The realization of how dangerous this... us... is grows larger every day. I could not bear it if anything ever happened to you."

"I couldn't, either." She truly believed she would not survive without him. "But I can't go without seeing you. I will simply have to work harder on the invisibility potion. Until I perfect it."

"And I will do more to attract less of Markham's attention." He placed a kiss on her neck. "I need to see you, too. These last few days without you have been very painful."

"Yes, they have." She had spent many times crying when no one was around. She dared not let anyone see her upset.

They stayed just like that for a little while. Gavin let out a purr against her when the tips of her wings caressed his back. "I love how our drawings look on the walls."

Her eyes flicked to the drawings. She had brought hers down with her yesterday, but she hadn't even noticed them on the walls. Her joy at seeing Gavin was the best kind of distraction. A slow smile tugged at the corners of her lips as her gaze fell upon one of his. "When did you put them up?"

"When I arrived here today. It just felt like something was missing. This way,"—he brushed a strand of her mahogany hair over her ear, then left his hand against her cheek—"even if one of us can be here and the other cannot, we will always be able to see each other." He placed a soft kiss on either side of her mouth.

Parthenia beamed at him. "It's a wonderful idea." She prayed things changed for them soon. Being without each other hurt too much, and it was hard not to wonder how long it would be until their reality changed. She truly wanted to escape the isle with him.

"I am glad it pleases you." He kissed the top of her head. "We have been standing this whole time," he said with a slight laugh. "Come." He sat down on the floor and tugged her gently into his lap. "How long do you have to stay here today?"

Curling up in his lap, she snuggled close and brushed a soft kiss across his neck. He let out a low rumble. "A couple of hours. They believe I am in the library researching."

Chuckling softly, he tightened his hold on her, his tail stroking her wings. "I did not tell anyone where I was going. I finished my duties, then left. At a normal pace, though, so no one would suspect anything."

"Perhaps we are getting sneakier." She sighed into him. Goddess, she had missed him, missed being in his arms. His presence. Just listening to him.

He laid his head on her shoulder, breathing in her scent. "What should we do with our time today, love?"

"Can we just sit here like this?" She left the forever remain unspoken because she couldn't voice it. The day would come, but sometimes it felt like it would never get here. And they were just biding time until someone discovered them.

"Absolutely, my beloved." He swept his tongue across the side of her throat. "I cannot think of anything I would like to be doing more."

Goddess, the day of their freedom could not come soon enough. She didn't want him to stop holding her until he had to let her go.

Again.

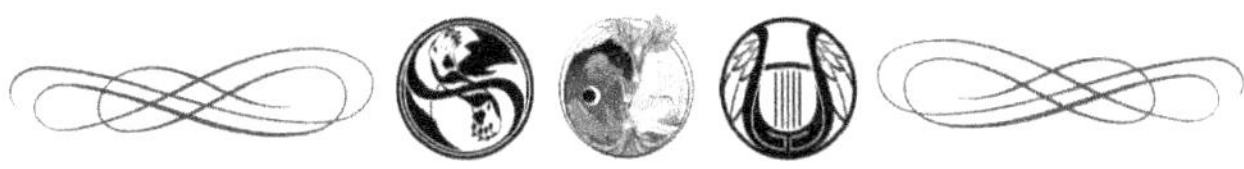

Despite Pierce's reaction to the bruises Jo had gotten the other day in her sparring session, she had felt horrible about what happened with Leo. She'd heard around the village that his shoulder had to be popped back into place. And that if she had pulled on his arm with any more force, she would have broken it.

Her bruises had healed, and she was entirely in control of her emotions. She suspected her conversation with Pierce about her father had helped. Not that she'd fully admit it. She strolled into the fighting ring and spotted Leo practicing with the bo sticks again.

His gaze flipped to her, and he stopped in the middle of a full-on swing.

She held up her hands. "I come in peace."

"No sparring, then?"

"After what happened the other day?" Either he was insane, or she had hit him in the nose more brutally than she initially thought—scrambled his brain or something.

Leo shrugged. "It was just another session."

Jo strode closer and inspected his nose at various angles, raising an eyebrow. No, it looked normal and still appeared to be in one piece.

He crossed one ankle over the other and leaned against the bamboo stick. "What are you doing?"

"Checking for brain damage," Jo smirked, and folded her arms across her chest. Nothing was visibly noticeable. Then again, she didn't expect to find anything.

With a snicker, he rolled his eyes. "My brain is fine."

"Are you sure? Because you just described the other day as *another session*, like it happens all the time." She tapped the bottom of her chin. Since he was insistent that he hadn't injured his brain; there was only one other plausible explanation. "Unless you're drunk. Have you gotten into the spirits this morning?"

"Jo, I'm fine." Leo grinned and cupped her jaw. "Now, stop worrying your pretty little head about it."

By the gods, what was he doing? She jerked her face from his hand and stepped back, putting a little distance between them. "I don't know what's going on with you but, whatever it is, just stop. I only came here to apologize to you about the other day. Nothing more."

"Really? That's it?"

"Yes. In case nothing else I've said has made it through that skull of yours. There is nothing between us. I have no feelings for you." Good gods, she didn't know how else to lay it all out for him. They'd had sex! A few times. And it wasn't even good! Did she need to tell him she'd faked an orgasm with him? Would he back off then?

"Come on, Jo. The heated passion of our spar, the way you keep stealing glances at me. I know you want me back. And I'm good with that." Leo closed the distance between them and stroked her cheek. "I mean, it was just a matter of time."

Balling up her fists, she backed up further and groaned. She hadn't looked at Leo, except maybe in pity. She pitied Leo if Pierce ever found out he was the one who put the bruises on her. Talk about something else she had to keep from him. Because whatever was going on now, she'd keep to herself. Besides, she could handle it, so she didn't need to tell him. "What part of *nothing* are you not understanding? And I mean nothing. Nada. Zero. Whatever you think you saw is complete and utter spourgiff shit."

"I know you, Jo. You're just keeping your feelings in. I can see it in your eyes. You're in love with me." He moved closer, grabbed her by the back of the neck, and leaned down to kiss her.

Before he got too far, Jo hauled back and punched him. Her fist connected with the side of his jaw, and Leo stumbled backward on his feet. "Stay away from me!"

Shaking her hand out, she stormed out of the sparring ring. Gods, that hurt. What did he have? A steel jaw? She was so pissed off; she had to get out of here. But she couldn't go to the basin like this because Pierce would know something was up. And she wanted to see him.

"Jo? Jo?" Her twin raced after her.

"Not now, Am. I'm not in the mood." Even if she was, she couldn't explain how Leo had gotten this idiotic idea in his head that she wanted him. At. All.

"Hey!" Ambrosia grabbed Jo's wrist. "Are you okay?"

"No, but talking about it isn't going to help either. Leo was being stupid or ignorant, or maybe both. I don't know. Either way, I need to get away from the village for a bit and cool down. Sound good?" And the long walk to the basin would soothe her so she could spend time with Pierce. As long as her knuckles didn't bruise or swell, she'd be good. Situation handled.

Ambrosia backed off. "Okay. I get it. Just be back in a few hours. We've got stuff to handle at the bar."

"I will." Without saying another word, Jo left the village and headed for the one place she would find peace. And it had nothing to do with the water.

Parthenia chewed on the inside of her cheek. Three days had passed since she had spoken with her mother. She hadn't seen the female around as she completed her daily chores, nor had she returned to the female's house for a single meal. Instead, she either spent time in her apothecary, the library, or at the treehouse with Gavin. She had quickly made it home.

The last healing potions made, she left there, along with several of her books regarding potions and alchemy. Gabby seemed to enjoy them. And she loved working with the female. Though Gabby had appeared somewhat distracted, they spent nearly an hour discussing herbs. She had promptly departed upon Gavin's arrival.

They hadn't spoken about what was bothering the female, though Parthenia knew from Gavin. They weren't that close. Inhaling a deep breath, Parthenia glanced out the window of her apothecary. Lunchtime passed by hours ago, making it an excellent time to collect her dresses from her mother's house. Cipriana commented earlier that a stench had followed her around. She could wash the clothing in the spring, but the last thing she wanted was someone coming up on her unexpectedly.

It just made more sense to get her other dresses without her mother around. Then she could change and comfortably wash all of her dresses. At least then she could get all the stench out, including the smells from her mother's house. A place she hadn't belonged in years.

Parthenia walked out of her apothecary and strode toward the collection of houses. It took but a few minutes to get to her mother's. She opened the door and poked her head inside. Empty. Just as she'd hoped. She entered the domicile, shutting the door behind her. The house had never been so quiet. It was pretty strange. Shaking away the eeriness that crept up her spine, Parthenia made her way to the bedroom she had once called her own.

She had reached her adult form three years past. Nothing with her body had changed since then. The same six dresses she'd had all these years still hung on the wall. It would be different having them in the apothecary with her. The only clothes she usually kept there were those she preferred to wear, not the white dress of her people.

As she stood in the doorway of her old bedroom, she thought back to how Gavin had described the land the night he'd seen it. *Clean, pure, calming.* Their views were still quite different. She strode across the room with a heavy sigh and collected the dresses.

"What exactly are you doing?" her mother asked.

Parthenia cringed. Her memories had her so caught up that she hadn't heard the front door open. Oh, poppies! She intended to avoid another confrontation with her mother. That wouldn't happen. No matter. She could handle this. She steeled her shoulders and faced the female. "I am gathering my belongings. What else would it be?"

"You have truly taken this a step too far, Parthenia. It is bad enough you have foregone our meals together, but now you are taking your dresses? Is this meant to teach me a lesson?"

"A lesson?" Parthenia scoffed. "What lesson do you think I would even attempt to teach you, Mother?" Better yet, why would she waste her precious time? No one could teach the female anything.

"That I do not appreciate all you do for this family."

"Family? What family? You are nothing more than the female who birthed me." Amara had stopped being her mother—no, that wasn't accurate. The female had only acted like a mother to her.

Amara's eyes narrowed. She stepped further into the bedroom. "Excuse me? I'll always be your mother. I raised you, fed you, clothed you, and this is the thanks I get!"

Raised me? Fed me? Amara hadn't done any of those things. Parthenia ground her jaw. No. She refused to allow the female to take credit that didn't belong to her. "In what realm did you do any of those things? None. Heron raised—"

A crack rang out as Amara slapped her across the face. "I told you that male's name is not to be mentioned in this house."

Her cheek stung, but she wouldn't take it back. Her father had raised her and provided for her. Parthenia glared at Amara. "Then I suppose it's a good thing I do not live in your house." Clutching the dresses tight, she pushed past the female and stormed out of the bedroom.

"Parthenia!"

She had nothing more to say to Amara. Ignoring the female's calls after her, she continued toward the front door. She didn't care what the others thought. Perhaps she couldn't tell Amara she no longer fell under her rule, but it didn't mean she had to act like it.

"Parthenia! Do not walk out that door!"

With her hand on the knob, she stopped. Her whole life, she had felt like less because of everything Amara had put her through. The number of times the female had punished her for mere accidents, scolded for no real reason, screamed at for anything the female thought was unbecoming. Nothing she had ever done would be good enough. Amara made it clear years ago that she hated her. She didn't know why. But, for once, she didn't care.

Gavin *loved* her. And she *loved* him. That was all that mattered now. Without even looking up, Parthenia opened the door and walked out of the house.

Chapter Seventeen

Jo wiped her sweaty palm down the front of her jeans. She hadn't gotten on stage in years, but she wanted to get up there and sing for the first time since she could remember. To say she was nervous didn't go far enough to describe her feelings.

Setting the music up, she gave herself a ten-second lead and climbed out of her booth. Jo got up on the blue-agate stage without looking over the crowd as the orchestral started. The song she had chosen tonight was "Meet Me on The Battlefield" by Svrcina. A song she loved to listen to but hadn't fully grasped the concept of the words.

Until now.

As Jo belted out the opening lyrics, all she could think about was Pierce and the way he stared at her with his ruby eyes. With so much space between them at night, it had been difficult to sleep. When she got rest, he invaded her dreams. Their extraordinary beauty often woke her—sometimes in tears. The more she tried to bury the pain at parting ways, the harder it became.

They were fighting what felt like an endless battle. Stealing moments where they could, and as often as possible. She knew they were both tired; even though they never vocalized it, just as she remembered what they continued to fight for.

Her voice carried across the building as she moved into the chorus. They would do whatever it took to protect each other—today, tomorrow, always. Keep their relationship a secret. Never speak of the other. Bury their emotions in the darkness. But when they came together, it was like the sun rising high above the battlefield. Rays of light breaking through the storm.

The sound of her voice lifted as the second verse resounded through the bar. The shape shifter laws forbid them from having a relationship. A sin that many were condemned for in the past. But they could change everything. Stand up and rise above it all.

Speak their truth.

And no longer hide.

Jo trilled out the chorus again. As she finished the song and repeated the chorus lines twice more, she buried her memories of Pierce down deep. To a place where she couldn't retrieve them until she removed the locks. It broke her heart, but they would do what they must in order to protect the other.

To stay safe.

The last of the harmony left her mouth as the music ended. It wasn't the hooting, hollering, and clapping that caught her attention. Instead, it was the sight of her twin. The female stood there at the side of the stage and gawked. Jo hopped off the hunk of rock and dropped next to her sister. She opened her mouth and snapped it shut as the female threw her arms around her and hugged her tightly. "Am? Everything okay?"

"That was absolutely beautiful." Ambrosia released her hold. "I just can't believe you got on stage. You never get on stage."

Jo shrugged. She couldn't explain the change. Well, maybe she could, but she chose not to. "I felt like singing today."

"Whatever the reason, I don't care. I'm just completely blown away."

"Thank you. I'm going back to my booth now." With a slight nod, Jo patted her sister on the arm. She didn't do well with compliments. Never had. Some females fished for them, while others knew nothing of their natural beauty. She fell in between. She knew how she looked but didn't need a daily reminder; they unnerved her.

"Right." Ambrosia's eyes widened, and she stepped back in the bar's direction.

Snickering, Jo strode to her booth and ascended the two stairs before someone else snagged her attention. One step away from freedom.

"That was amazing. Really, Jo. I didn't know you could sing like that."

She turned around and cracked a smile. "Thanks, Leo." Of all the people to show up, it had to be him. Why? He had never popped in before. What made today different? It couldn't have anything to do with their earlier conversation. She had changed sparring partners. That shouldn't be a big deal. At least not to him. To her—to Pierce—it mattered. Not that she'd tell Leo that. "I'm surprised to see you here."

"What? I can't come by and see a friend."

Not when that had changed lately. They used to be friends, and then he had made things awkward. Now, they were, well, she didn't know what, but not friends. As if to make herself clear, she descended the staircase. "No. How about you try that again? What are you doing here?"

"All right. You got me. I'm just passing through. Thought I'd come over and let you know how amazing that was, though. I could feel the passion."

"Thank you." If he didn't want to give her an honest answer, fine. So be it. She didn't have time to fret over it. Spinning on her heel, she started up the staircase again when something hard smacked her ass. Jo reeled around so fast she nearly fell off the step.

She steadied her footing at the same time as Bruce lifted Leo off the ground by the scruff of his neck. Her eyes widened as she watched the green-skinned troll drag the male across the room and throw him out the door. Oh, no! This wasn't done. Jo stormed down the aisle between the tables and exited the building, balling her fists up.

Once outside, she glared at Leo, who stood and busily brushed himself off. "What is your problem?!"

"I don't believe I have one."

"You don't have one?" Narrowing her eyes, Jo closed the distance between the two of them and shoved Leo. "Seriously? You don't have one!"

He chuckled. "No. I mean, why would I have one when the female who has been leading me on for months suddenly pushes me away?"

"Excuse me? I didn't suddenly decide anything. I've never found you attractive. Not once. Never. You were nothing more than a solution." Good gods, how had he gotten it in his head that they had anything more than friendship? Something they no longer had.

Leo crossed his arms. "Your body said otherwise."

"By all the gods, I faked it!" Jo screamed. Gods, she was so pissed off that she was airing their business. No one needed to know this.

"I don't believe you. And I'll prove it." He stepped in close and leaned in to kiss her.

Not this again. Jo slapped him across the cheek hard and kneed him in the gonads. This time she didn't care if her hand hurt afterward, as long as she got him to leave her alone.

With a squeak, his hands shot to his crotch as he doubled over.

Jo shoved her finger in his face. "Come near me again, and I swear by the gods and goddesses I will slice off your dick, and no female will ever want you!" Squaring her shoulders, she stomped to the door.

Reaching for the handle, Bruce opened it for her. "You should tell him."

She inhaled a deep breath and ran her hands through her crimson-colored hair. It wasn't necessary to ask. She knew exactly who Bruce referenced. It also shouldn't surprise her. He had been there when she first ran into Pierce and likely noticed when he popped his head into the doorway weeks ago. But it didn't matter. This was the last thing Pierce needed to know about. "I've got it handled."

Jo stepped into Zancle's Rock and headed straight for her booth without another word.

It had been some time since she and Gavin had any issues. Parthenia stopped at the bottom of the staircase, changed clothes as she'd gone back to doing, and slipped on the pendant Gavin had gifted her weeks ago. It was perfect. She would have worn it around Pteryrina if she could, but she couldn't. It would raise too many questions. Still, she wore it as often as possible.

As she'd done before, she made her way to the treehouse, keeping an eye out for anyone who might spot her. She flew below the top of the trees, using the leave to hide along the way. Landing at the base of the treehouse, Parthenia crouched down—

"This is where you've been going?"

Parthenia spun on the back of her heel. Her eyes widened. "Cipriana! What are you doing here?"

"Following you!" Cipriana crossed her arms. "I figured it was the only way I was going to get any answers."

"I told you it was for your safety. Why is that so impossible for you to accept?" No, no, no. She couldn't be here. Oh, goddess, how did she get rid of her?

"Because that's complete and utter crap. Tell me why you're here right now, or I'm going to the Elder," Cipriana hollered.

Gavin took a few steps forward out of the trees, revealing himself and making his presence known. "Because of me."

Cipriana turned toward his voice, her eyes bulging as she stared at him. She looked from him back to Parthenia. "Please tell me this isn't true."

Grimacing at her sister's words, Parthenia shook her head. Her sister reacted like this, of all the people she thought would understand. She strode around Cipriana to where Gavin stood and stroked his head, breathing in his scent before she faced her sister. She'd hoped he'd stay hidden while she dealt with the female, but since he hadn't, she wouldn't hide the truth. "Cipriana, this is Gavin, my mate."

Cipriana gasped. "Your what?!"

Gavin stayed on all fours as he addressed her. Her sister was taller than he was in this form, just barely taller than she was, but she suspected he didn't want to intimidate her by shifting and rising to his full height of eight feet. "I am her mate, and she is mine."

Cipriana blinked and focused her attention on Parthenia. "Let me get this straight. You weren't just breaking the law by coming down here. You broke the law by interacting with another species and another by mating with one. Have you lost your mind?"

Keeping a hand on Gavin's shoulder, Parthenia hissed, "No! I haven't! I'm well aware of our antiquated laws. They cannot instruct you who to love and choose for you. Or shall I go into how our species has fallen over the years?"

Cipriana squared her shoulders. "Fine. He's your mate, then let him prove it." She looked back at Gavin, eyeing him for the first time. "Tell me something about her."

Gavin glanced at Parthenia and smiled. "She spends most of her time in The Poppy Fields, which is why her scent is the way it is. She is very devoted to her work—what she accomplishes in her apothecary—though it sometimes frustrates her. Fruit tastes better when she has picked it with her hand. She dislikes the color white but loves the color red." He smirked a little. "And green. She is an excellent artist and cook, and makes a wonderfully flavored tea that I have only tasted once. Sometimes she hums without realizing it, and she has the voice of a heavenly being. She has six sisters and does not have a good relationship with her mother. And she misses her father very much."

With each word that left him, Cipriana's eyes widened more and more. Finally, when he finished, she just stood there, taken aback. Her gaze shifted between the two of them. "You told him about your mother?"

Parthenia shook her head. She'd only ever spoken of her father. As far as she was concerned, her mother was nothing more than the female who'd birthed her. But he'd likely picked it up from the connection they shared. She cast a grin at Gavin before fixating on her sister. "Does it matter? He's proven to you how well he knows me, has he not?"

Cipriana folded her hands behind her back and paced back and forth for a minute. She finally stopped. "You realize everything you're risking?"

"Yes. I'd risk it all for him. I love him with everything I am. Of all people, I expected you would understand this. If you wish to see change, stop fretting over what I'm doing and where I'm going. Focus on the problems we have in Pteryrina. The crops that are growing less and less, the continuous destruction of the poppies, and our drying pools."

Cipriana sighed. "I don't like this. What is he risking?"

Parthenia's shoulders tensed, and her gaze narrowed at her sister. "More than you know."

"I risk death. My King is a monster and a murderer who cares nothing for anything or anyone but himself." Gavin took a slow step toward her. "I understand your concern, your fear, and I do not fault you for it. But she is everything to me. She is my heart and my soul, what I have been missing for so very long. I would lie down my life for her without a thought."

Cipriana dropped her gaze to the ground and ran a hand through her mahogany-colored hair. "You risk death for her, and she risks it for you. Sounds like a great way to live."

"I would rather steal time with him than not live at all," Parthenia said. She truly hoped her sister could understand.

With sorrow in her hazel eyes, Cipriana lifted her gaze. "Par, you can't mean that?"

"I do. I hope you find the same one day, but if you cannot see past our differences, then you not only leave yourself to lead a lonely life, but you bring further harm to our species. We cannot survive the way we are going." She hated to point it out, but it was the utter truth.

Cipriana pinched the bridge of her nose. "I will say nothing, but you should be more careful. Fagonia notices every time you disappear for hours at a time."

Gavin gave a slight bow of his head. "Thank you. For keeping our secret."

"Yes, thank you, sister."

"Don't thank me yet. Even if Fagonia can't convince the Elder to punish you, you know well she'll convince your mother." She shook her head. "Goddess, I pray the two of you know what you're doing." Her sister said nothing more, just took off through the trees.

Gavin watched her go, then moved under Parthenia's arm, nuzzling against her. "So, that was one of your sisters. I have to admit, that could have gone much worse." He gave a light chuckle. "Is your mother so terrible?"

She needed to feel him in her arms a moment before she spoke. All this time, she'd successfully avoided any conversation regarding Amara. Leave it to her sister to force the discussion. "Yes. That's Cipriana. She's the oldest, birthed a few months before me. And, yes, it could've been worse." Not that it had ended as well as she would've liked. "My mother can be brusque."

"In what manner?" he asked gently. "Though I have picked up on some things. Sometimes, it is as if the thoughts you carry in your head are spoken out loud. That sounds strange, I know. But that is why I was confident in what I spoke."

"It doesn't sound strange. I think I get that with you sometimes." Parthenia blew out a heavy breath. "You remember the explosion I told you occurred in my apothecary? It was an accident, but my mother didn't see it that way." Parthenia swallowed before telling him about the punishment she'd endured because of that mistake. "My mother whipped me for the damage I had caused."

Gavin jerked back, staring at her in shock. "She did *what*? She *whipped* you? For a *mistake*?" He growled. "How could she be so cruel?"

Curse her sister for bringing up this subject. The female knew how she felt about her mother. Maybe it was best he knew, too, though—all of it. Her shoulders slumped. "My mother does not want me. She has never wanted me. Only Cipriana knows this. And perhaps Fagonia. My mother will take any opportunity to punish me for simply existing. Though it may never become public knowledge."

She could feel the heartbreak in him at the words she spoke. Anger shot through him, burning to his very soul for a female he'd never met. He shifted to his humanoid form and pulled her into his arms, winding them tightly around her. "I am so very sorry. You do not deserve that."

It wasn't okay, but she'd grown accustomed to how Amara worked. And it was no longer her home. Her mate was her home. "That is why I sleep in my apothecary. It became my sanctuary many years ago."

"I am glad you have that space. Everyone should have their own little sanctuary. This has been mine for quite some time." He rubbed her back, making no move to put space between them. "Why on earth would your mother not want you?"

"I don't know. All my mother has ever said was that she never wanted children. Though..." Parthenia paused. She enjoyed thinking about his sanctuary. In their time together, it had become hers as well. She had brought many of her things from her apothecary here, so they could work on potions and find the answers they needed about the barrier. She focused on the sound of his heartbeat as she continued. "Fagonia and my mother are sisters. I told you my father wanted nothing to do with Fagonia. I believe that is why my mother did not want me."

"Why would that cause her not to want you? I am sorry, it just seems so strange."

"If both sisters could not have children, then neither would." Or maybe her mother just didn't want children. She hadn't given it much thought in many years. And she truly wished to stop discussing Amara. "The reason does not matter. The female did nothing more than birth me. She plays no other role in my life."

"I see. I am sorry. It was not my intent to upset you." He kissed the top of her head. "I know how that feels. I once overheard my father praying to the gods for a better son. But my mother has not conceived since my sister and I were born. Once he realized I would never live up to his expectations, he played no other role in my life, either."

"I'm sorry, Gavin. I think your father is very wrong about you. You are the most wonderful male." She squeezed him tight around the waist.

He hugged her closer. "That is all that matters to me." Gavin nuzzled her neck. "I have missed you."

Their gazes locked on one another. "I missed you too. Shall we go up? I have more fruit with me and new herbs for Gabby."

"The fruit sounds wonderful, and Gabby will be delighted." He licked her neck and sent a playful smirk in her direction. "It has been a little while since we have raced."

"Yes, it has. And, perhaps this time, I will win." She giggled, released herself from his hold, and shot into the air. It was pretty different from the first time they'd done this. Her dress billowed in the wind, impacting her flight ever so slightly. She had on a short denim skirt and white tank top this time. It would cut down on wind resistance. Slightly.

Gavin laughed as he shifted back to all fours and shot up into the tree. His claws dug into the bark as he propelled himself up the trunk. When he reached the top, it was just moments before her. He shifted back and reached out his arms, plucking her from the air, and embraced her. "I truly believe one day you will beat me up this tree."

She chuckled. "Perhaps. Though, I suspect I may need to wear less clothing for that to happen."

He growled. "I would not have a single problem with that."

Naked flight. The idea had never crossed her mind. She blushed ever so softly and shook the thought away. "It's a good thing we don't get visitors." She brushed a kiss across his jaw and shrugged off her knapsack.

"Mmm, that is so very true. We will have to try that next time." He pressed a kiss against her neck as his tail stroked her wing. "Did you bring more books for me to look through? I found nothing in the last few that would help us."

"Yes. I also brought a couple for Gabby from my collection. More with herbs, though." She had had no luck either.

"Oh, she will enjoy looking at those for sure. She is off somewhere with Devin today, but I do not know what they are doing. I will let her know they are here, though."

"I thought she might. Perhaps she will have better luck with the invisibility potion than I have."

"Perhaps. That would be wonderful. She has become rather fond of you in the few times you have met."

"I enjoy her company as well. None share my affection toward potions and alchemy. It is quite a joy to discuss our attempts together."

"That makes me happy. And I am glad the two of you got to meet."

"I am too." She tilted her head. It almost amused her she'd met his sibling under such dire circumstances, and he may have met none of hers if Cipriana hadn't followed her. Almost. She didn't wish to repeat either experience. "I feel as if I should apologize for Cipriana earlier. I didn't expect her to follow me or question you the way she did."

"It is not your fault. Do not feel you have to apologize. I rarely speak of you to anyone, so that was rather nice. Circumstances what they are, I would not expect her to trust me. Gabby trusts you wholeheartedly, but she is just extremely carefree, mostly. She can be fierce, but usually only when the situation warrants it."

"I think Cipriana has just allowed her judgment to be misguided." She honestly expected the reaction to be different when he and her siblings met. Perhaps with the younger two. They were only eleven years of age, and their opinions were still very much their own. "Has Gabby said anything to you about introducing me to Devin?" Parthenia mentioned it once, but she had thought nothing more of it over the last few weeks.

"She has, actually. Devin told her as soon as she could. She has been busy lately but did not say what she was doing." He shrugged. "She has always been very secretive, but I am sure she has her reasons. I will try to ask her the next time I see her, though."

Gabby's head popped up over the floor of the treehouse. "You do not have to ask, brother mine. We were nearby, and I caught both of your scents."

"Gods, I did not even sense you coming." Gavin shook his head. "She has always been a master at stealth. To my knowledge, none have caught her at anything she has done."

"I have tried to teach him better, but he is hopeless," Gabby jested as she came up and shifted to her humanoid form. "Devin is with me," she said as another shape shifter joined them. She was the same height as Gabby, though she was a canine. Her fur was swirls of light brown and blonde, and her eyes were a bright teal, a perfect color match for the gemstone tourmaline.

At least their arrival occurred after her sister left. She didn't imagine that would have gone well at all. "Then, Gabby, perhaps you can teach me your ways. It would certainly come in handy, even if we succeed in an invisibility potion." Parthenia cast a smile at the female Gabby had spoken of before.

"Oh, I can only imagine." Gabby crossed the floor and hugged Parthenia. "How have you been?"

"Good. And you?"

"I am well. This is Devin. Devin, this is Parthenia."

The female dipped her chin in acknowledgment. "It is nice to meet you. Gabby has told me all about you. What is it you wanted to discuss?"

"It's a pleasure." Parthenia took a moment to collect her thoughts. "Gabby has told me you traverse the isle. In your travels, have you noticed the barrier that surrounds the isle?"

"Does it surround the entire isle?" Devin asked. "I had been trying to find out how far around it went, but I haven't come full circle yet."

"Yes, I believe so. I can only see a portion of it from Pteryrina. I do not suspect the dragon-shifters will allow us close enough to their territory to check." She wasn't sure about the other species around the isle, but neither of the sky people were truly friendly.

"Well, you know that would be one of those things we may not know until we try." Devin grinned widely.

Gavin looked between them, settling on Devin, and frowned. "You will not attempt that, will you? Are they not dangerous?"

"Home is dangerous. What do I have to lose by trying? If my presence angers them, I will leave."

"Do you think it would be possible for me to go with you?" Parthenia glanced over her shoulder at her mate and then back to Devin. He may not like the thought, but from what she knew of the war, it might be an option.

"I would not mind. What do you know of them? Do you know how magical they are, or if they can see through camouflage? Although, it may be better to appear as if we are not trying to hide from them. That could put them more on the defensive."

"I don't know much." Honestly, they needed to determine not only how far out the barrier went, but any close-up inspection might give them the key to opening it. "I know they are friendlier to sky people, but much like the sirens, they keep to themselves. They are massive in their dragon form, at least if what the books have told me is accurate.”

“We will take care, then. Perhaps if we just explain our intentions, they will allow us to pass,” Devin said.

“Perhaps. I don’t know how much of the land they watch. They may not have any guards below as they keep to the sky. However, we’ll need to be mindful of where we cross into their territory. A part of it borders Pteryrina. And our guards cannot see me.” She walked across the room and collected the map she had left. It no longer seemed important to keep it in her apothecary.

Gavin’s green eyes flicked back and forth between her and Devin . “I am going with you.”

Devin eyeballed him. “I will not advise for or against that, and you know that. You need to be mindful of how much they watch you, though.”

“I am mindful. Trust me.”

“Alright. Although it goes in your favor that Pierce has been preoccupied lately. He is usually the best at tracking.”

“Preoccupied? How?” Gabby asked.

“’Tis not important,” Devin replied.

The information that her mate was being tracked less warmed her heart. Now, if she could just ensure no one else followed her, then they may make it through all of this alive.

With her hand on the scroll, she stopped for a moment. They were all taking a chance at this. More so, if anyone saw her and Gavin together. But she didn’t suspect she’d be able to talk him out of it. She’d have done the same if he asked to go. Setting the scroll down, she waved Devin over and unfurled the parchment. Much of it was still incomplete. Though, perhaps the female could help her fill in the gaps. “Sirens control the eastern skies. Our main gates are near manticore territory. The dragon-shifters control the western skies. I don’t know where their gates are or what territories lie beneath them.”

“When we finish today, would you allow me to keep this for a day or two? I can fill in some of the missing spots.”

“Yes, of course you may. I’m limited to the outskirts of the market. Anything you can do to fill in the missing pieces would be quite helpful. That may direct us on how best to approach the barrier. From my readings, we still need to determine a catalyst to open it.”

"What exactly are you wanting to accomplish by breaking the barrier?" Devin posed. "What do you think is on the other side?"

Parthenia regarded Gavin and Gabby before turning her attention back to Devin. There was only one answer. "Freedom."

"Then we truly have the same goal."

"It would seem so," Parthenia said. It seemed many wished to leave. Even more than the ones she already knew of.

"If Markham could be killed, I would not mind staying on the isle, though I would leave the village. With him alive and no end in sight for his rule, getting out of here is the only option for many." Devin smiled at Gavin and Parthenia. "More than I realized."

"I completely understand. I don't know how easy this will be, so any information we can learn about the barrier would be helpful. Have you come across any in your travels who know more?"

"I may have. I would have to ask them to know for sure. And I cannot name them. But I can see if they might have more of the answers we seek."

"That would be a good idea." Parthenia peered at her mate and his sister. She rolled up the parchment. "I suppose then we should plan to check the barrier out after you fill in more of the map."

"Would you like me to do that first? We can meet back here in a few days."

Holding the parchment out to Devin, Parthenia nodded. "I think it best if we decide on a course of direction before proceeding forward. We need to account for as many variables as we can."

"Probably a wise decision to prepare for anything we may come across."

Parthenia grinned. It was rare to find a female who tried to plan. She hadn't met, well, any. Even if they failed in their ultimate endeavor, it would only provide them more information on how to tackle it again. "Yes. My thoughts exactly."

"Good. I will get right on this. Give me three days, then meet me back here if you are able. If something occurs, we can communicate through Gavin when to meet again." She raised an eyebrow at him. His only response was a dip of his chin.

"Three days hence, then." Though she could sense her mate's apprehension, Parthenia saw no reason for anything to interfere. But that didn't mean it wouldn't happen. As much as she planned, there was always something she couldn't plan for.

"Good," Devin said. "We should go, then. We have things to get at the marketplace, and it would not bode well for us to be late getting back to the village. Markham aside, my mother can get quite irritated if she does not have what she needs for meal preparation."

Gabby gave first Gavin, and then Parthenia, a hug. "Be safe. Both of you."

"We will, Gabby. You as well."

"The same to you, sister," Parthenia added. Things were unfolding and coming to fruition. She could feel it down to her core that things shifted in their favor. One step closer. "Oh, and Gabby, I'm leaving a few things here for you I brought along," Parthenia tacked on as an afterthought.

"Thank you, sister. Are there any herbs, or anything else, you would like me to bring for you?"

Parthenia blinked. The idea came out of nowhere. Why hadn't she thought of this until now? She searched for a blank piece of parchment and charcoal pencil, something she'd left here only a few days before. Quickly, she scribbled a few things down. Of all the herbs and spices she'd ever grown, there were some she simply couldn't get to bear anything. It likely had to do with the soil, not that she'd ever confirmed it. Despite all that, there was the apothecary in the market. She'd seen it from the tree she no longer visited. It was only three items, but she had an inkling these would work. She crossed back to where Gabby stood and handed her the list. "Do you think you can find these? I believe they may work for the invisibility potion."

Gabby scanned the list. "Oh, certainly. These should not be a problem at all."

"Thank you."

"You're very welcome."

Once they left, Gavin drew her into his arms. "Well. That was unexpected." He kissed her cheek. "I will not lie and say I am not apprehensive about all of this, but I am glad things are moving forward. Hopefully, we will figure things out."

She buried herself in his embrace. It was one of her favorite places. "I feel as if we're getting closer. Something is aligning in the stars. I can sense it. We may not end up with all the answers, but perhaps some."

He tightened his hold on her and laid his head on top of hers. "I believe that to be true. I choose to believe it will not be long now. Soon, we will be together for always. I will hold you in my arms as we fall asleep and still hold you when we wake. And…" He nuzzled her neck, licking it up to her ear. "One day soon, we will do more than just tease each other to orgasm."

Her feathers ruffled as a shiver ran the length of her spine. She traced small circles over Gavin's chest and pressed a kiss to his heart, bringing a purr out of him. "Mmm, I very much look forward to that day. And all the days we will have together without worrying someone will see us."

Gavin wrapped his tail around her, caressing her leg and over the curve of her rear. "I look forward to that day. And every day with you. Every moment with you, no matter how short-lived."

As another shudder coursed through her body, she trailed her hands around to the small of his back. Her fingers danced softly along the length of his spine until she reached his shoulders. She gripped his shoulders and leaned her head back. "As do I, my love. As do I."

He growled softly. Parthenia sensed the arousal that swept through him. Getting a grip on her hips, his thumbs caressed her stomach "When you call me that, I see an entire existence of happiness stretching ahead of us."

Oh, goddess, she would never tire of hearing his growl, purr, and having his hands against her skin. A small moan escaped her mouth as she stared up into his eyes. "I see it too. With my whole heart. I know soon, the world will be ours." Her body warmed, heat pooling between her thighs.

"Every moment I am with you, I feel like the world is already ours." He licked up her neck, nipping her ear. Kissing her shoulder, he grazed his fangs down and over her arm until he reached her fingertips. "Do you know what else I love?"

By all that was Demeter, Parthenia wanted to lick him from head to toe. The way he hungered for her, she starved for him. Although she was sure she knew exactly what he would say, she wanted to hear it, anyway. "Tell me, my love," she whispered, her voice husky.

He kneeled on the floor before her, licked and sucked each tip of her fingertips, growling as her breath caught in her throat. "I love every single taste of your skin against my tongue." Placing his hands back on her hips, he drew her closer to him and licked her hips and stomach. "And your honey." He swept his tongue over her belly button. "One day, I will do with my body what I have done with my tongue, and you will come on my cock, as well as in my mouth."

All the descriptions from the journal she had read popped into her mind. So many ways she and Gavin could take one another. Her on top. On her knees. With her in mid-air. She groaned in ecstasy as she played out the varying positions in her head. Parthenia stroked the back of his ears and nipped at his jaw. "One day, my love, I will show you all the things the journal has taught me and the number of things I can do with my wings." To emphasize her last words, she wrapped her wings around him and caressed his back and behind with her feathers.

Her head fell back as he hiked her skirt up around her waist, holding it there as he pulled her flush to him. He trailed his tongue down her stomach, inching lower and lower, and let out a loud groan as his tongue found her sex.

Punctuating what the journal had taught her, she used her wings to lift her and drive her sex more against his tongue. With an outcry of pleasure, she ran the tips of her feathers along the length of his cock.

His growl vibrated against her. He moved to the wall and held her against it. She hooked her legs tightly to his shoulders as they bunched between her thighs, scraped her talons across his back, and caressed his cock with her wings. Clutching right above her rear, he drove his tongue deep inside her sex, repeatedly plunging in and out. When she came, it gushed over his tongue and down his throat, covering his face, causing him to roar as an orgasm shot out of him.

Neither of them could have cared less that his release covered the floor. His growls and her cries of pleasure filled the room as he worshipped her sex. She didn't want him to stop tasting her, holding her, or physically expressing his love for her in the best way he could. She knew he would stay there until he sated her. And then she would do the same for him. Afterward, he would keep her in his arms until she had to leave. She prayed the day came soon, where parting from one another was no longer something they had to endure.

Chapter Eighteen

Ambrosia reached forward and wiped the top of the bar down. Her gaze fell across the crowd, those gathered at the various blue-agate tables around the room. Some occupied booths and others sat at the bar itself. At least when they weren't on stage, serenading their lungs out. She mostly tried to tune the singing out and focused instead on the patrons. It was easier to keep track of the drunks and handle them accordingly.

"Another shot," one of their regular patrons demanded.

Her eyes flicked in his direction as she strode over to him. Ambrosia peered over the bar and shook her head. The male was practically falling off the barstool. "I think you've had enough, Phillip."

"Nooo, not,"—He hiccupped—"enough."

Oh, yeah. Phillip had had more than enough. It might be time to offload him at the inn, where he could sleep his state of intoxication off. She glanced over her shoulder at one of her bartenders. "Hey, Giselle, watch the bar while I take Phillip here to Flight of Fancy."

"You got it, boss."

Ambrosia shook the thoughts away. She'd run Zancle's for nearly seven years, and she still wasn't used to being called that. Her sister was the only one who didn't call her boss. Then again, they ran it together. Except Jo only had to deal with the karaoke side of the business, which left her to handle everything else. It got tiring sometimes. None of that was something she needed to worry over right now. She tossed the wet cloth aside and stepped from behind the high counter.

Walking around to the other side, she helped Phillip off the barstool. "Come on, Phil. Work with me here."

"But, I'm not,"—He hiccupped—"ready."

"Yeah, you are." It took more effort than she would've preferred to get him out the door, but she succeeded. He leaned heavily on her as they headed toward the inn, which required navigating a variety of alleyways, much to her chagrin. How many times had she done this dance with their regulars? Way too often. Maybe she just needed a different job. No. Despite the occasional mishap, she loved her work.

What she felt had nothing to do with her work. Or the number of times she helped some drunkard to Flight of Fancy. It had everything to do with her relationship with Logan. Things hadn't gone stale between them; they'd just gotten weighed down over the last few weeks. They'd been different ever since—no, she refused to think about that. She couldn't. It hurt too much.

"Where we going?" Phillip slurred.

"I'm taking you to the inn." Like she could take him anywhere else? A few guilers appeared in the marketplace, but like her village, they kept the location of theirs a secret.

"Take me home," he crooned.

Gods, help me. It was bad enough she had to listen to it while she worked. She didn't want to hear it as she strived to get him to the inn. "I don't know where you live." But even if she did, she wouldn't take him home. Not that she was going to tell him that.

"Oh, that's easy. Skulls crow path to the beach. It's a straight shot."

Like that made any sense. He had to be confused. Ambrosia shook her head. She didn't have a reason to know where to find the guiler village, but she was curious. "Skulls crow path, huh?"

"No, no, no, no. Skulls crow path, no trail."

Oh, yeah, that made a big difference. Ambrosia's eyebrows knitted together as she thought over the maps she'd seen in the library back in Migas. Hmm, maybe Phillip had mixed up his words, and it wasn't Skull Crow but Crow Skull Trail. If it led to a beach, then it could be Diminutive Beach. At least that she'd seen. With him still relying heavily on her, she led him through the front door of the inn.

"You have got to be kidding me? Another one?"

"This process hasn't changed in years. I don't know why you're acting surprised." To be fair, she rarely brought them more than one drunk per night. Somehow, tonight was the exception. Phillip was the second, just the only guiler of the night. Then again, he was usually the only guiler that ever got drunk. Ambrosia smirked, passed him off to the innkeeper, and exited the building.

She stopped just outside and lifted her gaze to the night sky. Even from the marketplace, she could see the stars that sparkled against the dark hues of blue. It was quiet—she frowned. Ambrosia peered to the right, toward one of the back alleyways. That was strange. There was this pull, one that she usually only felt when she got close to Logan. It couldn't be right. He wouldn't be there. No. He would be at his cabin.

Then why did it feel like—she stopped and stared at a building shaped like the head of a beast. Its red eyes glared at her as if it knew something she had only just guessed. She blinked. It was the fight ring she'd heard about. Belly of the Beast. No way Logan was in the one place he promised he'd never return. She had to be feeling things. Shaking her head, Ambrosia spun on the back of her heel and headed back to Zancle's Rock. She had work to do.

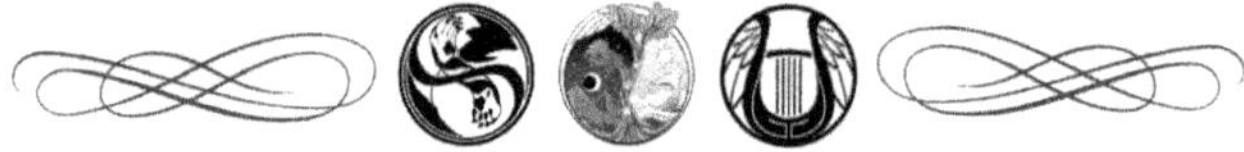

Logan leaned against the wall of Belly of the Beast. His gaze flitted from the cage where two trolls fought to the betting lines, back bar, and around again. His eyes stopped briefly on a pretty boy at the betting lines. Not part of the regular crowd he saw. Whatever. He didn't know why he was here. It was just some place to go, some place to get his mind off of things, not that it helped.

Three weeks had gone by since Ambrosia had the miscarriage, and things were different between them. They still spent every day together, still curled up together and said all the right words, but they hadn't been intimate since it happened. No matter how many times he tried to get her to talk about it, she refused. He still loved her; that would never change. But he was hurting too. Not that it stopped him from trying to be strong for her, but he wished he knew how they could be strong together.

He'd even pushed Derrick harder to talk to Lillianna. Not that it was the male's fault. She was likely skeptical of any Informant, something Pierce had probably taught her, and rightfully so. Unfortunately, not all of them were like his brother. Logan scrubbed his hand across his face and crossed his arms. There wasn't anything else he could do. He just had to be—over the stench of sweat, the aroma of vanilla hit him. Pushing off the wall, he scanned the crowd. His eyes met Ambrosia's.

With a dismissive wave of her hand, she turned and stormed off into the mass of spectators.

Shit. Shit. Shit. Logan pushed through the horde, shoving people out of his way as he ran after her. Pausing just outside the entrance, he sniffed the air and followed the trail her scent had left behind. He hit another alleyway and spotted her just ahead of him. "Ambrosia, wait!"

"No."

Damn it. There weren't a lot of options before him. Either he let her walk off, gave her a day to cool down, or chased after her. Running ahead, he skidded to a stop in front of her. "Please, let me explain."

Glowering at him, she shoved her finger in his face. "What is there to explain? You fucking lied! You promised me, *promised* me you wouldn't go back. And you did!"

"I know, and I am sorry, but I promise it was for a good reason. Though I came back, I have not gotten in the ring and fought." That much was true. Not that he hadn't wanted to, especially over the last few weeks, but he figured one broken promise was enough. He hadn't wanted her to know about this, except it was the best place to keep meeting Derrick. The male risked a lot just by getting together with him. That didn't account for anything else.

Ambrosia ground her jaw, her gaze dropping to the ground. She inhaled and exhaled a deep breath before lifting her eyes to him. "How long?"

Logan gripped the back of his neck. He'd hoped she wouldn't ask him that. She wouldn't like his answer. "Since I promised you, I would not return."

"So, you've been lying to me for almost our entire relationship?"

He opened his mouth and snapped it shut. They'd met close to three months earlier and had been together for about nine weeks. Although he'd gone to Belly of the Beast before he'd gotten into the ring, almost two months had passed since he found out about his mother's death and

Lillianna's existence. Ambrosia was right. Hades, how had he never looked at it that way? Because he'd become so focused on getting Pierce and Lillianna out, and he still wasn't any closer. Logan dragged a hand down his face and hung his head. "I was not trying to. This has simply been the safest place to meet my friend."

"I said you could use Zancle's. It has a back entrance, and shape shifters don't go in there, so there's no chance of you and this friend seen—"

"It is not that simple, Ambrosia." Logan sighed heavily. He was going to have to tell her more than he ever thought he'd have to share, but maybe that was the solution. At some point, he would mate her, officially, but that didn't mean he should hide anything from her, ever. "My friend is an Informant. To make matters worse, I am hunted. Meeting him at Zancle's would not just further endanger him, but it would also endanger you, and *nothing* in my entire being would allow me to do that. I am not just trying to protect him, but you as well. I could not handle it if something ever happened to you."

Staring at him, she blinked. "Why didn't you just tell me that? Instead of lying to me about going."

"I thought I was protecting you by not telling you. That was wrong. I should have explained my reasoning for continuing to go back." He caressed her cheek. Hades, he loved this female. Some days, he wasn't even sure he deserved her, but the gods had seen it fit to bring her into his life. "You and I are dealing with enough. I do not wish to add more pressure to that. While I cannot promise you, I will not return to Belly of the Beast, I can promise you I will not get into any more fights."

"I won't pretend I like you coming to this place, but as long as you can assure me there will be no more fights and no more lying, I can accept it."

Yeah. Leaning down, Logan brushed a soft kiss across her lips. He didn't deserve her or her forgiveness. "I can promise you both. No more fights and no more lying." It didn't resolve every issue they had, but this was enough for now.

Standing on her tiptoes, she stroked the back of his head and pressed her lips to his. "Thank you," she said against his mouth.

With a low rumble in his throat, he wrapped his arms around her and pulled her close. His tongue swept along the inside of her mouth as he deepened the kiss. Hades, he'd missed her taste. Not that he hadn't—nope, he couldn't think of that now. Not when they were kissing like they hadn't seen one another in weeks, which was what it felt like. Most of their touches recently were sweet but lacked all the passion they had toward one another, especially at the beginning of their relationship.

Ambrosia moaned and pressed up against his body.

That beautiful sound shot straight to his cock. He gently dragged his fingers down her spine, cupped her ass, and lifted her as her legs wrapped around his waist. Holy fuck. Was she wearing a skirt? Hades, he'd never seen her in anything other than shorts. How had he missed that when he'd first spotted her? Logan walked them further back into the alley, into the darkest corner he could find.

As she groaned into the kiss, her talons skimmed the small of his back, and she continued to stroke the nape of his neck. "Gods, I need you."

"Then do not stop kissing me." Their lips fused as he turned them around and pressed her back against the closest stone wall. They were utterly alone, and even though they were in some back alleyway, they needed one another. He slipped one hand beneath her tank top and caressed the scales along her spine. His other hand kneaded her breast, the material bunching up beneath his palm.

Arching her back, she pushed her breast more against his hand and moaned.

Hades, the sounds she made. Each one lit his synapses on fire, getting his erection harder. Not that he minded one bit. He brushed his thumb across her nipple and slid his hand down her side. While he'd love to bury his face between her thighs, the alleyway wasn't the best place for that. He would have to settle for using his fingers and then having her on his cock.

She rolled her hips, grinding against his erection, as her fingers skated across his shoulders, over his biceps, and raked down his back.

He growled as a shiver ran down his spine. Fuck. He loved the feel of Ambrosia's fingers as they sifted through his fur. Lowering his hands, he cupped her ass, grazing her thigh with his claw. He retracted his claws, slipped his fingers inside her underwear, and stroked her sex. He hissed at the heat radiating off of her. Hades, at this rate, he just needed to bury himself deep inside of her. Something that would appease them both until they could get somewhere a little more private.

Breaking the kiss, Ambrosia gasped and tightened the grip she had on his shoulders, digging her nails into his shoulder blades. She gyrated her hips against his digits as they had yet to enter her slick folds.

But he could certainly take a hint. He slid his fingers inside Ambrosia's sex. Hades, she was already so wet for him. He rubbed her nub with his thumb as he penetrated her sex over and over. Burying his face into the crook of her neck, he nibbled and sucked on her sweet, sweet skin. The hold she had on him tightened again, and pinpricks of pain shot straight to his cock. Fuck. His cock throbbed. He didn't think it was possible to get this hard, but he was oh-so-ready for her.

"Oh, gods, I need to feel you inside me. Now." Groaning, she rocked her hips against his fingers, and split her thighs further apart. She dragged her talons across his ass.

Fuck, yes. Slowly, Logan removed his digits from her sex, ripped the crotch of her underwear, and lifted his head. He licked both of his fingers, thoroughly cleaning them off. Locking their lips, he drove his cock into her sex. Hades, the way she sheathed him felt amazing. It was like feeling her for the first time all over again.

Her talons dug into his ass as their hips met thrust for thrust. She licked along the edge of his fangs. Her tongue entangled with his and the kiss deepened as if a new hunger rose between them. As if they had something to make up for. Like they were reconnecting after an extended time apart.

Logan threw a hand out against the wall and pistoned in and out of her, his pace increasing. The walls of her sex clenched around his cock, and her orgasm exploded all around him, setting his own off. He broke the kiss with a roar and bit her shoulder, hard enough to leave a mark without breaking the skin. It hadn't been something he could stop himself from doing. Her cries of ecstasy certainly convinced him, she didn't mind—not one bit.

As they rode their mutual releases out together, he licked the mark he'd made on her shoulder and buried his face in the crook of her neck. Both of them panted. His ears perked at the silence that still surrounded them. This wasn't the best place for them to do this. The only time Informants were outside of Métamorphe this time of night was when they were on week-long scouting missions. Since he had no clue what was going on, this was quite dangerous. No matter how badly they needed each other.

And he still wanted more. Not here in the alleyway, though. Logan stroked his tongue across his mark, pressed a kiss to her neck, and then brushed a soft kiss across her lips. "I am not done with you, but I think we should continue somewhere more private."

Through ragged breaths, Ambrosia nodded. "Inn. There's an inn."

"Perfect." He growled. No one needed to see his mate like this. Although he didn't want to leave the warm cocoon of her sex, they had to get to the inn.

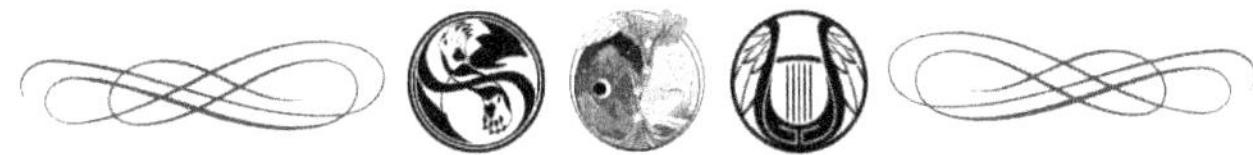

Devin got to the treehouse and shifted to her humanoid form before starting up the tree. When she got to the top, she stopped before breaching its floor. She could smell them both up there, hear the sounds of pages turning. "If I am not interrupting anything, may I come up?" The combination of soft chuckles reached her ears.

"You're not interrupting anything," Parthenia said. "Come on in."

Devin pulled herself up into the treehouse. She couldn't help but smile as she peered down at them. They were sitting on the floor in each other's arms, both with a book. Despite everything, dangers included, they indeed were a beautiful couple. She prayed to the gods regularly that everything worked out for them. That they would find the happy life they dreamed of. "So, I finished what I knew of the map. I have not been in all the territories, but I know where most things are."

"Oh. How wonderful." Parthenia tapped Gavin's hand around her waist as she set the book she was holding aside. He dropped a kiss to her neck.

Devin walked over and sat down on the floor. She withdrew the map from her bag, unrolled it, and laid it out. "Yes. I know a few of the endpoints for the paths you had marked here. The ones that lead away from the marketplace."

Parthenia leaned forward and traced her fingers over the work done. "I think I can almost imagine where the front gates to Pteryrina are from this. You filled a lot in."

"Just what I knew. I have not been everywhere or even inside all the other territories. I just know where the boundary lines are. This extensive area here,"—She traced one pathway marked—"is the forest that belongs to the fae. Their home is called Verdant Grove. Over here on this side,"—She moved her finger to the opposite side of the marketplace, not missing when Gavin peeked his head over Parthenia's shoulder to look too—"is the territory of the manticores. This other area is where the chimeras live. And here, in the middle of those two, is the shape shifter territory. Our village is called Métamorphe, which I am sure you already know from Gavin, but I would *never* advise coming inside the boundaries. Or even near them."

"No." Gavin shook his head. "Definitely not."

"I had a rough idea where the manticore territory is. Our front gates are here, just outside their territory, accessed via the beach." Parthenia pointed to the edge of the manticore territory. "Dragon-shifters have the other half of the sky. I can't say for sure where their gates are, but there's supposed to be a staircase somewhere close to the outer edge of the chimera territory. We may have to stay along borders to get to the beachside there."

"That would probably be a good idea. Without ever having met one and not knowing their temperament, I would not want to offend them by going where we are not supposed to."

"I agree." Staring down at the map, Parthenia bit her bottom lip. "It would probably even be best if we travel along the west border. I don't know what's here between their territory and the fae territory, but that'll put us the furthest away from shape shifter borders."

"We could cut around the west side of the market too, but still stay in the forest," Devin suggested. "Unless we plan on making multiple trips, I do not think we would make it around the entire border of the isle in one day."

"I don't think traveling the entire border would be necessary. I should have the invisibility potion perfected soon. Maybe, instead of meeting here, we meet in the treeline across from the hidden staircase. Here." She pointed to the tree right along the road that led into the marketplace.

"That sounds like a plan. Gavin and I can meet you there. It should make for a fun adventure," Devin commented.

"It'll be the furthest I've ever traveled. I usually stay along the forest edge around the marketplace."

Gavin reached over and squeezed Parthenia's hand, lacing their fingers together. "I have rarely strayed out of our boundaries at all. I have never traveled that far, either." Despite the dangers, excitement danced in his eyes.

"I'm glad we get to make this one together." Parthenia gave his hand a gentle squeeze.

Chapter Nineteen

As Pierce collapsed to the ground, he drew Jocasta into the crook of his arm, holding her as he attempted to catch his breath. "Holy Hades," he breathed out. Gods, sweat covered their bodies. And *shaking?* What in the—he shook his head. "Incredible. You." He blew out a breath. "I do not think I could ever tire of you." There was no *think* about it. He *would* never tire of her. He would never stop wanting to be with her, fucking her, holding her, or talking to her. Gods, he never wanted to be out of her presence, never wanted to be aw—NOPE. *Get those thoughts out of your head, Pierce.* They had long established that there was no possibility of that. Those thoughts had to be pushed far out and away from his brain.

Ragged breaths left her mouth as Jocasta curled up against him. "Amazing," she got out. They'd pulled several orgasms out of each other, their bodies wholly in tune with one another's demands and desires. They'd gotten together more frequently for about three-and-a-half weeks. Three weeks, four days, and two hours if one wished to be exact. He shouldn't know that. So what if it was getting harder to put the wall back up, more complicated to put distance between them? It was necessary, and they could only continue meeting like this.

Jocasta lazily stroked his chest over his heart. Hades, he loved when she did that. "I don't think I could ever get enough of you."

"Mmm ..." Even this tiny touch from her did things to him, though in a more muted way. He wasn't sure he had a single drop of cum left, and his cock was spent for now. "I enjoy hearing you say that." He wished things were different. So very different. He regretted his recruitment into his position; wished they had a different King and that he didn't worry so much about his sisters. He hoped they could leave the pack, go far away, and never turn back. Pierce shook the thoughts away.

"How has your sparring been going?" he asked, his fingers trailing gently up and down her side. It was only in the aftermath that things were so gentle between them. Sex was always rough and demanding. Except for that one time—Nope! Not going there, not even a little.

"Good. Duke is a much better partner. He doesn't go easy on me, but he never lets it get too far. His movements are very well-controlled."

Snippets of thoughts that weren't his own touched his mind, but he couldn't get a hold of what any of them were. Pierce smiled. Gods, he was getting used to smiling, but only around her. He didn't smile around anyone else. "I am glad you found someone new to spar with. I know you enjoy it." A shudder he couldn't stifle went through him. "I just cannot..." He took a deep breath and let it out slowly. Then did so again. "I have more time to spend here today than usual. Markham left the village early this morning, and I have no duties at home to attend to."

Jocasta shifted her head and laid it atop her hands on his chest. The motion shouldn't have pleased him as much as it did. "I do too. I'm not expected at the bar until later." Pierce's hand raised of its own volition. Starting at her ears, he caressed the back of her head, hair, spine, over the curve of her rear, and then back up to do it again. "Tell me about your siblings."

His hand froze at her request, but only for a second. It took him a moment to get the words out. "I am the oldest. I have four siblings. But I may as well only have three. In my heart, it does not matter what they accused my brother of or whether he is innocent, though I know he is. Communication is not an option, and my youngest sister, Lillianna, does not even know of his existence." Oh, gods, agony lit a fire in his chest. Outside of his arguments with Derrick, he hadn't spoken of Logan in a very long time. "Lillianna is sixteen years of age. My other sisters, Zinnia and Dahlia, are in their third decade of life."

Jocasta caressed his cheek. "It must be difficult not to speak to him. Even with your sisters there, I imagine it doesn't do much to ease the pain."

He closed his eyes and visions of how things used to be played in his mind. Running through the forest with Logan, catching small game, swimming in the river, their games in the caves, and play-fighting and wrestling. All the trouble they'd gotten into together. He squeezed his eyes shut tighter, slamming a steel door on the memories. "No. It does not. Nothing does." He hadn't meant to say that, but the words had come out, anyway. "After the king expelled him from the pack and my father disowned him, he forbade us to speak of him. My father is not one you would ever want to disobey." Why was it so difficult to speak of his brother? It shouldn't be. Especially as he hadn't even uttered the male's name out loud yet. "Two years before my father disowned him, Markham chose me to become one of his Informants. I tried to decline, but it is not something you can say no to. My brother and I had been so close before then—more than blood. Afterward, everything changed. I miss him." Oh, Hades, fuck, he did.

Pierce could feel more than just his heartache as Jocasta brushed a tender kiss on his chest, just above her hand. "I'm so sorry, Pierce."

As he opened his eyes and his gaze caught hers, the words spilled out. Not even a dam could've stopped them. "It frightens me sometimes, the possibility that Lillianna might learn of his existence. She would seek him out. She would be angry we hid the truth from her. And rightfully so. I fear she would hate me for keeping the secret from even her. I think Logan would hate me too, but he has so much more than that to hate me for. Out of all of my sisters, Lillianna is the one I am closest to. Her heart is very pure, but she is so ferocious. She despises everything about our life, and I betray my soul every time I do not encourage her hatred. Zinnia is frightened of doing the wrong thing, of getting punished. But she is a follower. She will do anything she is told to do. And our father tells her to do a lot. Dahlia is..." He shook his head. "Let me put it this way. If she were a bear, she would be Markham's perfect mate." He rolled his eyes. "She disappoints me, but I could never openly say that to anyone from home. The village is the perfect place for her."

It was the most he had ever said at one time.

"I think you're wrong about them hating you. I think your siblings would be angry, but they'd understand. Everything you have or haven't done has been to protect them. To keep them safe. My sister always tells me that no one but the oldest can understand the burden of being the oldest. I disagree with her. All these years, you've shouldered the weight of being the oldest, the example, living up to certain expectations, all so you can keep them safe. They would understand that. They would understand you had no simple decisions. That you've lived in a world of gray, not black and white."

"And yet I have despised every single decision I have had to make for the sake of safety." He laced his fingers with hers, rubbing his thumb over the back of her hand. He almost didn't say the words, but he risked nothing by telling her. And it felt good to talk. She was the only one he wanted to talk to. She never judged him, not even when the full brunt of his anger had shown. "Another Informant, and probably the closest person to what I could call a friend, Derrick... He goes to the fight ring in the marketplace. He speaks to Logan." He paused. "I do not know what they speak of. But Derrick hates Markham with a passion as well. I think he hopes to take him down. I have tried to make him understand it is not a possibility. But he persists anyway. The day I met you, I almost could not keep myself away the last time we were near there. The consequences would have been too dire had I made contact. I cannot do that." But oh, how he'd wanted to.

Jocasta sat there quietly for several moments. She kissed his chest, then flipped her gaze to his. "I think I saw your brother last night at the fight ring. My sister insisted on going. She refused to listen when I tried to talk her out of it. I couldn't let her go alone, and she disappeared within minutes of our arrival, along with the male I saw. I only glimpsed him, so I can't be sure, but with what I saw there, I can't imagine he would want you to seek him out. At least not there."

Pierce bolted upright, but kept her in his lap. His hands gripped her upper arms, but he forced himself to maintain control. He couldn't bear to harm her. "What did you see? Please, tell me. How did he look?" That she'd gone to the fight ring—which, according to what little Derrick had told him, was a ruthless place—was something that would probably haunt him later, but he couldn't think on that now. And he refused to think about how he never had, not once, asked Derrick the question he now posed to her.

"Bright aquamarine eyes, dark brown fur, really tall. Taller than you. The male looked like he was watching everything, studying everyone around him. His gaze locked on us, but it wasn't full of anger. It seemed like remorse. Then I felt my sister leave and, when I looked back, he was gone."

Logan had always been taller than him. The male had always watched, always studied everything around him. While his brother's fur had been dark as night when he'd left the village, on a rare occasion, he had seen that change in males, slight shifts in hues and vibrancy. The eyes, though, he had never seen another wolf with quite the same color eyes as his brother. A breath left him in a rush. He ran a hand over his head and face. "He has nothing to feel sorry about. Oh." He flicked his gaze to her. "Did he look alright? Derrick has told me some things about the fight ring."

"He didn't look like he'd gotten in the ring, if that's what you're asking."

Pierce swallowed hard and forced himself to release her, stroking her arms before resting his hands on his knees. He dipped his chin, acknowledging her words. Even if Logan fought there, the male was always more than equipped to handle himself. Pierce stared off. "As long as he is alright. I have not truly spoken about him in so very long. I think I have pushed my true feelings so deep inside me I did not understand how much I missed him or how sorry I am."

Jocasta ran her fingers up and down the nape of his neck. "Maybe, someday, you two can speak again on a more neutral ground. Until then, you can always talk about him with me."

He hugged her and pressed his forehead to hers. "Thank you." Pierce kissed her.

"I'd do anything for you."

He wanted to say it back, say he would do anything for her too because he would. Absolutely anything. Including dying. But he couldn't say that out loud. That was something he would have to keep to himself. He turned her around in his lap, so her back was to his chest, wrapped his arms around her, and laid his head on her shoulder. "I want to know more about your family, too." He brushed a soft kiss across her neck and caressed her naked skin.

He sensed two different emotions, both relief and hurt, and neither belonged to him. But they didn't linger. As if, like he always had to do, Jocasta swallowed them, tucking them away in a hidden place inside of herself. Leaning back, she got comfortable in his lap. "My mother, Lyrica, she's a strong, quiet, and humble female. She spends most of her time helping around the village. Even uses a portion of the profits from Zancle's Rock for the village. She always says it's just one way to give back. My sister, Ambrosia, we're twins. We look alike, but we're opposites. She's more like our mother. Except she's more talkative and always has her ear to the ground."

He trailed his fingers down her legs. "They sound like wonderful people. I can hear the love you have for them in your voice."

"Honestly, I don't know what I'd do without Am. Mindlink or not, she's kept me out of more trouble than I'd like to admit."

He frowned a little as he sensed sadness and regret that he didn't feel. "Oh, yes? What kind of trouble have you gotten into, my queen?" Regardless of the dangers of admitting his true feelings for her, painfully keeping them all to himself, he couldn't resist calling her that.

A soft chuckle escaped. "I was seven when I learned I could camouflage. And I thought it would be just the grandest idea to scare the groundskeeper while he was out with the spourgiff. We only had ten back then, but I spooked the animal and not the keeper. Ambrosia yanked me back just before its claws came down."

His eyes widened as he looked down at her, and then he laughed. It was more than just the chortle he'd previously uttered around her. This was a full-bellied laugh. "I am sorry. I am sure it was not funny back then. But I just got an image in my head and—" It took another moment for his laughter to settle. He laid his head on her shoulder. "You must have been terrified. If that ever happened to our yo—" He snapped his jaws shut, effectively cutting off the word that almost slipped out of his mouth. Truthfully, in the quiet hours of the night, he often thought of what a young of theirs would look like. What it would be like to live in a place where he could have one with her. They would never have that chance, though, to have young, to raise a family together. He didn't even know if he could procreate. He hadn't ever gotten anyone pregnant, and young were becoming so increasingly rare in his species, and he should not be thinking about young. Nope. Not at all. "I am glad you were not injured," he whispered.

"I think it's why Am keeps me so close now. She works at the bar, and I work at the karaoke booth. But she's always watching me."

"As I always watch out for my siblings. As well as I can, anyway." Logan aside... Pierce swept her hair over her shoulder and kissed her neck. His lips lingered against her skin. "Jocasta, there are things I wish to say to you I cannot. Saying them aloud would make it impossible to leave you when I have to. It is almost impossible as it is. I hope that by not saying them, you do not think I care for you any less than I do."

She leaned into him and inhaled his scent deeply. Closing her eyes, she sighed. "I don't. It doesn't mean it hurts less. I know how difficult it is to part ways. Every day, I stay here a little longer. Some days, it feels impossible to let you go. Not say everything I wish we could. But I would bear this pain just to have the time we have together."

"We will bear it together." He brushed a tender kiss across her neck, sliding his hands over her stomach, and then palmed her breast. "I will bear every bit of the pain because I will not give up a moment of my time with you. I could not stand not seeing you. You are mine." He nipped at her ear, then turned her head toward his, taking her lips in a deep kiss. "Mine." He growled.

"Yours. All yours. Just as every bit of you is mine. All mine." Stroking the nape of his neck, she fused their lips together.

He felt so much in the kiss. All the love she had that she tried to keep locked away. The ache that wrapped around her every time they parted. The emptiness she pushed aside to get through each day. Just as she had, Pierce conveyed his feelings for her in the kiss, too.

While he didn't verbalize it, he said how much he cared for her. How much it physically hurt to be parted from her, despite the necessity. The number of times he thought about her. Or how she stayed on his mind in the darkness every night, when sleep wouldn't come because he missed her voice, her scent, her very presence. He didn't say how much he dreamed of a life with her, of young, both things that could never be, or how she made it worth it to get up in the morning because he hoped to see her. The way she made his soul feel alive for the first time. Or how much he loved—yes, loved her. None of these things he said aloud, so he showed her the only way he knew how.

Pierce rolled her over on the ground beneath him, keeping his mouth fused to hers, his tongue warring with hers, as he entered her swiftly. Her legs wrapped around him as he slid in and out of her, each thrust hard but slow. He dragged the torture out, their lips and tongues and teeth on every part of each other. This time wasn't like the other times—except for that one time, that one other time they had poured their feelings into every stroke, lick, touch, kiss and thrust. The walls were down, and it was no longer just about lust but the love they had for each other.

Each languid kiss, each sensual touch, each long and drawn-out stroke where their hips came together told them of the depth of their desires and hopes. Things they didn't share with anyone else. Things they only spoke of in the quiet mornings when they got together.

Her head fell back, and a loud moan left her mouth, vocalizing her pleasure as her orgasm erupted all around him. His release exploded out of him at such a force he could have sworn his heart stopped for a beat. As her pleasure mixed with his, he uttered her name on a growl and bit down on her shoulder. His body shook with not one climax, but two, filling her until his seed spilled over. Their orgasms mixed with their sweat soaking the ground beneath them.

Through their lovemaking, he marked her. The way a male wolf did when he claimed his mate. As they stilled and he relaxed his jaw, he kept their bodies joined, placing licks and kisses over the mark he'd left on her shoulder. *Oh, how I love you,* he thought. Although he didn't speak the words, he prayed she heard them whispering in his head. And she would know. He was nothing without her.

Jocasta nuzzled his nose and brushed a gentle kiss across his lips. It was nothing long, nothing deep, just a simple touch of their noses and lips, letting him know she felt every part of him.

If he were someone who cried, he suspected the tears would roll down his cheeks now. The love he felt pouring from her was enough to take his very breath away. For so long, he had been cold, starving, lonely. His heart was a frigid hunk of ice. An impenetrable force surrounded his soul. But she warmed him from the tip of his tail to the end of his nose. She filled him up and took away his hunger like food never could. Gave him companionship, something he could hold on to, even in the moments when they weren't together. She had melted the frost from his heart and showed him it could hold and give love. Jocasta broke the barrier around his soul, piece by piece, shattering it and throwing each piece away. He loved this female more than he ever thought he could love anything or anyone.

He had no words. Nothing that sufficiently explained the emotions running through him. Nor could he speak the words he had.

Picking her up carefully in his arms, he carried her to the basin and entered the water with her. Pierce slowly and gently washed her, leaving not an inch of her lovely, precious skin, scales, and talons untouched. When he finished, she bathed him in return. She took her time, tenderly cleaning him from the top of his head to the bottom of his feet. The silence between them as they washed one another didn't feel as if they were scrubbing away the remnants of their lovemaking, of the hours they had shared. It felt as if they had taken a new, unspoken step together.

They spent the rest of the day together. They swam in the basin, ate a midday and evening meal, talked, laughed, and lay together in the grass, fully content in each other's company. When the light in the sky lessened, his heart broke all over again. He didn't want to leave her, but he had to go. Pressing his forehead to hers, he brushed a tender kiss across her lips. "I will come back as soon as I can. As always."

"I know you will." He felt two waves of pain as she said the words, one very different from his own. There was no other way, though. This was how things had to be.

Pierce kissed her deeply and passionately. Holding her body against his for a moment, he kissed her bare shoulder, over the mark he had left. Then he backed away. It took everything in him to put one foot in front of the other as he moved toward the trees. When he reached the treeline, he shifted back to all fours, then glanced over his shoulder at her. "So that you know, I would do anything for you, too. Give anything for you. Even my life." With that, he looked away and forced his body to move.

Leave. Walk away. From his life. His heart. Soul. Truth. Back to the village, where he pretended. The opposite of him. Where hatred, evil, and everything in between lived. Back to his family, yes. A sister that he had to protect. Though with each passing day, he was less and less sure he could go back to where he had to be instead of staying where he belonged.

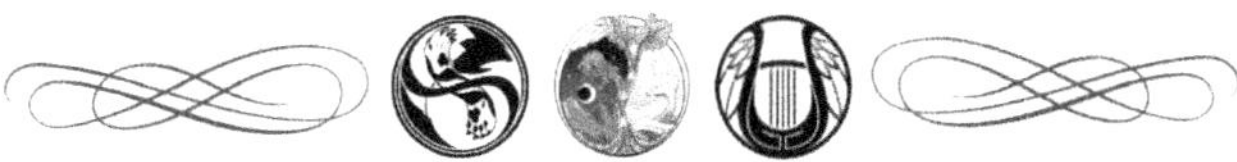

Jo stood there and stared at the various equipment in her booth. She and Pierce had parted ways a few hours ago, and already her heart broke. Of all of their goodbyes, it had been the hardest. Something had changed between them over the last few weeks. Although neither of them said the words aloud, she couldn't deny that they'd fallen in love. Even with the physical distance between them at the moment, she could still feel the emotions that came out of him earlier.

Maybe even then.

She'd started singing again. Something she hadn't done since her father passed away. Being with Pierce gave her strength. Her gaze flicked over the various songs she had to choose from. One, in particular, caught her attention. "Break In" by Halestorm. A slow smile settled across her face. It was perfect.

She got everything set up and descended the short staircase to the floor without another thought. Heading toward the blue-agate stage, she met her sister's gaze across the floor. Ambrosia had done so much for her over the years. Things she'd never really thanked her for—something she should probably do.

Despite all Ambrosia had done, she'd kept on with her life just the same. Not once altering her ways. Until she met Pierce, he changed everything. Jo smiled as her sister leaned against the bar and focused all her attention on her.

The music filled the bar, and silence settled across the patrons. Jo smiled, and her aria echoed around the building as she belted out the first verse. She poured everything she felt into the words—her love for Pierce, how much she missed him when they were apart, the loneliness of the nights forced upon them, simply because of what they were, and the laws of his King.

When they'd first met, they each had a wall around their heart, protecting themselves from any emotional pain. During their time together, they'd become beacons of light for one another, leading each other out of the darkness. Their souls had called out to each other, day after day, night after night, as they became one another's home.

The more time they'd spent together, the more she'd run to the basin where they'd meet. Each day, Pierce broke her wall down a little more. Slowly, the bricks crumbled beneath his touch, his voice, his eyes, the way he looked at her.

Jo moved into the chorus; her voice grew stronger with each word that passed her lips. Pierce had invaded every part of her. Their entire relationship was reckless, but neither of them had stopped themselves. No one had ever seen her the way he did. Maybe she'd been defenseless from falling in love with him, but she wouldn't have wanted it any other way.

With a passion she hadn't known in such a long time, she quickly slipped into the second verse. The first time there had been a difference between her and Pierce—it occurred when she'd broken down, talking about her father. Pierce had let her fall apart, then pieced her back together. It went well beyond that, though. She'd sensed the difference when they'd spoken about his family. The surrounding darkness had shattered, and they'd made one another whole—one piece at a time.

Her voice lifted as she went back into the chorus. There was no doubt in her mind. With each other, their walls came down, allowing them to fall in love. They'd given one another everything they had until all they heard was each other.

Jo positively beamed as she finished the last of the song. She didn't know if he could feel her emotions in his village, but she hoped he could. Like a whisper that was just for him, one that would go unseen by everyone else. Something that would make him smile in private. Because they had to protect one another and keep each other safe, this was how things had to be for them.

When the song ended, Jo couldn't stop the smile that crossed her face. Whether or not he'd felt it, she swore she could feel him. As if he stood right here with her, basking in the love they had for one another. As everyone clapped, she glanced across the crowd and her gaze stopped on her twin. Ambrosia stood right by the karaoke booth, applauding with everyone else.

That was beautiful, her sister said through their shared mindlink.

Thanks, Am. Seeing the bright grin on Ambrosia's face, Jo prayed it was a sign of the future.

Chapter Twenty

It was pretty early in the morning as Derrick sat with Gabby at the river. The summer months warmed as soon as the sun rose into the sky. Today would be a hot one. Gabby had curled up on the ground on all fours and just lay there, watching the water as it rushed by. He sat next to his mate in his humanoid form, slowly stroking the back of her head and the nape of her neck as she cried silent tears. He tensed when he sensed someone coming and partially sat up. The scent on the air belonged to his sister, so he forced his body to relax. His gaze returned to the water as Devina came through the trees, in her beast form as well.

"What is going on, Derrick? Why is she crying?"

"I am with child again," Gabby answered before he could say anything. Her voice was soft, and she didn't turn her head to look at Devina, just continued staring out at that water.

His sister blinked. "Please tell me I did not hear you correctly. Again? Are you serious?"

Derrick rolled his eyes but didn't speak.

"So, you two are still having sex?"

"Obviously," Derrick said, a bit of a growl on the edge of his tone.

"Could you not have waited until I had things figured out? I have been working my ass off..." Her words trailed off. "What are you going to do now?"

"First off, sister mine, I am twenty-four years your senior. Do not lecture me. You are barely out of adolescence. Second off, it is not like we planned this."

"Oh, like you did not plan the last one?"

Derrick snarled. "Shut your mouth about it, Devina. Now." Gabby hadn't moved past the loss of their child that had happened in the spring.

His sister inhaled a deep breath, exhaling slowly. "I am sorry," she mumbled. "That was heartless of me to say, and I did not mean it. I am just worried for both of you. Hades, all three of you."

"Yes. I know you are worried." He was too. He still hadn't located Migas Village, not that he'd had time to search. Markham kept him so busy with orders, most of which he couldn't pretend he hadn't done, that he'd barely had time to see Gabby. He had tried to be careful, but had not been cautious enough. There would be times they couldn't steal a moment away for a week or more, which had resulted in them not being able to keep their hands off each other. Neither of them had brought up the herbs either—ones that should've prevented this—but no longer did so. He also hadn't seen Logan since the day he'd spoken to him back in the spring. After Gabby's... He gave himself a mental shake, putting the thoughts out of his head.

"Does Gavin know?"

"No. She wanted to, but she could not bring herself to tell him. It broke his heart last time when..." He couldn't finish the sentence.

"Did you think it would not happen again, or ... Sorry, I am just trying to understand. Why on earth would you take the risk?"

"You have never known the love we share. True matings here are so rare. But it has happened to us. It is not something that one can deny, nor turn away. What has happened just happened. It was not intentional, but that does not change it."

"You two need to leave. Now. I do not care where you go, so long as you go."

Gabby turned her head to stare at her, tears still pouring down her cheeks. "How can you say that?" she whispered. "You know what leaving would mean. I cannot leave Gavin, and I cannot leave my mother."

"If you left, Gavin would follow you, and you know it. He has his reasons for not wanting to stay here, apart from you and your mother. As for Gemma..." Moving closer to them, Devina sat back on her haunches. "You know your mother wishes for yours and Gavin's safety above anything else. She would want this. If she knew you carried a young inside you, she would want you to go. To leave, find a place to hide, find the hybrid village even, be safe. Be happy. Raise your young *together*. Staying here, you are just waiting for the iron to drop. Markham will find out about the young. If he does not grow suspicious that the young is not fully feline during your pregnancy, there will be no hiding it once you give birth. You know what will happen then."

Gabby closed her eyes, fresh tears falling as she curled more into herself.

Derrick let out a harsh sigh. "She will not go. I have tried everything to convince her, but she will not."

"The number one reason is that you refuse to go with her, Derrick. Because you refuse to go, it prevents her from even thinking of going."

"I cannot put her at further risk, Devina."

"And how is staying here, staying with her, continuing to have sex, *not* putting her at risk?"

"You really should stop speaking of things you know nothing about, Devina. Miss, *I will never have a mate.*"

"To me, it is an intelligent choice, one that I fully intend to follow through with. Unless things change within the pack, I cannot protect myself from much, but I will not be in the situation you two are in. I do my best to support you both, and I would not want to speak against what you are doing. Speak against your love. At least, I am trying. Regardless of my decision, I understand love. Perhaps not this type of love, but I understand. That does not change how foolish it is. Especially if you refuse to leave the one place you are in immediate danger."

"I am an Informant. Markham will *not* let me go. He will have me hunted down until I am found, and he will have me killed. What then, for Gabby and the young? Will he let them go when they are found with me? Or will he rip the young to pieces before doing the same to her? Tell me, please, how my going with them would be a *good* choice."

His words only made his mate sob harder. He hated himself for speaking them. They were at an impasse, and he didn't know how to move past it. If Gabby and their young could be safe, he would take the pain that came with that separation. She was unwilling, or perhaps unable, to even consider it. And she feared leaving her brother and mother behind in the hands of her father. And Markham. But that, at least, even if he did not say it aloud, he could understand. While he didn't wish to leave Devina and their parents behind, his sister refused to leave. Though he'd never asked their mother and father, they would never leave their daughter behind in this place. Staying would further ensure he could protect them, at least as much as possible, and keep Gabby and their young safe as well. He turned away from his sister, wrapped his arm more around his mate, and stroked her head.

"Gabby has decided she will no longer leave the village. At least for the time being. She is afraid..." His words trailed off. His mate was terrified that shifting, that too much activity, would cause this pregnancy to go the same way as the last one.

Silence stretched between them for several minutes before Devina stood up. "I must go. I have plans to meet someone. Hopefully, I will find something out today. At least, more of a solution. If anything pans out, I will let you know. For now,"—she paused—"be careful. Just, gods, be careful."

Derrick watched his sister briefly as she left the same way she'd approached and then stared out at the water. He couldn't stay here much longer. He didn't care so much about finding Migas anymore. Even if he did, it wasn't a natural solution for them. They both had their reasons they couldn't leave. No, ultimately, they had to find a way off the isle. It was the only way. The only way they could escape Markham, get Gabby's mother away from her father, and be free. If only he knew how to accomplish it.

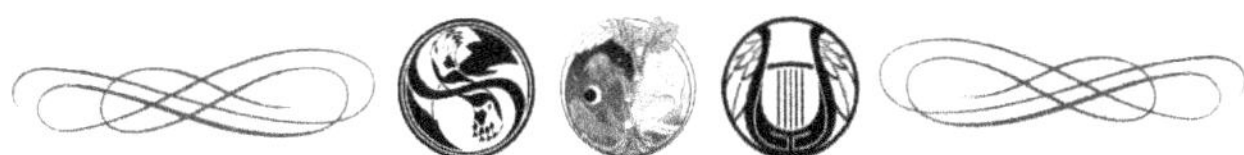

Gavin remained tight on Parthenia's heels as they made their way through the forest. Their trek following the path his mate and Devin had laid out earlier had proven relatively easy. If he and Devin ran and Parthenia flew, it would've impeded their pacing. At least this way, they avoided traps of any kind along the route. Devin was in the lead, Parthenia took up the second position, and Gavin held the back.

Parthenia tilted her head, attempting to look beyond Devin as she slowed her pace. Hopefully, they had reached their destination. "Are we at the edge?"

"Very close, yes," Devin replied. "We must take care. We could run into anything."

Gavin took a step closer to Parthenia. His instincts were on high alert, and there was an uneasiness about him. He'd never strayed far from the village. Few did without permission, really, for fear of punishment. And the path they took could turn dangerous at a moment's notice.

"Be of ease, Gavin. We are all more than capable," Devin said.

"I know we are." Despite the knowledge, he couldn't shake the apprehension.

"Should we then take the invisibility potion?" Parthenia asked. "Or wait until we are closer?" The potion wouldn't last longer than an hour. Although Devin and Gavin could camouflage, this gave them an additional layer of protection. Parthenia had recommended they get as close as possible before indulging. They needed all the time they could to study the barrier. Search for weaknesses or a break.

"Yes, now would probably be a good time. It would not be wise to get any closer before we do."

Parthenia shrugged her knapsack from her shoulders and dug out the three vials she'd brought along for their mission. She handed one to Devin, another to Gavin, and uncorked the third for herself. His mate had perfected it. No one above would even know she'd left. Not that she'd been able to sneak up on him at the treehouse. He'd caught her scent before she'd even made it to the top.

They each drank the potion and became nothing more than a part of the background. It felt strange going invisible without using his ability.

"We should be as quiet as possible," Devin whispered. "The potion will not keep any guards from hearing us."

"And mindful of our steps," Parthenia added. "We do not wish to leave tracks." At least as much as possible. Even if they made it back to the forest unseen, none of them knew much about dragon-shifters.

As Gavin left the shelter of the trees, he caught his first glimpse of the water. He had never seen what Devin called the ocean. It was breathtaking; what they could see of it, anyway. Small waves rolled over the top of the water. The white grains of sand squished beneath the pads of his paws. It was soft and cold all at the same time and grittier than the soil. The surrounding air smelled fresh and a little like salt.

The closer he got, the more apparent the fog became. Almost as if clouds from the sky manifested on the ground. They hovered above the water and continued to the sky and beyond with no end in sight. There was a bridge, which meant there had to be something on the other side.

"Come. Look at this. The slats of the bridge." Devin's voice came from closer to the overpass.

Gavin shifted to his humanoid form and kneeled at the edge of the structure's edge. He frowned as he looked down at the first slat. It was a bright green color with what appeared to be an engraving in the middle of it—an emblem that was a mixture of color: black, brown, tan, and white. It also featured a tail and paw shifting into a hand.

The next one was a different color, with another emblem in its middle.

Gavin felt it as Parthenia came up behind them. "The one with the lyre and wings that belong to us. Sirens, I mean."

"This first one could be ours," Devin said. "The others belong to different species, at least from what I have learned on my travels around the isle." She named each one. One emblem to represent each species on the isle. They were all connected.

Gavin reached where he felt his mate and captured her hand within his own. "They repeat. I wonder how far across the bridge we could go?"

Parthenia squeezed his palm. "There is only one way to find out."

"Derrick and I were having a discussion the other day," Devin stated. "He agreed with me. None of our species will survive without unity. Markham proves that daily, but this bridge proves it even more. We are dying out. He should believe that more than most. He is the last bear in existence."

"Markham is a fool," Gavin uttered. "No one would disagree with that, outside of his favored pets." Taking a tentative step onto the bridge, they moved together until they stood in front of the fog. It appeared dense, so he slowly reached out, placing his hand against the mist. It was cold to the touch, but his fingers went straight through it.

"None of us will survive if we continue to divide ourselves. But how do we get anyone to listen?" Parthenia had shared information with him regarding her species. They weren't any better off than theirs. They had kept much to themselves. He sensed Parthenia extend her hand to the fog and a small puff of it emerged midair, as though she cupped it in her palm. That was odd; the fog reacted differently to her. Gavin frowned.

Sensing Devin to his left, he watched as the mist seemed to form over the shape of her hand. "How strange," he said, primarily to himself. "What do you think that means?" He pushed his hand further into the haze; there was no resistance. Would they be able to get through? It couldn't be that simple.

"I don't know," Parthenia replied. "We need to walk until we can't." She squeezed his hand, telling him they were in this together. Or if they got through to the other side—wherever it led them.

He tried hard not to allow the hopefulness to sink in. There were no guarantees that they could pass over, and giving into the hope would only give way to further disappointment if they could only go so far. Gavin reached out and found Devin's shoulder and clasped it. Putting one foot in front of the other, they started across the bridge. When they had gone forty yards, a current crackled in the air before them.

Parthenia hesitantly reached out again. A spark danced across her skin, almost as if it was scanning her. A light shocked her fingers. "Ow," she muttered. The electric waves were gold flecked with green and black. "I don't think this is part of the isle. I think one species created this."

A curse shot from Devin as the fog swirled. The same thing must've happened to her. "What do you mean? What could create this? And why?"

"I don't know why. I'm not even certain of the how. Most barriers require a catalyst or key to both lock and unlock. Even one with magic such as this. As for the who ..." Parthenia paused. "Those colors I have only ever seen in siren materials. I believe my species created this."

"The true question is," Devin posed, "was it to keep us in or to keep something out?"

"We must find that key."

"Thank you, Gavin, for stating the obvious," Devin teased. "At least now we have more of an idea of what we are up against. Parthenia, do you think there are any texts at your home that might give us more information?"

Parthenia leaned her forehead against his chest. He could tell she was holding tears at bay. Even knowing that her species had created the barrier was no answer at all. Or hardly one. She sighed and straightened her body. "There is a possibility. We have a vast library. Gavin and I have gone through perhaps thirty or more texts in the last month, but there are hundreds more."

"I will do anything and everything that I can to help as often as I can get away. If it would be possible, I could even bring some to Gabby. I know she would love to help as well. She refuses to leave the village right now, though. She truly fears her condition."

"Her condition?" Parthenia paused. "Will it be safe for her? I mean, to read them in the village. Gavin told me books are forbidden."

As Gavin realized what her words meant, the scent of his fear practically leeched off of him, permeating the air. Gabby hadn't told him again. And shape shifter pregnancies were frightening enough without the risks his sister and Devin's brother took.

"One at a time should be alright," Devin stated. "I can bring each one back to the tree at first light, before inspections. Derrick usually does the one for their hut, and, as long as he can remain composed, it should be fine."

"Is Gabby with child again?" he asked softly, a slight tremor in his voice.

Devin didn't respond, but there was no need. If this pregnancy came to fruition, and Gabby showed, he would never forget what he had seen Markham do to the last couple that had been in Derrick and Gabby's position.

Parthenia gave his hand a squeeze. "Yes, that seems a good idea. We have kept many books there as it is. I will bring as many down as I can."

"Good," Devin said. "I will spend all of my free time going through however many I can. We will find the answers we seek."

The fog shifted and enveloped Parthenia during their conversation, almost as if it was hugging an old friend. "The barrier was erected not long after our war with the half-breeds. Perhaps if there is someone old enough on the isle, they can offer aid in our search."

"Who are you thinking?" Devin questioned. "The oldest creature I know is Markham. From what I have gathered, he is somewhere in his fourth century. They killed many of our own off when he took control. There are substantial gaps in the ages of our species. The ones that are left."

"I don't know. Much has been retracted from our histories, which don't align. But I can't imagine Markham is the only one."

"No, he cannot be." Devin paused. "I know of a village where others have sought refuge. Our kind has not gone near it. From what I have heard Markham's Informants say, a great feeling of dread overtakes them if they get anywhere near it. I believe something or someone protects it from anyone who would cause its inhabitant's harm. Perhaps I could find it and see if anyone there may have some answers. It may well be a long shot. I do not know who may live there. Or what?"

"You cannot do that alone. That is far too dangerous," Gavin commented.

"I have done much alone that is far too dangerous. And I am still standing."

They'd taken a risk coming this close to the fog. Even approach the bridge right in dragon-shifter territory. Though it relieved him that no guards waited or lurked nearby. "We must trust she will be safe," Parthenia said. "There are places we can't go. If I'm discovered, even on the isle..." Her words trailed off.

Gavin frowned. He glimpsed images from her of what it meant when a siren lost its wing, what a siren went through during unnatural death. Losing a wing wouldn't just be painful; it would be deadly. "We should go back. We have been here too long," he mumbled, his voice strained.

"I agree," Parthenia said.

Gavin tried to hide the ache in his heart. He gripped Parthenia's hand tightly as he kissed the top of her head. Wrapping his arm around his mate and holding her close, he turned them back toward the forest.

The invisibility potion wore off just as they hit the forest's edge. It had succeeded in its job. He could tell she felt his grief. Something he hoped to conceal, but failed to hide.

"We should go back to the treehouse. We can regroup in a few days, but I'll leave books there tomorrow." Parthenia shifted her gaze to Devin.

"Of course. I will see what I can find out until then." Devin clasped Parthenia's shoulder, and then did the same to Gavin. "Hold on to your hope, brother." She shifted to all fours and took off into the trees.

Parthenia watched for a moment as Devin left. Her shoulders slumped as she heaved a deep breath. "We will be fine. We have the potion now, and it will help."

All he could do was nod, unable to find the words to say. He held Parthenia against his chest and stroked her hair. Whether he was trying to ease her, himself, or both of them, he couldn't have said. "Everything is going to be alright. We will figure this out. I am sure of it." But the hope he tried to hold in his heart didn't quite reach his tone of voice.

She hugged him tightly and cocooned them in her wings. Closing her eyes, she inhaled his scent. "I'm sorry, my love. I didn't wish you to see that. Ever. But it won't happen."

He laid his head on top of hers, breathing in deep, allowing her scent to fill him up. "No. It will not. I will not allow it." He kissed the top of her head. "I cannot lose you," he whispered. "I would not survive it."

"Nor would I, but that won't happen. We'll find all the answers we seek and a way off this isle." She pressed a soft kiss to his chest, over his heart. "Come. We cannot linger any longer. Let us go to the treehouse."

He nodded against her and shifted to all fours. Once she had climbed onto his back, he made his way to the treehouse. He hoped with everything in him, it wouldn't take much longer for them to find the answers they needed.

Chapter Twenty-One

"Are you sure this is a good time?" Logan glanced down at his mate and dropped a kiss on the top of her head. They'd spent the last hour in a room with Santos, the Elder of Migas. Her village was his now, too. His head still reeled from the conversation. Not just because the elder granted him sanctuary, but because there was a high possibility the male would give it to his sister and brother, as well. But there was something else, something that Santos had said that still made little sense to him. *Evil does not always win. All you have to do is look to the sky to see the tides of change.*

Had the male been trying to say that one day Markham would die? Over the years, it was something many hoped for. Even then, they prayed their so-called king met his end. Most wouldn't have the opportunity of a better life as long as Markham ruled. As much as he wanted to understand Santos' words, he focused on his following actions. Not just with getting his brother and sister out of Métamorphe, but meeting his mate's family for the first time.

"I'm positive. It's a perfect time. Mom already has afternoon meal ready, and Jo should be back in the village soon."

He scanned their surroundings as they walked across the wide-open clearing. Everything was so different here than from Métamorphe. The houses appeared structurally sound, nothing like what he'd grown up with. That didn't include the buildings across from the homes or how the houses sat angled from one another. Hades, this would be a good place for his family. He grinned as they passed different people, who nodded at both of them. He didn't know any of them, despite that, they acknowledged him. It was so strange. "Have you told your mother or sister anything about me?"

"I told them I was bringing a guest. I didn't say who."

Logan raised an eyebrow as his fingers danced along her hip. "Any reason?"

"Well, I've seen little my sister lately, and I didn't want to end up answering their questions twice."

Given the number of things it had taken him time to tell her and how he'd kept any information regarding her a secret from Derrick, he couldn't fault her reasons. "I can understand that."

"I probably would've told my sister by now; there isn't much we hide from each other. But even when she's physically present, she's not there. I think she is seeing someone."

"Oh? What makes you think that?" From what she'd told him, not only did she and her twin live with their mother, but the two sisters also worked together. It would stand to reason that, as often as they saw one another, the possibility of a male in their lives would have certainly come up.

"A lot of things. I've seen changes in her recently, plus she disappears a lot during the day. The only time I see her now is when we're at work. Even there, things have changed."

"What changes?" Logan tucked Ambrosia into his side as they slowed their pace a bit. The day they'd met, something Ambrosia's sister had done upset her. She'd complained a few times since then about her twin, though it occurred less over the last few months. Part of him thought that had more to do with—No. His mate didn't need to pick any of that up from him.

"She doesn't drink as much as she used to. She gets up on stage and sings, something she hasn't done since we were kids. Not to mention Jo just seems happier. And she doesn't spar anymore. She used to do that here. But a couple of weeks back, she changed sparring partners, which couldn't have made me happier, and the guy she spars with now, they run around chasing his son."

Although he hadn't yet met Ambrosia's twin, her suspicions made perfect sense. Since they met, he'd gone through changes, some more visible than others. It was the same with Ambrosia. He noticed them even if she didn't. "I am certain when she is ready to talk to you about whatever the cause is; she will."

"I know. I'm just used to knowing things. And it's kind of strange not having to spend so much time taking care of her."

"It simply means there will be more time for you and me, especially as we will live here together." With a low growl, his gaze met hers, and he leaned down to brush a soft kiss across her lips. "And I cannot wait."

"Me either," she mumbled against his mouth.

There was a lot to get accustomed to in Migas. Not just moving in with his mate, but the differences in things he'd have access to and how he'd be able to survive going forward. Plus, what he hoped would occur in the coming days with his youngest sister and older brother. Things were finally coming together. Soon.

"Hey, Logan, before we get to my mom's house, can you do me a favor?"

"Anything for you, my love." And he meant that. The worry emanating from her made him stop mid-step. There was something that weighed on her mind. He'd thought it was *that*, but that didn't seem to be the case.

"Can you just keep that you knew my father to yourself? I don't want to upset my mom and my sister at all. At least not right now, you know?"

They'd spoken about it once before. It made sense to keep that information to himself. Maybe, eventually, when they all knew one another a little better, he could tell them what he knew of Galenus. Not to mention, his brother might have a few stories to add in there, too. Logan brushed another tender kiss across her lips and stroked her cheek. "I can certainly do that."

"Thank you." She smiled up at him. "I love you so much."

"I love you too, Ambrosia. I am grateful every day that you fell into my arms." That day had indeed altered his life. The influx of emotion from others quieted so much easier whenever she was nearby. She was his shield against the chaos of the outside world, and he couldn't imagine going another day without sleeping next to her at night.

"A day I'm sure we'll both remember for the rest of our lives." She smirked.

No more fitting words had ever been spoken. The images that Logan saw flash through her mind had little to do with their fiery exchange. It was more their first time together. A low rumbled sounded in his chest. He kissed her again. "I believe we should go on before afternoon meal becomes less of a priority."

"I agree." She slipped her hand into his and laced their fingers together. "However, I took the entire night off, so maybe we can head to the cabin afterward and remind ourselves again how we first met."

Oh, yes. Yes, they absolutely could. Logan bit back the growl that threatened to come out and reminded his dick to be a good boy. Just in case, he wrapped his tail around his hip between his thighs, so he didn't embarrass himself in front of Ambrosia's mother and sister. That was something he very much wanted to avoid.

They started forward, and he tried to take in the differences in the houses as they passed by them, but he couldn't stop thinking about the next few days. Hades, he prayed Derrick could finally talk to Lillianna. Everything else would follow. He'd love for his family to be there when he officially got mated.

Ambrosia slowed her pace and pointed to a house just ahead of them. "That's my mom's house."

"It looks very nice." At least, from what he could see of it. The house appeared bigger than the log cabin he'd built. Although, a lot of the homes he'd seen as they made their way to her mother's place looked like that. It was just something else that stood out as wholly different from Métamorphe. The homes here wouldn't likely need the roofs repaired anytime a storm came through, as the huts did in Métamorphe. Not to mention, they were all well-protected. Even if the entrance to Migas wasn't well hidden, the houses were in the center of the village, not the outskirts like Métamorphe. He shook his thoughts away. There were so many differences, and he could track them all day long and still find more.

"I suppose so. I guess when you know nothing else, it just doesn't seem like anything more than home." She shrugged as she led him up the staircase, across the front porch, and into the house itself.

Unlike some houses he'd seen, the door didn't have any decoration or color to it, other than the standard dark wood color. Still, it was gorgeous to him, especially with a small front porch and a lovely bay window he could see through. That was all before they even stepped across the threshold. Not too far beyond the doorway, he stopped and peered around. To his immediate left sat a piano. On the other side, two chairs and a couch filled the living room. To his right, there was a small round table, enough to seat four comfortably, and then the kitchen. He spotted the hallway beyond that, leading to the bedrooms. From where he stood, he'd gather three. Hades, the hut he'd grown up in, wasn't even close to the size of this place.

His gaze flicked from the empty hall to the female heading toward them. He hadn't noticed which direction she'd come from, though if the smells in the house were anything to go by, he'd guess the kitchen. He studied the older female for a moment. So, this was Galenus' mate. She shared little with Ambrosia, except for the eye color. It was the same bright amber that reminded him of the sun. And maybe the talons. Other than that, the older female had brown hair and multi-colored blue scales just above the top of her talons. Damn it. He was staring. He needed to stop, and he had to get any thought of Galenus out of his head.

"Mom, this is Logan. Logan, this is my mother, Lyrica," Ambrosia said.

"Oh, my goodness. It is so lovely to meet you." The female beamed and threw her arms around Logan.

His eyes widened ever so slightly, and his arms lifted. What the fuck was he supposed to do? Ambrosia asked him *not* to say anything about Galenus, but the male's mate hugged him. Wait, he hadn't touched her. *Whew.* He'd done nothing wrong. Yeah, the male may be dead, but he still respected him. "Um, it is lovely to meet you as well." He glanced at Ambrosia. What did he do with his arms?

"Okay, Mom. Let the guy breathe," Ambrosia stated.

Lyrica released her hold and took a step back. "My apologies. I was just so excited when my daughter told me she was bringing home a guest."

"No need to apologize. It is alright." He had no other words. "You have a beautiful home." How was that possible? Why couldn't he think of anything else to say?

"Thank you." She gestured to the table. "Come now, let us sit. I know Jocasta will be home shortly, and lunch will be ready soon as well."

Food would be a good thing. It would give him something to occupy his mouth with when he couldn't get words to come out. His eyebrows knitted together. He really shouldn't be this nervous. Although, the more he thought about it, the more it made sense. He wasn't just meeting his mate's mother, but also Galenus' mate, and he had to keep everything he knew about the male to himself. He had to watch what he said. Hades, he hadn't had to worry about that in a long time. Not saying anything about Ambrosia to Derrick had been easier. At least, it had felt that way.

They were moving. Why were they—right. Lyrica had told him to sit. Logan followed his mate and her mother to the table. He pulled a chair out for Ambrosia first before he sat down.

"So, Logan. Ambrosia tells me you are good with wood."

"I suppose that is true." That wasn't what he meant to say. It was pretty accurate. She'd seen the work he'd done in the cabin, not to mention the cabin itself. "Yes, it is something I am capable of." Okay. That sounded better. Maybe not as well as it could've come out, but at least he didn't make his mate sound like a liar.

"He's just being modest, Mom. His work is quite stunning. He'd put half the males in the village to shame."

"Then, maybe you can show the males around here a thing or two," Lyrica commented. "I am positive many would appreciate it."

Had he blushed? His cheeks were hot. He might've blushed. Not that he was sure it would be noticeable through his fur. Thankfully, if Ambrosia felt his emotion, she didn't point it out or say anything. Hades, he loved that female. "I would enjoy passing that knowledge on." His brother hadn't ever really gotten into it. No one in his family had. It wasn't like he could've done a lot with it, but he'd done what he could. Mostly, he whittled smaller items. A lily for his mother. A toy for Derrick's sister, Devina. There were others, but those stuck out the most. Although he'd made some furniture pieces for their hut, Ailwin had likely destroyed them after he left—no way the male would've allowed them to remain in their family's home.

"Tell me about your family, Logan. Do you have any siblings?"

How did he answer that? He didn't want to lie, but he also wanted to talk about Dahlia as little as possible. Honest. That was the best way. "I have four. One older brother and three younger sisters."

"Wow. It sounds like—"

The door opened and shut. "Sorry, I'm late."

His nose twitched. A smoky aroma with a distinct sweetness filled his nostrils It couldn't be, but it smelled like it. Logan flipped his gaze to the female at the door, and as discreetly as possible, he inhaled deep. His eyes widened. Holy Hades! Eighteen years had passed since the last time *that* scent had invaded his nostrils, but sure as shit, Ambrosia's twin sister smelled like his brother. He tilted his head and narrowed his gaze. Was that? No. His eyes zeroed in on her shoulder. Really, he needed to stop staring at her like this. But, holy fuck, that was a mark. One likely given to her by his brother. Logan grinned. Oh, this day just got a lot better. He crossed his arms and leaned back in the chair.

Ambrosia glanced at him. "Um, Logan, this is my sister, Jocasta."

"It is wonderful to meet you, Jocasta." He couldn't stop smiling. It seemed his brother had over one reason to leave Métamorphe. At least once he got Lillianna out. With this new information that landed in his lap, getting Pierce out was inevitable. He canted his head. Ambrosia's sister had said nothing yet, but she eyed him. Had Pierce told her about him? Spoken of him? Perhaps. He was getting a lot of shock from her, which made sense. It wasn't as if Ambrosia had told her about him. Hmm, did Jocasta realize he recognized Pierce's scent all over her? Impossible to tell.

"Um, yeah, you too. Logan, right?" Jocasta ran her fingers through her hair, sweeping it over her shoulders, hiding the mark. "So, you're, um, the guest that Am has told Mom and me all about."

"Yes, that would be accurate." Well, that answered that question—every single one. From what Ambrosia had told him earlier, she only had suspicions, which meant Jocasta had kept a secret of her own. And it made perfect sense. If Markham discovered one of his Informants had a relationship that he hadn't approved was bad enough. Tack onto that, Jocasta was part shape shifter and Galenus' daughter... Yeah, no wonder she'd said nothing.

"Tell me more about your siblings," Lyrica stated.

His gaze shifted back to Ambrosia's mother. It amazed him how quickly his nerves settled. "Pierce is my older brother. He is passionate but stubborn to a fault." Was it mean to throw his brother under like that? Yes, but he wanted to see if he could get Jocasta riled up enough to admit the truth.

"Mom, is there anything I can do to help with lunch?" Jocasta asked as she disappeared into the kitchen.

"Well, I've finished most of it. Though, if you wish, you can always put a salad together," Lyrica replied.

"Great. I'll do that." With a brief nod, Jocasta started milling about the kitchen.

He had to stifle the smirk. Yep, he'd ruffled Ambrosia's twin a little. Not enough for her to admit something about Pierce yet. Logan grinned. "He was always a bit of a troublemaker. When we were younger, he came up with most ideas for things we should try. Nearly everything was something he suggested."

Lyrica chuckled. "I am certain you both scared your mother many times."

"That we did." No matter who came up with the idea, they'd always gotten into trouble, together and equally, most of the time. He was a bit more daring, pushing the boundaries to see what he could get away with. Not that Pierce ever argued against it. At least not until they got older. That was when things changed.

"And what of your sisters?" Lyrica asked.

Logan reached across the table and took one of Ambrosia's hands in his own. "I have three. Dahlia, Zinnia, and Lillianna."

Something clanged against the kitchen floor.

Their rapt attention snapped in Jocasta's direction.

"Are you alright?" Lyrica questioned.

"Yes, sorry, Mom. Too many things in my hands." Jocasta offered a faint smile and returned to getting things together.

He wasn't so sure about that. Something else was going on, some fluctuation in her emotions. Concern. Shock. Her desire to protect threw him off. Was she trying to protect Pierce? From who? Unless ... No. There was no way she believed that. He'd never turn his brother in. Logan peered back at Ambrosia, who still stared at Jocasta. He raised an eyebrow. This might be part of that mindlink thing she'd told him about.

"You have to love when you are not part of a conversation." Lyrica snickered as she focused back on him. "Tell me about your sisters."

With a slight chuckle, Logan nodded. Absolutely. Though he believed Ambrosia would tell him later. Or at some point. Despite their one problem, they attempted to talk about everything. It didn't always work out that way. He'd never had much of a relationship with Dahlia. She'd been a lot of trouble, not something he wanted to tell Ambrosia's mother. Zinnia had been a child when he left. And he knew nothing about Lillianna. He sighed heavily. "To be honest, Lyrica, I have not seen Pierce, Dahlia, or Zinnia in a long time, and I have not even met Lillianna."

"Oh, well, I can certainly see how that might prove difficult to know much about them."

"If that's the case, then how can you describe Pierce as stubborn?" Jocasta asked, crossing her arms somewhat defensively.

Hades, it would be so easy to question her about her interest in just one of his siblings. He glanced at Ambrosia out of the corner of his eye. If she caught onto anything, she didn't give it away. "He was an adult when I left. Dahlia and Zinnia were both still rather young."

"Does that mean you think less of him?"

"No. On the contrary, I respect the choices Pierce was forced to make. If I had been in his place, I would have done the same." He offered her a genuine smile. "We have both always been protective." It had probably only grown since then, especially given what he'd learned recently. "Even after all of this time, I do not believe that has changed."

Jocasta dipped her chin in acknowledgment as she focused on putting a salad together.

"Let me check on everything. I believe we should be close to ready to eat." Lyrica stood.

"Why don't Logan and I set the table while you do that?"

"That sounds like a wonderful idea, Ambrosia." Lyrica disappeared into the kitchen.

Although he spoke little about himself, he hoped he gave both Lyrica and Jocasta a good impression. He didn't want either of them to think badly of him. Not when they would be related soon. Standing, Logan pressed a tender kiss to the top of his mate's head when she returned with the plates. A long time had gone by since he'd spent time with family, but he looked forward to all the changes coming his way.

Chapter Twenty-Two

Parthenia bit the inside of her cheek as she stepped through the willow leaves and ascended the staircase. Her mind swirled with everything they'd seen on the bridge. The golden color of the electric waves flecked with green and black inside the fog had danced on her brain her entire flight back to Pteryrina. How did a siren build such a massive barrier? Or had they only created the token that made the barrier? Either way, Devin's question echoed in her head. Why? Was it to protect Prisma Isle or to keep something in?

She rubbed at her temples. Seeing the barrier up close had indeed given them something. More questions. Demeter and all the books they still had to go through. She sang the notes for the secret door to open with a heavy sigh. Once inside the library, she doubled up the dosage of her cleansing potion. She was sure she needed to work on the potion some more. No matter how hard she tried, someone almost always seemed to pick up hints of Gavin's scent on her.

Of course, she'd spent the night with him last night. That would surely make a difference. They'd both needed it, especially after her thoughts darkened at the end of their trip. She hadn't meant for them to go there. It wasn't something she could change. At least something good came of it. Rubbing her temples again, she passed rows upon rows of books and made her way toward the front doors of the library. It added a lot to her plate, but today was a fresh start.

Parthenia pushed open the heavy wooden doors of Antekilio and descended the stairwell. A few books sat in her apothecary that she could read through while she ate breakfast. Maybe it seemed like a lot of work, but she was definitely up for the task. They'd find some answers regarding the barrier between the four of them. They had to.

"Where have you been?"

Her foot had just hit the second step when she heard Fagonia's nasal voice. Good Demeter. She couldn't get to her apothecary without running into the female. Just once, it would be nice not to be constantly monitored. "In the library. Where else would I be?"

"All night?"

"Yes. All night," Parthenia said, her voice even as she blatantly lied. Fagonia didn't need to know otherwise.

"If that's true, then what is this odor wafting from you?"

"That would be sweat. Some of us work around here." Parthenia smirked. Really, she shouldn't antagonize the woman. It wouldn't make things better. Just worsen them.

"Exactly how did you sweat in the library, unless you were running around stacking books all night long?" Fagonia crossed her arms.

With her feet now on the ground, she spun around and faced her aunt. "It happens when you're flying around reading volume after volume to find answers to your problems." Of all the things she had to say, it had to be that. While it was true, it showed she'd researched how to resolve the problems with The Poppy Fields and The Reflection Pools. While she had, nothing she had found provided her any answers. She just kept coming back to the same conclusion.

There was something wrong with Prisma Isle.

"Oh? So then, you've found out how to address the loss in The Poppy Fields and The Reflection Pools?"

Parthenia narrowed her eyes. Technically, yes, she had, but no one—and she meant *no one* in the village—wanted to listen to her. None of them were prepared for what needed to happen.

"No? That's what I thought. Maybe I should just go report this to Elder Vasilia and see what she thinks." Fagonia spun on the back of her heel and started forward.

"It's the same fucking answer I've been saying for months now. But you have to be right, don't you? Keep telling everyone that I'm wrong and that our losses have nothing to do with what's going on with the isle, right?" Goddess, she was so damn tired of Fagonia pulling this shit. Not that she'd ever spoken her mind with the woman before.

Her aunt halted and faced her. "Whatever is going on down below has no impact on us up here. It has been like that for centuries, and it remains true today."

"Bullshit," Parthenia snapped. Whatever happened on the isle affected all of them. Not just sirens and shape shifters, either. They were all impacted by it. It was time someone saw Fagonia for the destructive female she was. "We're all linked, but you refuse to acknowledge that. I guess it's easier to convince everyone otherwise because then they'll think you're less of a burden on our people than you appear. Instead of helping in any kind of way, eventually, you'll lead us all to our deaths. But that seems to be what you want."

"Parthenia!" a voice screeched from behind her.

Oh, no. No, it couldn't be. Parthenia glanced over her shoulder. Yes, it was her mother. She noticed a small crowd had gathered. Damn it. Her focus on her aunt prevented her from seeing any sirens approach the clearing in front of the library. Her eyes flicked from one face to the next. Blair. Ariadne. Cipriana. Fantasia. How much had any of them heard? From what she could see by the looks on their faces, it was enough.

There was no way out of this. And if what she believed was coming, well, then she might as well make it worth it. She turned her attention back to Fagonia. "My apologies. I meant to say that you were nothing *but* a burden on our people."

"Parthenia!" Her mother hollered again. "Apologize to your aunt. Right now."

Like that was going to happen. Parthenia opened her mouth to refuse and caught sight of their Elder approaching. Well, this just got worse. Initially, she expected a private punishment at home, but with their Elder now involved, that made it public. Goddess, she prayed Gavin didn't feel any of this from her. Two months had gone by since he'd gotten punished in his village. She remembered what that felt like. Damn it. She had to say something. She couldn't just keep her mouth shut.

"Is there an issue?" their Elder asked.

Her mother bowed her head to their Elder. "Yes, Elder Vasilia. My daughter seems to have forgotten her place and how to address those older than her."

She hadn't forgotten. At least not to the people it mattered with. Her mother and her aunt weren't on that list. Although no one addressed her punishment, she didn't miss the smirk that settled on Fagonia's face. She'd bet anything that the female did this on purpose.

"You know our laws, Parthenia. Your punishment is your mother's decision."

"Yes, Elder Vasilia." She offered a slight bow of her head. What else could she do? All she could do was acknowledge what was coming. Nothing more. Parthenia peered over her shoulder at Cipriana. Her half-sister flicked her eyes from her to their Elder. No. She couldn't do it. Yes, their laws placed her under her mother's responsibility until the day she mated. But she couldn't tell any of them about Gavin. Cipriana only knew because she'd followed her one time.

"Very well." Their Elder eyed Parthenia's mother. "Amara, what is your decision?"

Amara inhaled and exhaled a deep breath, clasping her hands in front of her. "As her verbal assault was public, so should her punishment be as well. Twenty lashings with the scourge."

Her mother's weapon of choice. She'd had it used on her twice before. However, this would be the first time it had ever been public. In the past, her mother punished her in the privacy of their own home. Not that she'd been home in the last couple of months. There wasn't anything she could do. Demeter, give her the strength to keep Gavin from feeling her pain.

"Very well. Cipriana, will you please assist Parthenia in getting changed into the appropriate attire?"

"Yes, of course, Elder Vasilia," Cipriana said.

"Thank you." With a slight nod, Elder Vasilia fixated on her. "Parthenia, I expect you in the temple in ten minutes. Everyone else should gather now." And, just like that, they all dispersed in various directions.

Cipriana grabbed her hand and dragged her off toward her apothecary. Yeah, she'd have the right dress in there. It was among the things she'd packed from her home. Her sister said nothing as they walked. That wasn't a good thing. The quieter her sister was, the worse the tongue lashing she was about to receive. Great. She'd have to listen to her sister go off before she got a physical lashing.

"Your grip is a little tight," Parthenia uttered as Cipriana practically shoved her through the door of her apothecary.

"Good. I'm glad." Gritting her teeth, she slammed the door shut behind them. "Why didn't you say anything about Gavin?"

"I couldn't. There's too much at risk if I did." It wasn't hard to understand the direction her sister's thoughts took—their laws. She fell under her mother's rule *until she got mated*. While they had mated, she couldn't share that information with anyone.

Cipriana pinched the bridge of her nose and lifted her gaze to Parthenia. "Too much risk. You're about to be whipped, and telling them about your mate is a risk?"

"Yes. Because if word got back to Gavin's King, he would kill him." Parthenia swallowed the lump in the back of her throat. It was the first time she'd ever spoken those words aloud. She'd barely acknowledged them in her mind. Although she knew their truth, it wasn't something they ever focused on. They concentrated on how much they loved one another. "I'd gladly take a whipping if it keeps him safe."

Her sister sighed heavily. "Okay. I'm not happy about this, but I understand."

Good. No one could change it now. Parthenia had one option—try her hardest to shut her emotions off from Gavin. Try to hide the pain from him. Inhaling and exhaling a deep breath, Parthenia strode further into her apothecary. She set her bag down on the table and retrieved the right dress from a hook on the wall. "You'll have to pin my hair up."

"I know the drill."

For the next few minutes, the two of them worked together in silence. Parthenia changed into an off-white dress with a bareback hooked around her neck, and her sister slowly pinned her hair into a chignon. She allowed as much calm and peace as she could to wash over her. She didn't fear what was coming, but it would be painful. Her mother had likely searched for a reason to punish her, and she'd unintentionally given it by going off on her aunt.

Instead of thinking about the lashing, she let images of her and Gavin's time together flood her mind. Their time in the springs. His reaction to The Reflection Pools and The Poppy Fields. The number of times they'd been intimate together—how they pleased one another physically. The different ways they comforted one another in difficult times. More than that, she thought of everything that they wanted for their future.

All of those memories allowed warmth and love to flow through her. This was just one more hurdle for them to get over. And she could do it for him. Inhaling and exhaling one final deep breath, she glanced over her shoulder at her sister. "I'm ready."

With a slight nod, Cipriana left the apothecary first. Once they were both outside the door, she faced her. Cipriana took both of Parthenia's hands in her own and squeezed them. "Fantasia and I will take care of you afterward."

"Thank you." She started toward Demeter's Temple. They used the temple for three purposes. Meetings, which they had whenever the Elder deemed necessary—ceremonies or celebrations, usually if someone had gotten mated or they welcomed and anointed young. And punishment, but only when it was to be made public.

Gods, no matter how hard she tried, she couldn't keep her thoughts from drifting to what she was walking toward. Parthenia swallowed to wet her throat. *Demeter, please give me strength.* Gavin didn't need to sense what was about to happen. She probably wouldn't keep him from feeling it, but he didn't need to sense her emotions beforehand. Her gaze flicked to the library as they passed it, and she swallowed again.

Deep breath. One more deep breath. Parthenia focused on her and Gavin's happy memories. On the good things. On their love. It was the only way she'd get through this. Cipriana squeezed her hand one more time before they entered Demeter's Temple. They couldn't walk through the temple connected. This was a punishment. No one could show her support until her mother completed the twenty lashings. Nor was she to be shown mercy.

Parthenia strode down the long hall with her sister by her side. It wasn't much, but it was more than she could've hoped for as they headed toward the back of the temple. There was a reasonable likelihood the lashing would injure her wings, which would prevent her from flying out. Usually, they would have flown in, but the temple rules also forbade it as retribution.

Her eyes fell to the fourth and final set of doors leading to the area designated for punishment. Both were wide open as she and her sister approached. She held her head high and crossed the threshold. A broad, angular slab sat in the center of the arena with a handhold and strap at each end. Without once looking over at the small group of sirens gathered in the stands, she walked with purpose toward the waiting stone slab.

As expected, she kneeled in front of the rock and leaned against it. Turning her head to the side, so the cold stone pressed into her cheek, she grabbed onto the handholds as she spread her wings. Her gaze fell to Cipriana, who stood off to the side, hesitating. Her sister had to do this. Parthenia bobbed her head. They could do nothing to stop this. It had to be done. Another moment passed before Cipriana strapped her wings down and backed away to join the others.

The first crack of the scourge rang loudly in her ears—the metal barbs connected with her skin, burning as they raked across her back. A single tear rolled down her cheek, but she refused to make one sound. She drew every memory she had with Gavin to the forefront of her mind and cycled through them in rotation. Maybe she couldn't stop the flow of tears each time a metal bearing tore into her body, but she didn't have to utter a single peep that revealed the depth of her physical suffering.

She'd be damned if she gave her mother or her aunt the satisfaction.

Each new strike made it more challenging to hold on to her carefully composed rotation of memories. She couldn't count the lashes; otherwise, her self-control would fracture. All she could do was cry at the pain wracking her body each time the barbed ball ripped a piece of flesh from her back or one of her wings. Gavin had suffered far more wounds to protect her—to protect them both. She could do this for him. Tears continued to stream down her face.

Her grip on the handholds tightened with each new stinging lance across her bare skin. Blood trickled from multiple wounds, staining her dress. She didn't have to see it to feel the wetness upon her back and the stickiness in her feathers. With images of Gavin still cycling through her mind, she winced as the barbed hook of the balls struck her again. Although she hadn't tracked the number of lashes, certainly they had to be close to the twenty-mark. Demeter, please, they had to be close. She didn't know how much more she could take.

Quietly, Parthenia sobbed. Her lips trembled. She tightened her grip on the holds. Please, *please*, let it be done. She couldn't break. She just couldn't. Fat tears poured down her cheeks and onto her neck. Someone yelled, but she couldn't determine who or even understand the words.

Gavin. Gods, Gavin. She didn't want him to feel this, but she couldn't stop the agony that ripped through her as the barbs lashed against her back repeatedly. Gods, they weren't done. They weren't done. *Please, please, please*, she prayed. She couldn't take any more.

They had to finish. They just had to. Parthenia sagged against the slab of stone. She just couldn't.

"Parthenia," Cipriana said.

Her name registered, but nothing else. She couldn't make out the words coming from her sister's mouth. Everything was blurry, but she made it through since her sister stood right here. Gods, she made it through it. She couldn't, gods, she couldn't keep her eyes open. *Gavin, please forgive me,* Parthenia thought before the darkness claimed her.

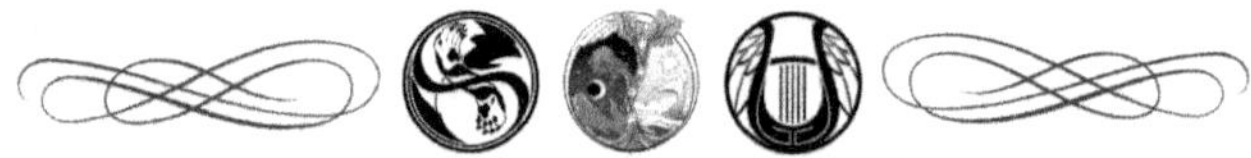

Logan's ears perked up. He knew the noises around his cabin since he had lived here for nearly ten years. Someone was nearby. His gaze shot to Ambrosia. "Stay inside and lock the door." Offering no more information, he exited the cabin and shifted to all fours. Sniffing the area, he descended the short staircase. A familiar acrid stench permeated the air. He moved forward with a low growl, prepared to defend his home and mate.

"Logan," Evan's voice called out in a sing-song tone. "Come out, come out, wherever you are." The barely discernible sound of paws crossing the ground, weaving through the trees, reached Logan's ears. "Do not be shy. I have missed your company."

This was his turf. No way Evan thought he had an advantage. The male couldn't beat him eighteen years ago. They may be close in height and weight, but time could strengthen a male, especially when one got into enough fights. He focused on the sound of Evan's movements. The last thing he wanted to do was kill the male in front of his mate, but he would do what needed to be done to keep her safe.

It wasn't hard to tell when Evan stopped walking, maybe even figured out where he stood. Indeed, Evan could smell him. And Ambrosia, too.

"I cannot wait to see the prize I get for bringing your head home," Evan called out. "Your father will be so happy to see it. He may even reward me.

Maybe I will not even have to pay this time. Hmm, I wonder if I will get my pick."

Evan's words almost got to him. Except he sensed what the male felt. His claws dug into the ground just a little. He could tell the satisfaction running through the male at both accidentally locating him and the prize he believed waited on the other side. It was enough to help him maintain control. And enough to ensure he killed the male painfully. And it didn't make him budge. It was imperative he kept the upper hand and forced Evan to seek him out.

Evan wove in and out of the trees as he slunk closer. "Dahlia gives it up freely. She has turned into quite the little slut, if I say so myself. But she is fun. Zinnia, not so much. She feels good, but the sex is rather boring. Now your baby sister, ooh, you have not met her, have you? Have you not had the pleasure? I have. Many, many times." He chuckled. "She is a screamer."

Oh, gods. Lillianna. No, he hadn't met her yet. But he would soon. He would get her out of that pit. And ensuring one less Informant returned would be his pleasure. Evan didn't feel any fear yet. Logan would enjoy making sure the male did. He bit the growl back and focused his senses on the soft sounds of Evan's footsteps. Most may not have heard Evan's movements, but Logan's hearing was one of the best, as was his sense of smell. Combined with his empathic ability, it made him a deadly foe. One Evan should fear. With all of his senses at work, his gaze shifted in the direction he expected Evan to come from. Logan prepared himself, ready to slap away the smirk he knew the male wore on his face.

Evan let out a low chuckle within the edges of the trees. "I smell a female. That scent is rather delicious. Where do you hide your plaything? Is she in that cabin, I see? I know she is. I can hear her. Smell her. When I am done with you, maybe I will have some fun with her." He chuckled again as he left the trees and entered the clearing.

Logan's eyes flipped black. "You will not get near her." He lunged at Evan, prepared to dodge the anticipated paw swipe. Striking Evan in the face with his claw, Logan knocked the bastard off his feet.

Evan fell back with a snarl but was up on his paws in moments. Blood dripped into his eyes. He ducked the next attack and launched his body into Logan's, throwing both of them back. Evan's jaws latched onto one of his hind legs, and he held on, striking out with his claws and catching Logan on the side.

He swung his front claws at Evan's muzzle and kicked at him with his free hind leg until the male released his hold. No time to shake the pain off. He got back to his feet and charged at Evan, throwing him into one of the nearby trees. The sound of snaps filled the air as the male's ribs connected with the trunk. Logan didn't stop as he sliced across Evan's belly with his claws.

The male howled out in pain as blood spilled from his abdomen. Although he attempted to move, he failed to get his body out between Logan's claws and the tree. Evan's jaws snapped at his neck, but he jerked his head out of the way just in time. The male shook the blood from his eyes and swiped his claws again, connecting somewhere with Logan's body. There wasn't time for him to look.

Growling low, Logan struck the male's muzzle again and again. Once for Zinnia and once for Lillianna. Then he used his paw to hold Evan's muzzle out of the way, giving him perfect access to the male's jugular. "Do not worry. I will send your head back to Markham." He wrapped his jaws around Evan's throat and ripped it open, crimson liquid spilling everywhere.

Slightly panting, Logan took a couple of steps back and winced as he sat back on his haunches. First, he needed to tell his mate that everything was okay. Then, he could finish separating Evan's head from his body, bury the head, and burn the remains until he could appropriately deliver the male's head to Métamorphe.

Yes, that was the order in which he would take care of things.

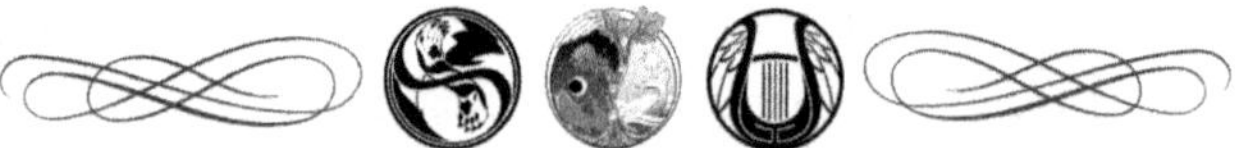

Ambrosia sat in the oversized chair, one leg bouncing as she stared at the crackling fire. It had taken every ounce of willpower not to go outside and check on Logan. Although he'd carried her inside when she'd gone out to check on him a couple of hours ago, he'd gone back out to deal with the body. And practically demanded she stay inside. Like it would be any safer. Other than that, the male had been an Informant, so she didn't know who specifically had found them. Or if others would be on their way.

What made them think it would be safe to spend the night here? Yes, they'd been spending time here together for months now without incident, but that didn't seem to be the case any longer. It wasn't as if they needed to stay here. He received sanctuary earlier that day, and their home was likely ready.

They had gone months without being discovered, and Logan had lived in the cabin for years before that. One Informant stumbling on them didn't mean more would come. That should comfort her, but it didn't. No, seeing her mate walk through the door would comfort her. What was taking so long? She got up to her feet, clasped her hands behind her back, and paced the length of the living room.

Two minutes. She'd give Logan two more minutes, and if he didn't come through the door in that timeframe, she was going to search for him. Maybe she wasn't as skilled as her sister, but she could fight if it—

The front door opened. Logan entered the cabin in his humanoid form.

She raced across the room and launched herself into his arms, her legs wrapping around his waist. "Oh, thank the gods."

"I am sorry, my love. I did not mean to take so long." With a slight grunt, he held her against his body for a moment. He shut the door and walked over to the chair she'd recently occupied. Logan sat down in the chair, adjusting her so her legs were across his lap.

Curling up to him, Ambrosia inhaled and exhaled a deep breath as she focused on the steady beat of his heart. "I'm just glad you're okay." That he wasn't hurt more than he'd been during the initial fight. Gods, she just needed to lie against him like this for a little while until her nerves settled. "It was an Informant, wasn't it?"

"Yes, it was." He stroked the back of her head, gently running his fingers through her hair. "But he was the only one. I made sure of it."

Good. That was good. Not that it meant others wouldn't find Logan or come across the cabin at another point. If she didn't know better, she'd think this place was cursed. Between the Informant and her—no, she couldn't think about that. It would only lead to tears and, if she started crying again, she didn't know if she'd stop. Weeks had passed since that happened, and those memories still crept in. There was only one way to get them out of her head. "What did you do with the body?"

"You do not need that image in your head. It is bad enough you saw the body. That is not something I ever wanted you to see."

Ambrosia sat up. She reached up and caressed his cheek. "Please, tell me." The last thing she wanted to do was explain why. But she had to give him something. Something that would get him talking. Even if he was trying to protect her, this wasn't knowledge he had to hide. "I just need something to occupy my mind."

"If you truly feel you must know, I will tell you."

It was better than what sat on the edge of her mind as it was, and she didn't want him to see it either. Neither of them needed the reminder of her failure. "Please…"

Nodding, he blew out a heavy breath. "I retraced the path he had taken. I did not want to burn the body close to the cabin, so I went as far away as possible."

There was something he wasn't telling her. Something he'd left out. Not that she deemed it essential. There would be only one reason to burn the body some place the male's scent already existed. Protect the cabin. Maybe deter others. "You don't think he might've been a scout, do you?"

He gingerly ran his fingers through her hair, playing with the ends of her tresses in silence for a couple of minutes. Maybe longer. Logan sighed. "I do not know. I do not think so, but I did not want to take any chances."

Right. Less of a risk to her and Logan. But if they genuinely didn't want to take any chances, then they'd be wise to leave. Ambrosia swallowed the lump in the back of her throat. That would be the best thing for them. Right? "Maybe it would be best if we returned to Migas then."

"With as dark as it is, it would be too risky to leave now. We will wait until morning." Logan kissed the top of her head. "Do not worry, love. Nothing will happen to you."

That wasn't what scared her; quite the opposite. She was afraid that something would happen to Logan in his efforts to protect her. He believed they'd be alright, and she trusted him. Ambrosia slowly nodded. They would be fine. "We should clean and tend to your wounds."

"Soon, love. Let us just sit here a little longer."

"Okay." As long as he was comfortable, she was okay with staying put. Being curled up to him like this helped ease her fear, so if he wanted to keep sitting here, then she wouldn't argue. At least not for a while. They could always come back to it after she addressed his injuries. Yeah, that's what they would do. For now, they'd stay right where they were, snuggled together in the chair in front of the fireplace.

Chapter Twenty-Three

Jo dove into the falls' waters and swam a couple of laps from one end of the basin to the other. How did she approach this, tell Pierce she had formally met his brother? Oh, and not on accident either. No. Nope. Logan was in a relationship with her sister. By all the gods, how had that happened? *When* had that happened? These same questions ran rampant through her head for the last day.

She'd said nothing of Pierce when she'd met Logan the day before. Though she had noticed a twitch of his nose. Had he caught Pierce's scent on her? While she'd done her best to hide the mark on her shoulder, he might've glimpsed it. Despite how much she hated to do it, she'd kept it hidden. No one had seen it. At least, she thought no one had.

Attempting to calm her nerves, she swam back toward the front of the basin. Movement tickled her ears and drew her attention from the water. Pierce was—what in the gods? Her eyes narrowed as she sat back on her heels and crouched down on her haunches as much as possible. "Leo? What're you doing here?"

"Where else would I be?"

No. No, no, no. Jo wasn't doing this with Leo again. The guy rarely came here for his scales. He was one of those that traveled to the beach. "You need to leave, now."

"Why would I do that when you're here?" Completely naked, he ran a hand through his sapphire blue hair, got into the water, and strode toward her.

She tried to step back. It wasn't like there was a lot of anywhere she could go, but she needed to put space between them. Her feet didn't budge. The water constricted around her arms. What the fuck? They never used their abilities on each other, but it was like a rope held her in place. The harder she struggled against it, the tighter it got. "Leo! Stop it! Let me go, now!"

"I don't—" His blue-green eyes zeroed in on the mark on her shoulder. With a loud hiss, he closed the distance between them, grabbed her crimson-colored hair, and yanked her head back. "You dirty whore! How dare you—"

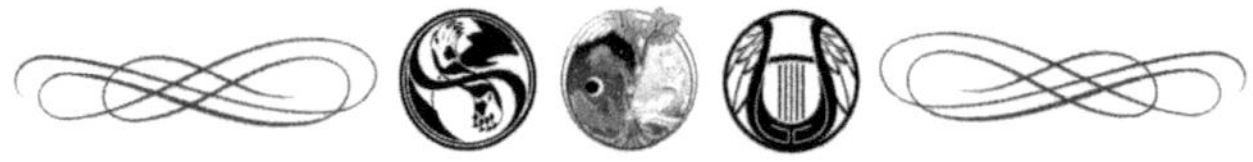

A terrible feeling had twisted in Pierce's gut all morning. He couldn't seem to shake it, no matter how hard he tried to push it from his mind. When he finally left the village, he took precautions, ensuring no one followed him before speeding to the basin. The closer he got to the clearing, the stronger Jocasta's feelings of anger and fear became. The scene he came upon made him absolutely livid. It was more than rage; he was murderous. His eyes flashed an inky black as he sped across the grass and reached the water just in time to hear the words coming out of the male's mouth.

A loud snarl emanated from him as his jaws latched onto the male's arm, jerking him out of the water and tossing him onto land. He landed with a hard thud and scrambled back. "Oh no, you don't," Pierce growled as he stalked toward him. He saw nothing else but the male before him as he got closer. As Pierce lunged forward, his jaws latched onto the male's arm again. Scales broke free into his mouth and he spit them out. He was going to tear this fucker apart for harming his queen.

The male didn't cry out. He created a force of wind that knocked Pierce back, though not much, and shot a glass-like ball of water at him. The slight sting didn't bother him one bit. Out of his periphery, he spotted Jocasta tugging her clothes back on. Moving toward the male again, he swiped a paw at his chest, opening gashes from his shoulder to his waist. Pierce lunged at him, clamping onto the male's calf. As his jaws locked on, he landed hard on the ground, hearing a snap. Not that he cared. Suppose the male broke something, good. If it were on him, he would deal with it later.

Blood ran down his chin as he ripped a chunk of flesh away. His growl was loud as he forced himself to take a step back. The male's death should not be swift, but slow and painful.

And then Jocasta was there, right between him and the male who writhed on the ground. "Pierce, stop. Please, you can't kill him." She stepped closer to him. "It'll draw—" Her eyes widened at the sound that registered two seconds too late. She turned just in time for a blast of water to hit her square in the chest, sending her flying into a tree. Her head banged against the trunk before she hit the ground.

A smirk spread across the male's face as Pierce's heart froze in his chest. *"NO!"* he roared. He rammed into the male, causing him to land flat on his back. As his paws slammed hard against the male's chest, he felt the heart beneath it lose a few beats. His claws flashed once, twice, three times. Blood splatted everywhere, but he would spill every drop. Someone yelled, but he didn't register who it was or what they said. He locked his jaws around the male's throat and was about to rip it out when something significant crashed into him, throwing him to the side.

Pierce jumped to his feet and whirled around—Logan stood over the hybrid he'd nearly killed. He snorted, his nostrils flaring as he maintained his position and protected the male from Pierce. He called out to a female who dropped to Jocasta's side without looking. "How is she?"

"Bruised ribs, for sure, but she's got a gash on the back of her head that needs cleaning. What about him?" The female glanced over her shoulder.

"I cannot look." Pierce's eyes stayed on Logan. "Not without endangering him again."

Pierce's chest heaved as he panted, his teeth still barred. A snarl came out of him. What in Hades' name was Logan doing here? This was the worst possible reunion they could have had. The last thing he ever wanted was for his brother to see him like this. Again. But he didn't regret doing it. And he was not done. "Move."

Logan stood his ground. "That is not something I can do, brother."

"I know what he wished to do." Pierce growled. "I could smell it. He would have killed her when he was through." His jaws snapped as he tried to get at the male, but Logan blocked his way. Pierce heard a groan and felt a pounding in his skull that wasn't his own.

"Pierce?"

His head jerked to the side. "Jo," he breathed out.

"Good, you're coming around," the other female said as he sped across the clearing to her side. She backed up as he shifted to his humanoid form and kneeled, taking Jocasta gently into his arms. He barely registered it as the female strode over to where the unconscious male lay on the ground.

"Jo? Speak to me, my queen."

She reached up to cup his cheek. Blood smeared across his face. "Oh, gods, I'm sorry. I'm so sorry."

"No, my love, do not apologize. This was not your fault." He leaned into her touch. His eye color changed back and a slight tremble echoed through his body. Oh, gods, he could have lost her. The pounding through her temple was still present, so he tried to stifle his growl as he checked the marks on her.

His glance shifted to his brother. The female stroked along the male's head as she kneeled, presumably checking for a pulse. "He's injured badly. I can dress it until we get him back to the village. Only Santos can handle this."

A low growl rumbled in Logan's throat. "Are you sure we just cannot leave him?"

Crossing her arms, the female frowned. "That's not funny."

His brother peered at them. Sorrow poured through him. He wished to say so much, but he couldn't just yet. Right now, Pierce had to focus on his mate. "Where can I take you? To bandage you up? I will not leave you like this."

Jocasta blinked back tears. She swallowed, saying nothing for several moments, then fixated on him. "Help me up, please."

He helped her carefully to her feet, but he kept his arm around her, holding her against him. He couldn't bear to be parted from her right now.

The other female tore the bottom of her shirt and dressed the male's wounds. She rose to her feet and glanced from Logan, who simply nodded at her, to him and Jocasta. "Logan has a cabin about fifteen miles from here. You can take her there. He's got supplies to treat her. We'll handle this."

Pierce looked over at his brother, and the female, who could only be Jocasta's sister. They looked so much alike. "Thank you," he mumbled. He cared not what happened to the male. Hopefully, he would succumb to the injuries Pierce had given him.

"You're welcome," the female said.

His gaze dropped to Jocasta. "I am going to carry you there. You should not be walking just yet." Standing, not to mention just breathing, was causing her pain.

Jocasta nodded to him. She looked back at her sister, and something unspoken seemed to pass between them.

"Fine," the female said. "I'll come up with something."

"We can say he was in the fight ring. I have seen him there a few times," Logan said.

"Fine, but if he dies, I will not lie."

"Then I will move fast, my love." Logan lowered his body so they could place the male across his back. He shifted his gaze to Pierce. "Be careful. There was an Informant out this way just yesterday."

Pierce picked Jocasta up into his arms as gently as possible, cradling her against his chest. An Informant. Out this way. He cursed to himself. "He no longer lives, does he?" Evan had not returned to the village yesterday, and he was being searched for.

"I plan to send part of him back to Markham."

"I need to speak with you, Logan. We have much to talk about."

"Yes, we do. I will come to the cabin once we have dealt with *this*."

Pierce nodded, not voicing the obvious—he would have dealt with it had Logan not stood in his way. "I will see you soon, brother." He looked down at Jocasta. "Do you know the direction I need to go?"

"Yes. There should be a broken tree north of here. That's the path we take."

He headed in that direction, going as swiftly as he could without jostling her as much as possible. He kept his eyes straight ahead. "Please tell me you are alright." His voice cracked as he spoke. He sensed the throbbing in her head, but she was alive.

"I'm so sorry, Pierce. I feel horrible. I should've told you sooner, but I swear, I swear I thought I had it handled. It should've never come to that."

He tried so hard to hold his growl in, but he didn't quite succeed. Not that he aimed his anger at her. It was at the male who had dared to touch his female. The male who had dared to put his hands on, leave marks on his queen. "It is still not your fault, Jocasta. He made his choices, and he suffered the consequences. Though I would have finished the job had Logan not stood in my way." The context of her words finally, fully, registered with him. *Told you sooner. Had it handled. Should've never come to that.* "How long? How long has he been coming after you?"

Jocasta blinked back tears she could no longer fight. "Weeks. I punched him when he tried to kiss me. He left me alone for a few days until I changed sparring partners. Then he showed up at the bar later. Bruce kicked him out, but I thought I had cleared things up. I told him outside to leave me alone. To back off. Even slapped him and kneed him in the groin." She shook her head ever so slightly.

"Try not to move, love," he said when he felt the stab of pain go through her.

"I don't understand. It should've worked. It should've deterred Leo."

Still putting one foot in front of the other, he bent his head down and gently kissed her cheeks where her tears fell. A drop of blood dripped down. How much blood had he gotten on himself? Evidently, it was a lot. "Males like him are never deterred, no matter what you do. Trust me. I know many like him."

"It's my fault. I should've told you. I'm sorry."

"Do not think like that." Part of her thoughts drifted through his head. The guilt she felt for not speaking up sooner, or how things would have ended differently if she had. She hadn't been afraid he would lose; she'd been afraid word would get back to Markham. And he would suffer for it. Not that Markham would have cared if all he found out about was a dead hybrid. But if he discovered any more... "Truly, it was easy to read him. It would not have mattered what you did or what I did. He would not have stopped. He may still not. If he retaliates, I will take whatever punishment comes to me. I do not regret what I did. Remember, I would do anything for you. Anything to keep you safe." He bent his head and carefully kissed her lips. "You know how I feel for you," he said against them. He wouldn't survive if anything happened to her; he couldn't survive without her any longer.

"I do."

A decently sized cabin came in sight, much bigger than any of the huts in the village. It had a large front porch with three small steps. A small clearing surrounded it with the forest lining it. Pierce crossed the clearing and went carefully up the stairs. He didn't stop to look at the handiwork or study the carvings on the handrails. Not that he needed to inspect it to know who'd done it. He held her in one arm as he opened the door.

The inside was cozy and warm, but straightforward. Pierce didn't have the mental capacity to let his eyes wander too much, but it was hard to miss much of anything. A fireplace was built into the far left wall. A couple of chairs sat opposite it, with a small table in between. To the right sat a table with chairs that would easily seat six people. Each with detailed carvings. The kitchen area was inside the house, not something he was used to. A couple of bowls of fruit sat atop the counter, two knives laid out beside it as if Logan and her sister had been in the middle of morning meal. Beyond that was a long hallway that led to additional rooms.

"I am going to set you down while I look for things to bandage you with," he said.

"Okay," Jocasta replied. She didn't look around much as he set her carefully on her feet. The pounding in her head limited the movement of her neck. She took a few baby steps as she ventured a little further inside.

As he moved across the room to check the cabinets for supplies first, he couldn't help but run his hands over the pieces of furniture. It hit him in a rush just how much he had missed them—missed seeing them. The skill and care that went into them rivaled no one else he knew. After his banishment, their father set fire on everything in the home that Logan had built by hand. He couldn't save any of it.

Pushing forward to the cabinet, he opened them one after the other until he found one fully stocked with what he needed. Turning around, he saw Jocasta weave a little, so he rushed to her side. "Hades, I am sorry. I should not have left you standing." He practically tossed what was in his arms onto the nearby table and then picked her up. Carrying her carefully to one chair, he eased her into it. "Let me get a look at this." He moved one of the other chairs behind the one she was on and sat down.

Biting his tongue to hold back a growl, he carefully parted her bloody hair to see how severe the cut was. There were a few minor scrapes along the nape of her neck. Blood matted around the worst of it, a gash at the base of her skull. He was as careful as possible as he cleaned the blood from the back of her head and neck. While he did so, her fingers stroked the meticulous detail of the table. The design was quite intricate.

He gently massaged her shoulders, hoping to ease the tension still in her neck. Once he got a good look at the gash, it didn't seem like she would need stitches. A bandage, for sure, though. He took care of it, probably bandaging it more than truly necessary, then placed a kiss over the top of it. "I am so sorry."

She lifted her tank top enough to check her ribs. "You have nothing to apologize for. If you hadn't come along…"

His chest tightened at the thought of what could have—would have—happened had he not been there. Had it gotten any worse before he'd intervened, not even Logan could have stopped him. "I was more worried about causing him pain than anything else. After what I saw him doing…" Pierce growled. "He meant that shot for me. And he felt it was funny that you got in the way instead." He got up off the chair and kneeled in front of her. Her ribcage had already turned a lovely shade of black and blue—no deep breaths for her. There were faint bruises on her arms as well. It physically hurt him to see the marks she wore. "Are your ribs broken? I want to check, but I do not want to hurt you anymore."

"No, I don't think so. I think my ribs are just bruised."

"I would have taken this for you. You did not deserve to be hurt. Most especially, by the likes of someone like him." He brushed light kisses around where the bruises were, careful not to touch them. "Do you hurt anywhere else?"

She stroked the back of his ears and let out a small sigh. A tender smile touched her lips. "No. I'm okay. I will heal."

"That you will heal is not the point." Her bruises may not have bothered her, but they bothered him. A lot. He should have been there from the beginning. He should not have had to run from miles away to get to her when he had a feeling something was going to go wrong. She should not have been alone in her fear. He wanted to lay his head upon her, but feared hurting her accidentally. Pierce got up and sat behind her instead, reclaiming his chair. After placing a kiss on his mark on her shoulder, he rubbed them. "My brother made this table. And the rest of the furniture. I can tell just by looking at it. It has been way too long since I laid eyes upon his handiwork."

Her shoulders relaxed beneath his touch. She didn't move too much, but she surveyed their surroundings. "It's quite beautiful. I officially met him yesterday. My sister introduced him as her mate."

"Mate? Gods." Logan had mated. He had moved on with his life in the aftermath of what had happened to him. Logan had found happiness, as he should have. As he deserved. "I am glad to hear it. And I thought that must be her. You two look too much alike to not be related." He sighed. "I wish I had not marred the meeting. That should not have been our reunion, either. Almost two decades, and the first time he lays eyes on me again, I have my jaws on someone's throat." He tried and failed to keep the venom out of his tone.

"I had planned to tell you this morning. I said nothing about you when we met, though Logan got a funny look on his face. Our elder gave him sanctuary in our village."

"He looked well," he whispered. "The brief look I got of him. The change to his fur suits him. And if you met him after I left you yesterday, he probably smelled you on me. He always had an extremely keen sense of smell, even for our species." He kissed the side of her neck. "What does it mean that he got sanctuary in your village? You have not told me much about it. Will they better protect him there?" He hadn't said it aloud, but it worried him that there was such easy access to the cabin, especially considering the Informant that had already found his brother here. Thank the gods things had not gone differently.

Slowly, she readjusted in the chair. "Our land is protected. Informants do not come near our land. Based on what Logan said, the one he saw yesterday is the only one who has come the closest. Even if Logan had not addressed the issue, he would not have survived if he came closer to the village. Our Elder and his warriors protect those granted sanctuary."

He let out a sigh of relief and kissed her neck again. "Good. That pleases me. I hope he accepts the sanctuary. I know who it was that was killed. He was no loss."

"I believe he has. He spent a lot of time with our Elder."

"I have prayed to the gods for his happiness and safety since the last time I saw him. I..." Pierce blew out a heavy breath. "Gods, I have missed him." He couldn't admit it aloud, but he was insanely nervous about speaking to Logan again. He didn't know what Derrick had told him either, just that Logan knew of their mother, sisters, and Lillianna.

She caressed his cheek, and he leaned into her touch. "I can't imagine having gone that long without speaking to my sister. We share a mindlink and the longest we've ever gone—" Her words stopped, and her eyes became rather focused. A wince crossed her face.

Frowning, he reached up and placed his hand gently against her cheek. "What is it, love?"

It was another moment before she responded to him. "My sister. She says Logan is on his way back."

Nerves shot through him, and he swallowed hard. He had much to atone for, much to regret and apologize for. He and Logan could have been twins, as close as they'd used to be. Being parted from him, not able to speak to him, even speak about him, had made him sick. Not a day had gone by that he hadn't worried over his younger brother if he was alright and safe. He inhaled a deep breath and exhaled slowly. It didn't matter if he hadn't had a choice in any of it. He had betrayed his brother in the worst way by never seeking him out. "I am glad he agreed to speak with me."

Jocasta stood and climbed into Pierce's lap. Cupping both of his cheeks in her hands, she lifted her amber eyes to his. "Regardless of what has happened in the past, he is your brother. With just the short time I spent with him yesterday, I can't imagine he wouldn't want to speak with you. Pierce, I'm certain he still cares for you."

Being careful of where he placed his hands upon her, he held her against him, pressing his forehead against hers. "I hope you are right."

"I am." He could feel how positive she was about it, and he tried to turn her positivity into his own, though he didn't quite succeed.

Heavy footsteps approached. "I suppose I will find out sooner rather than later."

She brushed a soft kiss across his lips. "I'm going to make some tea and give you guys some privacy."

He nodded, then caught her hand, bringing her gently back to him, and kissed her again. "I do not know what I would do without you." Getting off the chair, he pressed another gentle kiss to the top of her head before she disappeared into the other room.

As Pierce faced the door, the footsteps got closer. The last words he'd ever had with his brother over eighteen years ago flashed through his head. It had been a few days after Markham had punished Logan for turning down the Informant position. But Logan hadn't been the only one punished. Pierce had never cared what had happened to him. He would never get the nightmarish images of what had occurred to their mother out of his head. Never get rid of the horrible picture of his brother dragged out of Markham's hut and chained down at his side.

"You should have just said yes. You think I do everything he tells me to? I pretend more than most in this godsforsaken place."

"No," Logan said. "I could not."

Pierce scoffed. "That is bullshit! You need to go back there and tell him you changed your mind. Before this gets worse."

"There is nothing that could ever make me wear that brand. I am not our father, and I am not you."

I am not you. No, Logan was not. He was a better male than Pierce had ever been. He'd made Logan think he blamed him for what had occurred to their mother. And then Logan had left Métamorphe and never been able to return. Pierce had never accused him. Not once. He just hadn't wanted to lose his brother. He clenched his fists, trying to force his nerves to settle as the footsteps crossed the porch. It didn't work, and he scrubbed his hands over his face as the door creaked open.

Pierce hadn't cleaned up, so he still had blood upon him as his brother entered in his humanoid form. Logan stopped in the doorway, stared across the room, and smiled. It broke him. Crossing the room, he wrapped his arms around Logan in a firm hug. If his brother pushed away, so be it. "Too long. Way too long. I am so sorry, Logan." For words, he had so rarely spoken in his lifetime; he said that a lot today.

Logan returned the embrace. "Way too long, but you have stayed safe. That matters."

"As have you." Still hugging him tightly, he grinned. "And I hear you have mated as well. Congratulations are in order." He pulled back but kept hold of the male's shoulders, getting a good look at him. "You look well."

Logan eyed his brother. "As do you. A ceremony has not been performed, but yes, I have mated. It has certainly impacted me."

"I can tell that it has." He gave him another once-over. "The color change suits you." Pierce squeezed his brother's shoulder.

"Ambrosia seems to have a like for the change."

"We have not had a ceremony either. With current circumstances, it is not a possibility right now." He beamed as he glanced over his shoulder at his mate. She milled about the cabinets as she worked on the tea preparation. Sensing his look in her direction, she cast a smile back at him and then returned to her work. "She is the best thing that has ever happened to me. I believe she has saved my life."

"I can see as much. But I believe you saved each other. At least from what I have been told." Ensuring the door was closed tight, Logan gestured to the chairs. "Come, let us sit."

They crossed the room, and both sat backward on the chairs. Pierce sighed. "I know Derrick has been to see you." He didn't even know how to apologize that he hadn't come. "I wanted to come, but I could not risk it."

Logan folded his arms across the back of the chair. "I understand why you did not."

"Whether you understand, I expected you to be angry at me, and I would not have blamed you. It was not right." He wanted to say how much it pained him to turn Derrick down. How many times he had gotten near the fighting ring, only to turn around and leave. He knew if he got close to Logan, it would be that much harder for him to return home. And he couldn't risk being seen by anyone. Lillianna's life depended on it. He wanted to say all of that, but didn't. Logan would feel the emotions from him.

Logan's gaze dropped to the floor for a moment. "I was angry. For a long time, Pierce. In one moment, I lost everyone. Every person I cared about. My anger subsided some as the years passed. I used it as fuel to build this cabin. Then I met Ambrosia. She helped me see things I had not considered before. My anger changed to regret. Regret that I did not get you and our sisters out. Perhaps if I had, our mother would not be gone. Zinnia would not be lost to us. I am sorry I did not try sooner." He shook his head. "I try not to think of what has not transpired but what I can do now."

That his brother held onto the same feelings that he had—so much guilt and regret—shook him. They had both taken responsibility for something that had not been their fault. Pierce reached out and squeezed his shoulder. "Do not apologize. There is no need. You had no control over any of it. Had you tried, you could have lost your life. That is something I could not bear. I had no control over it either. But knowing that does not change how I feel about any of it." He dropped his hand, then lowered his head, staring at the floor. "How much has Derrick told you?"

Logan scrubbed a hand down his face. "He told me enough. Enough that I have been working on getting you and Lillianna out of the village. I pray Zinnia is not entirely lost and will leave as well."

Pierce glimpsed at him. Derrick had told him that he'd shared information with Logan regarding Lillianna and their mother. Fresh sorrow hit him. "Will they accept us? Me? I have made many enemies over the years, Logan, by my title alone."

"They will accept us. They will accept you. One of them already has." Logan nodded in Jocasta's direction.

He nodded, then let out a sigh. "I never got to give Mother a ceremony. Father is solely at fault for her death. I blame no one but him. He would ruin us all, given a chance. Even now, he is trying to get rid of Lilli. She goes through too much." He lifted his gaze at Logan again as his brother let out a growl. "Jocasta is my life. But, even if they will not take me, please do what you can for Lilli. She is not safe there. If she cannot get away, there may well come a day when I can no longer protect her at all. She is mine, as if she were my young."

Rolling his shoulders, Logan got himself under control and squeezed Pierce's shoulder. "I have already asked for sanctuary for you both. Besides, I do not think Ambrosia would allow it to occur any other way. She has seen too much change in Jocasta to alter her course. If everything goes according to plan, in but a few days, you and Lilli will be free. I promise you that."

Pierce sagged in relief. "Thank you, brother." Keeping Lilli safe had become increasingly challenging, especially considering her age and beauty. The more scouting missions Markham sent him on; the more opportunity the Informants left at the village had a chance to harm her. Not that they always waited for him to be gone, as had occurred, but a couple of months ago. The last time he had walked in on something, he'd come close to ripping the arm off the male before they took him to the ring and beat him. Not to mention what happened when Markham put a stop to fights.

Would it be possible? Could they be free? Could Lilli have the life she deserved, far away from the attacks and abuse? He smiled over at his mate. She took her time, longer than needed to make the tea, but he didn't need to ask why. "Sleep has never come easy, but even less so without her next to me. I look forward to the day I do not have to be parted from her any longer."

"I believe that goes both ways, brother. They need us as much as we need them."

"You may be right. It is a strange feeling. One I never expected to experience."

Logan grinned. "That it is. At some point, it became one I do not know how I lived without."

"I feel the same. Until I met Jocasta, I did not know what I was missing. Despite my life, I never realized how truly empty I was. She has given me a reason to keep breathing." And it was the truth. Lillianna gave him purpose. He would do anything for her, and he loved her as he would if she genuinely were his own young. But the mated love was different. It was something one could never understand until one experienced it for themself. Because of her heartbeat, his heart kept beating.

"Our mates can do that. Make us see things more clearly and give us a new life. It is what Ambrosia did to me. It is why my fur changed color. And, brother, I am happy you have found it. I am happy Jocasta has revived you. We have endured enough pain. It is time we experience joy."

"She brings me that and more. I notice things that used to be a blur. The stars in the sky, how bright the sun is, how the water runs in the river. Everything just seems brighter." He smiled at his brother. "I am happy Ambrosia has done that for you as well—that you have found someone to ease your pain and anger and bring you happiness. Your smile has been missed." As they spoke, a new hope filled him. He realized he didn't feel the need for revenge against his father any longer. Not even Markham. If he could just get Lilli safe, maybe even Zinnia too, and keep Logan safe as well, that would be enough.

"I have missed you as well. And I am glad we have gotten to talk. It eases me in ways I cannot explain."

"You do not need to explain. I understand completely. Not a day has gone by when I did not think or worry about you. It brings me joy to see how well you are, despite everything. I am so very sorry I did not come to see you sooner."

Logan flicked his gaze from Pierce to the surrounding room and the hallway leading to more rooms. He looked back at Pierce. "You do not need to apologize. We have come together now, and we will work together to make a better future for our family."

"Yes. Our family." Pierce beamed at his mate. "Our entire family." He cut his eyes back at Logan. "I will do whatever needs to be done."

"That is good, as I expect Derrick will bring Lillianna to the market any day now. I have no intention of allowing her to return once he does."

"Thank the gods. Please, do not. I cannot speak of you to her, not yet. She has not learned to shield her mind, and Markham's powers grow stronger every year. We are watched, listened to when we are in the village together, and she has never been permitted to leave." He reached across and squeezed his brother's shoulder. "When she is gone, I swear to you, I will follow."

"I expected nothing less. I do not have hope Zinnia will follow, but I ask you to speak to her, anyway. Perhaps you can convince her it is what is best."

"I already have plans to do so. But not until Lillianna is safe. Zinnia is too attached to Dahlia, and Dahlia would not be above throwing Lilli at Markham's feet." He sighed. "Her soul is darker than I care to acknowledge sometimes. And she hates me. Lilli too."

"I would not ask you to do so until Lilli was safely out of harm's way." Logan stood. "I should begin toward the market. Take as long as you need to here with your mate. Jocasta can tell Ambrosia when we may return. Under the circumstances, the bar has been closed for the day, so Jocasta does not need to come back to the village right away, which may be best at the moment."

Pierce let out a low growl as the meaning of his brother's words registered. He didn't need Logan to go into details. "Perhaps once he has healed, he will think twice about coming near my mate again. He will not get a second chance at recovery." He didn't need to explain any further what he meant. Rising from his chair, he drew Logan into another hard hug. He didn't know when they would see each other again. A few days was the best-case scenario.

Logan returned it. "Be safe, brother."

"You as well, brother. And thank you for the use of your cabin. I truly appreciate it." Besides being a little more sheltered than they were out in the open in their usual meeting spot, Jocasta needed to rest.

"You are always welcome here." With that, Logan released the hug. He nodded to his brother once more before he left.

As soon as the door closed behind him, Pierce sat back down, sagging in the chair. He put a hand over his eyes, squeezing tight as tears threatened. Seeing his brother again, how well he was doing, the conversation, and the love they had shared, eased him more than anything ever had. He had lost hope long ago that what they had just shared would ever be a possibility.

Jocasta stepped between his legs, wrapped her arms around his shoulders, and stroked the back of his head. Nothing needed to be said.

He laid his head upon her shoulder, one arm around her back while the other stroked her hip. As a few tears slipped down his cheeks, the sensation burned his eyes. He hated crying; strived never to let tears escape, especially in the presence of others. To his father—in the village at large—tears were a sign of weakness, and they didn't allow weakness. These tears held happiness within them, though. Happiness and relief.

He felt the smile cross Jocasta's face. She would have known the conversation had gone well. He knew she would have attempted not to listen, but being in such proximity, coupled with her excellent hearing, she wouldn't have been able to prevent eavesdropping, at least for most of what he and his brother said. Not that she would repeat any of it. But she was grateful, too. He could feel the emotion swirling within her; grateful she wouldn't have to worry about him so much. That they could soon hold one another in their arms and that he would soon be free.

He was beyond grateful, too, for everything that was being done for him and his little sister. He couldn't wait for the day when he no longer had to worry about leaving his love again.

Taking the hand from her hip, Pierce gently cupped her cheek. He stared into her eyes, those pools of amber liquid that saw straight through to his soul. He pressed a soft kiss to her lips. "I love you, Jocasta. I can hold the words back no longer. I love you."

Tears pricked the corners of her eyes as she beamed brightly at him. "I love you too, Pierce. With all my heart."

Oh, gods, how that made his heart swell. A smile spread so tightly across his face it made his cheeks ache. "When my sister and I are free, I want to mate you officially in front of my true family. I want to shout to the world that you are my queen. My everything."

With a gentle nod of her head, tears rolled down her cheeks, and then she nodded again, more fanatically. "Yes. Absolutely, yes. A thousand times, yes. We will be mated, and everyone will know you, and only you, are my king."

A rumble of satisfaction left him, and he kissed her again, deeper this time. "That pleases me greatly." He nipped at her lip, then licked his own as he stared at her. "How much pain are you in, my love?" He noticed the throbbing in her head subside a short time ago, but with his arms around her, his lips against hers, all he felt from her was utter pleasure. Perhaps the pain would appear at some point, though he prayed it wouldn't, but not right now, not when they had finally declared their love for one another.

"I don't feel any pain."

He growled against her lips as he stood, picking her up into his arms. Her legs wrapped around his waist as he gripped her rear. He kissed her as he carried her through the hallway and into a bedroom. There was a place set up for sleeping, but sleeping was far from what they would be doing. Logan's scent was faint in here, and he didn't think it was where the male lay his head at night.

Laying her on the bedding, he slowly undressed her, being as gentle as possible with the bruised parts of her. He worshiped her body, and she honored his. When they joined, the union was perfection. As they laid in each other's arms in the aftermath of their lovemaking, each of them stroking the other, he knew he would have to leave her soon. However, the knowledge didn't pain him much as it usually did. It wouldn't be for long. Soon, they would have the chance to be together for good, and they would never have to leave each other again.

Chapter Twenty-Four

Six days. Six days where Devin had left the village as early as permitted. Searched. Gone home before curfew so Markham wouldn't punish her. Yeah. Six days. After hiding in the shadows of the marketplace, camouflaged, listening to rumors for months.

Desperation was not an emotion she appreciated. She had no choice, though, and she had to do this alone. Gavin and Parthenia were not an option. Pierce had his own issues going on, his own problems to endure, not to mention his Informant duties. Derrick was the same, with the added emotional turmoil over what he and Gabby were going through. And it wasn't like she could enlist Gabby's help, not with her condition. Gods, Devin prayed the female didn't lose her young again.

Unless she fled the village with Derrick, perhaps it would be less cruel for her to lose this young, too. Considering what would happen to the three of them if the pregnancy came to fruition. If anyone discovered their relationship.

Continuing through the trees, she noticed the markers, those subtle things that would be invisible to the eye unless you searched for them. Her ears pricked up, her nose wrinkling a bit as the scents in the air changed. Frowning, she moved forward through the trees. There was nothing here. The trees just ended. No. This could not be right. It was here. It *must* be here. She *had* to find it. It was the only way.

She scoured but couldn't get any further. It was as if the forest had just disappeared. No. This *had* to be it. It just *had* to. But there was nothing here. Devin let out a huff of frustration. She was about to give up, turn and leave when a breeze hit her. Upon the breeze came the most amazing scents. It came from beyond the trees. There *must* be something here. As she moved closer, the trees shifted, curling and entwining upon themselves, until an archway formed. It started tall, then shrank down to a height that would accommodate someone of only her size. As it opened, she looked beyond and into a clearing. About sixty yards past the opening were buildings, houses. Hybrids were everywhere.

Oh, gods, she'd found it.

"Greetings, young one." A male of an indiscernible age stepped out from a nearby hut. The male clasped his hands behind his back as he strolled in her direction. His robe billowed with each step of his taloned feet.

Devin regarded him carefully as he came closer. Like no one she had ever seen before, he was a strange male. With his talons, perhaps he was part siren? On all fours, he was about two feet taller than she stood. If she were in her humanoid form, she would be the taller of the two of them. She didn't feel threatened as he came nearer, but she had a distinct impression that it was because she meant this village and its inhabitants no harm. She bowed her head slightly, unsure why she felt inclined to do so. "Greetings."

"I know you seek answers, child. So tell me your questions." He offered an acknowledged bow of his head in return.

How on earth did he know? "I seek information about the barrier surrounding the isle." And perhaps more, but she would see how this conversation played out first.

"There is much to know of the barrier that surrounds the isle. Some of which I cannot share. Tell me what you specifically seek, and I will know what guidance I can offer you."

Devin sat down, still staring up at him. She hadn't asked for entrance into this place, and he hadn't invited her. Not that she could blame him, though. He had an air of being in charge, and she was an outsider. "Does the barrier surround the isle? And is there a way through?"

The male stood in silence a moment, a gentle breeze playing with the ends of his bright red hair. "Yes, the barrier surrounds the entire isle. There is no way through from our side."

She sighed and quietly cursed to herself. Shaking her head, she stood back up, then sat back down. She didn't want to go back and tell them it had all been for nothing. "I suppose I have no other questions. Regarding the barrier."

"You seek other information," he said.

"Merely about something that I do not think there is a satisfactory answer. Others think differently. But with little hope of a solution."

"You may ask your question. I cannot say whether my answer will be illuminating."

Devin weighed her words. She didn't get the sense that he would betray her, but one could never be too careful. Nor could she say aloud that she wished *him* dead, but... "Eternal freedom from the shape shifter King." She wouldn't call him *her* King. He wasn't worthy of holding the title.

"Freedom can be granted, though I do not believe you would accept sanctuary. There are others you would not leave behind in Markham's care, are there not?"

"You know of him." It was a statement, not a question. "Yes, there are. For some of those that seek freedom, sanctuary would suffice. For others, mere sanctuary would not ease their fears. Fear is a potent deterrent."

"I am aware of him. I worked best with his predecessor." He paused. "I cannot interfere with destiny. Sanctuary is all I can offer to those of a good heart that would seek it. However, all is not lost." A small smile crossed his face. "Ambrosia, please come out."

"Greetings, Santos." A female, taller than she was in this form, came out from behind the hut the male had emerged from. She had burgundy hair pulled back, amber eyes, and bird-like feet. The female brushed a wisp of hair behind her ear and bowed her head.

"Perhaps you may be of some aid to the young shape shifter."

"Yes, Santos."

He bowed his head ever so slightly to Ambrosia before turning his attention back to Devin. "I trust you will speak to no one of our location. Ambrosia, here, may offer more insight to your first endeavor." With that, he bowed his head once again to Devin, turned around, and walked back toward the hut.

She kept her head cocked, watching as he went back to the hut he'd come out of. He was a strange one. Intriguing, but odd. Devin turned her head and looked up at the female. As their eyes met, she frowned as a flash of memory went through her head, one she hadn't thought of in many years. "I-I was asking him about the barrier around the isle."

"Yeah. I kind of overheard. But Santos isn't wrong."

"What is it you could tell me? I would appreciate any help."

"Well, I can't exactly tell you anything, but I may know someone who can." A mischievous grin crossed her face. "But you have to take me with you."

Devin thought for a moment before answering. She had nothing to lose. Without answers, hope was truly lost. "I would agree with that."

Ambrosia opened her mouth when the sound of paws pounding against the ground rang out. A canine skidded to a stop beside her. He blinked at Devin, then sniffed. "Devina?"

Though it had been so very long, and his fur had changed, his scent and his eyes had not. Devin had been very young the last time she'd seen him, but she remembered. "Oh gods, Logan. You are here? You are alive?" Well, obviously. "I cannot believe this. It is wonderful to see you."

"Yes. They granted me sanctuary just a day ago." He sniffed the air, peered around, then focused back on her. "It is wonderful to see you as well."

Ambrosia rested a hand on Logan's shoulder. "I'm so glad to hear you two know one another." She beamed. "She's agreed to take me with her to that village I told you about a few days ago."

Sitting back on his haunches, Logan glanced at Ambrosia. "She has, has she?"

"I came alone. Why does that surprise you?" Devin smiled and glanced at Ambrosia. "She says she can help me with something. Information I am seeking."

"I told Derrick of this place, but I know he would not leave without his mate or you." He nuzzled Ambrosia and let out a low growl as she stroked his head. His gaze flicked back to Devin. "I trust you will keep her safe."

"I'm not completely incapable of taking care of myself," Ambrosia smirked.

"Derrick does not speak to me about what he does when he leaves the village. And it is not safe to speak of such things inside the boundaries. Perhaps he was just waiting for the right time." She was going to have an honest conversation with her brother, though, that was for sure. If he knew of this place, he could have saved her heaps of trouble as she'd tried to figure out where it was. Not to mention, he'd said nothing to her of Logan. Not a damned thing.

"Perhaps."

"I hope he and his mate find safety. I have been searching for the same thing, among others. But, yes, of course, I will keep her safe. I am well trained."

"I must take my leave of you, but maybe we can talk when you both return," Logan said.

Ambrosia opened her mouth, then snapped it shut, saying nothing.

"I would like that. Much has changed. But I am glad to see you doing well." She smiled. "And mated. Congratulations."

"Then I will see you both soon." He nuzzled Ambrosia one last time and licked her neck. He glanced at Devin. "Thank you," he said, then ran out through the archway.

Ambrosia watched him go. "I'm Ambrosia, by the way. I know you heard Santos call me, but I go by Am. At least, most people call me that. We should head out ourselves. I don't know how long Crow Skull Trail is."

"I go by Devin." She nodded and stood. "I will follow you. Do you enjoy talking, or do you prefer quiet? I can go either way, and I do not pry."

"Oh, I'm a talker," Ambrosia freely admitted. "But I listen as much as I talk. One of the many reasons I'm considered the go-to in the marketplace. Besides the fae. But they don't talk to everyone. They mostly listen." She started in the direction Logan took to leave the village.

Devin followed. "I have heard that. So, how did you and Logan meet? It has been many years since I saw him last. Many rumors have floated around."

Ambrosia smirked. "He caught me in his arms." She laughed softly. "I was climbing a nearby ridge, and I miscalculated a step and fell. He caught me before I cracked my head open."

"Well, that was lucky." Devin chuckled. "I have wondered about him. He and my brother used to be very close. I called him brother as well."

"I heard Logan mention Derrick. Is that your brother?"

"Yes, Derrick is my brother. I was not aware he had met with Logan. But, then again, he has a position in the village that makes it difficult for us to spend time together. And it is dangerous to speak inside the boundaries on things that do not line up with our laws."

Ambrosia nodded. "I know of the shape shifter's 'so-called' laws. Though, from what I heard you say to Santos, you don't seem all that fond of them yourself."

"Oh, no. I am not. I say not in the village, but that is out of self-preservation and nothing more. Wrongful accusations result in horrific punishments and deaths. Too much, and too many, has been lost because of Markham's laws. Too much would be lost were I not there to help those who cannot help themselves." And she didn't say that to brag, but as the truth. "As I told Santos, sanctuary is not something I can accept."

"He has a way of knowing who will and won't accept it. Not that it ever stops him from questioning them, but I suppose that's simply to confirm what he believes." She paused. "I understand about self-preservation. I know all about that."

"If you will forgive my nosiness, may I ask why?"

Ambrosia inhaled and exhaled a deep breath. "My father was a shape shifter. He lost his life when he was betrayed by Markham eighteen years ago. My sister and I have stayed well hidden, despite that we work in the marketplace."

A shape shifter? She hadn't even guessed. "You hide your lineage well." Devin's steps slowed. "Eighteen years ago?" She frowned. He couldn't be the same, but she remembered only one that year. There had been others, but only one had stuck with her. Though she had been young and only in her third year, she could be wrong. "What was his name?"

"Galenus. And I take more after my mother. My twin sister carries more of his genes."

Devin stopped as a chill went through her. "*Galenus* was your father?"

Ambrosia paused in her steps. She raised an eyebrow and sighed, then shook her head. "He didn't do it."

"I witnessed your father's murder. I know Logan is innocent, but I—" Oh, gods... She didn't know the male had had children. But how could she have?

Ambrosia's amber eyes widened. "I'm sorry, what?"

Devin didn't speak for a moment. She didn't know quite what to say, but the words came out, anyway. "I was a climber from the moment I could walk. It was unusual for my form, driving my mother insane, but I could not help it. I loved to climb and see how high I could get into the trees, no matter the weather. I also learned to camouflage when I was still a nestling, but I had not been doing it for very long then." She paused. "I was high in a tree that day. As soon as I sensed others, I camouflaged. I witnessed all of it."

Ambrosia leaned against a nearby trunk. "Oh, gods."

Devin didn't utter a word for several moments. "I am truly sorry," she said finally. "It makes up for nothing, but I am truly sorry." She shifted to her humanoid form and sat down, leaning back against a tree. "I was only in my third year. I was petrified and did not know what to do." She paused. "It is no excuse. I have only told two other souls the truth. One of them was my brother. That was because he awoke me from a nightmare when I was calling out in the night. It was a while past Logan's departure. Markham had given his Informants orders to hunt and kill as soon as he returned to the village that day. He had named Logan a traitor. To go against him is death. Derrick ordered me to secrecy."

Ambrosia dug her elbows into her knees and hung her head. Once her breathing returned to normal, she lifted her head. "If you ever meet my sister, please say nothing. We had very different relationships with our father. His loss." She swallowed. "It affected her greatly."

How could it not have? "I will say nothing. You have my word. I did not mean to say anything just now. When I am comfortable around someone, the words just spill out." She paused. "I would not give the details unless that is something you wished to have. They have never left me."

"No, absolutely not. I share a mindlink with my sister, and I'm afraid if I knew the details, I wouldn't be able to keep them from her."

"Understood. I will not give them. And I will say nothing to your sister. I became adept at keeping secrets a very long time ago." She sent her a small smile. "If it makes you feel any better, there are those in my village, though few they may be, who have never forgotten. And he was given a death ceremony."

"He was?" Ambrosia blinked.

"Yes. He was. I was not there, and only one person was in attendance. But I know they gave him as proper a ceremony as was possible."

Her shoulders sagged. "It helps. Very much." Ambrosia pushed off the tree. "Thank you for telling me. Even if I can't share it with my mother and sister, it still helps."

Devin followed suit, shifting back to all fours. "I am glad I could bring you some comfort," she said as they started forward.

"While Santos didn't ask this, not that he ever asks much, but how come you're looking for a way through the barrier?"

"I have loved ones who wish to leave. It is the only way for them to gain true safety."

"And sanctuary isn't enough?"

"No," Devin said simply. "I do not believe so. Not for two of those in question, at least."

"I'm sorry to hear that." Ambrosia slowed her pace, canted her head, and pointed out a couple of stakes between trees about twenty feet to their right. There was something on top of the stakes. "Do those look like crow skulls to you?"

Looking where she pointed, Devin studied what was on top of the stakes. "Yes, I think so. Are we close?"

"At least to the trail. According to what I was told, we take that, well, until it ends."

"Well, let us see what we find." Hopefully, it wouldn't take too long, but this was too important to turn back from.

As they continued toward the trail, Ambrosia glimpsed at her. "So, do you have a mate?"

"Oh, no. The path of mating is not for me."

"Oh? How come?"

She took a minute to answer. "I have seen a lot, though my life has been short. Maybe, in the past, things were different for my kind. Perhaps before Markham took over. Santos stated he worked better with Markham's predecessor but, if there ever was a time when he was not the ruler of my village, it was a very long time ago." She paused. "In the life I have lived, I have seen a rare few true matings between two shape shifters. Though, children continue to be born in the village, if you catch my meaning. Most of the shape shifters I have seen fall in love and mate have had to do so in secrecy. Those that do are always eventually found out and suffer significant loss. Many mates and children have been stolen before their time. Perhaps those stolen moments of brief happiness are worth it to some. But I have lost enough in my lifetime not to wish to look for something else to lose."

"I can understand that. My sister used to feel the same way."

"Oh? Not any longer?"

"Nope. Not any longer." Ambrosia dragged a hand down her face. "I found out this morning that she has a mate."

Devin raised her eyebrows a little. "You do not seem overly thrilled by that. Though I suspect there is more to that story."

"I know little about the male, so I can't pass any judgment on him. There was simply a situation that Logan and I had to handle on their behalf. I guess I don't know; she seemed different the last couple of months. Better. And I don't have all the details from this morning. All I know is what we came upon."

"You can share, but do not feel obligated to do so. I could give you an unbiased opinion if you would like." She would give it a shot, though, if Ambrosia wished. She was adept at doing so, but it was easier to know the people in question.

"My sister has been spending time with a shape shifter. I didn't know; no one did. She never mentioned it. Then, this morning, she called me through our mindlink for help. She sounded freaked out, so Logan and I got there as fast as possible. I found my sister knocked out and Leo on the ground when we got there. Logan couldn't get through to Pierce. He had to body slam him to keep him from killing Leo. Jo comes around, explains nothing, just begs me not to say anything."

She considered the female's story, taking a few minutes before speaking. There had been a few imperceptible changes she'd noticed in Pierce over the last few weeks, but nothing that showed he'd met someone. Unless... "Well, without knowing the context of what came before the scene you came upon, I can tell you one thing. I know Pierce, and I know him well. Despite certain things, he has never been so angry enough that he would take a life if there were truly no cause. If he has been seeing your sister, and she was unconscious, but he was attacking another male with such ferocity, then there was a reason." She had seen that ferocity in him before. But only regarding Lillianna, and the rage was always justified. "Pierce has never, to my knowledge, taken a life where no true crime had been committed."

"I don't care that he was attacking Leo. The male is a chauvinistic, arrogant prig who likely deserved what he got. What bothers me is that the first time Logan crosses paths with his brother again in years was like that. Although,"—Ambrosia sighed—"it is good to know that this isn't likely a common theme with him. That's the last thing my sister needs."

"That was the—oh, gods. They had not spoken with each other yet?" The subject of Logan wasn't something they'd discussed in the time they'd spent together. It was a painful subject for him. More painful than others, in some ways. "Although, in some ways, that makes sense. There are things to consider that, well, it's not my place to say. Suffice it to say; there are many demons there. And Pierce has an obligation that supersedes any other. But, no. In his heart, Pierce is a very kind male. He just cannot show that in our village." She looked over at Ambrosia. "So, seeing each other? Or mated? Or do you know? And I am aware I am being very nosy."

"By the way, he was acting, I'd say mated, sans any formality, for obvious reasons. I've seen Logan like that one time. And he was protecting me from a threat. So, I'd have to say mated."

"Hm. Well. That certainly sheds some light on a few things." Devin cracked a grin. "If he has found his mate, that brings me joy. He is one that truly deserves happiness. But I will pray for him. If Markham were to find out, it would not go well for him. He breaks more than one of Markham's laws by doing so. Not that I put much stock into them, but the punishments are genuine."

"I know Logan has already requested sanctuary for him, as well as their sister."

Though Pierce cared about Zinnia too, she had to be talking about Lillianna. Not to say Zinnia didn't suffer, but Lilli suffered the most. This evening, she would pray to the gods that things would turn out alright and that both received sanctuary.

There was another pair of stakes ahead. "Are you seeing this?" Ambrosia asked.

"I am. Perhaps we have reached our destination?" She hoped as much. The walk had been long, and her day was already even longer.

"I mean, I've seen a few already, which officially makes this the strangest trail I've ever taken, but I don't know how long it is."

"I have not yet been to this part of the isle, nor do I know anyone else who has. But the surrounding scents are changing."

"I'll take your word for it. And I'm in completely unchartered territory here. I go two places, well, only if you count the market as one."

"Many do not leave my village often, if at all, but I travel as often as I can. There is a curfew, though, which makes things difficult sometimes."

"Curfew?" Ambrosia stopped dead in her tracks. "What happens if you don't make it back by then?"

Devin didn't speak for a moment. Without looking at the female, she said, "Nothing that is not worth it if there is a chance to find the information I seek. Lives depend upon it. That makes everything endured worth it."

"Then I pray this Elder can give you the information you seek."

Yes, so did she.

Ambrosia started moving again and picked up speed as best she could. They didn't get more than another half mile before they both heard a swooshing sound as something flew toward them. An arrow landed in the ground, right at their feet, stopping them where they stood.

"State your purpose," a masculine voice called out.

Devin surveyed the trees, but didn't find who'd spoken. She glimpsed at Ambrosia. "We mean no harm. We seek only information. If we are not welcome, we will turn and go." Gods, she hoped they didn't turn them away, though.

Ambrosia frowned. "We only wish to speak with your Elder."

Leaves rustled as the figure moved through the trees. After a moment, a male siren with green wings touched down on the ground with ease. Ambrosia's eyes widened. "He will grant your request," the male said. "Come with me."

"Thank you," Devin said as she followed him. The male said nothing as he led them forward. After a moment, Ambrosia did as well, her gaze flicking over to her. Although the sighting surprised her, she didn't outwardly reflect it.

As they walked, her thoughts swirled around in her mind. It wasn't normal for a siren to be down here. When she'd spent time with Gavin and Parthenia, talk of Parthenia's home hadn't come up much. But as much as she'd traveled around the isle, Parthenia was the only siren she'd ever met. They just didn't leave their home. Well, some did. Did he know anything about the barrier, how it was made? Parthenia had said it was siren made. She wanted to ask him, but he didn't seem too keen on talking.

The path continued for another half a mile before the treeline opened up into a large clearing. In the background, the gentle sound of waves crashing resounded. Wooden huts sat sporadically along the shore to both the east and west. Scattered trees of varying heights dotted the land. Devin inhaled a deep breath, a small smile lifting the corners of her mouth. She loved the ocean.

The creatures that meandered around the village seemed humanoid in appearance. Each had some unique deformity. They strode through the huts to the west and passed by a group of young using air to play with a ball. Devin glanced around, beaming at all of it, but most especially the young. The innocence of them, their freedom to play and be themselves, was a beautiful thing. But in her village, young never kept their innocence for very long. And it was so very heartbreaking when someone tore it away.

The male stopped in front of a hut and led them up a small ramp. "Felix will see you."

Devin glanced at the male. "Thank you for your assistance. And for not shooting us. Your home is a lovely place."

"It was not my decision." He scowled and turned away.

"He's friendly," Ambrosia smirked and rolled her eyes. She eyed Devin and the open doorway. "Shall we?"

Everyone had a past, and everyone had a reason for their demeanor. The male was a protector of his home, and he didn't know them. She grinned at Ambrosia. "Yes, let's." As they went inside, her gaze went immediately to the humanoid creature across the room, hunched over something on a table. He stood about a foot taller than she was in this form. His skin was the color of eggshells and appeared to have a bumpy texture. Bones protruded from the tops of his shoulder blades, similar to what Ambrosia had, but more pronounced. He had no hair atop his head, either. "Hello. Felix, was it?"

Felix scratched the top of his head before he spun around to face them. Oh, he was blind. It didn't seem to affect him, though. "Oh, yes, yes, come in. Please, sit." He gestured to the chairs in the front room as he approached. "Things are moving as expected."

"They are?" Ambrosia asked. With a tiny shrug, she stepped forward and sat in one chair referenced.

Devin shifted to her humanoid form and took a seat. Even if she left right now, she would arrive back to the village late. Just barely right now, but late all the same. It would no longer make any difference. So, why not take her time? "I apologize for our interruption. May I ask what you were working on?"

"Star charts. The stars are realigning. Change is coming, and it is inevitable." The laugh lines etched into his face as the corners of his mouth lifted. "Perhaps even long overdue," he said as an afterthought.

Devin cocked an eyebrow. "In good ways, bad ways, or both?"

"That depends on the person. What may seem a righteous path for one appears wrong for another. Either way, we cannot change destiny."

"And it is always the darkest before dawn." She offered a faint smile. "Without offending, may I ask how old you are?"

His eyebrows furrowed, and his face lit up. "I celebrated my three-hundred-and-eleventh birth *solaris* the summer past."

"Congratulations. That is quite a feat."

"Oh, thank you. Though, at some point, all good things must end." His smile never left his face.

"If it would not offend, how long do your species live?" She tried not to get hopeful here.

"Oh, not nearly as long as I have. I have witnessed many deaths and births. I shall miss them, but my purpose is near finished."

Meaning he was near death, though he didn't seem to be saddened by it in the least. "Do you know anything about the isle and the barrier that surrounds it?"

"Yes, I know many things."

"We would appreciate anything you could tell us. True freedom is the goal, but there is no possibility for some as things stand now. I am doing what I can to aid them in what they seek. I have been to the barrier, and it is impenetrable. Truly, I know nothing about it except the sirens likely created it. No one I have spoken to or listened to knows if that is true, how to get through it, or how to destroy it."

He tilted his head and scrutinized her with his white irises. "We do not wish for its destruction. We are ill-prepared for that. Though, it has not entirely served its purpose either. The stars are realigning. They indicate that may soon change."

Who was "we?" His species, or more like him, who watched the stars? "I understand. The needs and wants of a few do not outweigh the necessities of the whole."

"Oh, yes, quite true. Sometimes sacrifices must be made for life to continue."

"Is there any possibility for a few to pass through without destroying it?"

The male sat in silence for some time before he spoke again. "The key is not on the isle. It has been separated for many years. There is a prophecy: *Like no other, one so pure; With a touch of gold; That holds the cure; Will one day return to the fold.* The stars are realigning."

"You keep saying that," Devin repeated the words of the prophecy to herself. "What does the prophecy mean? In simple terms, if you do not mind."

"She is coming," he said, explaining nothing else. "Sirens have many prophecies. Perhaps, if you know one, she may help."

"I know one, yes," Devin repeated the words to herself again, committing them to memory. "May I ask another question?"

"Oh, yes. I do not get outside visitors often."

"Where I am from, we get none. But I travel when I can, and I have met many." She hesitated. "Do you know anything about dark magic?"

His wrinkled face scrunched, and the smile left his mouth. "One must handle magic of any kind with great care. It is a give-and-take relationship. Not all understand that. If not properly used, it will rebound on itself." He paused. "Even dark magic needs balance. More so than natural magic because of its nature. It is geared to take life, not give it." Felix rolled up the sleeve of his shirt and ran his hands over the bumps that ran the length of his arm. She wanted to ask, but it seemed too personal unless he volunteered. "All magic comes at a cost. Dark magic, black magic, however one deems it—the cost can be far greater than imagined."

That indeed lined up with her suspicions. "The dark magic I have encountered has certainly not been used properly. It is used to gain power and instill obedience and fear. And it has been used to take many lives that did not deserve to be stolen." So many lives. "What might be the catalyst for it to rebound on itself?"

"I cannot say. Nor can I say when. However, we guilers understand the true cost and value of magic more than most." He lifted his arm so they could closer see the bumps. "I was but a mere boy when this occurred." He flicked his wrist, and the charts floated in the air and over to where she sat. "I lost my eyesight when I took a life that was not mine to take. Though the sacrifice was necessary to protect my people."

"Sacrifice is sometimes necessary for change." She hesitated. "Without your eyesight, how do you see?"

"My other senses have heightened. I feel what I cannot see. I listen closely to know when I am not alone."

Devin ran her hands over the bumps on his arm; close, but not quite touching. When the star charts landed in her lap, she moved her attention to them. She placed her hand upon the deep blue parchment, running her fingers along the raised dots each one had. "These are incredibly beautiful. I have seen nothing like them."

He sat there quietly and clasped his hands together in his lap. "I believe they will be in excellent hands with you. I no longer require their assistance."

Her eyes widened. "You would give me this gift? Why? How do you know I will be worthy of it?" She couldn't have said if she were.

"Destiny."

Silence stretched between them for a moment as she focused on the parchment, running her fingers over the dots. "You know much that you do not—or cannot—say aloud."

"Yes, though I do not have all the answers. There are things I do not need to know to trust they are right."

"That makes sense. I know that feeling well myself." She lifted her eyes to him. "Thank you for this."

"You are quite welcome. If there were no other questions, I believe you should both get on your way before night falls. We are close to the fae forest, and some, well, they like to play tricks."

Devin cracked a grin. She had met a few fae over the years. "You are right. Thank you very much for speaking to us. You were accommodating. And thank you, again, for the charts. I will do my best to put them to good use."

"I am quite glad." Felix stood and escorted them to the door.

Devin peered at Ambrosia. "Would you mind carrying these while we head out? I prefer to travel in my other form."

"Of course." Ambrosia took the charts and rolled them up.

Unsure how he would receive it, she reached over and gave the male's hand a gentle squeeze. "I wish you well. And maybe, someday, we may have another chat. I rather enjoyed my time here."

"I enjoyed it as well."

She gave him one last smile, then released his hand. "Take care, Felix." Grinning at Ambrosia, Devin shifted back to all fours and started towards the door.

"For as long as I have, I will." He offered them one last nod before he turned toward the back room of his hut.

Ambrosia stopped in the doorway and glanced over her shoulder. She paused, then dipped her chin before striding out the door after Devin.

As they walked back through the village, Devin didn't hurry. She watched the goings-on around them, curiosity and smiles crossing her face. She spoke when they were back on the path lined with crow skulls. "That was certainly informative. Thank you. For bringing me here."

"Thanks for letting me come. It was intriguing." Ambrosia said nothing more until they were far enough away. She whispered, "Makes me glad that guiler had one too many spirits."

"Oh." Devin chuckled and shook her head. "Well. Spirits loosen the tongue."

A small chortle escaped. "Yes, they do." Ambrosia took in their surroundings and eyed the point of the sun. "You didn't say when your curfew is, but I suspect if you don't leave now, you won't make it. I know you wanted to speak with Logan, and you promised him you'd get me back in one piece, but it's okay if you want to head back to your village. I can get back to mine on my own."

"It is alright. I will not make it back in time. I realized that while we were talking with Felix. It is why I took my time." She paused. "The punishment will not change now, no matter how late I am. If I do not return tomorrow, then they will hunt me down."

"Well, Logan and I have extra bedrooms if you'd like to stay with us. At least then, I can ensure you have a good meal or two. He never spoke much about life in the village, but I could tell our lives are very different."

"Life in the village is difficult. That is for sure." She was about to decline the offer, but why? It was the truth; the punishment would be the same no matter how late she was. Perhaps a bit more brutal the longer she stayed away, but she'd been near death at least once and still come through it. Plus, a break would be nice. It sounded very nice. "I think I would like that. That sounds lovely. Thank you."

"You're welcome. You'll be our first guest."

"I am honored." They retook the path and headed back toward Migas.

"You know another siren?" Ambrosia asked.

"One, yes. She is a fairly recent acquaintance."

"I wonder if that's who people have seen around the edge of the forest," she mused aloud. "Is that why it didn't shock you to see the male siren?"

Seen around the edge of the forest? Hades, she would need to warn Parthenia to be more careful. "I thought it was strange, but not much surprises me anymore. It just seems to be more common than I thought for them to leave their home. I know there is much about the isle I do not know."

"I didn't think there were any. Guess I was wrong." Ambrosia shrugged.

"Who has seen her?"

"No one person has. I've only heard rumors in the market that people have seen one."

"I will let her know." If anyone discovered them, both Parthenia and Gavin would lose their lives. "It is imperative the wrong people do not discover her."

"I'm surprised one even came down to mingle with us 'commoners.'"

"Hmm. Perhaps the one I have met is just different from the rest. That is never the attitude I have gotten from her. Quite the opposite."

"Oh?"

"Yes. She is mated to a friend. The brother of my closest friend."

Ambrosia stopped walking. "I'm sorry, mated? To your friend? Another shape shifter?"

Devin stopped as well. "Yes. I will name no names, and I said it only because I trust you. They risk much. In my opinion, too much. But it is their lives and their love. Not mine."

"I don't need names." She was quiet for a minute. "Sirens and hybrids were in a war almost three-hundred years ago. Hybrid-sirens left. Most fled to Migas. You said the barrier was siren made, right?"

"That is the suspicion. I do not know if my friend has confirmed it but, when we were there, she said that is what it seemed like."

"She is coming. Return to the fold. That's what the elder said. If your friend is right, what if he means a siren will be returning home? And that's the key?"

She thought about that for a minute. Returning home. "Do you think the prophecy referenced the male in the guiler village?"

Ambrosia opened her mouth, then snapped it shut. "No. Felix said, '*she.*' It would have to be a female. I know little about sirens. We don't learn about anything other than the abilities we may get and the war. Everything after that is about hybrids."

"I will ask my friend when I see her next. Perhaps she will shed some light on it."

"I've got to say I'm curious enough to ask to join you, but I won't put Logan at risk. No offense to your friends, but I just want to keep him safe. It's bad enough he goes to that fighting ring."

"I took no offense. I do not know if she would meet you or not. That is something I would have to ask her." She stole a brief glance at Ambrosia. That didn't surprise her. "I can imagine why someone who has gone through what Logan has would need an outlet like that. Though I have heard of the place, I have not gone there myself. I can fight, but I only do so when necessary. It is not something I would wish to engage in otherwise."

"When we first met, that may have been likely, but he has only returned once with scrapes and bruises from a fight. He hasn't fought since."

"Perhaps he is healing from his past, then. He looked well. I do not have many memories of him. But he was always very kind to me. His sisters, not so much." Not counting Lillianna, of course. "But they are who they are. He and my brother Derrick were as close as brothers. What happened pained him."

"Derrick is who he meets. We're expecting that he'll be able to help get Lillianna out soon. I believe he's healing. His fur has changed color since we met. I don't know if he's fully healed, but having his family back might help. Before we left, I noticed a slight difference in him."

"I was not aware my brother was meeting with him until Logan said something. His duties in the pack make it hard for us to speak, and it is too dangerous to do so inside the boundaries. He rarely speaks to me about what fills his days. Markham has ways of drawing information out if one cannot shield their mind. I do so in the village. Speaking about certain subjects is unwise. Eyes and ears are everywhere." She let out a sigh. "I was not speaking of Lillianna before, though, but of Dahlia and Zinnia. Those two and I have never gotten along. Lillianna is lovely and innocent." Despite the circumstances. "I will say a prayer to the gods for her and Pierce. If they can get away and stay safe, I would call that a miracle. And I think reuniting the three of them would help a great deal." She paused. "It took me a moment to recognize Logan at first, with the change to his fur. But his scent is unique, and the particular shade of his eyes is rare in canines."

"He told me of them, but he made it seem as if they only couldn't save Dahlia. Are you saying that's not true? That one of his other sisters is lost?"

"Oh, no. Zinnia is not lost. At least, not in how I think you mean. She is well, but a follower. She cannot help herself. Though she does not harbor the evil inside herself that Dahlia does. But she yearns for acceptance from those who do not deserve her attention. She only wishes to fit in. To not fit in brings punishment. So, I think fear has a part to play in all of it as well." Devin shrugged a little. "Who knows? I know that when their father tells her to do something, she does it without question. Any hesitation she may have to do what they ask of her grows less as more time passes."

"Oh, thank the gods. Logan keeps hoping Pierce might talk her into leaving once we get Lillianna out. If she's not back at the village with him, then he's probably working on getting one bedroom ready for her." She sighed. "He deserves to have his family back."

"Everyone deserves to have their family. I hope it can happen to him. Pierce goes through too much in the village, and Lillianna ..." She sighed. "Getting them away from there would be very good."

"Devin." Ambrosia paused. "I feel like the only way to ask this is to be direct. What exactly have they gone through in the village?"

Devin didn't speak for a few moments. "It is not my place to tell someone else's tale. But with Lillianna, if she can get away and make a home with you, be gentle with her."

Ambrosia was quiet for a couple of minutes, then offered a simple, "Thank you."

"Of course." They were getting close to where she'd found the entrance before. Ambrosia went directly to the spot, and the trees immediately readjusted to an intertwining archway. They strode in together, and the lines closed behind them. She followed Ambrosia toward the clearing when a voice called out.

"Ambrosia." A female no taller than four feet rushed in their direction.

"Yes, Delenia?"

"Santos wishes to speak with you."

"Um, okay. Let me just show Devin to mine and Logan's place, and I'll return."

"Of course."

"If you give me directions, I am sure I can find it on my own. That sounds urgent."

"I would be happy to show her the way." Delenia smiled.

"Thank you, Delenia."

"Of course."

Ambrosia nodded to Devin. "I'll be at the house shortly. Did you want me to take these with me?"

"That is alright." She shifted to her humanoid form and held her hands out for them. "Thank you for carrying them. And I will see you soon."

Ambrosia handed the scrolls over to Devin and strode off toward the hut.

Delenia grinned at her. "This way, please." She started toward a group of houses and zigzagged through them before stopping in front of a tall cabin-style home with a small front porch. "We are here."

"Thank you very much for your guidance. It was much appreciated. Good day to you."

"You are welcome." The female left.

Devin went up the porch steps and knocked.

"Come in," Logan called out.

Opening the door, she entered, raising her eyebrows a bit at the look on his face. He stood in front of some furniture, just staring at it. "Having a conundrum?"

"It does not feel right." He gawked at it, seeming to be deep in thought.

"May I make a suggestion?"

"Yes, please."

Devin surveyed the room and the furniture for a moment. "Stop over-thinking it." She carefully placed the scrolls in a chair and moved the furniture around a bit. "They will not care where each piece sits. They are going to care about the company."

He stood there, watching as she moved everything around, and sighed. "My mother always told me where to put everything. I suppose I just wanted it as perfect as I could get it."

"Something tells me that your nerves have little to do with where the furniture sits. And do not expect a miracle here; you know we have little in the village of what we could consider furniture."

He rubbed the back of his neck. "I know. I guess Ambrosia told you I know about Lillianna."

"She did." But how much did he know? She didn't speak as she finished moving the furniture around. Tilting her head to the side, she considered the arrangement. "I will say a prayer for a miracle this eve that the situation works out. And I will keep to myself what she told me."

"Thank you, Devin."

"You are welcome."

Logan gazed at the furniture placement. "I am nervous about meeting her. I know very little about what to expect."

"Do not be nervous, though; I know that is easier said than done. She will adore you, as younger sisters often do their older brothers." Devin paused. "I will tell you nothing, as the experiences are hers to give, not mine. But I advise you to go slow with her. Be gentle. She is not much younger than me. Even so, I took her under my wing whenever I could." It wasn't as often as she would have liked, and less so since she'd helped her friends with their escape plans. And Pierce had been gone more often from the village as well. Now, she knew it was because he was mated and hoped to escape. She prayed it worked out.

He peered out the window, registering the sun's position. "I did not expect to see you as the day wore on. I can sense my mate on the grounds, but I am surprised to see you."

She glanced at him for a moment, then looked away. "Ambrosia is speaking with Santos. She was called there as soon as we returned. A lovely female showed me the way over here." Devin shrugged. "While I was gone with your mate, I realized I would be late getting back to the village, anyway. So I took my time. How much I am late will not change that I am late."

"I suspected as much. Santos has already spoken with me." He walked over and sat at the table, gesturing for her to do the same. "Although both Derrick and Pierce echoed most of your words, I feel much is being left out about Lillianna."

Devin sat at the table across from him. "There is. But it is not my experience to tell. I would not want another to tell mine without my consent. I would extend the same respect to her. She may be but an adolescent, but she deserves that. Just know it has not been easy for her. She may need a bit more time than others to adjust if she can flee to here. I do not feel comfortable saying more than that."

Logan sat there quietly for a minute, then changed the subject. "Was your trip with Ambrosia fruitful?"

"It was, actually. Very insightful. Thankfully, worth the risks. And quite fun." She smiled. "Your mate is lovely." They *had* almost gotten shot with an arrow, but she didn't want to tell him that. He'd been nervous enough, letting Ambrosia go as it was. Although, *almost* might push it. She had a feeling the male shot the arrow in a warning.

Logan raised an eyebrow. "There is something you are not saying. I can feel it."

"I promise, if someone harmed her, I would have told you immediately. They gave us a warning shot when we came upon the village, that is all. Someone shot an arrow at our feet. But then, they permitted us to meet with the Elder of the village. It proved to be very informational. I may have, hopefully, found just what I was searching for."

He barely held back a growl, taking several moments before he spoke. "That is good. I am glad." He nodded. "Derrick told me you do a lot of traveling across the isle."

"I do. Whenever I can, the isle can be fascinating, and the village is stifling." Sure, that was a good word for it. "I rarely get sidetracked and end up being late, though. Being punished is not my goal. Sometimes, depending on the situation, the repercussions are worth it."

"I cannot imagine anyone would have that goal. I wish there were a way to free a few from the unjust laws Markham has instituted. Though I can sense the value in rolling heads."

She raised her eyebrows and let out a soft chuckle. "Oh, yes. There is value in that, for sure, when it is warranted. That was not particularly what I was searching for, though. But I may have found a way to free a few who are in more danger than most."

"You are seeking a way off the isle? Like Derrick."

"Yes. Not so much for me, though I know my brother does not want to go without me. For him, Gabby, and another couple in more danger than them."

"The only way that would be possible would be if a shape shifter mated with another species."

She cocked an eyebrow at him. "What about a shape shifter mating with a siren?"

His eyes widened. "In all my time away from the village, I have not once seen a sky person on the ground."

"I used to say the same. No longer, though. She is lovely, very kind, mated, and in love." Devin shook her head. "What they are doing is very dangerous, but it is not my place to deter them. I am just doing what I can to help them. Besides, there is no betraying a true mating. Or so I have heard. Once your soul has found its other half," she shrugged, "that is it. I do not know about all of that personally, but that is by choice."

"You do not wish to find a mate?"

"I have seen too much. You know what mating is like within our species, the rarity of true mates. With the way, Markham has twisted things." She didn't need to say the words. Most who had found their true mate had done so outside their species. They were eventually discovered, slaughtered in front of each other, their bodies displayed publicly as a warning to all. Logan was quite familiar with the ways of Métamorphe. He had suffered too much because of Markham's tyranny. "As I told your mate earlier, perhaps those brief moments of happiness are worth it to some, but I have lost enough in my lifetime not to wish to look for something else to lose."

"I can understand where you are coming from. Though, perhaps, if you get off the isle or Markham's reign ends, there is always the possibility you may find it even if you are not looking. It is near impossible to fight."

"That is true. Right now, I refuse to see it as a possibility for me. I think it is why I keep to myself." She stared at him for a moment. "I always wondered what caused Markham to accuse you of Galenus' death. You do not have to tell me; I have just always been curious. It was not something I thought about for many years after. But the entire thing was so cruel to so many." And watching it happen had given her bitter, gruesome nightmares well into her adolescent years. Had she not been born a natural mindblock, those nightmares alone would have brought about her death. There weren't supposed to be any witnesses to what had happened to Galenus.

Logan inhaled and exhaled a deep breath. "I am an empath. For a long time, only my mother knew. It was not until my teenage years that Pierce found out. Still, we kept it a secret. Then, Pierce became an Informant. It strained our relationship. I do not know how Markham discovered my ability, but he did. He wished me to join his group of Informants. I refused. I would not use my empathic ability to help him torture those in our village. Galenus' arrival seemed perfectly timed while I was away."

"And so for that, he sentenced you to death." It was challenging to keep the venom from her tone. Gods, she hated that demon. She eyed the table, realizing she'd been slowly tracing the carvings upon it with her finger. "I have met one other empath on my travels around the isle. They have used their ability to help heal others, which is beautiful. Markham would wish to twist such a gift—well, I expect nothing less. He twists everything. Even the beauty of mating."

"That he does. I still pray that he will perish for all the pain he has caused one day. He deserves nothing less than a horrific death. My ability is how I have stayed hidden for as long as I have. It is easy when you can feel what others do." He paused. "You said there is another?"

"I agree with you on Markham wholeheartedly." She lifted her gaze to him. "One that I have met, yes, and quite by accident. I was in the market one day and went the opposite direction for a while instead of going back to the village right away."

"I did not think there was another. Though we try to stay hidden, especially in sizeable crowds. Emotions can get overwhelming." The front door opened, and Ambrosia entered the house, shutting it behind her. She gave a slight nod to Devin and strode to Logan. She wrapped her arms around his shoulders, and he nuzzled her neck. "Is everything okay, my love?"

"It's better now. I just came from Jo. I stopped by Mom's after I left Santos."

"How is she?"

"Afraid, mostly. Jo thinks Pierce will be upset with her. I tried to explain he wouldn't, but nothing I said helped."

"The situation you spoke of earlier?" Devin asked.

Ambrosia faced her. "Yes. My sister finally told me everything, and you were right." She sighed and sat on Logan's lap. One of his arms came around her waist as his hand stroked up and down her arm. "Leo, the male Pierce attacked, made multiple passes at her—tried to kiss her once, smacked her ass another time, and then tried to kiss her again. This time, he showed up at the basin, naked, and—"

Devin's eyes darkened, and she let out a low growl. She cleared her throat.

Ambrosia shook her head. "She told Santos all of that, but she also had to tell Santos that Pierce is an Informant. Jo feels like she betrayed Pierce. I kept telling her she didn't, that going to Santos about Leo was the right thing to do. But she's freaked out because Santos wants to talk to Pierce."

Devin nodded slowly. She didn't know what the implications of Santos wanting to talk to him were, but the situation was daunting, judging by the look on Ambrosia's face. "Well, no matter the outcome, though I hope all goes well, I am glad Pierce was there to keep it from going further. That is one situation that is guaranteed to throw him into a rage, especially if it is someone he cares dearly for."

"Me too." Ambrosia shifted a bit in Logan's lap. She caressed his cheek, and the darkness that had been in his eyes disappeared. "I keep thinking I should've told you to let him kill Leo."

Logan swallowed and nuzzled her neck. "It is best he did not. This gives Santos the chance to speak with all involved and punish Leo as he deserves. You know this."

"It doesn't make it any easier. After everything my sister has suffered, she deserves to be happy. And so does Pierce. He's brought out so much in her."

"I know, love. We simply need to trust in Santos's judgment. Is that not what you said to me when you first brought me here?"

"It is." She sat there a moment longer, then flicked her gaze back to Devin. "I feel like a horrible host. Would you like something to drink while I get evening meal going?"

"That would be lovely. Anything you have is fine. But, please, allow me to help with the meal. I feel as if I am putting you out." She cut her eyes at Logan. "I believe I forgot to mention. Your mate kindly offered me a bed for the night. Is that alright with you?" Not that she wanted to hurry to her impending punishment, but this was his home as well.

"Absolutely. You are welcome to stay. There is a spare room at the end of the hall."

"It isn't necessary, but I'm also not one to turn away help when offered. And right now, all we have is tea and water. I didn't have time to get a jar of milk today." Ambrosia glanced over her shoulder. "Love, why don't you get the oven lit while I show Devin the spare room so she can put the scrolls up?"

"I can do that." He pressed a kiss to her neck and lifted her off his lap before he stood.

Ambrosia looked to Devin. "Shall we?"

"Yes, let's." She nodded a "thank you" at Logan before gathering up the scrolls and following her down the hall. "You have a lovely home."

"Thank you." Ambrosia smiled as they headed to the back bedroom. "You wouldn't believe we just moved in yesterday."

"Yesterday? Gods, well, you have done a wonderful job with the place." She looked over at the furniture. "Logan is very talented. Pierce told me once that he misses seeing it."

"Yes, he is. His workmanship, I've always adored how creative he gets." She stepped into the spare bedroom. "Though I'm certain Pierce got to see some of it earlier. My sister got hurt, and we thought it was best for her wounds not be treated here. Logan has a cabin about sixty miles from here. We told him to take her there. After we got Leo back, Logan went to the cabin, and I believe he spoke with Pierce."

"Oh,"—Devin grinned—"that makes me thrilled. I am glad they got to speak finally."

Ambrosia shook her head. "This was the first time they've been able to speak since he left the village."

Gods, she couldn't imagine. That had to have been genuinely emotional for them both. Devin gazed around the bedroom. There was a bed, nightstand, and lantern. The bedframe was plain, but the nightstand had carvings on it. It was all quite beautiful. She stroked the carvings on the nightstand. "I hope your sister was not injured too badly. Will she be alright?"

"She will. Pierce did a good job cleaning up her head wound. And her other physical injuries could've been much worse. I'm grateful they aren't."

"I am grateful as well." Too often, she'd seen females in her village break beyond repair from it. "What about those that are not physical? Will she be alright? Situations like that are very hard to move past."

"I got the feeling it'll take time. My sister may not go to the basin alone for a while. Either that, or she'll look for someplace new to go. We're part merfolk, so we have to go somewhere with salt water to keep our scales moist." Ambrosia sighed. "I don't know. I've seen her come alive since she got with Pierce. So, I hope this doesn't damage all the progress made."

"I hope not either. I have seen changes in Pierce as well. Though they are almost invisible, they are there. I am going to say a prayer to the gods for them tonight."

"Thank you. Logan should have the oven fired up by now."

Devin reached over and gave Ambrosia's hand a brief squeeze. "Well, let us make some food then."

"If you're ever in the market and you need something, stop in Zancle's Rock. I'll help any way I can. Even if you just need information." Ambrosia grinned.

Devin smirked and let out a soft chuckle. "I shall do so, especially after our adventure earlier. It was quite entertaining. However, I should warn you I told Logan about our near miss. But I made it quite clear it was a warning shot, and you were unharmed. I think it upset him, though."

A small laugh escaped. "I'm sure I'll hear all about it later." She turned back down the hallway and strode to the kitchen, Devin following.

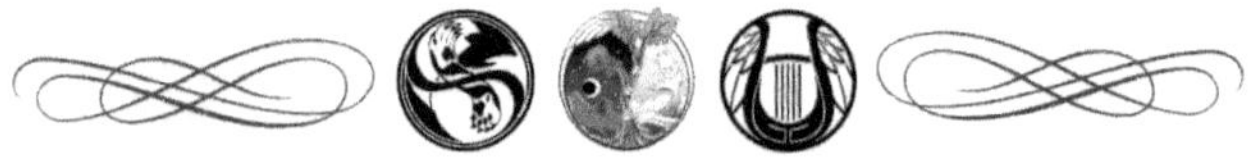

Jo paced the length of the living room of Logan's cabin. She hadn't seen Pierce since the day before. They'd agreed to meet here instead of the basin, as they had been. After they'd parted ways and she'd returned to her village, she went immediately to their Elder. There had been no other choice. It was something she should've done weeks ago, but there was no point in looking back now. Leo was on the mend and would already be back home. It didn't make her any less nervous to tell Pierce what she'd done. There had been a lot she'd meant to leave out, but Santos had a way of pulling out the truth.

She sensed Pierce near the cabin, then heard him bounding up the steps. The door opened, and he came inside in his humanoid form, smiling widely. His face lit up when he laid his eyes on her, but then a frown crossed over his face. Closing the distance between them, he took her into his arms. "What is wrong, my queen?"

Chewing the inside of her cheek, she tightened her hold around his waist. How could she tell him? It had to be revealed by her. She hadn't betrayed him, but she'd done what needed to be done. She opened her mouth to speak, except nothing came out. Jo swallowed the lump in the back of her throat, then somehow found her voice. Her Elder requested to talk with him. It was her duty to take him to her village. "It was the only way. I had to make it right."

His entire body became like stone, even his tail stopped moving, and his ears made not one twitch. Shifting his gaze from hers, he stared off somewhere into space. His hands clenched into fists, his claws digging into his palms. "If your Elder wishes to speak with me, then we should go."

He'd never sounded like that around her. Not once. Not even when they held everything back. Tears rolled down her cheeks. No, no, no. She wouldn't lose him. Not for Leo. They had one law. And Leo had been the offender. Not Pierce. "Please, don't." She couldn't even get all the words out.

"Jocasta." His tone of voice hadn't changed. "I cannot bear to think of what might happen when I walk into that village when I go in front of your Elder. Logan said he had already requested sanctuary for Lillianna. Do not let him forget she is still there." He turned away from her and toward the door. "I will not say goodbye to anyone. It is not something I have in me. I would prefer to just get this over with."

It was the way he said her name that broke her in two. More tears trickled silently down her cheeks. She had gone to Santos for *them*. She had requested sanctuary, but he hadn't decided yet. Even though she'd told the truth, she had betrayed Pierce. She'd told Santos about his position as one of Markham's Informants. There had been no other way. "Please, let me explain."

"There is nothing to explain. That is your home. Those are your people, your family. That is where your duty lies. You did what needed to be done. There are no actions that do not come with consequences. I will take mine. Let us go, Jocasta. I will let you lead, as I do not know the way." He paused for several long moments. She hadn't been able to bring herself to move. "Please. Let us just go."

Nothing she could say would make a difference. Pierce wouldn't hear her out. His village had damaged him so much that he always thought the worst. And she hadn't once spoken of life in her village. Gods, she'd never forgive herself if she lost him over this. She swallowed and nodded. She couldn't pretend the journey wouldn't be the quietest one she'd ever taken. And the longest. Because it would be the heaviest. Wiping at her face, she ambled past him, which only made her wipe at the tears again. Gods, she loved him so much. She prayed this would not be the end.

As they walked, Pierce said nothing, and no matter how many times she tried, she couldn't find the words. It felt worse than the day she'd lost her father. Pierce was so far away. At some point, her tears stopped because she had nothing left in her to cry.

He was taking her heart with him. Every step shattered her soul a little more. Although she tried to convince herself it would all work out, she no longer believed it when they arrived.

To Be Continued...

In Book Two
Chaotic Tranquility

Chaotic Tranquility

Gavin felt Parthenia nearing the treehouse. His excitement and relief at seeing her again was overwhelming, but it wasn't enough to overpower his fear. She was walking, not flying, because it hurt too much to do so. They hadn't seen one another since the morning after they'd made their trip to the barrier. That had been nearly three days ago. Then, afterward, whatever had happened to her—he'd felt it all. As he'd sat at the top of the staircase, pining after her but unable to reach her, he'd sensed her wake and felt her excruciating pain. His mate's suffering had eased somewhat. Perhaps someone had tended to her. Parthenia had thought of him, and her body had relaxed. When she'd radiated calm, she'd fallen asleep. Though it had been a natural sleep that time, not her passing out. Gavin had stayed there for as long as he could until the sun had nearly set. Then he'd fled back to the village, arriving just in time.

She hadn't shown up to the treehouse the next day. Hadn't been able to move without pure agony assaulting her. Today the ache wasn't as great, but periodically he felt a searing sting lance his shoulders.

As her presence drew near, her yearning fluttered through him, to see him and to hear his voice. He longed for her just the same. The sensations grew more and more intense the closer she got. As her pain hit him anew, his eyes turned black. Squeezing them shut, he tried to calm the roaring rage inside and get his eyes to change back to their normal color. He didn't know what had happened to her. Nor did he know how badly she had gotten hurt.

Gavin took several deep breaths, but they did little. As she got within feet, he eyed his reflection in the silvered mirror Gabby had placed on a shelf. Nope. Black as charcoal. Gods, his body shook. He needed to calm down. *Now.*

It wouldn't happen. He was halfway down the tree before he'd even registered leaving. As he leaped the last ten feet onto the ground, he shifted to his humanoid form. Parthenia stood at the base of the tree in one of her white dresses. "You are hurt. What has happened?" Closing the distance between them, he went to take her into his arms and she winced away. He'd barely touched her shoulders. He snatched his arms back, letting them fall to his sides. "What has happened to you?"

As she stared into his eyes—which he knew were still jet black—he sensed the direction of her thoughts. She felt as though she shouldn't have come, injured as she was. But he could also sense how badly she'd wanted to see him. Parthenia swallowed, her throat working as he watched. It was still another moment before she formed words. "I was punished."

Gavin growled. "Punished?" He reached a hand out; despite the rage that coursed through him, the caress he gave her cheek was gentle. "Why?"

"I said some things to Fagonia I shouldn't have."

His jaws clenched tight together, and he barely held back a snarl. Though she said aloud that it was Fagonia, her thoughts pointed in a different direction altogether. Her mother. "I want to see. No. I need to see. Show me."

Showing him wouldn't change what had happened, and he could sense that Parthenia didn't think it was a good idea. All the same, she exhaled a soft breath and slowly turned around. Her dress hid most of what she'd endured, but it didn't hide all of it. With a grimace, she untied the top of the straps to her dress and let the back slide from her skin, gently clutching the front to her breasts. Although she tried, her wings didn't extend very far. It was enough that he could see.

Hot tears spilled from his black eyes as a loud roar emanated from him. Balling his hands into fists, he dug his claws deep into his palms. He felt nothing from them, not even when blood trickled through his fingers and dripped onto the ground. No. All the pain he felt right now came from her.

Large gashes that were still healing covered her back. On several spots lay angry, red welts. Something had ripped small chunks and holes from her wings, tearing out her feathers. "Whoever has done this to you ..." Oh, gods, he would lay them to waste. He couldn't get any more words out as his throat seized up. He faced the tree holding the treehouse. She had told him she'd brought more healing potions here. He needed to get her one immediately. Touching the trunk, he glanced over his shoulder at her. "Close your wings, love. Do not hurt yourself anymore. Stay right here, and I will be right back."

Letting her wings fold into one another, Parthenia shook her head. "I know what you're thinking, and no. I can't take the potion."

All he could do for a moment was stare at her. "Why would you not? You need it to heal. You are... you are in so much pain." He let out a growl, but his wrath wasn't towards her.

"Because she will see. I can't." A tear rolled down her cheek. "They will know I didn't stay put. If they find that out, they will never let me out of their sight. If I take the potion, then I cannot return, and we may never find all the answers we've been looking for. Gavin, we have spent *penumbras* pouring through books. I can't let that happen. I just can't."

With his body sagging a bit, he gripped the bark of the tree, leaving a gouge in the wood. His eyes clenched so tightly shut he felt as if they were trying to fuse. He let out a low, keening cry, his chest heaving as he tried to draw breath. "What can I..." He let out a deep, shuddering breath. Her pain and her tears were shattering him apart. "Can I tend to your wounds? If you cannot take the potion, may I at least do that for you?" Then he remembered. "Gabby. She brought more herbs here, the ones for pain. Let me give you those."

"Can you... can you retie my straps first, please?" she whispered.

Gavin could only nod. Blinking furiously to get his eyes to lighten to their normal hue, he pushed off the tree and went to her. He took great care as he re-tied her straps. Taking her face gently in his hands, he brushed her tears with his thumb. "Do you think you could hold on to my neck? I could take us up to the treehouse. I will go slow so as not to jostle you as much as possible." His voice was soft, but still strained. He fought to hold his anguish back. She didn't need to feel that from him, not now, but it was so difficult.

Her gaze held his for a minute. "I think so."

Turning his back to her, Gavin shifted to all fours. Putting his front paws on the trunk, he peered over his shoulder at her. "Put your arms around my neck, lock your fingers together, and grab my back legs with your talons. I will wrap my tail around your waist, too. I will not let you fall, beloved."

Briefly dipping her chin, she followed his instructions. With a small wince, she placed her arms around his neck and interlaced her fingers. Lifting one leg, she curled her talons around his leg, and then did the same with the other. The pull on her back was a bit more intense at that point, but it was tolerable.

"I will go slow," he reminded her. "Tell me if it hurts too much, and I can slow down." He brushed his cheek against hers as he wrapped his tail around her waist. She rested her head against him just a touch, and he inched up the tree. It was going to seem to take forever, but if it gave her a chance to rest until she had to go back, it would be worth it. "When we get up there, will you allow me to dress your wounds? Or is that not allowed either?" he asked through clenched teeth.

"They are only allowed to be cleaned to prevent infection."

He bit the inside of his cheek to stop the growl from coming out. He didn't want to risk her losing her grip if his body vibrated. Rage surged through him. "Do they need to be cleaned?"

"Likely. They have not been cleaned since yesterday."

"I will clean them after I have given you the herbs." He spoke no more words until they had gone further up the tree. Flickers of images from her reached his mind, but he could tell she was trying to keep the details from him. He had probably terrified her already with his eyes. Part of him didn't want to ask, but the other part of him needed to know. "Will you tell me what happened?"

"If you feel you truly must know, I will tell you, though not before we reach the top."

Gavin simply nodded and continued to climb. He wasn't sure how long it took before they reached the top. Moving over only so far as she would need to step off, he then stopped so she could dismount at her own pace.

It took several minutes, but she climbed off with minimal twinges. Parthenia stepped in further to give him room to climb in. After entering the treehouse the rest of the way, he shifted to his humanoid form, took her hand, and helped her lower herself to the floor. After pressing his forehead to her knuckles for a moment, Gavin made his way around the room. It took him a minute to find the herbs Gabby had left, and even longer to find what he'd need to clean her wounds. He grabbed a jar of water to mix the herbs in as well. With their texture, it was easier to drink them than to chew them. Not to mention, their taste left a lot to be desired.

Gavin glanced at the silvered mirror in passing. His eyes were still black. It was rare that his eyes changed like this, and they had never stayed dark for so long. But then again, he'd never been quite this livid. When he'd collected everything, he lowered himself to the floor in front of her. Keeping his eyes downcast, he worked on readying the herbs.

Parthenia inhaled a heavy breath. He flipped his gaze up to meet her stare, then turned back to his task. "Do not worry over me, my love. My anger will pass." Even when his eyes returned to normal, even when the trembling in his body settled, and the constriction in his chest lifted, he would never forget what had happened to her. When he was done with the herbs, he held the jar out to her. "Drink all of it, if you can. When they have worked and your pain has eased, I will do what I can for your wounds."

"I wish you didn't have to be angry, though I understand why you are." Gingerly, she picked up the jar from his hands and took a sip before taking a larger gulp.

The taste was horrid, but the herbs did the trick. His voice was still quiet and weary. "My mate has had violence done to her. I cannot go after the ones that harmed you right now, and I cannot do anything to take your injuries away. How could I not be angry?" Taking her free hand in his own, he stroked her palm and fingertips. He would wait until he sat behind her to ask her for the details. She was in enough agony, not to mention everything she would feel from him. His eyes were still black, but she didn't need to see his expression or his tears when she told him.

"I would've waited longer, but I missed you too much. I simply had to come." She drank the last of the remedy in the jar. It wouldn't take long for it to take effect.

As he moved his fingertips up and down her forearm, the touch of her skin allayed him a little. "I am glad to see you. I have missed you so much. That you are in pain, though..." He let out a breath. He could feel the ache in her body taper off. "Will you allow me to carry you home when you must return?"

He sensed the protest on the tip of her tongue but also that she really didn't want to turn his offer down. It would certainly be better than walking, and they would be able to further enjoy one another's company.

"Yes. I would like that. Thank you," Parthenia said.

"Of course, my love. I cannot do what I wish, so I will do what I can to keep you from further pain." He brought her wrist to his mouth and stroked it with his tongue. The last thing he wanted to do was cause her any more discomfort by touching her too much. "Let me know when you are ready for me to clean your wounds."

The tension further eased from her shoulders. Combined with the herbs, he could feel the first bit of relief he'd felt from her in days. A deep sigh left him. His trembling passed as her tension left. The constriction in his chest settled into a dull throb. He was too in his head to know if his eyes returned to their normal color or not.

"I am ready."

Gavin moved behind her, dragging the supplies to clean her wounds with him. Sitting cross-legged on the floor, his chest tightened again as he scanned all of her injuries. Lifting a shaking hand, he clenched it to steady himself. He inhaled and exhaled slow, deep breaths. In. Out. In. Out. Trying again, Gavin worked on her, keeping his touches as light as he could. "Will you tell me?"

Silence stretched between them. "Fagonia was outside the library when I returned after our trip to the barrier. She questioned me on my whereabouts. Somehow, it turned into a verbal fight. I said that her insistence that The Poppy Fields and The Reflection Pools had nothing to do with the isle was our downfall. Our argument drew everyone's attention. At which time, I called her a burden to our people. I may be right, but it was the wrong thing to say."

He was quiet for a minute once she'd finished speaking. "Perhaps, if they disliked the truth so much, they should have looked at the perpetrator. Not who called them out. Everyone should be allowed to speak the truth." What was he saying? No one in his village could do so either. "Why does Fagonia care so much where you go?"

"I am responsible for The Poppy Fields and The Reflection Pools. We continue to lose lots in the fields, and the second pool has lost water. They think I am being derelict in my duties. That instead of finding answers, I am causing more problems."

"What is happening with those is not your fault. Any more than what happens in my village is mine. We cannot grow crops within our boundaries since well before my birth. Trees grow even though they appear to be dying. But nothing else. And the difficulties with pregnancies." None of that had been anything he'd yet told her. Gavin shook his head. "What good does misplacing blame do? They should assist you in finding a solution, not chastising you for something that you have no control over."

Parthenia half glanced at him over her shoulder. "I do not believe we are the only ones suffering. The problems you've just stated in your village seem to confirm my suspicions. Something is happening on the isle. Something that is the true cause."

"If they are happening within the other species as well, Devin may know. She travels around the isle more than anyone I know, but I do not know if she speaks to the other species or not. What do you think the cause might be?" Neither of them had thought to ask her. Even if they could confirm suspicions, they'd be the only ones who knew. But at least it would allow them to focus on other areas.

"I have found none. But the more I study it, the more it feels as if the isle is losing its power." She paused. "Regardless, no one cares to hear my thoughts. And the argument with Fagonia was simply the ammunition my mother needed."

"If the isle is truly losing its power, it does not seem to have any effect on Markham. The village, yes, but not him. His power only appears to grow. Each *solaris*, it appears he is stronger." Which really made little sense unless there was something else at work with Markham. He couldn't have said what, though. Once he finished cleaning the wounds on her back, Gavin moved to her left wing. Her last words confirmed his thoughts from what he'd caught from her earlier. "So, your mother did this to you."

"Yes. I'm certain she has been looking for a reason over the last *cycle*. This simply presented her with the opportunity. And because of the nature of the argument, the punishment..." Her words trailed off. "It demanded to be public as well."

It felt as though fire burned within them. Gavin jerked his hands away from her wing as they curled into fists. "*What*?" he growled.

"It was..."

Images of her memories flickered through his head. Thoughts of the moment her mother and Fagonia had agreed to a public lashing. Her sister stepping forward to object. Her refusal to reveal his existence, even though it may have stopped her punishment.

Fury surged through him so much that his vision shorted out for a moment. He picked up one bottle of medicament in his hand and threw it against the wall. It shattered, covering the floor beneath it in liquid and shards of glass.

Parthenia jolted at the sound of the crash and cried out as a pang lanced through her shoulders, radiating down her wing. Tears rolled down her cheeks as she squeezed her eyes shut tight. She swallowed, taking shallow breaths as she tried to gain control of the erratic throbbing at the base of her wing. For a brief second, an image of a spiked metallic whip popped up in his head.

Oh, no. What had he done? Another keening cry, louder than the one he'd uttered on the ground, came forth from him. He couldn't have even said where such a sound came from. It was one he'd never uttered before today. His claws gripped the wood beneath him, and he leaned over until his forehead pressed against it. His chest heaved and fell, quick gasps leaving him. He couldn't breathe. He had caused her pain. His emotions and his anger were out of his control, and it hurt her. "I am... sorry. I am... oh, gods, I am so sorry," he sobbed out.

Parthenia reached out and stroked his back. "It's not your fault. Please, please, do not blame yourself."

The tremors through his body slowed as her fingers sifted through his fur. "It *is* my fault. I cannot seem to control myself. I have never been like this. Oh, Parthenia, I am so sorry. I should not have startled you. My action caused you pain. I would never..." Well, he couldn't say he *wouldn't* cause her pain because he just had. "I would never mean to cause you pain." Forcing himself upright, Gavin faced her. As gently as he could, he took her face in his hands, rubbing his thumbs over her cheeks where her tears had fallen. "I am so sorry," he whispered.

"I know you wouldn't." Closing her eyes, she pressed a tender kiss to the inside of his palm and lifted her gaze to his once again. "I don't blame you. The pain, until I fully heal, simply cannot be helped."

He stared into her eyes, his thumbs slowly caressing her cheeks. "I wish to hold you, but I know I cannot. Is there anymore I can do for you?"

Her gaze dropped to his broad chest and flicked back to his eyes. "I believe there is. Lay down, please."

"On my back? Or otherwise?"

"Yes, on your back. Just don't move until I am settled." Once he'd laid on the floor, she crawled on top of him bit by bit. He stayed utterly still as she adjusted herself. It took several minutes, but she lay atop him in a way that didn't cause her any discomfort. Her head rested just over his heart, her arms tucked in close, her wings and shoulders relaxed, and one knee right above his hip. "If you keep your hands on my hips, we should be fine."

He let out a contented sigh. Settling his hands on her hips, Gavin kept them still, but stroked her skin through the slits of her dress with his thumbs. Closing his eyes, he breathed in her scent that surrounded him, letting the beat of her heart resonate through him. "I wish there were a way for us to run away now." The words came out all on their own. Thinking about wishes that had no hope just yet of coming to fruition made his heart ache all over again. But it was too late to take them back. "One day, hopefully soon, I will whisk you away from all of this. And I will never allow harm to come to you, never again." He gently kissed the top of her head. They both wished for that more than anything.

"Yes, one day soon. We will leave and never look back."

There was a comfortable silence between them for a while before he spoke again. "I would like to have a family with you one day. Even if Markham is defeated, I would not want to stay here. I do not want to raise young here. There has been too much darkness." It was nice to speak about the future. Speak of what they believed would happen. Soon Devin would find the answers they needed to get past the barrier. And they would find the answers to their other issue. Not that it was the right word for it. Though, perhaps it was a good thing they couldn't take their lovemaking further. They still enjoyed and satisfied one another, but they needed to find a way off the isle before they brought young into their lives. So, not an issue, just a delay.

"I do as well, but I agree with you. This isn't the place to raise them. I'd like for us to find a place of love and acceptance. I believe that is where we should raise them."

"Our young, when they are born,"—Because he refused to believe that they wouldn't find the answers they sought; refused to believe that a true future for them wasn't possible—"will be free. To grow up in safety. Make their own choices. Speak their minds. Love who they wish for when that day comes. Without punishment. Without repercussions. They will have two parents who love them, and they will know our love knows no bounds. They will have my sister and her mate." A sudden tear pricked at the corner of his eye, but he didn't want to move his hands except for the soft strokes of his thumbs, so it stayed where it was, not yet traveling down his cheek. "They will have all of us to teach them right from wrong. To show them how things should be. To give them the life that they deserve. They will never know the pain we have."

"Yes, they will. They will have an abundance of love. As we all will." She shifted her arm just a touch. With her thumb, she gently caressed his chest. Unhurriedly, she inched her hand closer to his collarbone and continued to trace an indiscernible pattern through his fur. A quiet purr came out of him, and he tilted his head to the side to give her better access. "I do not wish you to get angry again, but I thought about you when it was happening. You gave me strength. I endured because of you."

That news gave him a strange sort of happiness. But the rest of what she said made him feel as if his heart were constricting again. The tear that had threatened slipped down his cheek, followed closely by another one. He still refused to move his hands. His throat tightened, and he swallowed hard to clear the lump. Gavin forced his thumbs to linger as they brushed against her hips. He felt unworthy to be touching her perfection at all. "You should never have had to endure that," he murmured. "I should have been able to come to you. I should have been able to put a stop to it."

"I know, my love. But I would have done whatever was necessary to keep you safe." Possibly keep them both safe, and be able to leave and still come down to see him. This was their current reality. Until they could change the outcome, this was what they had to do. Parthenia's fingers rose a little higher and gently ran the length of his neck.

"Mmm." He tilted his head a little more, his purr a little louder now. "I do not want you to feel like you have to sacrifice yourself for me. Endure pain because of me. But I would take every death blow thrown at me in order to protect you. So, I cannot fault you for that." Her fingers inched a little higher. "I love to feel that peace from within you."

"It's all your doing. Your purrs, the gentle beat of your heart. It's like the perfect lullaby."

The corners of his lips lifted just slightly. "Then we will stay like this for as long as we have."

"I very much like the sound of that."

He could feel how comfortable she was, the most she'd been in days, and he didn't want her to move any more than she did. He lightly nuzzled her head. "Do you know how long until you need to return?" As much as he despised she had to return at all, it was necessary.

"Before evening meal. Cipriana and Fantasia will come to my apothecary with dinner for me."

"If you would like to rest, I can wake you in enough time to get you back there." Before he'd even finished speaking, her fingers stilled, and she'd fallen asleep. He watched her as she slept. The slow rise and fall of her body with each breath she took. The feel of her on top of him, her hand against his neck, and the peacefulness he felt within her all helped keep his anger at bay. He kept his breathing slow and even, not moving his hands from her hips. Every once in a while, he would glance at the view of the sun that he could see out one window. While she slept, he enjoyed her dreams about a little girl with his emerald green eyes. There would come a day when that dream, as well as all their others, would become reality.

About the Authors

Author of the Love's Worth Series, **Brigit Rosé,** lives in a world of romance. She has taken her life experience and made it into one endless love story. When she's not writing, she's singing loudly and off-key, hanging out with friends, or playing with her 2 fur babies. She can usually be found with a kiss in one hand and a twist of line in the other, exactly the stories she likes to read and write. If you'd like to know more about Brigit, you can find out more on her website: https://kbfennerrose.com

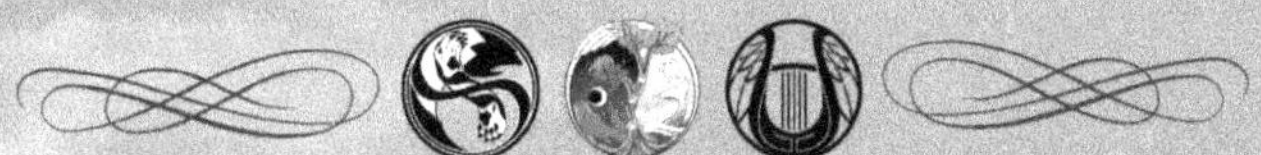

Nikki Haras has had a passion for writing since she was a small child. She will use whatever means necessary to get the words down that swirl inside her head, bleeding ink onto the page and breathing life into the characters who demand to tell their stories. When she's not immersing herself in her fantasy worlds, she's a full-time mom of three children and three fur babies, but you can usually always find her with a cup of coffee in one hand and a pen tucked into her messy bun. Always plotting the next amazing scene, fantastic new story, or immersive fantasy world to bring to life. To find out more about Nikki Haras and her upcoming book releases, you can find her on Facebook.

Other Works by Brigit Rosé

Love's Worth Series
UnHinged
ReIgnited
The Lucent Chronicles
Grace's Beast
Shattered Wonderland
The Mystic Chronicles
Detached

UNDER Krys Fenner

Co-authored

Prisma Isle Series
Perfectly Reckless
Chaotic Tranquility
Rebel Tides
Siren's Curse
Silencing the Shape Shifter
Insider's Guide
Prisma Isle Puzzle & Coloring Book

Coming soon

Blood & Bondage (The Empyreal Den Chronicles)
Hunted (The Atlis Chronicles)
Bloodline (Prisme Isle Series Prequel)
Kingdom of Embers (Prisma Isle Series)
Darkness Reconciled (Prisma Isle Series)